ABSOLUTION

SCATTERED STARS: EVASION BOOK 3

ABSOLUTION

SCATTERED STARS: EVASION BOOK 3

GLYNN STEWART

FAOLAN'S PEN
PUBLISHING
faolanspen.com

This edition published in 2023 by:

Faolan's Pen Publishing Inc.

22 King St. S, Suite 300

Waterloo, Ontario

N2J 1N8 Canada

ISBN-13: 978-1-989674-36-9 (print)

A record of this book is available from Library and Archives Canada.

Printed in the United States of America

1 2 3 4 5 6 7 8 9 10

First edition

First printing: June 2023

Illustration by Elias Stern

Faolan's Pen Publishing logo is a registered trademark of Faolan's Pen Publishing Inc.

Read more books from Glynn Stewart at faolanspen.com

1

TRACE HATED everything about the situation.

The pale blonde teenager hated being back in the Icem System. She'd run away from home for *reasons*, after all. She especially hated being back at Denton, though she had to admit she'd never actually *seen* her home planet from orbit before.

By the time Tracy "Trace" Bardacki—then Tracy Finley, prior to her adoption—had been in orbit of Denton, the reality of the "help" she'd received in running away had become clear. She hadn't had access to windows or cameras.

She'd been kidnapped, trafficked and slated to be sold as a virgin. Then she'd met her dads. They'd rescued her—Trace had *escaped* on her own, but she was still clear on who'd *rescued* her.

They'd saved her, protected her and destroyed the monsters who'd kidnapped her. Then they'd adopted her, and she'd found home for the first time in her conscious memory.

So, she absolutely *hated* the fact that they were walking through the hallways of Icem's main orbital, an orbital elevator mid-station above Denton named Icem High Home Station, toward a meeting with her original foster parents.

She hated *everything*. She hated the station. She hated that she was afraid. She hated that her dads were stressed.

She even hated the outfit she was wearing. Not in itself, per se—a friendly babysitter in her preteen years had instilled a laser-sharp sense of low-cost fashion into her, and she figured she'd done a good job with the long skirt and light sweater combination she was wearing over her shipsuit—but in that she'd spent so much thought on what to wear to meet her former "parents."

"Breathe, Trace," Evridiki "EB" Bardacki murmured to her. "No matter what happens, you're not going anywhere you don't want to."

"I know, Dad-E," she admitted. "But I'm still…" She swallowed.

"Afraid," Dad-V—Vena "Vexer" Dolezal—finished for her. Her second father—EB's fiancé and the navigator on their ship—gripped her shoulder.

"We're all a bit concerned," Vexer continued after a moment. "But you're not going anywhere you don't choose to, Trace. Like EB said. This'll just…lay things out clearly and make sure there's no trouble in the future."

"Nothing changes unless you want it to," EB confirmed. "So, all I'm really expecting out of this is a very expensive dinner on someone else's credit."

Trace giggled at that, but she looked past her adoptive dads and shivered as she realized they'd arrived. The Glorious Dragoon Restaurant loomed in front of them, marked by a twice-life-size statue of a figure she recognized as a Napoleonic War–era cavalryman.

"I'd *heard* about this place," she told them. "The Vortanis had *one* dinner here—with the party leader after Sarah got elected to Parliament."

And the party leader, so far as Trace knew, had paid for that. Her foster parents had been on the high side of "comfortably affluent," but even *they* hadn't come to the Glorious Dragoon on their own budget.

The best restaurant on or off the planet had a reputation and charged the prices to uphold it.

TO TRACE'S SURPRISE, stepping inside the ten-meter-tall façade of the restaurant—clearly originally three storefronts in the three-story promenade—put them into a surprisingly small and ordinary waiting room, with an artificial stupid hologram greeting guests cheerfully.

"Welcome to the Glorious Dragoon," the hologram greeted the three of them. "Do you have a reservation?"

"Meeting another party," EB told the machine.

That was the only thing he *said*, but Trace was learning to follow the electronic datasphere around her. Thanks to her neurosurgeon former foster father, she had a unique set of hardware and software in her head—experiments that were almost certainly illegal and *definitely* unethical.

Combining those with the extra hardware that the Siya U Hestî trafficking cartel had put in her head to allow her to act as an unknowing data courier, and the software that EB had "borrowed" when he fled his home system of Apollo one step ahead of assassins...

She had discovered a natural talent for computers, too, but the hardware and software went a long way toward making her a competent hacker and data analyst. Even at thirteen, she had enough software running in her headware that she could "see" the data transfer as her dad sent their reservation code over to the AS.

"Of course," the hologram confirmed. "Em Bardacki and two guests. If you will follow me."

To Trace's surprise, the hologram stepped off its plinth and started walking across the room. A moment's examination revealed a series of concealed projectors to allow it to do just that—but given that the *projectors* were the most expensive part of a virtual greeter, the hologram moving across the room was *showing off*.

"Hey, why do they get to go in?" someone barked from the seats.

"Because they, Em Bathory, have a reservation for *now* instead of in thirty-six minutes," the AS said primly. "Please be patient and you may enter the restaurant when we are ready to seat you."

"You don't meet many snide stupids," EB murmured. "This might be interesting."

Trace's nervousness stole her speech, and she followed her dads and the hologram up and through a door that looked like it belonged in a stable or a barn. The couldn't-be-real-wood door slid sideways at the hologram's gesture, and they were waved in.

"Ah, Em Bardacki, Em Dolezal, young Em Bardacki," a graying older woman greeted them, stepping up to them as the sliding door closed behind them.

"Welcome to the Glorious Dragoon. Do you need to store coats or bags before I take you to your table?"

Trace barely registered the woman. Her attention was taken by the restaurant itself, which spilled out before them like an opulent fever dream of gold braid and woven tapestries. There had been a passing mention of the Palace of Versailles in some of the history classes she was working through—and if it had looked like *this*, she suddenly understood the French Revolution.

As a matter of esthetic taste, let alone political power.

THEIR HOSTESS GUIDED them through a maze of tapestries, curtains and furniture that Trace began to realize wasn't nearly as cohesive as the designers had likely thought it was. Unless she had *badly* misjudged her classes—and she was distracting herself by checking the station datanet—they'd mixed and matched similarly overly lavish styles from effectively *all* of Europe from roughly seven centuries of style.

If they'd *just* managed to mirror the pre-Revolution Palace of Versailles, it might have worked. As it was…it was a chaotic jumble that at least managed to convey a sense of luxury and sumptuousness.

But not style, consistency or sophistication.

Still, the chaos gave Trace the distraction she needed to get through the maze to their table—a claw-footed monstrosity that she suspected didn't belong to *any* late-second-millennium style at all. The chairs around it were high-backed creations of wood and velvet—and they were *empty*.

The immediate anticipation shattered like a broken vase, and Trace found herself gasping for breath. The stress was still present, but she wasn't going to be facing the Vortanis that exact instant.

Of course, she was *now* going to have to face them at some unknown point in the immediate future. That wasn't exactly better.

EB reached over to grip her hand firmly.

"Grab a seat, Trace," he instructed before glancing over at the hostess. "We were supposed to be meeting another party. Have you heard from them?"

"The reservation is for six in total," the woman replied brightly, gesturing at the empty chairs around the table. "We haven't heard anything from the other parties, no.

"Should I have a server bring you menus?"

"Just waters for now, I think," EB told her. "We wouldn't want to start without our hosts, after all."

The hostess nodded and stepped away, vanishing into the chaos of the Glorious Dragoon's layout with a speed that suggested an ulterior motive to the cacophony.

"If nothing else, *I'm* not paying for dinner in this place," the captain said with a chuckle.

"What do we do?" Trace asked.

"We wait, for now," Vexer told her, taking a seat to one side of her.

She realized that her dads had flanked her protectively and drew reassurance from that.

"Either our hosts arrive or something odd is going on here," EB said. "I'm starting to wonder if we made the right assumptions after all."

Trace had *no* idea what he meant.

"Are you thinking trap?" Vexer asked. "We're not armed."

That wasn't true, though Trace wasn't going to *admit* to her parents that she had a self-targeting stunner hidden in her small purse. Her dads were relatively sensible men, but they had multiple reasons to not poke through her stuff to find the weapon.

Plus, she'd have been *very* surprised if she was the only one of the three with a stunner.

"Whatever *we* may have on us," EB told her other dad, "*Reggie* is in the concourse, and *Reggie* got himself registered as private security, authorized to carry heavy stunners and light blasters."

Reginald Kalb was *Evasion*'s weapons tech, responsible for the defensive turrets on their freighter. He also had some kind of past he didn't like to talk about—hardly unique aboard *Evasion*—that had left him very, *very* capable with small arms.

Not that anyone had told Trace that Reggie was playing backup. Somehow, that made her feel better—even if the absence of their hosts was making all three of them twitchy!

2

EB LEANED back in the ridiculously ornate chair and tried not to let his daughter see how worried he was. Vexer almost certainly saw right through, but his darkly handsome navigator and fiancé always been able to do that.

He'd *thought* he was being paranoid when he and Reggie had come up with the plan for Reggie to be nearby. The Vortanis had been the only people he'd thought the message could come from, which was why he'd come at all.

Any other possibility was a trap, and if he was being honest, almost everyone who was likely to try to trap *Evasion*'s crew was dead.

It took less than sixty seconds for an artificial stupid, made to look like a sixteenth-century tailor's mannequin, to deliver their drinks. A ping in his headware informed him that the water was from a specific mountain spring on the surface of Denton.

And that it was costing them eleven hundred Icemi reals per half-liter bottle.

EB sighed and poured water for his family, still watching the rest of the restaurant as he pinged Reggie.

Our hosts are missing, he silently advised the weapons tech. *Situation unclear; keep your eyes open.*

All he got back from Reggie was a wordless acknowledgement, but that was all he needed.

Everyone aboard *Evasion* was running from something. EB had made a strict rule of not asking questions, but he knew most of the secrets now. Vexer had been indentured starship crew in a system where only the nobility was truly free. The ship's doctor, Lan Kozel, had been covert ops and a *bioweapons* specialist. EB himself had been an ace pilot in a war he didn't like to think about anymore.

And EB was about seventy-five percent sure that Reggie had been a pirate. Whatever attack of conscience or outside threat had driven him into exile wasn't EB's business, so long as the man stayed within the rather fuzzy lines the crew drew for themselves.

"Of course, it's the sort of place that charges for water," Vexer said drily. "I mean, *most* stationside restaurants do, but…"

"*Eleven hundred reals?!*" Trace exclaimed. "That's extortion."

"That's 'the best restaurant in the star system,' Trace," EB conceded. "Water is all we're getting for now. We wait."

"We didn't set this appointment," Vexer noted. "So, making us wait is making a point, isn't it?"

"That's one option. The other is that something has happened to our hosts," EB replied. "So, we wait."

And while he waited, he was going into the news feed and doing something he probably should have done in advance. Sarah Vortani, after all, was a public figure. There was a decent chance that—

"It's not the Vortanis," Trace said sharply, clearly having followed the same thought process. "*Assistant Minister for Justice* Sarah Vortani is on the wrong *planet*, Dads. She's on Tarsus, in a scheduled meeting with regional security administrations."

"And given the press release, that meeting has been scheduled since before we left Estutmost," EB finished, finding the same information his daughter had a few seconds later.

"So, if it isn't Trace's ex-fosters, who in *voids* made the damn invitation?" Vexer asked.

"I don't know," EB admitted. He hadn't made that many friends in this region of space. Enemies aplenty, unfortunately, but few friends— and none he could think of that would approach him so vaguely.

"The Vortanis made sense, though I wonder now if we should have taken the invite *here*"—he gestured around at the ridiculously ornate restaurant—"as a red flag. As Trace said, they aren't regular diners at this level."

The arrival of a human server interrupted their conversation. The waiter was an older Black man wearing an elegant tailed coat in a style from the wrong century to match the eighteenth-century decorations.

"My name is Akachi Léopold Favreau, and I will be taking care of you tonight," he introduced himself. "We are still waiting on some guests, I see, but would you like me to have menus brought so you can review the appetizers, perhaps?"

"It is starting to appear that our hosts may have stood us up, Em Favreau," EB said slowly. "Let's stick with the water for now, as we may need to leave." He shrugged.

"That is extraordinarily unfortunate," Favreau replied. "Let me talk to the floor manager. The Glorious Dragoon could not possibly send you away hungry because of another's malfeasance!"

The waiter bowed slightly and, like the hostess before him, seemed to almost magically vanish into the chaos.

"That...was not the response I expected," Vexer replied. "I'm going to stick to the water, though."

Trace hadn't even touched her water, staring blankly off into space as she clearly scrolled information in her headware.

"Trace?" EB asked gently.

"I..." She swallowed and blinked, looking over at him and finally taking a gulp of water. "I kind of assumed the Vortanis just replaced me. I was a prop for Sarah's career, nothing more."

"Except?"

Trace flipped him a news article. No—a news *archive*, an entire listing of articles over the year since Trace had left Icem.

Over the course of the year, brand-new Member of the Icemi Parliament Sarah Vortani had made the kidnapping of children and the failures of the foster system her defining cause. She'd pushed hard for reforms of the foster system to move toward more permanent placements and adoptions—on a slogan of "Kids need families, not just homes."

She'd also spearheaded an initiative to crack down on human trafficking, kidnapping and grooming—which had led to her becoming
the Assistant Minister for Justice, EB presumed, from her involvement
in the law-enforcement side.

Trace's kidnapping had derailed Sarah Vortani's career—into
making sure it didn't happen to anyone else!

"She's still using me as a prop," Trace said bitterly. "I go missing
and she uses it as a springboard to a *ministry*."

EB held his tongue. He could see a few different interpretations of
Sarah Vortani's actions—and while Trace's was probably the most
uncharitable, that didn't mean it was untrue. She knew the woman and
EB didn't.

"Twenty minutes into the reservation," Vexer observed. "Whoever
invited us to this isn't coming, EB. So, I guess the question is: what
kind of trap did we walk into?"

"I'm not sure," EB conceded. A silent ping to Reggie confirmed that
the other man was still outside and hadn't seen anything of concern.
"Reggie's highest-priority report is that there's a mobile ice cream
truck moving through the concourse."

He was considering the situation when their waiter reappeared, a
determined expression on his face.

"My floor manager and I have checked and confirmed you were
invited guests, not the reservation-maker," Favreau told them. "Our
reservations are in high demand, Captain Bardacki, and we expect
people to keep them.

"We certainly do not expect people to use them to inflict unexpected financial burdens on potential future customers," he said with a
wry smile. "We have decided to comp your waters for the evening and
one entrée of your choice apiece."

He produced menus out of his sleeve with a flourish.

"Regardless of how you ended up in the Glorious Dragoon,
gentlemen and lady, we pride ourselves that *everyone* leaves with a
positive experience!"

EB took the menu with a bemused expression—and the suspicion
that the blithe "we checked" covered a larger degree of investigation
than Favreau implied. They didn't want him to leave angry, but given

that a single entrée at the Dragoon was a day's wages in a lot of places he'd been...they'd presumably made very sure he wasn't deceiving them.

Unfortunately, he didn't even need to *ask* to know that they wouldn't tell him who had made the reservation. A place like the Glorious Dragoon wouldn't give that out to anybody who didn't have a warrant.

And even a cop with a warrant might find the record had been "accidentally deleted."

For the moment, he sighed and began to skim the menu. One way or another, it appeared he was going to get to eat at the Dragoon on someone else's budget.

3

GINERVA "GINNY" Anderson had kept the watch while EB took Trace and Vexer out for their appointment. Now he saw her waiting by the hatch linking High Home Station to the nova freighter *Evasion* and couldn't help but feel a sense of relief.

If Ginny was outside the ship, nothing had gone wrong aboard. She wouldn't leave her engine and machinery rooms unless everything was ticking along smoothly enough that her environment and engine techs could handle it.

Including Trace, EB's forty-thousand-cubic-meter freighter had a crew of nine. Everyone had their own role and area of the ship—though the vast majority of the ship's volume was dedicated to cargo.

"Nobody showed," Ginny guessed.

"Nobody showed," EB confirmed. "Trace, go rest."

He got a somewhat mutinous look from his daughter, but the afternoon had been emotionally draining for her, too. With a sigh, she flounced off deeper into the ship.

Reggie stepped up to join the remaining trio at the access to the ship and grumbled wordlessly.

"If someone set a trap, they did it damn poorly," Vexer noted. "It *feels* like someone was actually going to meet us and didn't make it."

"And it wasn't the Vortanis," EB said. "Apparently, our Trace's former foster mother is on the other *planet*. Being very publicly busy. Unfortunately, the other half of the matched set isn't quite so much a public figure."

Dr. John Vortani was a high-end neurosurgeon and a man that EB would very much like to punch in the face. His experimentation on Trace had saved her life by rendering much of the extra headware the Siya U Hestî had stuck in her head impotent, but that didn't make it any more ethical.

"So, what do we do?" Ginny asked.

"What we always do," he told her. "In the absence of whoever invited us here, I'm going to look for a cargo tomorrow. Something taking us farther out-Beyond and well away from this region!"

Vexer chuckled.

"Were you thinking about getting married here?" he asked. "I know the Black Oak Island Sanctuary is gorgeous and, well, we *are* here—and it would mean something to Trace, I think."

EB grimaced. "It would," he conceded. "But between our mystery invitation and the Vortanis being in the same star system, I don't think sticking around here is wise. And, love, *most* planets have somewhere gorgeous to get hitched."

"I wanted to float it," Vexer said with an acknowledging nod. "But I agree. We traveled almost thirty light-years to get here and make that appointment, and there was nobody there. It makes my skin crawl."

"Well, let your skins crawl back inside the ship," Ginny told them. "Cargo exchanges are closed for the night, and they're not going to open up for strangers!"

Someone with an account in good standing could access the exchange's information systems outside working hours. Since EB hadn't known what was going to be happening at dinner, he hadn't *opened* an account, and it was too late by station time now.

"Morning," he agreed. "In the morning, I'll find us somewhere to go to get out of here."

THE REALITY OF "STATION TIME," of course, was that it was a fiction agreed to by the residents and visitors to any space orbital. Its primary purpose was to allow most businesses to have office hours for only half of a standard twenty-four-hour day.

There were businesses and work that went on for all twenty-four of those hours. This was a working cargo-transfer station, after all, with standard ten-meter-unit cargo containers in eternal cycles between the ships, the space station and the orbital elevator.

Cargo ran every hour of every day. Security ran every hour of every day. And, it turned out, so did the on-station post service.

"Ser, we have a package delivery for you at the access hatch," Tatiana "Tate" MacNeal told him. Tate was the ship's Jill-of-all-trades, though her primary role was cargo handling and administration.

Ninety percent of cargo handling was done by robots and control arms. For the remainder, Tate was as broad-shouldered as EB himself and significantly stronger with it. She was the single most intimidating member of his crew—at least when Reggie was behaving himself.

"A physical package?" EB asked, trying to get out of bed without waking Vexer. "From who?"

"It's weird, boss. They want you to sign for it personally and they're willing to wait."

Just what kind of postal service *was* that?

"All right. I'll be down in a minute."

TATE WAS DOING her best loom at the uniformed courier standing impassively outside the hatch, and they were gamely ignoring her. The uniform was unfamiliar to EB, but he knew the type of enby wearing it at a glance: ex-soldier, earning a paycheck by virtue of being basically completely unflappable.

"Captain Evridiki Bardacki of *Evasion*, ship out of the Redward System, Captain Bardacki out of the Apollo System?"

That was more information than EB would have expected to be on the mailing information for a package. Void, only the origin point of *Evasion* was listed on her registration documents.

Both Redward and Apollo were back in more civilized stars. The Rim was the outer five hundred light-years of the three-thousand-light-year-wide sphere of "mapped and civilized" space—a zone that Icem was several hundred *more* light-years outside.

Maps in the Rim and Coreward from there were constantly updated, managed and exchanged. Out here, they were trade secrets.

"I am Captain Bardacki," EB confirmed. "You need a signature?"

"Signature, image, thumbprint," the courier reeled off, holding out a datapad. "This was a high-priority, high-security package. We don't see the like often."

That was when EB realized that the courier wasn't carrying a stunner. The holster built into their uniform held a very real and very deadly heavy blaster pistol.

High security indeed.

"Who sent the package?" he asked, surveying the datapad.

"Arteve Escrow, Limited," the courier told him. They sighed. "You won't get more than that, Captain. Arteve takes the privacy of their clients very, *very* seriously."

EB signed the datapad and handed it back to the courier.

"Here you go. Enjoy."

EB nodded absently as he took the package. It was a padded envelope about the size of his outstretched hand, and he stared blankly as the courier gave him a crisp salute and headed toward the station.

"Any ideas, boss?"

"No," he admitted to Tate. "And I'm going to have Lan put it through a scanner before I open it."

He suspected it was safe, though. He still didn't know *who* had wanted him in the Icem System, but he was quite sure the package had to do with his missed dinner appointment.

4

LAN'S MEDBAY had the best short-range sensors aboard *Evasion*, and the doctor cleared the package as being safe before EB took it to his office. Something about the whole affair told him he didn't want an audience when he opened the envelope.

Alone in his office, with most of the freighter's crew asleep and the station as close to midnight as a space platform ever got, he studied the padded envelope with scant favor. A stylized *AEL* logo in the top right corner fit with the courier's description.

Escrow agencies held packages and cargos and monies "in trust," to be released on specific conditions. Usually, this was for large transactions, to make sure the money was in hand before the purchase was handed over.

Another use for them, though more common in spy fiction than real life, was for "dead man's mail." If a client didn't check in for a specified period—or the escrow agency had confirmation the client was dead—the package or letter was sent to a designated recipient.

Thanks to the medbay scanner, he knew the package contained two datachips. Nothing else. Not even a physical note. Just...two datachips.

Sighing, he tore the envelope open and dumped the two chips out on his desk. Each had a single word written on it in unfamiliar hand-writing. Whoever had sent them had at least put passing thought into how the poor recipient would interpret the message!

One chip was labeled *DATA* and the other was labeled *VIDEO*. That was about as clear as one could hope for.

Accessing either chip was a matter of tapping the block of plastic and silicon to direct his office systems to open *that* one. His entire desk surface was in range of the chip reader; it just needed to know what he wanted.

The *VIDEO* chip contained, unsurprisingly, a single video file. EB waited a few seconds for a malware scan he'd appropriated from his old employer, the Apollo System Defense Force, to finish running.

While backward by the standards of the overall galaxy, EB's home-world was significantly more advanced than the Beyond worlds he was traveling through now. Nothing coded here was likely to make it past the ASDF scan, so when the video came back clean, he activated it without hesitation.

There was a momentary blip, almost enough to make him worry, and then the holographic image of a man he'd never expected to see again in his life appeared above his desk.

"If you have forgotten who I am, Captain Bardacki," the man drawled, "Lady Breanna introduced me as Ansem."

The holoprojector shrank a man EB knew to be easily two meters tall down to a fifty-centimeter-high figure, but somehow that didn't remove the air of menace radiating from the broad-shouldered and shaven-headed enforcer who'd served as the crime lord's bodyguard.

"Lady" Breanna Tolliver was the head of the Siya U Hestî. Currently, she was living in a high-security prison in the Nigahog System, where EB had happily delivered her. In the process of ending Tolliver's threat to Trace and freeing several hundred kidnapped people, though, he'd collided with Ansem personally.

He'd shot the big man several times—and then, while trying not to die, Ansem had given him the codes he needed to free the prisoners before Tolliver could dump them into space.

EB owed him enough to listen to the video message. Not much *more*, all things considered, but that much. Ansem was boosted enough to be hard to kill, some mix of cybernetic, genetic and biological modifications that made a blaster shot through the stomach a merely inconvenient and life-threatening condition.

Rather than unavoidably fatal, as it was for most people.

"My name is Anthony Seminole Hadzhiev," the enforcer continued, "and if everything goes according to plan, the time I am spending recording this message is wasted energy that I should spend doing other things."

He snorted.

"But I didn't like to live without contingencies *before* you shot me and put my boss in jail for a long, long time," Hadzhiev concluded. "I do appreciate, Captain, that you didn't have someone pick me up and chain me while I was unconscious recovering. Slipping out while everyone was occupied later was straightforward, but you could have made my return to free life a lot harder."

He stared blankly off into space for a few long seconds.

"That said, there was a *reason* no one was watching the ship I stole," he admitted. "Just about everything but life support failed after the second nova, so I spent a good week just jury-rigging her back together enough to get me to a star system that wasn't Nigahog." He chuckled. "I didn't figure that Nigahog was a good place for me to try to lie low."

"But..." Hadzhiev shook his head. "I suspect, Captain Bardacki, that you understand the meditative aspect of working with your hands. I've spent longer than I suspect you realize trying not to come face-to-face with who I was and what I'd done to survive.

"Fixing a ship requires a pretty specific mindset, Captain, one that leaves you a lot of time to *think*. And to look in the mirror. And when I looked in the mirror, it wasn't just the scars from where you shot me that I didn't like."

He paused again, staring off into space before refocusing on the hologram pickup.

"I'm the one who sent you a message in the Estutmost System," he admitted, though EB had figured that out by now. "We have business to finish. Siya U Hestî business that needs to be...*wrapped up*, let's say."

EB didn't like the sound of that. He'd already run into Siya U Hestî remnants in Estutmost, where their attempt to kidnap Trace and access the datavault still in his daughter's head had complicated the already-messy war he'd ended up dragged into.

He'd be a *lot* happier once he was clear of everything to do with the Shadow and Bone forever.

"Like I said, I'm expecting to have this conversation in person," Hadzhiev told him. "But the long and short of it is that, at any given moment in time prior to your assault on the Cage, about five hundred kidnappees were in transit toward or away from the station.

"Lady Breanna and I always believed in contingencies," he continued. "So, there were a series of commands and codes that would redirect the ships carrying them. I know that those codes unlocked specific navigational data in our ships, directing them to a fallback facility secret even among the Siya U Hestî.

"I knew this facility existed," Hadzhiev said. "I've even *been* there. But I do not, thanks to Lady Breanna's information-control protocols, know exactly where it is. It is somewhere in the Icem System, but that is a system with two habitable planets."

He shrugged.

"That said, I figured that it would be easier to rescue hundreds of Breanna's victims from one central location than from scattered freighters and bases across a dozen star systems. So, I activated those codes, Captain Bardacki. By the time we meet, I believe all of the ships in question should have arrived in the Icem System and made it to the base."

EB wasn't sure he trusted Ansem—Hadzhiev—as far as he could throw his own starship. But what the man said made *sense*, in terms of rescuing the last round of victims of the Siya U Hestî.

"It's hard to be certain what to say in this recording," Hadzhiev concluded. "Hopefully, you'll never see it." He coughed. "If you are watching this, then I almost certainly trusted the wrong person, asked the wrong question or otherwise ended up imprisoned or dead.

"If that is the case, I..." The enforcer paused and took a deep breath. "I leave the fate of an unknown number of innocents in your hands, Captain Bardacki. You will need three things to find them:

"Firstly, you will need to know the ships transporting them and their origin systems," Hadzhiev told EB. "That information isn't available to anyone outside Lady Breanna's personal circle. So far as I know, everyone who could have sent the retreat signal except me is imprisoned or dead.

"The list of ships and where I believe they were at the time they received my message is on the other datachip in the escrow package," he said. "If I am dead, you are the only one who knows which ships, coming from where, were carrying those prisoners.

"All of them will be on ice by the time they reach Icemi," he warned. "That was part of the protocol I activated. Everyone will be in cryo-stasis." He exhaled slowly. "And unless the Bastion's people are less paranoid than I expect, the crews of those ships are likely now dead.

"A price I dislike but I see no choice but to pay."

EB shivered at the flat calm in Hadzhiev's voice. He wasn't sure how many ships they were talking about—the number of victims in play could be carried by as few as two or three ships or as many as a dozen.

But he agreed with Hadzhiev's assessment. If Breanna had a secret fallback, this "Bastion," its people would kill anyone who reached the place who they didn't trust.

"The names and origins of the ships will only do you so much good without the ability to pick them out from the background chaos," Hadzhiev continued after a grim moment. "There are standardized protocols for our ships to pick up scramble codes, emissions and variant identities when they arrive in-system.

"Those protocols are automatic. Without a copy of them, you will never be able to identify the ships in any sensor data you acquire. Without the original list of ships, the protocols are useless. You will need both—and you will need a full set of historical sensor data back to about at least a few weeks."

EB exhaled a long breath. The latter he should be able to get from the government—if he found somebody he could trust—but he had no idea how to get Siya U Hestî scramble protocols!

And that was assuming he believed Hadzhiev's story. It wouldn't be that much work to set all of this up as a long con of some kind. It wouldn't be worth the effort as a trap, EB suspected, but Hadzhiev could easily be trying to lure him into some kind of misstep.

"I have a few contacts I hope to have reached out to before we meet," the enforcer told him. "But who knows what the sequence of events that would result in you having this datachip will be. So..."

Hadzhiev swallowed.

"Janessa Ali was an ambitious Level Seven in the Siya U Hestî," he told EB. "Her contact information will be on the data chip. She's smart and she's dangerous—but she's for sale and she stays bought. Put enough money on the table, and I'm sure she'll sell you the scramble protocols.

"To screw her boss over, if nothing else."

The Siya U Hestî had been *such* a warm and friendly workplace, EB reflected.

"For the sensor data, you'll need to talk to the Icem System Defense Force. The officer I'm planning on reaching out to is Commodore Wu Lim. They command one of the ISDF's nova gunship squadrons and, well, they know who I am for all the wrong reasons," Hadzhiev concluded with a chuckle.

"Weirdly, the fact that Wu Lim has a stick up their ass and a hate-on for all I was and did works in my favor this time. You'll like them, Captain Bardacki. And once they know what's at stake, they'll help us."

There was a final long pause.

"I don't know if there's enough in this recording to clear the way for you," Hadzhiev admitted. "The data on the other chip should give you everything you need, but I'm *hoping* to bring Wu Lim to the dinner reservation.

"That'll make all of this a waste of time, so I should go make some calls." He paused. "But if you are seeing this, Evridiki Bardacki, I am probably dead. Between old enemies I deserve and new enemies I'm going to be making, I'm high on a lot of people's hit lists.

"I'm not aiming for redemption, freeing these people. Some form of absolution, maybe. I don't need anyone to forgive me. Don't *want* anyone to forgive me. I know I can't make what I was and what I enabled right.

"But I can save these people. If you're seeing this, then I might be saving them from beyond the grave—but by void and stars and the life the Siya U Hestî took from me, I beg this one favor of you:

"Save them for me if I cannot. Because I was a dumb kid like your Tracy once, and none of them—*none of them*—deserved where fate has left them."

5

EB DIDN'T MANAGE to get back to sleep after that. He didn't even try, spending the next few hours sitting in the mess room, drinking coffee and mentally spiraling through a dozen different scenarios and options.

By the time the rest of the crew drifted in for their next meal, he'd settled on the bare bones of a plan—and had breakfast and coffee waiting for everyone.

Trace was the last to come in, the young woman glancing around and clearly recognizing that something was going on.

"Did someone call a family meeting or am I just late waking up?" she asked.

"Neither," EB told his daughter with a chuckle. "I could have called a meeting, I suppose, but it seemed easier to just have food and coffee waiting for everyone so we could all talk."

Trace made a face at the coffee and grabbed the hot chocolate that EB had put out for her, then took a seat next to Vexer and looked expectantly at him.

"Is this about that package?" Lan asked, the soft-featured doctor delicately slicing their pancakes into perfect eighths. "It certainly seemed interesting enough."

"Package?" Vexer asked.

"We got a courier package while most of y'all were sleeping," Tate told the XO. "For EB specifically and requiring a signature."

"That's…never a particularly *good* sign," Reggie observed.

"It's not," EB agreed. "In this case, the package was from an escrow agency, and I think we've all been involved in enough crap and watched enough mediocre movies to guess what that means."

He had his people's full attention and he smiled thinly.

"Dead man's mail," he confirmed in answer to their questioning gazes. "A passing acquaintance of ours left me as his final contact. He was also supposed to be our host for that dinner at the Glorious Dragoon, but it appears something went wrong before then."

"Who?" Ginny asked. "I'm not thinking of many friends we have in this area who wouldn't reach out more openly."

"He wasn't a friend," EB warned. "And that's why I'm more than a bit twitchy about this mess. The message was from Ansem—Lady Breanna's bodyguard who gave us the codes to stop her dumping her prisoners into space."

Several of his crew shivered and he felt guilty at the sight of Trace's expression. This whole meeting was going to be rough on his kid, and he met her gaze.

"Trace, this is about the Siya U Hestî," he warned her gently. "And about the kids like you. If you're not feeling up to it, you can grab your chocolate and—"

"No," she cut him off. "If we're getting involved in that mess again, I have to know. I'll survive."

EB nodded. His kid was tough, but he wished she didn't have to be. *He'd* never wanted to engage in violence again after fleeing his homeworld—but he also had to keep his people safe. That was more important to him, in the end.

He'd prefer to keep violence as far down the list as he could manage…but he had to admit what his skillset was. He was a fighter pilot and an electronic-warfare specialist. Violence was an option he was *good* at.

"Ansem…" EB sighed. "I'm just going to play the hologram for you all," he decided aloud. "I have some thoughts on what to do next, but I want to make sure we're all on board."

He put a holoprojector puck on the main mess table and started the playback. The quarter-scale image of Anthony Seminole Hadzhiev materialized above the table, smiling sardonically at EB's crew as he began to speak.

HADZHIEV'S RECORDING ended and EB looked around at his crew. His family. His husband-to-be and their adopted daughter, and the people who'd joined his ship to run away from something.

"This is almost certainly a trap of some kind, isn't it?" Lan finally asked. "But he knows the bait to hang out if it is, doesn't he?"

"If the man's *dead*, that sure suggests he was doing *something*," Reggie pointed out. "And..." The weapons tech trailed off, then coughed as he realized everyone was looking at him.

"Look, people like...Ansem. They *have* consciences, often enough," the tech said quietly. "They just got real good at shutting them up. And then you get a big shock of some kind; either you get told to do something you just *can't* do—or, well, someone shoots you.

"Or both."

EB shivered at the tone of Reggie's last two words. His suspicions about just what Reggie had been up to before joining *Evasion*'s crew were firmer now, but in a few sentences the blond man had told him all he needed to know about *why* Reggie had given up his past life.

He clearly hadn't originally meant to say "people like *Ansem*," after all.

"I don't think we can trust everything Hadzhiev is telling us," EB told his crew. "But...we have a list of ships and locations. Tracking them down isn't impossible, after all. We should at least be able to confirm that they were Siya U Hestî ships from the datavault."

There was only one datavault he could be referring to and his people knew it. Thanks to Trace's nonstandard headware infrastructure and EB's old hacking programs, they had complete access to the status update she'd been supposed to deliver.

"I can do that," Trace said quietly. "But...it makes sense they'd have...people in transit."

"It does," EB confirmed. "We pulled a lot of people out of the Cage, but it seems like we didn't finish the job." He swallowed. "I...feel like we should."

"Everywhere we turn, we collide with the Shadow and Bone," Vexer warned. "We want to get out of their territory, not pick a fight with what's left of them."

"The ship isn't called *Evasion* because I'm out here to pick fights, Vexer," EB replied. "But..." He shook his head. "There are times I don't think we can run. That said..."

He put a copy of Hadzhiev's second chip down on the table and then placed his hands on either side of it, palms down, as he surveyed his crew.

"Two things," he noted. "One, I'm not going to the fucking Siya U Hestî for fucking *anything*. We will find a way to find these ships and trace their courses without talking to this Janessa Ali.

"Two..." EB exhaled a sharp sigh. "I will not knowingly take this crew and this ship into danger without agreement. I believe that there are hundreds of innocent people sealed in cryo-stasis somewhere in this star system.

"I do not believe that we can just hand this over to the authorities," he admitted. "Not without knowing more about what happened to Hadzhiev, anyway. But if you aren't all on board, I'm not going to risk us all."

"I can compare against the datavault and start poking at the station systems to see what we can extract," Trace offered. "These people were kids like me. Afraid, dumb, mistaken—lied to... The Siya U Hestî don't believe anyone is coming for them, and they've convinced their victims of the same.

"Let's prove the *fuckers* wrong."

EB glanced around the room and met Vexer's gaze.

"I would love to go a month without getting in a fight," EB's fiancé said. "But hell, I owe you a wedding gift, and I figure a few hundred innocents saved from assholes counts."

EB chuckled.

"I'm in," Ginny said instantly. "Damnation to all slavers."

The techs chimed in, and then Reggie was the only one still silent. EB arched an eyebrow at his weapons tech, who met his gaze and chuckled.

"Thought my answer was clear enough, boss," Reggie said. "I've got a hell of a lot more karmic debt to pay off than anyone else on this ship. *Of course* I'm in."

6

TRACE LEFT the adults sorting out the rest of the plans and focused on the piece of it she could handle. Adults, especially *her* adults, had uses —and the planning was one of them.

The first step was to go through the data on the chip Hadzhiev had sent them. She swiftly had it hanging in the air in front of her—an illusion created by her headware, given that she was sprawled on the bed in her tiny room.

She only cared about one piece of it: the list of ships. She knew the datavault had extensive lists of ships—not just the Siya U Hestí's own fleet of transports and raiders but also local military, paramilitary and mercenary ships.

That database had allowed her to identify a bounty-hunter ship before she'd even realized that the vault was leaking into her awareness. She'd removed much of the general information from the vault in her head, leaving behind such minor things as "security codes" and "contact addresses for black market weapons and hacking software," but she'd saved *everything* into *Evasion*'s memory.

The datavault itself wasn't physically much bigger than the datachips Hadzhiev had supplied. It was a bit higher density, but there was a lot of empty space on both chips.

There were nine ships listed on the chip. None were even as big as *Evasion*, ranging from ten-thousand-cubic-meter tramps—built on the cheapest and most ubiquitous version of the interstellar nova drive—up to thirty-thousand-cubic ships that were about as large as most local construction got out in the Beyond.

They were coming from six star systems, all on this side of the Fasach Expanse—a large area without stars that was difficult for ships to navigate through. A nova ship had to discharge static every six jumps at most, which limited them to a range of about thirty-six light-years. There was only one place to discharge in the Fasach—the rogue gas giant where Trace had run into *Evasion*'s crew.

One of the nine ships, from the information Hadzhiev had supplied, should have been traveling from that planet, the Diomhair, toward Nigahog. All of them were, eventually, supposed to stop at the Cage—but since the Cage was no more, they would likely have been diverted before Hadzhiev sent out his message.

Any of them that *had* made it to the Cage would have met Nigahog's Extraterritorial Enforcement Agency. The NEEA wasn't well regarded by *Evasion*'s crew, Trace knew, but she was confident that they would have captured any ship showing up at the Cage and freed its kidnappees.

The data included the courses the ships had been following, she realized. Given a bit of time, she figured Dad-V could confirm Hadzhiev's estimate of where the ships would head to Icem from.

Her main task was confirming that the ships *were* Siya U Hestî. Pulling the list from the datavault, she ran a quick comparison.

Nine ships. Eight matches—and the captain listed in Hadzhiev's data for the last ship matched a woman commanding a different, smaller, ship. Trace guessed the woman might have upgraded since her original datavault files had been created.

The concept of a *woman* commanding one of the human-trafficking ships felt strange, but given that the Siya U Hestî was run by a woman —and it had been a woman who had groomed and kidnapped Trace herself!—she knew there had to be some.

Even if it made no sense to her.

A gesture hung the two lists in the air next to each other, with fist-sized models of each ship floating through her bedroom above her head. None of them, thankfully, were the ship that had carried *her* from Icem to the Cage.

Trace clenched her fists, trying to neither focus on nor suppress the memories of that hellish flight. She'd realized early on that being obedient and playing along would give her the best chance of escape. That had let her avoid some of the unpleasantness visited on some of her fellow "passengers," but it had come with its own costs.

Exhaling, she let her fears and nightmares pass through as best as she could.

Seeking a distraction, she pulled up a link to *Evasion*'s sensors and the traffic-control network for High Home Station. She didn't expect to get lucky, but she was still a touch disappointed that there was no sign of any ship by those names.

She figured that with an example, she and Dad-E could reverse-engineer the scramble code that Hadzhiev had mentioned. *Finding* an example, though... That wasn't going to be easy.

Once she found her calm, she'd go back and rejoin the adults with what she'd learned. Right now, though, she was more comfortable in the computers and her own head than she was around people. Even her family.

Still linked into the station's systems, Trace plugged in the name from the chip: Commodore Wu Lim. She figured that a system defense force Commodore had to have some kind of public record.

She wasn't expecting to find Wu Lim's name in the station news, and she shivered as she saw the headline.

SHUTTLE CRASH KILLS TWENTY-SIX.

Digging deeper, Trace grimaced. Commodore Wu Lim was explicitly called out as being a senior SDF officer aboard the shuttle when a thruster nozzle had burned through its liners. Between the flare of the rocket failing and the pilot taking too long to adapt to the loss of the nozzle, the spacecraft had lost control and slammed into High Home Station itself.

Like most major planetary orbitals, High Home had started as a conveniently located and suitably sized asteroid. Between natural rock and human-added armor, the transshipment station could withstand significantly more force than a standard orbital shuttle could.

Trace very carefully did *not* look at the pictures of the crash. The only thing she *really* needed to know was that their planned contact was dead.

What came next... That was for her dads to sort out. Trace hadn't found much useful, really. But she'd at least found *something*. Even if it was bad news, it was better to *know* than guess.

7

IT TOOK ABOUT twenty minutes for EB to settle all of the immediate concerns and send his people off to their usual duties—or, in Tate's case, her quarters to sleep.

That left him alone in the mess hall with his plate of now-cold pancakes and only barely warmer coffee. He took a long sip of the latter, grimacing at what lukewarmness did to its already mediocre flavor.

He was eyeing the pancakes, debating whether it was worth reheating them versus eating them cold, when Trace came back into the room. His daughter looked strained, but she took a seat across from him and smiled wanly at him.

"Any more of that chocolate, Dad-E?" she asked.

"I can manage something," he promised. "Need fresh coffee for myself and to warm these pancakes."

She chuckled and nodded, her smile warming a bit.

"What did you find?" EB asked as he slid the plate into the heater and started water boiling for the chocolate. There was about a cup's worth of coffee left in the pot, and he replaced the tepid liquid in his cup with it as he prepared hot chocolate mix for Trace.

"The ships are what Hadzhiev said they are," she told him. "Siya U

Hestî—Shadow and Bone to the last." She shook her head. "I can't say for sure that they're..."

"Carrying victims," EB concluded for her as she searched for words. "We can't know that, but it seems likely. Would they have been where he said, too?"

"I think so," she said carefully. "I'm not entirely clear on how he communicated with them, so I don't know when they'd have got the order. I figure Dad-V can check courses and such?"

"He can." EB eyed her. She was hesitating around something. He finished her chocolate and dropped it and his fresh coffee on the table before going back for his pancakes.

He let the silence fill the room, warm and comfortable with just him and his daughter there, as he took his first few bites. The pancakes were far from well served by being cooled and reheated, but he was honest enough to admit that *his* pancakes didn't have that much to lose.

"You found something else," he concluded as Trace stared into her hot chocolate without drinking it.

"I did a search on the Commodore he told us to go to," she said quietly. A ping in EB's headware told him she was sharing a file. A news article.

"They're dead," Trace finished bluntly. "Shuttle crashed into High Home Station."

EB was silent, running through the information in the article and considering the situation.

"Accidents like that happen," he observed softly. "More out here than Apollo would tolerate."

More out there than *anyone* liked tolerating, but while the star systems of the Beyond had access to the Standard Colonial Database—a collection of freely shared schematics and scientific literature spread across all of human space—many had difficulties finding the combination of resources, parts and skills necessary to keep everything running at full form.

That said, rocket thrusters were often used for final station approaches *because* they were simpler and even more reliable than the reactionless Harrington coils that provided thrust for most ships. A thruster's nozzle liner *could* fail, but inspection should prevent it—and proper pilot training should have stopped it resulting in enough loss of control to *destroy* the shuttle.

"You don't believe it was an accident," his daughter said, then finally took a sip of her chocolate. "*I* don't believe it was an accident. Hadzhiev said he was going to talk to this Wu Lim, then Wu Lim is dead and he's gone silent?"

Trace was only thirteen, but she'd seen far more ugliness even while living with EB than he would have wished. Her paranoia was well founded, and EB didn't disagree. He nodded silently and finished reading the article.

"The message was recorded five days ago," he said quietly. "We were supposed to meet Hadzhiev last night—and Commodore Wu died the night before that."

He shook his head.

"What was the commander of a nova gunship squadron even *doing* on an under-maintained civilian shuttle?" he asked pointlessly, then sighed and answered his own question. "He was trying to avoid notice. And he failed."

Trace nodded grimly.

"Thruster nozzles haven't been covered in what Aurora has been teaching me," she admitted. Aurora Narang was *Evasion*'s engine tech, working with Ginny to keep the ship flying. "I can just about do daily maintenance on a Harrington coil, if I've got the parts and someone to ask questions of. But I only know what a *thruster liner* is from a passing discussion of early rocketry in my history class."

"Thrusters use action-reaction and hot gasses to achieve acceleration," EB said simply. "Hot enough that the inside of the directional nozzles slowly burns away. So, we line them with material that is more heat-resistant and made in one piece for easy replacement—the liner.

"They *can* fail, but they're supposed to be inspected." He sighed. "And it doesn't take much of an explosive to breach one while the rocket is firing."

"So, someone knew what shuttle Wu Lim was on *and* decided they were a threat," Trace guessed. "That's…not a great sign for our safety, is it, Dad?"

"There are a lot of things in this universe I am afraid of," EB admitted, reaching out to take his daughter's hand gently. "But I am far more afraid of the Vortanis trying to take you away than I am of anyone trying to sabotage *Evasion*.

"And I have plans for *that*, too," he said with a smile. "We're going to be fine, Trace. And we're going to find these poor kids and finish what Hadzhiev started."

"Even if it means we go talk to this Janessa Ali?" she asked.

He grimaced.

"Maybe," he conceded. "First, though…you and I are going to break out the best of the old electronic-warfare toys and start prodding station systems. I'm *guessing* that the Glorious Dragoon's systems will be easier to crack than Arteve Escrow's, but one of them is going to let us in, my dear.

"And once it does, it's going to tell us where Lady Breanna's ex-dog was hiding."

8

TRACE HAD TAKEN to the hacking software and all of the surrounding information and skills like a fish to water. Some of it, EB suspected, was a consequence of her foster father mucking with her headware. Her in-head software was much more flexible than any he'd seen before, which allowed her to take advantage of features he hadn't even known his electronic-warfare programs *had*.

Still, neither the restaurant nor the escrow agency had basic security. Both clearly outsourced information security to high-quality third-party contractors—and he wasn't so lucky that they'd both hired the *same* consultants.

After over half an hour of poking at assorted avenues of approaching the two businesses' systems, EB went to get a drink of water and consider the problem.

"We could ask?" Trace suggested. "The escrow agency knows that the package was for you, for example. They might be willing to let you know information about the sender."

He shook his head.

"Not how they work," he told her. "They won't hand over anything they weren't specifically instructed to. That kind of by-the-letter instruction-following is their stock-in-trade.

"We might be better off talking to the Dragoon—they, at least, appear to be irritated that Hadzhiev invited us and bailed. But, again…" He spread his hands.

"Discretion is part of their 'stock-in-trade,'" she quoted back to him.

"Exactly." EB stared blankly at the wall. "If I knew *when* the big guy had dropped off the package at the escrow agency, we could see if the cameras outside the office are more vulnerable."

"Well, how long would he have waited after recording?" Trace asked. "We know when he recorded it."

Five days before. Hadzhiev could have spoofed the time stamp, EB figured, but there was no *reason* for that.

"It also seems likely that he gave them the package before he spoke to Wu Lim," she continued. "Which, unfortunately, I figure was before they died."

EB nodded slowly and smiled.

"So, we know he dropped the package off at least two days ago and no more than five," he agreed. "You keep poking at Dragoon's systems," he told her. "I'll see if I can get into station surveillance."

The irony, of course, was that private system security aboard High Home Station was better than that of the station's overall infrastructure. Companies that made privacy part of their appeal hired the best. Outside of militaries and critical infrastructure, most government systems ran on the lowest bidder.

While the defensive systems and power plants were concealed behind significantly better security, internal surveillance had even shoddier security than he was expecting. His Apollo-written software sliced through their firewalls like they weren't even there, and he shook his head.

"Something to keep in mind, I guess," he murmured.

"Dad?"

"Station Security's surveillance systems are secured with, roughly, wet tissue paper," he told her. "So, if we're on High Home Station, we can pretty much assume we're being tracked."

"Huh." Trace, quite sensibly, looked concerned at that.

"But for now…" EB quickly fed the holographic message that

Hadzhiev had sent them into a facial-recognition suite he'd kept tucked away for a rainy day. *He* wasn't going to watch three days' worth of recorded security footage if he could avoid it.

To his surprise, he had a match almost immediately.

"Looks like our friend went straight to Arteve after recording the message." He pulled the footage his program had found and watched the big gunslinger walk into the office like he owned the entire space station.

EB had only encountered "Ansem" twice, once as Lady Breanna's escort and the second time as a troubleshooter sent to stop him freeing the prisoners in the Cage. Both times, the man had possessed a certain *swagger* that EB knew he didn't share.

Even after EB had called fire from the ships outside down on their shared position and then shot Hadzhiev repeatedly, the man had radiated a degree of power and confidence few shared. Every ounce of that was still present as he'd entered Arteve's office, for all that he *had* to be less certain of himself.

A thought struck EB as he ran through the footage at high speed, and he checked the time stamp on the holographic message.

"Huh."

"Dad?"

"He recorded the message *in* Arteve's office," EB told Trace. "I plugged in the scan by days and picked up about eleven hours more than I meant to. Which worked out for us, it seems."

Hadzhiev had been in the office for just over two hours, he assessed, before leaving and heading elsewhere in the station. For all of High Home Station's other failings, the surveillance network was station-wide, and EB could follow the other man through his five-day-previous journey.

The probably-ex-criminal had wandered into a food court and eaten a meal that EB skimmed by. Hadzhiev might have met someone there, but that wasn't really relevant to EB. He needed to know where the man had been staying.

And after his meal, that was where he had gone. A mid-tier hotel on the resident's ring, well away from the usual places where outsiders to the system would stay.

"Got it," he said aloud. "Blue Holiday Hotel, Ring Two."

He shut down his link and smiled at Trace. "A place to start, at least."

"You're going back aboard?" she asked.

"I am. And I'm taking Reggie, I promise," he told her. "I need you to check in with Vexer and get him to calculate those updated origin points."

"I..." Trace trailed off and he stepped over to grip her shoulder reassuringly.

"You don't need to see him," EB assured her. He wasn't sure if Hadzhiev would trigger his kid's trauma, but just digging back into the Siya U Hestî seemed to be setting her on edge.

He needed her to heal, with a power and certainty he'd rarely felt. He'd taken her in and he was going to protect her—but it had been *under* his protection that she'd killed a person for the first time.

EB knew he couldn't keep her out of everything—she had her own personal stake in all of this. But he was going to keep her safe.

No matter what.

"I'll go find Reggie," he told her. "I'm not going alone and I'm not going unarmed. We'll find out what happened, Trace. And then we'll make plans from there."

He wasn't seeing a lot of choices at the moment, but he'd *make* them if he had to.

9

ICEM REGARDED itself as civilized space—and however backward *EB*
might regard the system, he supposed they had at least some point.
There was an active system-wide police presence. There was an orbital
elevator on each planet, and each planet even had a proper asteroid
fortress.

One asteroid fortress. And their production of Harrington coils,
antigrav units and nova drives was limited enough that apparently
orbit-to-orbit shuttles used rockets to save money.

But they were also one of the two systems in the region with *any*
kind of nova-capable force, too. On the other hand, with less than sixty
million people in the system, their infrastructure, resources and
general *civilization* lagged well behind even the Outer Rim.

Still, self-image was important—and because the Icemi regarded
themselves as civilized, blasters were heavily restricted in populated
cities and on space stations.

EB wasn't sure how Reggie had acquired the licenses necessary to
carry one, but *EB* hadn't. That meant that he went in front, carrying the
almost universally acceptable personal stunner, while his self-identi-
fying goon followed behind with an actually lethal weapon.

He even mostly trusted Reggie to use the stunner the man was also carrying *before* resorting to the blaster, outside of the situation having obviously already reached that level of violence.

The area of High Home Station they were walking through didn't feel like the kind of place that was used to situations getting that far. It wasn't the nicest area of the station—there were areas and hotels in the visitors' section of the station that had *water features*, after all—but it had something the visitors' rings and decks didn't.

This place held people's homes. Everything from a small but noticeably higher level of cleanliness to the clearly amateur but heartfelt murals painted on the corridor bulkheads told EB that.

"Why are there even hotels in this kind of area?" Reggie muttered. "You don't *want* strangers in this chunk of the station."

No one was *actively* looking daggers at them, but EB could tell that the majority of the people around them knew at least some of the others. As Reggie noted, it wasn't a place for strangers. This was where the people who kept High Home Station running day to day and week to week lived.

"Because these people have families and friends who live on the planet or other stations," he pointed out. "Most of the people who'd stay in a section like this are looking to stay close to people they know. The hotel won't turn anyone *away*, I'm sure, but their clients mostly aren't strangers."

"Which makes our friend more visible here...but also makes it less likely the hotel is being watched or has an existing channel to report to anyone," Reggie guessed. "Huh."

"It's a balancing act of risk," EB agreed. "I'm not sure it's a path I'd have taken, but it seems to be Hadzhiev's course here."

There were *three* Blue Holiday Hotels on High Home Station, he'd learned in the last hour or so, but they were all in places like this one: small commercial sectors tucked away in the residence sectors of the station. They were next to the spaceborne equivalent of neighborhood pubs and grocery stores, not ship sutlers and spacers' bars.

This one shared an exterior façade with images he'd seen of the other two on High Home—and likely with the other twenty-odd franchises across the system's two inhabited planets and their orbital platforms.

The front of the hotel was painted a soothing eggshell blue, with a columned portico extending a meter and a half out into the corridor to shield guests from nonexistent rain. A holographic greeter stood off to one side of the entrance, to answer questions from potential visitors.

"So, how are we planning on finding this guy?" Reggie asked. "He's not going to be staying under his own name, is he?"

EB grunted. He'd followed that chain of thought himself, and it hadn't ended anywhere productive.

"No," he admitted. "But we know he *was* here. I'm going to gently poke their systems and see if I can find any sign."

"Their systems," in this case, being an automated hotel directory that would allow a visitor to contact a guest if they knew their name and room number. The security was *supposed* to stop anyone pulling the directory straight from the file, but EB had hacked military recon drones.

The hotel's firewall barely slowed him down—but he paused as he accessed the files. There was active code running that shouldn't be there. He managed to isolate it, but he wasn't sure he'd stopped it sending a message home.

"Someone bugged the directory," EB told Reggie. "It just phoned home, so we should probably get moving away from the hotel for a moment."

Whoever had left the snippet of code would know that the directory had been downloaded, but they wouldn't be able to locate or identify EB—he didn't think.

"Let's go grab a burger," Reggie suggested, gesturing toward the pub. "Unless you think we're going to be assassinated between here and there?"

"No. Food sounds good."

He needed to review the data, anyway. And keeping his eyes on the hotel might tell him just *who* had left that little trap behind.

EB WAS HALF-EXPECTING to see a squad of station-security officers descend on the hotel. He put the odds at slightly over sixty percent that the trap code was at least semiofficial and belonged to law enforcement.

No tactical teams or mob enforcers descended on the quiet neighborhood strip mall. Everything seemed to continue on as if completely normal, and EB eventually focused on his stolen data.

The food wasn't much of a distraction. The fries, burger and coffee were roughly exactly what he'd expected: perfectly serviceable, neither particularly good nor notably bad. It was a local pub, with no pretensions of grandeur but a steady audience to serve.

"I see our friend wasn't overly concerned about being found," EB said after a few seconds.

"Oh?" Reggie asked. The weapons tech had taken the seat facing the door and was failing at pretending to relax. Something about the situation was setting EB's companion on edge more than EB expected.

"He's on the list as Anthony Seminole," EB explained. "That's two-thirds of his real name." He chuckled wryly. "I considered just walking in and *asking* for him by that name."

"It's two-thirds of the name *he gave you*," Reggie corrected sharply. "Which means he wanted you to be able to find this hotel. Which means it could be part of a trap."

"It could." The captain eyed Reggie for a few long seconds. "What's up, Reggie?"

"An older gent who is trying to look normal but is boosted to about seven out of five showed up at the same time as our burgers," the tech said. "He isn't the *only* boosted local who has wandered past, but he's been sticking around and talking to folks.

"I don't think any of the locals have picked up on it, but I know a cop gladhand-for-info when I see it, boss."

"And you're only mentioning this now..." EB asked.

Reggie snorted. "Because I wanted to finish my burger? And because I wasn't *entirely* sure until he started walking our way."

EB wasn't certain what metric Reggie was using to class the stranger as "seven out of five" or where Reggie would put his own set of augments on that scale. Glancing across the main corridor, though, that descriptor helped him pin the stranger down almost instantly.

There was a certain smoothness to the movements of anyone with physical augments. The type of augments that made someone count as *boosted* had limited—but real!—noncombat uses, but most people limited themselves to the standard array of headware and a few special-purpose implants.

EB was probably one of the least modified people he knew, especially since every person he knew with a uterus had at least *one* more implant than he did. Reggie, on the other hand, had a limited but capable set of combat boosts of his own.

The stranger was about on par with Reggie, EB judged. And that meant that, whoever he was, he was no beat cop.

"He's going to come to our table," EB said with a sigh, studying the body language. "Cop, I think, and he's IDed the only strangers who are *still* here since the alarm triggered."

"What do we do?" Reggie asked, his twitches smoothing away. That was dangerous. That meant he'd brought his boosts fully online.

"We talk, Reggie," EB said firmly. "We talk. Nothing more."

EB WAS IMPRESSED, at least, with the man's bravado. The stranger wore a mediocre suit, the kind with oversized shoulders sufficient to conceal body armor and a shoulder holster, but other than that and the boosts, he looked like any other graying sixty-odd businessman.

That didn't stop him walking right up to EB and Reggie's table and smiling down at them.

"Excuse me, may I join you?" he asked brightly.

EB arched an eyebrow.

"I'd say that was...an unusual request," he pointed out, "except that I flagged you as a detective before you even entered the pub. So, I don't get the impression we have much choice, do we?"

"I suppose the choice, Captain Bardacki, is whether we have a civil conversation here or a *less*-civil conversation at the station," the man said, his tone still bright. "It would be difficult to make charges of hacking stick, but I certainly have enough evidence to bring you in for a chat.

"I suspect, however, that you can help me, and I'd rather keep things...*civil*."

"Have a seat, Detective," EB instructed, mentally ordering the server stupid to swing by their table and take the man's order.

"Senior Detective Prasada Everest, High Home Security Homicide," Everest introduced himself. He glanced at the stupid as it rolled up and asked for his order.

"Water, please," he told the bot. "Nothing else."

It chirped inquisitively at EB and Reggie, who gestured it away.

"Homicide, huh." That fit EB's expectations—and his fears. "And what does a homicide detective want with a pair of random strangers enjoying a burger?"

"You're looking for Anthony Seminole, I'm guessing," Everest said calmly. "No one else of sufficient interest to require hacking the directory has stopped at the Blue Holiday in the last couple of *years*, let alone recently."

"This place is that boring, is it?"

"I *am* High Home Station's Homicide team," the detective replied. "And I have *been* the Homicide team for eleven standard years. The only reason I'm even being promised an assistant is because the Board realizes I have to retire eventually.

"Between those eleven years and the ten before that where I had a senior partner, our Homicide team has carried out barely two hundred investigations—and over *half* of them turned out to actually be accidental deaths."

Everest snorted.

"I double as backup for our Organized Crime team, which is *much* busier," he said wryly. "But the Seminole case... Yeah. That's my purview, so why don't you tell me why you were looking for Anthony Seminole?"

"I haven't said we were," EB pointed out.

He got A Look from the detective, one that suggested that however quiet the Homicide team on High Home might find their docket, Everest was still damn good at his job.

"Well, if you *are* looking for him, you'll *find* him in the morgue at High Home Primary Medical," Everest said flatly. "Seminole is the victim in my current investigation, which is all the information *I'm* going to give you unless you decide to start sharing yourself."

That had been reasonably obvious, and EB considered the situation for a few seconds before he sighed and leaned back in his chair. Swallowing down the last of his coffee, he pointed the mug at the cop.

"Anthony Seminole invited me to a dinner reservation on this station to discuss what he described as 'unfinished business,'" EB explained. "To give you an idea of the apparent importance of this, we were in the Estutmost System when we received the invite."

"And you came here to have dinner with the man?" Everest asked.

"I didn't realize it was him at the time. I thought the invitation was to do with my adopted daughter, who is from this system." EB had no real reason to *lie* to the detective, though he wasn't going to tell the man everything, either.

"I received some communication from him that confirmed he was the person who contacted us, but I hadn't heard from him otherwise since we got here, and he didn't make the dinner invitation. I suspected he had met an ugly fate, but I needed to *know*."

Everest grimaced. "About as ugly as you can think. Shot at close range with a projectile weapon loaded with explosive rounds."

Given what EB remembered of Hadzhiev's reaction to being repeatedly shot with a blaster and the general level of boosts the Siya U Hestî soldier had possessed...that was about the level of killing that the man would take.

"Someone knew who they were after," he murmured.

Everest chuckled grimly.

"I see you were familiar with Seminole's level of augmentation," he noted. "I'm not entirely sure sixteen grams of high-density explosive in the upper torso would have been enough to kill him on its own, but neither was the shooter. Two shots to the torso, one to the skull, followed up with a close-range electromagnetic pulse to burn out his cybernetics."

EB exhaled softly. "That's a lot of killing," he admitted. "I wouldn't expect a weapon like that to be aboard the station."

Projectile weapons were generally regulated alongside blasters—

but the kind of weapon that could put sixteen grams of explosive into a target was usually just straight-up illegal.

"No. I also wouldn't expect three explosive rounds and an EMP to be fired off without triggering an alert," Everest told him. "And yet we didn't know about the murder until a cleaning stupid entered the room about sixteen hours after the event.

"Surveillance doesn't show anyone entering the room, which means we are looking for someone *very* skilled at editing our footage on the fly. You can see, Captain Bardacki, why your hacking of the directory drew my attention."

"I haven't said I did any such thing," EB replied.

"But you don't seem surprised that Em Seminole is dead," Everest said. "And it's more than just that you haven't heard from him. So, tell me, Captain, who wanted Anthony Seminole dead?"

"A lot of people, I suspect. He was Siya U Hestî."

Reggie inhaled sharply, clearly surprised that EB would give up that piece of data. EB, on the other hand, felt no reason to keep it secret. Hadzhiev was *dead*, after all.

"Someone got in close and took him out with a weapon basically designed to kill him, specifically," EB continued. "That tells me that he was almost certainly murdered by another Siya U Hestî operative. Likely another enforcer or senior agent like himself. I am not under the impression that his identity, let alone his implants, were common knowledge in the Cartel."

Everest steepled his hands and studied EB.

"Your encounters with the Siya U Hestî are relatively common knowledge in law enforcement in the area these days," he observed. "Which at least answers the question of how *you* knew that he was Siya U Hestî. But why would his compatriots have turned on him?"

"I don't know," EB lied. *That* was information he wasn't prepared to yield yet. He had every reason to believe that reaching out to the Icemi government was what had betrayed Hadzhiev's presence to the Bastion.

"I don't *know*," he repeated after a moment, "but the Siya U Hestî are coming apart at the seams, and that kind of internal conflict leads to violence with criminals. That's how it goes, as I understand it."

Everest sighed and nodded slowly.

"That's true, as far as it goes, but I have the feeling you're not telling me everything, Captain."

"I've answered your questions," EB said carefully. "And you've told me of what I feared, the fate and fall of Anthony Seminole. What more do you need?"

"Are we free to leave, officer?" Reggie asked firmly.

"I appreciate your information, Captain Bardacki," Everest conceded. "I know more than I did an hour ago. But I still don't know who killed the man."

"Neither do I," EB told him.

"In answer to the question, though, you are free to leave," the cop said. He slid a physical card—a small sliver of paper with a tiny information chip concealed in it—over to EB.

"If you happen to…*remember* anything else that might be relevant, let me know," he told them. "We don't like people getting killed on our station, Captain Bardacki. Even criminals."

10

AT THIRTEEN YEARS OLD, Trace was not at all clear on what she wanted from life yet. So far, she was sure she didn't want to leave *Evasion* again, and that was about it. She also *really* wished that her own trouble would stop following the ship around.

While EB might have had his own conflicts with the Siya U Hestî, Trace was certain that if *she* hadn't been with them and had a datavault of all of the Cartel's secrets in her head, the crew would have escaped their notice a while back.

Now, though, they were in her home system—one misplaced phone call from Trace having to deal with the foster parents she'd run away from! Not helped, she realized, by the fact that Sarah Vortani appeared to have put a lot of money and almost all of her influence behind trying to find Trace.

That was not what she had expected, and she found herself watching an old interview from just after she'd run away, where the raven-haired and pale-skinned then-MP had all but *begged* anyone with information to come forward.

"I wasn't the mother I should have been," Sarah Vortani told the interviewer. "I can't make that right, but I *can* make sure Tracy is safe. I hope."

The tone, the body language, *everything* in the interview was off from what Trace was used to with her foster mother. Trace may have been a prop for Sarah Vortani's political career, but her running away and subsequent kidnapping had apparently struck the woman *hard*.

Another interview queued up on her search, from more recently. In this one, Sarah was calmer, back in the political mode that Trace was more familiar with.

"I have accepted the post of Assistant Minister for Justice with great reservations," she told the interviewer. "We now know that my foster daughter was kidnapped and taken from our star system by a human-trafficking cartel.

"I failed her, and I can't undo that," she said flatly. "But what I might be able to do is make sure that no other child shares that fate. I have been given several mandates as I work to support Minister Cartwright, but high on my priority list is working to make certain that our anti-organized-crime forces are properly coordinated and equipped across the star system.

"I presume that Minister Cartwright will continue to be the face of the Justice Ministry and our system-wide law-enforcement presence," Vortani continued. "But our gang unit leads and our police chiefs should expect to hear from me shortly.

"We like to think our systems and our protections are perfect, but Tracy Finley was groomed, kidnapped and smuggled out of this system under our very noses." She shook her head sadly. "I can't promise it won't happen again. I *will* promise that we are going to move the stars and void itself to Make. It. Stop."

Trace shivered and turned off the interview. Even *she* wasn't sure if she could read Vortani's actual feelings on the matter, but the face of it was that her kidnapping had changed her former foster parent's entire political course.

She didn't remember exactly what Sarah Vortani's main platform items had *been* before she'd run away. She was quite certain that the justice portfolio hadn't even been on the woman's radar, for all of Vortani's time as a lawyer.

But a quick data search told her that a first-term Member of Parliament being appointed even *Assistant* Minister was a major coup.

Vortani might have detoured from her plan because of Trace's kidnapping, but it had served her well.

Trace still had no interest in going *back* to her foster parents—EB and Vexer had adopted her, and there wasn't even a trace of temporariness there. She was staying with her dads. But she was surprised and gratified to see that Sarah Vortani appeared to have actually *cared* that Trace had gone missing, rather than simply replacing the living prop the way she'd expected.

She wasn't *supposed* to be looking at the news, though, and she looked up guiltily as Vexer stepped into the "office"—a converted storage closet near the office where she could work in quiet—to check on her.

"How did your run at the station sensors go?" he asked.

"Short and pointless," Trace replied. "The station's onboard surveillance has all the security of damp cheese, but the sensors and traffic-control systems are locked down. Physically disconnected from the communications systems and the station datanet."

Vexer softly whistled.

"That's...harsh," he observed.

"I think they know how crap their security software is," she admitted. "So, they removed it from the equation for the systems they absolutely *needed* to be secure."

"Makes sense." He squeezed her shoulder. "What took so long, then?"

"Got distracted by news about the Vortanis," Trace admitted. "Apparently, Sarah was actually looking for me. Like...seriously." She sighed bitterly. "As usual, it's worked out for her politically."

"Hence Assistant Minister," Vexer said. "I get it, Trace. If *any* of Estuval's Dukes were here, let alone Duke Baard..."

He shivered. So did Trace, when she remembered the very rough summary she'd been given of Vexer's home system. The Dukes of Estuval owned *all* orbital and space traffic in their system, *including* the crews. Vexer had been chattel, a highly technically trained not-quite-slave.

So, if his old Duke had been around, she figured Vexer would be hiding in the ship. Or, potentially, borrowing heavy weapons from Reggie.

"Did you recalculate those courses for Dad-E?" she asked, changing the subject.

"Yep," Vexer confirmed. "Looks like Hadzhiev made it to Poberin shortly after we left Nigahog. He sent out his recall order, then came here." The navigator stared blankly into space for a second, then a file update appeared in Trace's headware.

"At least two of the ships likely knew about the Cage's fate before they got his message, so those are wild cards," he noted. "Otherwise, I make the timelines about the same as he did. Last of the ships should have been here a week ago."

"So, they all made it to this Bastion," she guessed. "So, they're here...or were, at least."

Trace thought about the situation for a moment, then checked the data Hadzhiev had provided compared to the files from the datavault.

"Hadzhiev didn't give us a lot on the ships," she murmured, "but the *datavault* contained pretty thorough details on the Siya U Hestî ships, plus the data I pulled from the computers in Estutmost appears to have the Estutmost scramble codes."

There was a thoughtful pause.

"And just what are you thinking about doing with that?" Vexer asked.

"We can't get into the traffic-control data, but *Evasion*'s sensors are decent, right?"

"Built in the Rim by folks who owed EB a favor, from what I can tell," he agreed. "Low end of Outer Rim military grade, but given that even the Icemi *SDF* is running SCD tech..."

"Our scanners are probably just as good as traffic control's," Trace guessed. Icemi Orbital Traffic Control had significantly larger arrays and more scanners to work with, but the resolution on *Evasion*'s scanners was higher.

"For some purposes," Vexer said slowly. "You want to see if any of those ships are *here*, don't you?"

"I have full physical specs on three of them," she told him. "And enough information on several of the others to run through the scramble code and see if we have any close matches."

"It's not likely that the scramble code for Estutmost is going to be remotely similar to the code for Icem," he warned. "EB could probably explain the logic better than I could, but I think those codes have to vary a *lot* to work."

"It gives us a place to start," she said.

"That it does. Give me five to grab a coffee and meet me on the bridge?"

TRACE WAS STILL LEARNING MOST of the various roles and systems aboard *Evasion*. To the extent that she *had* a role on the bridge, it was mostly internal communications—summarizing and relaying information from the rest of the crew to her dads.

She could run the data analysis herself, but she still needed Vexer to run the sensor sweep. And, when she was being more honest, she recognized that her data-analysis skills were still rough.

Even her hacking, if she was being particularly forthright, was seventy percent using EB's hacking programs and twenty-seven percent using the codes and information included in the Siya U Hestî datavault.

Trace could do a lot of things on *Evasion* semi-competently, but she was still learning. Having Vexer look over her shoulder as she ran the data analysis made her feel a lot better.

Especially when she came up blank.

"There's a handful of ships over here"—she haloed them in the shared headware feed—"that are rough matches for a couple of our targets, but that's because they're Icem-built ten-kilocubic tramps."

Less than a quarter of *Evasion*'s size, those tramps were the backbone of trade in the Beyond—but almost entirely in their sheer numbers rather than any great efficiency or unique value. Basically, any ten-kilocubic built in the same yards would get a rough match with any other ship built a few years on either side of it.

"Yeah, I don't think they're our traffickers with a fresh coat of paint," Vexer agreed. "I'm not really surprised, Trace."

"Why?" she demanded.

"Two—no, three reasons," he said. "Firstly, the last of them would have arrived a week ago. Cargo ships don't make money sitting still. Without a good reason, none of them would be sticking around.

"Secondly, I doubt the Bastion is on Denton. There's over forty-five million people around here, which means we've got orbitals, we've got transports…" Vexer shook his head. "No, I don't think that the Siya U Hestî's secret base is here. It *might* be on Tarsus, but I'm figuring it's somewhere around Deus."

Deus was the system's inner gas giant, home to a small number of cloudscoops and discharge stops. Given how quiet the gas giant was in terms of traffic, Trace could see his point. It was the best place to hide a space station or major facility in her home system—short of the outer gas giant, Machina, which had *no* traffic at all.

"What was the third reason?" she asked.

Vexer sighed.

"If the Bastion is as secret as Hadzhiev's message suggested, they may have killed the crews and destroyed the ships to keep themselves hidden," he admitted. "They *probably* removed the trafficking victims first, if only to have them on hand for later sale, but the ships and their crews represent a security threat the Bastion's people wouldn't tolerate."

She grimaced.

"That…is awful," she said quietly. "But fits with these assholes, doesn't it?"

The last senior Siya U Hestî official they'd met had unleashed a swarm of autonomous killing machines to try to cover their escape. It hadn't worked out for them—Trace had turned the robots on the Siya U Hestî—but they'd been willing to risk having the robots kill an entire city to allow them to get away.

The leaders of a crime syndicate weren't known for caring about collateral damage.

11

EB FOUND his fiancé and his daughter on the bridge when he came back aboard *Evasion*. He gave Vexer a quick kiss, then dropped heavily into one of the free seats with a sigh.

"Any luck with the sensors?" he asked them.

"No," Trace told him, her voice tired. "We used our sensors to get a look at who's around right now, but none of the transports are here. Dad-V figures they either never came to Denton or already left."

"Or the Bastion's people killed them," Vexer added grimly. "I ran the numbers, and Hadzhiev's idea of where the ships should have been makes sense to me. They all should have been here by the time we got his message in Estutmost."

"Local traffic-control sensors and their records are air-gapped from the datanets," he continued with a glance at their daughter. "I can see a couple of ways to get the *current* data, but historical data is harder."

"We might be able to physically access the traffic-control systems on High Home Station, but that's asking for trouble and would only get us Denton history," EB said thoughtfully. "And the security on High Home Station seems to have a pretty good idea of how bad their digital security is.

"They're *definitely* watching for people breaking through their fire-walls, and they're not above using it as a trap."

Vexer studied him for a moment after that, then chuckled grimly. "You walked into it?" he asked.

"Oh, yeah," EB admitted. "I don't think they pinged my access to the surveillance cams, but when I hacked Hadzhiev's hotel, I managed to bring the local Homicide detective down on me."

"Homicide?" Vexer echoed. "So, his message was a literal dead man's mail."

"Yeah. Hadzhiev is dead and, from the sounds of it, took a lot of killing to do it. Except that his killer isn't on the surveillance feeds." EB had checked, looking to see if the local security had missed something.

They hadn't. *Looking* for a missing person, EB had found traces that someone had walked into the hotel around when Everest had said Hadzhiev was killed. But they'd been expertly sliced out of the footage, on a moment-by-moment, pixel-by-pixel basis.

"I've never seen anything like it," he admitted. "I've seen repeated footage, spliced layers, masked faces, that kind of thing—but everything else in the footage is perfectly normal. But if you look hard enough, there are artifacts that show something was edited.

"And, presumably, that something was a person entering the hotel, carrying a weapon that is *spectacularly* illegal on High Home Station."

"You might be understating it, boss," Reggie told him. EB glanced up to see his weapons tech walking over to the command console, a matte-black carrying case in his hands. "I had to go looking. Not many guns *I* know of that can do what the cop described, but..."

Reggie put the case on top of the console and opened it, gesturing every eye in the room to the massive hand cannon inside.

"This is a fifteen-millimeter special-purpose-munition revolver," he said grimly. "This *particular* version is an Armadillo Armaments SPM-Fifteen Ghostmaker. Five chambers individually loaded. Cylinder has powered rotation and can switch to a specific round in under a quarter-second."

EB was reasonably sure he couldn't fire the gun one-handed. He was *quite* sure that Trace couldn't fire it with *both* hands.

"You figure it was something like this?" he asked Reggie.

"There aren't a lot of pure projectile weapons being made these days," the other man told him. "This is designed to be used by boosted shooters and give them a moderately portable counter to hostiles in armor.

"That said, it ended up being banned in the system where they *built* it, which is pretty common. It has four different varieties of armor-piercing round, two of which will breach a station's exterior hull—and one of which might have done so *from the Blue Holiday.*"

EB considered where the hotel had been and shivered.

"So, armor-piercing and EMP rounds?" he asked softly.

Reggie nodded, tapping the top half of the case. Distracted by the sheer size of a handgun nearly half a meter long, EB had missed the massive bullets in the other half of the carrying case.

"I have *one* full box of ammunition for this thing," he observed. "Light-armor-piercing explosive round, standard power-armor-piercing round, tank-armor-piercing round, and discarding sabot penetrator round." He tapped each cartridge—each ten times as long as they were wide—as he spoke.

"Also, general high-explosive, electromagnetic pulse, tangleweb and an area stun bomb," he concluded. "Eight rounds—one of each!—in the carrying case. The supply box has four of each. I have forty bullets for the Ghostmaker."

"Can even *you* fire that?" Trace asked, the teenager staring at the massive handgun.

"I'm boosted enough that, yes, I can fire it one-handed," Reggie said calmly. "Which tells us a few things about the killer."

"Oh?" EB asked. He had some pretty specific thoughts himself, but he suspected Reggie had more bitterly won experience with this kind of situation.

"He was boosted. Beyond any civilian justification," the tech noted. "If he managed to carry and fire a gun like this without it drawing huge attention, he was more boosted than Detective Everest.

"Second, he had access to some seriously esoteric firepower. There's no equivalent to the Ghostmaker in the SCD, though the *tech* to build something like it is there. My quick-and-dirty check says that nobody in the local systems builds anything like this. Closest I found records of is back in Tatare."

He spread his hands. "So, either our killer had a tool *custom-made* to take down Hadzhiev, or he had a specific type of rare esoteric special-purpose firearm imported from the other side of the Fasach Expanse.

"Third." Reggie ran his hand over the gleaming barrel of the hand cannon. "Hadzhiev knew them and trusted them enough to turn his back on them. This is *not* a weapon you can quick-draw. I don't care *how* boosted our killer was. Hadzhiev would have outdrawn them if he'd seen them drawing it."

He chuckled.

"Voids, *Trace* would have outdrawn someone pulling this out," he admitted. "They likely had all the tools and tricks to make it a fast and deadly draw, but they still needed to either sneak up on Hadzhiev or make him think he was safe."

"I was thinking the same," EB said grimly. "On top of that, our killer has access to digital overwatch unlike anything I've seen before. That said, I've fought Hadzhiev." He shook his head. "There is no way they snuck up on him, and there's no way they outdrew him. Which means his killer was someone he knew, someone he thought was safe.

"And Hadzhiev did not strike me as the type of man to think *anyone* was safe."

The bridge was silent and EB glanced around at his people.

"So, Hadzhiev himself is a literal dead end," he concluded. "It sounds like we're not going to get historical data from the system scans without a contact, but Hadzhiev's contact died in a freak accident.

"We're out of good options, people, and I only really see two left."

He didn't like either of them, but they were the choices in front of him.

"One, we write the whole situation off," he said quietly. "Hadzhiev may have been playing us. He might not have been, but we're short on data and places to go. There will be other people looking for those trafficking victims—we could probably hand everything we have over to Detective Everest and let him find the right assets to find and free them."

"We have every reason to believe that contacting the Icemi government is what *killed* Hadzhiev," Vexer pointed out, his voice equally soft. "And almost certainly killed Commodore Wu Lim, too. This Bastion has the local system wired up forward and back again, I suspect. Giving Everest the information may just kill *him*."

"That's a possibility," EB agreed. "And not something I'm dismissing, Vexer. But we're down to one option that isn't leaving, and I want to make sure we all realize that we *can* walk away."

"I was one of those kids once," Trace whispered. She looked up at EB and he met her gaze. "Can we, really?"

He exhaled.

"The other option is that we deal with the devil again," he warned. "If we can't run and we've no more clues of our own to follow, the last choice we have left is to go to Janessa Ali.

"Are we ready to step into bed with the Siya U Hestî again? Even hiring a *former* Cartel member as a mercenary?"

"We don't have a choice," Vexer said. "If Ali is the only lead we have left, we have to follow it. We're the last hope those poor kids have."

EB was still holding Trace's gaze. There was no demand in her eyes. No requirement. Simply...the knowledge that *she* had once been aboard a ship like those diverted to the Bastion. She had been a foolish child, fooled and kidnapped.

Just like the hundreds of teenagers now trapped in cryo-stasis somewhere in this star system.

"Okay. I'll make the call."

12

EB WAS sick to death of playing nice with monsters. The Siya U Hestî were slavers, kidnappers, murderers, pirates, thugs, drug dealers—all of the oldest tricks of organized crime run with absolute ruthlessness and the best technology available in the region of space he'd found himself in.

Before he'd arrived there, he'd been making a very real attempt to never engage in violence in his life again. He'd been an ace pilot for the Apollo System Defense Force in their war against Brisingr, awarded and honored for his skill at killing.

And when that war had ended in disgrace and betrayal, his own government had secretly authorized their enemies to assassinate their heroes as part of the peace deal. Faced with the ruins of his dreams, his honor and the nation he'd pledged them to, he'd fled to the stars and sworn himself to pacifism.

The Siya U Hestî had forced him to put that aside. He'd had to choose between either taking up his old trade in a new form or losing his people and what honor he had left.

So, he'd destroyed them. Killed or captured their leadership. Turned their central headquarters station over to police forces from Nigahog, the arguably most powerful system in the area.

That hadn't, it seemed, been enough. The Siya U Hestî had managed to mess up their next contract, attempting to kidnap Trace after she was trapped behind the front lines of a war he'd been paid to supply.

And now Ansem Hadzhiev had once again put the Siya U Hestî front and center of his path. He didn't have it in him to walk away when hundreds of innocents were trapped in the hands of an organized crime cartel. The thought of kids like Trace being put *in storage* to be sold later to help rebuild the organization… It made his blood boil.

People like Janessa Ali had run that system. A Level Seven, according to Hadzhiev, she'd have been in charge of a segment of the Siya U Hestî in Icem—divided either by geography or industry. Just what, exactly, Ali had done for the Shadow and Bone hadn't been included in Hadzhiev's data dump.

Only that she had the scramble codes and could, potentially, be bought.

EB spent a full ten minutes going through his communications and computer systems, making sure that his call couldn't be traced back to his ship. An encrypted relay connected him to a private server-for-hire aboard Icem High Home, which then relayed under a *different* encryption to a second private server-for-hire on a different orbital.

There was more obfuscation involved on top of that, as both servers-for-hire promised a default level of encryption and secrecy as well—his encryptions and concealments were inside that wrapper to make him harder to find.

The extra seconds of the disguise weren't going to cost him much. The com code Hadzhiev had given him was for an office in orbit of Tarsus, a bit over two light-minutes away.

With a five-minute round trip for light, a live conversation was difficult at best. Still, he wanted his messages obfuscated. Anyone from the Siya U Hestî would almost certainly be able to track down *Evasion* relatively quickly, but any delay would work in his favor.

Plus, he was procrastinating.

Grimacing, he brought up the holorecorder and checked over his unadorned shipsuit. He didn't look particularly wealthy or intimidating—which was the *point*, normally, but could fail him today.

There was only one way to find out, though, and he turned on the recording.

"This message is for Janessa Ali," he said calmly. "My name is Evridiki Bardacki and I want to make a deal. I understand that you have certain data from the former Siya U Hestî Cartel operations in Icem that I wish to purchase.

"Contact me on this line and we can discuss further. Payment will be in third-party-assayed precious metals."

He ended the recording and hit transmit. Third-party-assayed precious metals were the so-called "stamped elementals" of interstellar trade. Marked with their purity and an indelible seal from the company doing the assessment, they ranged from gold and silver all the way up to stabilized reactive metals and rare earths.

Given that Icem didn't have the same currency as Estutmost or Nigahog, the last two systems he'd been in, the use of elements was a necessary part of interstellar trade in the Beyond. Even in the Rim, there were banks and systems that managed to make themselves the regional currency of exchange.

In the Beyond, things were not so organized. It was that lack of interstellar communication, banking and mapping that *made* it the Beyond and not part of so-called "civilized space."

EB had certainly seen Rim worlds as reliant on the Standard Colonial Database as any system in the Beyond, after all. It wasn't just technology and distance that separated the Beyond from the Rim.

A soft chirp informed him that five minutes had passed, and he didn't have a response yet. Snorting at his own optimism in setting the timer, he took a deep breath and stretched. He'd barely begun to roll his shoulders, though, when a *second* chirp informed him that he *did* have a response.

He checked the time. Direct lightspeed lag each way was two minutes and fourteen seconds. His security relays added two seconds each way, creating a total round-trip loop of four minutes and thirty-two seconds.

The reply had taken five minutes and forty seconds to arrive, which meant that Ali—or whoever had answered—had received his message, watched it and replied inside of a minute.

There was a reason the five-minute timer had been optimistic. Somewhat hesitantly, EB hit Play on the message.

An elegant woman in a long burgundy dress appeared in miniature above his desk. Perfectly coiffed and maintained black hair fell to her desk, contrasting with the dress and drawing attention to a perfect heart-shaped face and olive-toned skin.

One perfectly groomed eyebrow was raised a clearly calculated amount, and Janessa Ali appeared to be studying something behind the pickup.

"You are known to me, Captain Bardacki," she said slowly. "While you are hardly on my list of people I expect to hear from, you somehow have my private personal-contact code.

"That makes any attempt at prevarication irrelevant, I suppose. Depending on what information you are seeking, Captain, it is possible that I can arrange it. The Siya U Hestî, as you may have postulated, no longer exists in the Icem System. The complications inherent in that are relevant to any discussions we may have."

She shrugged, the motion smooth and elegant in a manner that spoke of intensive training in body language and deportment.

"I require more information," she concluded simply. "This code will remain accessible for the moment, but we are both maintaining security measures."

The image of the crime lord froze, leaving EB staring at her and grimacing. It was a good thing that he'd decided to have the message exchange alone, because he suspected that Ali had the same training as the woman who'd deceived Trace into getting onto an orbital transport.

Or, potentially, had *trained* that woman.

Schooling his features to some level of even, he activated the recorder again.

"Em Ali, I was given your contact information by a gentleman I think we both knew as Ansem," he told her. "Thanks to him, I am now aware that a number of kidnapping victims were still in transit when the Cage fell.

"I don't believe in leaving a job half-done, Em Ali. I want to find and rescue those children. According to Ansem, you have the information I need—the signposted Siya U Hestî scramble codes and patterns for the specific days the ships carrying them would have arrived."

He considered for a moment, then realized he needed to at least put an offer on the table.

"I am prepared to pay two hundred and fifty grams of stamped lanthanum for those codes," he concluded. "I can provide you with the date ranges I need once we have a deal."

EB fired the message off and leaned back in his chair. Five minutes each way, plus however long it took for Ali to make her decision and check whatever she ended up checking.

Two hundred and fifty grams of stamped lanthanum was ten percent of what he'd been paid to smuggle enough weapons to change the course of a war through a close blockade. Converted to local currency, it was probably enough money for someone to disappear entirely—or, conversely, to create a "legitimate" business to slowly funnel crime proceeds through as they went legit.

It depended on what Janessa Ali was after and how much she valued the data he was asking for. He assumed she was smart enough to know that, given multiple days' worth of the scramble codes, EB could reverse-engineer the algorithm creating them.

If the Siya U Hestî was truly gone in Icem, that wouldn't matter—no one would be going out to maintain the concealed beacons. They'd continue to run for a while, until their solar panels and batteries failed, but no one would be looking for them or using those scramble codes.

Five minutes became six this time. Then eight. Then ten. He was starting to check in to cargos in case he did end up having to leave when Ali's response finally arrived.

She looked very thoughtful in the recording and leveled him with a carefully calculated smile that might have had some effect if he'd been remotely attracted to women.

"That is not data that I would put up for sale," she observed. "But if Ansem gave you my contact code, I think I know what you're after. And I don't think I want to talk about any of this via even encrypted transmission across two planetary systems.

"Come to Tarsus, Captain Bardacki. The address for an office you can contact me through is attached to this message. Once you are here, we will make an appointment and we will talk in person.

"This is not so simple a negotiation. It is a conversation that must take place in person. I look forward to meeting you, Captain Bardacki."

There was an edge to her smile he suspected wasn't supposed to be there.

"You did, after all, change my life already."

13

EVASION EASED her away out of the docks of Icem High Home Station with her crew in various degrees of trepidation, turmoil and concern. There were too many questions being asked for EB to be entirely comfortable about the entire situation, but at least he knew where he was going.

Flying was always relaxing for him. While Denton orbit was far from *busy* by any objective standard, there were still enough ships, small craft and space stations to make the journey away from High Home Station require most of his attention.

All of the nova ships he saw were armed, though only a handful were actually warships. Like *Evasion* herself, most of the freighters expected to have to manage their own safety. Few of the other freighters had enough firepower to really discourage a warship—even one of the ten-thousand-cubic-meter gunships of the Icemi SDF—but most pirates out in the Beyond wouldn't *have* warships.

Evasion was better armed than the Icemi SDF gunships—but she was also four times their size and devoted twenty-five of her forty kilocubics to cargo. EB's ship probably had as much cubage devoted to weapons as the gunships did, and *her* guns were not based on the Standard Colonial Database.

Of course, the ISDF had six four-ship squadrons of the nova gunships. They could outfly *EB*'s ship, and while he could outshoot any given gunship, twenty-four of them was a bit much for his armed freighter.

"To Tarsus, then," Vexer commented as they cleared the orbital fields above Denton. "I make it about four hours."

"Same," EB confirmed—though he downloaded Vexer's course into the computer. That was the difference between the ship's *pilot*, who was in active control as they moved through the crowded space above an inhabited world, and the ship's *navigator*, who plotted the course to the next planet.

"We could nova," Vexer pointed out. "Two and a bit light-minutes; we'd only have a ten-minute cooldown and probably be ready to jump again by the time we docked."

Any jump, however short, required the nova drive to cool down afterward. For the standard class one drive, like the one propelling *Evasion* through the stars, the minimum cooldown was ten minutes—which stayed about the same up to about a fifteen-light-minute jump before it started growing.

The class two drives, with their *one*-minute minimum cooldown, critical for the nova fighters EB had once flown, were almost completely unknown in the Beyond.

"No, we'll take the long way," EB said. "And keep our eyes peeled and the sensors wide."

He chuckled.

"It also gives Em Vortani time to return to Denton, since her ship is scheduled to depart in about two and a half hours," he told his fiancé. "Just because it turns out we weren't called here by Trace's ex-fosters doesn't mean I want to *meet* them, and being on different planets sounds *perfect* to me."

Vexer shook his head.

"Where is this office, anyway?" he asked.

"Planetside, in the city of Alexandra," EB replied. "We'll dock at the orbital, and I'll take regular transport down, I think."

There was only one station above Tarsus. There were about eight million souls scattered across the chilly, barely habitable planet—and the orbital elevator attached to that station hauled the rare minerals that were the main purpose of the colony up for easy transport.

"Alone?" Vexer gave EB a dark look.

"Not alone," he assured his lover. "I'm not sure who I'm going to take with me, yet—other than *not Trace*, anyway!—but I'm not foolish enough to walk into the lion's den without backup."

"No matter how pretty the lion is," Vexer replied.

EB shrugged. Vexer was more...*broad* in his tastes than EB was. EB didn't see the appeal of Janessa Ali to anyone, where Vexer certainly could.

"She was a Siya U Hestî Level Seven," EB noted. "Whatever she calls herself now, I suspect her actual *work* hasn't changed much. She's a criminal running some scale of criminal organization. 'Lion' is understating the threat, I suspect."

"Almost certainly. You realize she's going to know *Evasion* is your ship, right?"

"And you're going to sit in orbit and make sure all of my guns work," EB told Vexer with a chuckle. "That's why I'm thinking Reggie again," he admitted. "We know the guns are in decent shape, and the automatic systems can target and fire reasonably well.

"It's a lot harder to fly the ship, and you're the only other fully qualified pilot we have."

"I don't like sending you into trouble while hanging out on my own," Vexer said.

"I'd prefer not to walk into trouble, regardless," EB replied. "I don't trust this woman. I'm going on a recommendation from a dead man—and I'm not sure I trust *him*."

"At least you're not *completely* detached from reality. This situation stinks, love. Hadzhiev's message seems perfectly calculated to lure you in."

"That hasn't escaped me," EB conceded. "On the other hand, Hadzhiev is most definitely *dead*, so that limits the amount he could gain from anything."

"Janessa Ali, on the other hand, is very much alive, very much in possession of information we need—and very much in possession of her own agenda. Even if she isn't actively working to harm us, she is going to make sure *she* benefits."

"That's dealing with mercenaries and criminals," EB said. "Hopefully, she'll just take money. Even if it's a *lot* of money, I'm prepared to pay for the data we need."

"The problem, love, is that people like Ali don't deal in money," Vexer warned. "They deal in *favors*—and people like her don't want the type of favors we generally want to provide."

EB considered that, then nodded his understanding.

"You're right, of course," he said. "But we're not walking away from this mess, so we talk to the lioness. There are favors she can ask that I'm prepared to do to get several hundred kids out of cryo-stasis and slavery."

There were hard lines he wasn't prepared to cross, but when push came to shove, he'd get his hands at least a bit dirty when that was on the line.

14

TRACE DIDN'T EVEN BOTHER ARGUING that she should go with EB down to Tarsus. She'd learned on Estutmost that the remaining leaders of the Siya U Hestî would, quite literally, kill for the information update that had been loaded into her skull.

She didn't have most of it *in* her skull anymore, and she was sure there had to be more up-to-date versions of it out there, but it had been less than a month between her escape and the fall of the Cage.

Trace hoped that this Janessa Ali took that as a warning. People who got on the wrong side of her adoptive fathers tended to lose—fast and hard.

For herself, she sat in her "office," going through the sensor feeds when she was supposed to be doing coursework with her education stupid. Tarsus was a frigid ball of frozen rock, with an average surface temperature well below zero degrees and effectively no liquid water.

But it was just close *enough* to Icem itself and just volcanic *enough* to have areas of habitability. The equatorial zone was hardly pleasant, but it was livable. The native life had fascinating attributes and adaptations, she remembered from her school on Denton, which was one of the reasons humans settled Tarsus.

With Denton only a few hours' flight away, it took something of value to get people to live on Tarsus. *Denton* wasn't the most pleasant of worlds by most standards, she now knew, but it was much warmer and more livable than Tarsus.

But while Denton had good soil and even areas that could be terraformed into perfect replicas of Earth—like the Black Oak Island Sanctuary she'd grown up in—it lacked in easily accessible surface minerals. With only a few trojan clusters in Deus's orbit available for asteroid mining, a habitable, low-gravity planet with surface deposits of rare earths and other valuable ores was useful.

So, Tarsus was not only inhabited but it also had a full orbital elevator with a centerpoint civilian station and counterweight asteroid fortress. Trace hadn't realized how rare those fortresses *were* in the Beyond before she'd left Icem.

The education program in her home system was quite vague on the local stars. She'd known more about Greek city-states of several thousand years earlier than she had about the inhabited star systems within a few weeks' nova travel.

"We're heading in to Teamster Station," EB said over the ship's network. "It looks more than a bit rough, about what I expect of what's not much more than a glorified mining colony.

"We're not the only nova ship floating around, but most of the ships here look sublight to me," he continued. "There is no way that our 'friend' doesn't already know which ship we are and where I'm coming from, but let's play things nice and chill.

"Ginny and Tate will go aboard station to check out the supply options while Reggie and I head for the orbital elevator. Everyone else, I need you to stay aboard ship and out of trouble."

Trace grumbled. She figured she was capable of going aboard station without drawing attention or getting into trouble, but she knew where Dad-E was coming from. He was going to go talk to a crime lord, and he didn't need to be worrying about everyone behind him.

She wasn't giving Janessa Ali the credit of assuming the woman was an *ex*-criminal. The woman might no longer be Siya U Hestî—and Trace wasn't even certain she was going to give Ali *that* grace—but she was almost certainly still a criminal.

Which meant that there was *no way* she was going to be able to focus on the educational stupid and its series of recorded lectures on the early interstellar diaspora. Sighing, she waved the screen off and stood.

If she was going to be sitting around, staring at the sensors, she might as well do so with company and a sandwich.

SOMEONE—TRACE wasn't sure who but she had guesses—had rigged the wallscreen in the mess to show the exterior view of Teamster Station, with green stick figures marking where their two parties currently were.

Aurora was currently standing at the counter, making sandwiches. The sallow-skinned raven-haired woman was the second-youngest member of *Evasion*'s crew, though Trace didn't find her overly personable.

Joy, on the other hand, was sitting at the table watching the display and playing with an empty coffee cup. The oldest of the "non-officer" crew, Joy had lighter hair than Aurora and a brighter personality, which made the Black environmental specialist a generally more pleasant companion than the engine tech.

"Oi, Aurora, you got the makings for two more of those?" Joy asked.

"I've made mine," Aurora pointed out, stacking two onto a plate. "I can leave the fixings out if you want."

Joy met Trace's gaze and obviously rolled her eyes. It seemed Trace wasn't the only one who had problems connecting with Aurora.

"I mean, you *could* do some folks a favor while you're standing there and throw some ham on bread," Joy noted.

"Or you could use your own perfectly good legs and hands to feed yourselves," Aurora replied.

There was an undertone to both women's voices that Trace couldn't quite follow. She didn't think it was hostile. More...resigned? Like they'd had some version of this conversation a thousand times and both of them had accepted that the other wasn't going to change.

"Leave the stuff out; I'll make ours," Trace asked.

Aurora gave her a look and a sour expression but nodded and gestured to the bread and pre-sliced meats and vegetables sitting on the counter as she took a seat at the mess table.

"Be my guest."

The green icons for Ginny and Tate weren't going very far onto the station, Trace judged as she began to assemble sandwiches—two for herself, one for Joy. They were looking for chandleries and sutlers and seeing if there were any supplies *Evasion* was short of that Teamster Station had for cheap.

Given that they'd just left Denton, Trace doubted it, but her understanding was that Ginny was always going to check.

Her main attention, though, was on the two green figures marking EB and Reggie making their way toward the central section of the station, where the unimaginably strong cable of the orbital elevator ran through a cylindrical gap built for it.

"It takes longer for that elevator to go down to the surface than it took us to get here from Denton," Vexer's voice said loudly. "Always a bit of a sore spot, I feel. A Harrington-coil shuttle is faster but so much less efficient."

Trace glanced over at her second father. She gave him a quick smile —and added a fourth sandwich to her assembly line.

"All he's going to find down there is trouble," Aurora predicted. "Only people you can trust less than governments are criminals."

"I come from a place where I wouldn't distinguish between them," Vexer replied. He took a sandwich from Trace with a grateful nod as she carried plates over to the table. "But *most* places, as I understand it, governments are a bit less...*draconian* than the Dukes."

"Aye." Aurora stared blankly into space. "We weren't going to not get involved, so it was this or the government. I'd have gone to the SDF. Might fuck it up, but they're less likely to stab us in the back."

Trace felt a small—very small, admittedly—surge of affection for the prickly environment tech. Regardless of anything else, even Aurora was entirely on board with rescuing the trafficking victims.

"Boss thinks local government leaks like a sieve," Joy pointed out. "So does Reggie. They figure that's how Hadzhiev got whacked and that we'd be in *more* danger talking to the SDF than to an ex-Cartel flunky."

"Ali's no flunky," Trace said quietly. "She *was* a Level Seven, in charge of all their affairs on Tarsus."

She'd looked that up in the datavault after EB had decided to go talk to the woman.

"Knowing what I know about the Siya U Hestî and about Tarsus— plus a large dash of cynicism and a bit of reading on the flight over— they've been trafficking the young and dumb into the Tarsus mines for years.

"There's *supposed* to be labor regulations and inspections and laws and such, but..."

She spread her hands.

"Those only apply to the mines the inspectors *know* about," Vexer finished for her. "It wouldn't be the first time that trafficking victims found themselves working in what *looks* like an entirely aboveboard operation, doing labor for pennies."

The mining was done with the full power of the SCD's extraction tech, which meant it was safe and environmentally friendly and all those wonderful things...to a point. It required humans to supervise the drones and fix the machines and guide the scanners and extractors, and while that work was mostly safe, it was hard, both physically and mentally. *Usually*, that meant it was well compensated.

"Not all trafficking is about sex or power," Joy said grimly. "Some-times, it's just about some asshole who wants to shave two percent off this year's payroll budget."

15

THE DESCENT DOWN the elevator had been about as boring as EB had expected. The transfer pod was decently sized and had a bar with surprisingly good beer and food. There wasn't much else to recommend it, though it served its purpose well enough.

Anyone who wanted a more luxurious ride down to the planet would take a shuttle. EB was hoping to avoid drawing too much attention—but he realized that had been wasted effort as they exited the transfer pod on the ground.

"Captain Bardacki?" a stranger greeted him. He was cut from much the same mold as most of the people around them, stocky-shouldered workers worn and pale by hard work underground.

"And you are?" EB replied, studying the man. He figured he knew why the man was there and who sent him—and if Ali was sending people to pick him up at the elevator base, he should have just flown down.

Hindsight was always perfect, though.

"You can call me George," the local told him, in a tone that said that *George* wasn't his name. "Ali sent me. Come with me, please? We've set up an appointment for you with the lady."

You ready? Reggie's mental message appeared in EB's headware. *I can take him if we need. Politely, even.*

EB wasn't even sure what taking the man down "politely" would entail, but he also didn't see a need.

Why waste time? he asked Reggie, then turned back to George.

"Lead the way, Em George. No reason to make the lady wait."

And if George had known that the only person EB had known recently who used *Lady* as a title was Breanna, the monstrous queen of the Siya U Hestî, he might have hesitated to use that particular descriptor for Janessa Ali.

As it was, the big miner led them through the concourse to a waiting ground car. There was a chill in the air—even there on the equator, the temperature outside rarely rose to double digits Celsius, and the water in the atmosphere sank that chill deep into his bones.

Somehow, EB suspected that the cold air and dark skies of Tarsus were a warning for what was to come.

GEORGE DROVE them through a city that was not quite what EB had expected. Part of him had been expecting a mining town writ large, with dull gray concrete barracks as far as the eye could see.

With any examination, that logic fell apart. Alexandra was a city of over a million people that served as the main administration and transshipment hub for an entire planet. One in every eight permanent residents of Tarsus lived in Alexandra—and while the nature of mine work probably meant that at least a quarter of the people on the planet at any given moment *weren't* permanent residents, Alexandra was home and capital to the people who were.

A series of graceful towers soaring half a kilometer tall each formed a perfect circle around the main downtown core. There was no way the structures had not been designed to flow into each other, forming a marker that as rough and primary-industry-driven Tarsus might be, *this* was still a planetary capital.

Other, lesser towers likely held the administration of the mining companies and their support services, but somehow, EB was unsur-

prised when they were driven to one of the gracefully curved mono-
liths declaring Alexandra's claim to sophistication.

The tower base was surrounded by a small park, with a surface
area for vehicles large enough for maybe a dozen ground cars. EB
hadn't seen any sign of public transit sufficient to allow even *one* half-
kilometer-tall office tower to function without parking, so he was
wondering what was going on as George parked the car and got out.

"Move," he instructed. "Sensors are *supposed* to wait until everyone
is out, has checked the trunk and so forth...but they aren't always as
good as we'd like."

The instruction told EB the answer, and he got out of the car with
disturbed alacrity. Reggie clearly hadn't quite followed what George
meant, but he left the vehicle behind EB swiftly enough.

Fortunately, they were well clear of the marked parking space
when the system activated and what *looked* like solid concrete turned
out to be an elevator. The vehicle descended into the ground, where
presumably an automated system stored it with the rest of the vehicles
required to staff the tower.

"Come," George said quickly. "The lady is waiting."

THE INTERIOR of the tower gave EB much the same impression as the
outside. The building was named Pourewa Tekau Ma Whitu—Tower
Seventeen in Māori, his headware informed him—which suggested a
fascinating combination of imagination and the lack thereof.

Pourewa Tekau Ma Whitu was decorated in what a corporation
almost two thousand light-years and a thousand standard years from
Māori origins clearly thought to be the correct style. EB wasn't
convinced the living palm trees, water features or murals of volcanos
and rafts were an *accurate* presentation of that culture, though.

A quick headware search of the datanet told him that each of the
Towers Twenty was named in a different language, based on the
distant ethnic backgrounds of the original survey team.

He wanted to call it tomfoolery and pageantry—except that he was
well aware how small a portion of his own ancestors had actually been

Greek, despite Apollo's pretensions to descent from Athenian philosophers.

The high-speed elevator tucked behind the palm trees was ordinary enough, at least, and it swept them halfway up the tower with a distinct lack of fuss. George led them through a plainer but still luxuriously decorated corridor to a set of double doors.

The sign burned into the wooden doors declared this to be HANFORD AND COLLIER BARRISTERS, but George barely slowed down. He waved a hand at a concealed scanner, likely accompanied by a headware command, and the doors swung open.

"Ah, with Captain Bardacki, yes?" a delicately featured woman behind a heavy desk that was *definitely* armored greeted them. She leveled a beatific smile on the three men. "Thank you, George. I'll handle the gentlemen from here."

Their escort grunted and stepped back out of the way. EB paid attention out of the corner of his eye, but George left the office almost immediately. That probably...wasn't a sign either way, really, but it made EB nervous.

"Do you need a drink, Captain? Em..."

"Kalb," Reggie said crisply. "No, thank you."

EB let his escort speak for both of them—the secretary certainly didn't seem surprised or taken aback by Reggie's doing so. She was clearly used to bodyguards and had instantly classed Reggie there.

"Em Kalb, my scanners show you are carrying a heavy blaster," she said after a few seconds. "While Captain Bardacki's stunner isn't a concern, I do have to ask you to leave the blaster here."

She produced a safety deposit box from beneath the desk.

"You are welcome to secure it and recode the security box," she offered. "But I can't let you see Lady Ali, carrying a lethal weapon."

Do it, EB ordered.

Reggie didn't argue. He drew the blaster—a big ugly thing, as befitted an energy weapon designed to take down people in light power armor—and placed it on the woman's desk.

"I don't need the security box," he said calmly. "I think you all know better than to let it go astray."

The secretary smiled and rose from her seat. Like Detective Everest on High Home Station, the grace of her movements told EB she was augmented. If Reggie was trying to intimidate her, just *moving* was a solid counterargument on her part.

"Come," she told them. "Lady Ali is handling a call at the moment, but I have instructions to set you up in a meeting room where you can wait for her. It shouldn't be too long, but I can bring you drinks or even a snack if you—"

"No, thank you," Reggie repeated before EB could say a word.

They'd come this far on trust...but there was a limit. EB figured they might be being impolite, but he was prepared to come across as paranoid.

He did, after all, have very real enemies, and he suspected he was waiting for a meeting with one of them.

16

JANESSA ALI WAS, if anything, even more gorgeous in person. This time, she wore a jewel-blue sheath dress that outlined her figure frankly and drew the eye carefully away from the artfully designed concealed holster on her left side.

The dress, EB judged, had pockets that were equally invisible. Her dressmaker was *incredible*.

"Em Ali," he greeted her when she finally swept into the meeting room and took a seat across the small real wooden table.

"Captain Bardacki. Em Kalb," she greeted them. "You didn't mention that Ansem was dead."

EB blinked, taken aback.

"I presumed you knew," he admitted. If nothing else, he wouldn't have reached out to her at all if Ansem was alive.

"The nature of your message made me suspect, but no," she said softly. "I did not know that Ansem was dead until I investigated after our discussion. That does make for an...*interesting* track record for people in my line of work who meet you, doesn't it?"

"Oh?" he asked carefully.

"Ansem. Chey. Lady Breanna... Quite the trail of corpses you've left in your wake."

EB grimaced. He hadn't killed Hadzhiev—he wasn't even sure who *had*. He'd take the blame for Kunthea Chey, the Level Eight on Estutmost, but mostly because *Trace* had killed Chey and he didn't want that to get out.

Lady Breanna, though...

"The last I'd heard, Breanna Tolliver was in a moderately uncomfortable prison cell on Nigahog," he said mildly.

"Then your news is out of date," Ali told him. "Breanna Tolliver is dead. A fellow prisoner cut her throat in the showers." The elegant woman shrugged casually. "Presumably, someone paid richly to make sure she didn't decide to get talkative."

"I did not know that," EB admitted. He had expected that Nigahog's prisons would be better managed and secured than that, especially for a prisoner as important as the head of the Siya U Hestî. On the other hand, he knew intimately that money and computer access opened a lot of doors.

"Well, consider that information a freebie, then," Ali said calmly, "so that you understand just *why* I am just a touch twitchy interacting with you. Everyone else in my former organization who has dealt with you is dead."

"I want to make a deal, Em Ali," he told her. "So long as nobody tries to hurt me or my crew or family, we trade information and money and we all walk away."

"The problem, Captain Bardacki, is that I'm still not sure *what* you're after," Ali said. "Scramble codes are valuable things, restricted by time and space to make them more valuable. Were someone continuing to use Siya U Hestî for a new operation, giving up those codes would make them vulnerable."

"Frankly, Em Ali, I'm not convinced you aren't still Siya U Hestî," EB pointed out.

"Level Eight Alistair Hammond made very certain of that," she said coldly. "He did not *survive* his attempt to secure direct control of the Level Sevens in Icem...but neither did any remnant of our former organizational structure.

"I have resources and personnel that used to belong to the Cartel, but most of the connections and networks that *made* the Siya U Hestî are gone. At least here in the Icem System."

"You'll forgive me if I don't weep."

Ali snorted.

"Given your involvement in matters, I'd be surprised if you thought differently," she admitted. "But the Cartel has been my career and my life. Its destruction hardly serves *my* needs, though I can see that many would not agree.

"So." She leaned back in the chair, studying the two men across the table. "You have told me you want the scramble codes. I can tell you now: those are *not* for sale. Equally important, I doubt they would be of use to you. Even the beacons themselves do not keep track of the ships that request and receive the scrambles. The entire point, Captain Bardacki, is to render the ships anonymous even to us."

"But with the code sequences, a rough arrival time and the identities of the ships in question, I can back-calculate what they would have been disguised as," EB said. "With that and enough other information, I can establish where a ship went.

"One ship I might get wrong," he conceded. "But with a list I know were headed to the same destination, I can use the aggregate effect to locate that destination."

"I see." Ali continued to watch him in silence for a few more seconds. "And this list of Siya U Hestî ships came from where? And the ships are going...where?"

"If we are not making a deal, Em Ali, I am not certain I want to reveal that information," EB told her.

"The problem, Captain, is that your previous activities suggest that we are working at cross purposes," she said calmly. "Those ships, after all, are quite likely coming to an operation I am either involved in or looking to take control of."

EB was feeling worse about the possibility of working with this woman by the moment, but she was also the only option on the table. It was clear that she wasn't going to give up the codes without knowing exactly what he was after—and that he was going to need to phrase his plans in a way that would benefit *her*.

"More, I think, in the order of removing a competitor," he suggested slowly. "Thanks to Ansem, a number of ships in transit at the fall of the Cage were redirected to a backup facility Breanna was maintaining.

"Those ships carried cryo-stasis-frozen kidnapping victims. Hundreds of them." He met Ali's gaze flatly. "I clashed with Siya U Hestî over their trafficking operations and my daughter. Given the information I have, I cannot stand by and abandon those victims.

"I am going to find those ships, and I am going to find Breanna's Bastion, and I am going to save those people," he told her. "If we make a deal, you can profit from this. If you try to stop me, well…"

He shrugged.

"You noted yourself what happens to Cartel leaders who cross my path," he concluded, smiling winningly at her.

"I suppose I walked into that," she said. "But I will warn you, Captain, I am a dangerous person to threaten."

"And I imagine the presence of a secret Siya U Hestî facility in your star system, one with unknown loyalties now that Breanna Tolliver is dead, constitutes a threat."

There was a long silence as she didn't quite glare at him.

"You are correct that I do not know the loyalties of the people at the Bastion," she conceded. "And with Lady Breanna's death, they become a wild card. And while I knew the Bastion existed, I did not know it is in Icem."

She raised a hand.

"We still do not *know* it is in Icem. I know you believe it to be and think that you can trace it, but that is not a guarantee."

"I know that Ansem believed it is here," EB told her. "And that he, unlike either of us, had been there."

She sighed and nodded.

"Fair. That is as much of a guarantee as we're going to get, isn't it? Combined with Ansem's death, that does suggest you're climbing the right tree, doesn't it, Captain?"

"It does," he said. "Sell me those codes, Em Ali, and the Bastion will cease to be your problem. *I* will also cease to be your problem."

Ali steepled her hands and regarded him with unreadable dark eyes.

"I have already told you, Captain Bardacki. The codes are not for sale. A deal, however, is still possible."

"Then I am still listening," he said carefully.

She smiled thinly.

"I want the Bastion, Captain. I don't care about the prisoners you want to rescue. The facility, its systems, resources and supplies, though, will make a significant difference to my efforts to consolidate my position. Plus, as you say, it is a threat to me."

EB didn't *want* to help Ali consolidate her position. He was, however, perfectly capable of packaging everything he learned about her over the course of the "deal," wrapping it in a neat bow and handing it over to the Icemi police.

It might not be enough to change anything, but it would be a useful salve to his conscience.

"You have something in mind," he said.

"I do," she confirmed. Her smile suddenly reminded him of something *very* predatory and probably venomous to boot. "The simplest option is that *you* provide *me* with the dataset of ships and arrival times, and in exchange, I make sure that the trafficking cargo is delivered to a neutral port for release."

"Not a chance in hell," EB replied brightly. "Some trust is required for us to operate, but I will see to the safety of the Siya U Hesti's victims personally. I'm not going to hand the data over to you—though I'll note that I don't think *you* have everything you need to use it, either."

"No, we will need system-wide scan data," she conceded. "I have some thoughts on how to acquire that, but first we will need to put the pieces you and I each have together. If neither of us is prepared to release custody of our own data, then I see only awkward options."

"A compromise is clearly necessary," EB agreed. "Appropriate stewards and technicians meeting on neutral ground. I imagine it is possible to rent time on a data-processing center aboard Teamster Station?"

He suspected that Teamster didn't really qualify as "neutral ground" by any real meaning of the term, but it was closer to it than anywhere in Alexandra.

"That will work, I believe," she said. "The arrangements will be made, and I will have one of my trusted people meet you there. Assuming that we have a deal?"

"If you turn on me..."

"I don't need that cargo, Captain Bardacki," she told him—and he *knew* she was using the euphemism to test his nerves. "So long as I end in control of the facility, I am content. You take your poor, *poor* victims with you, and I take Breanna's fallback base.

"We both win."

"We have a deal," he ground out.

"One question," Reggie asked before Ali could say anything. She looked at the man in surprise, as if she hadn't expected the bodyguard to *speak*.

"What?" Ali asked, her tone sharp.

Reggie conjured a holographic image of his SPM-15 Ghostmaker into the air in front of him. He gestured toward it.

"I'm a weapons expert, Em Ali," he said, his tone surprisingly respectful. "Something along these lines was used to murder Ansem— an extremely specialized weapon, one that was probably custom-made in this star system.

"Any idea who would have such a weapon or where it would be sourced?"

Ali looked at the rotating image of the monster revolver, and a thoughtful expression crossed her face.

"I don't know that gun," she admitted. "But someone custom-making specialized weapons rings a bell. There was a woman—a Level Six, angling for Seven last I saw her—who made her own toys like that."

She shook her head slowly.

"She usually did it to make her involvement in things *harder* to detect, since most people assume a projectile weapon was a hunting gun," Ali noted. "But something like that"—she gestured to the Ghost-maker—"wouldn't fool anyone on *that* reasoning. Custom weapons to take down a difficult target were basically her signature."

"What happened to her?" EB asked.

"She fell into the orbit of central authority," the crime boss said.

"Ended up working for Ansem, and then Breanna herself for a time. But...working in the orbit of the core of Siya U Hestî was never a *safe* path.

"Jessica Vargas was her name," Ali concluded. "She fell afoul of her new bosses and vanished, five years ago now. We had mutual acquaintances, if not *friends,* and none of them were sure what happened.

"Just one day, no one ever heard from her again." She chuckled. "Vargas wasn't the first *that* happened to in my line of work. Won't be the last, either. But while I doubt a dead woman killed Ansem..." She studied the holographic gun for another moment. "I wouldn't put it past her to have left a few toys floating around the system. Something like that would have been her idiom."

"Hrm." The hologram closed down and Reggie leaned back wordlessly.

"I take it you didn't have Ansem killed," EB murmured.

"You're not wrong to wonder, I suppose," Ali admitted. "And no, I did not have Ansem killed. If he'd been smart enough to come to me *first* with his clever plan, we'd have already dealt with the Bastion."

"I suspect, Em Ali, that Ansem was hoping to maintain control of the situation to make sure that the cryo-frozen prisoners didn't fall into the hands of someone they didn't matter to," EB told her.

"You ascribe a bit more warmth to a Level Nine than I would," Ali said. The door to the meeting room opened and revealed the same boosted woman as before, summoned by a silent signal. "Vortex will see you out, Captain. Either she or I will contact you once we've arranged what I regard as safe passage for our code-wrangler and an appropriate facility.

"I'd ask that you remain around Tarsus until then, if you'd be so kind."

17

"SO, we're just going to hand a covert installation, full of who knows what in terms of resources and data, over to Ali?" Vexer asked after EB had filled everyone in.

"She makes my skin crawl," Trace added. "Reminds me of…"

She trailed off. Everyone knew who she meant, thankfully, which meant she didn't need to finish the sentence.

"She wants to be Breanna's replacement," she muttered.

"Given her use of the title *Lady* and suchlike, I agree," EB said flatly. "Unfortunately, I suspect she realizes I'm likely to hand over everything I know about her to the Icemi police when we're done working together.

"I haven't promised I won't—but she's making sure that we don't have enough data to hurt her. She doesn't want us to have the scramble codes, because that will expose the ships she has moving through this system already."

"I was wondering why she was so protective of it," Reggie observed.

Trace wasn't sure what her father was thinking, but it made a vague sense to her.

"Reading between the lines of what Ali told us, right now, the former Siya U Hestî in this system are having a lovely little civil war," EB explained. "If Ali is the last one standing with access to the scramble beacons, then she has a clear advantage. Even just the transit between Tarsus and Denton can be useful to fly anonymously.

"I haven't seen a mining colony yet where someone wasn't carving off a slice of the highest-value items and smuggling them out to avoid paying taxes or selling at local prices."

"But the flight from Tarsus to Denton is too short," Trace reminded him. "And there's enough sensors above both to make switching beacons detectable, aren't there?"

"They'd head out to Deus," Vexer said with a sigh. "Would take a while for a sublight ship, but it might be worth it to raise cash without oversight. Launder it through mining consortiums they control. Arrives on Denton on a ship with papers that say it's never been to Tarsus, and the extra gems or whatever get added to legit shipments where taxes and assaying fees have already been paid.

"I don't know what the markup between gems or rare earths bought at the mineshaft on Tarsus and the same sold to manufacturers on Denton, but I suspect it's worth it."

There were advantages, Trace supposed, to being local.

"Taxes on the Tarsus mines are a major driver of government revenue," she told them. "They talk it up in school as part of why our personal income taxes are so low—the system is supported by the mining operations in multiple ways."

Vexer chuckled.

"Well, that's an interesting story to tell the schoolkids," he observed. "Probably true enough as it goes. Thanks, Trace."

"We're talking about forms of smuggling we're comfortable with," Lan said quietly, the doctor locking their gaze on Trace. "It's possible Ali is still involved in human trafficking, isn't it?"

There was a long silence.

"Yes," EB admitted.

"Without the Siya U Hestî interstellar network, she can't do what they did," Trace told them, grimacing as she considered both the datavault and her own experiences with the Cartel. "They had an abso-lute hard rule: nobody was trafficked in their own star system. They figured it was too easy to track people when you had quick access to identification databases they were in.

"That's *why* the Cartel was interstellar." She shivered. "They did other smuggling and the rest of the list of crimes, but they were primarily spread out so that they could make sure their victims were put to…work in an entirely different star system."

She hated that she knew that much about the people who'd groomed and kidnapped her. Given a chance to use it against them, though, she'd grab that knowledge with both hands.

"So, she might be trying to build a new network, but my impression is that Ali's solid control is currently limited to Tarsus," EB said. "It would be hard for her to source trafficking victims on Denton right now, which means she's limited to the rest of that list of crimes."

He didn't look much happier than Trace felt. She wasn't sure that working with Ali was a *good* plan, but she didn't see any other choices.

"What do we do now?" she asked.

"This is where Reggie gets less useful and I get more so," Lan said calmly. The pudgy ship's doctor grinned around at their companions. "You are a great asset, Reggie, but you are a brute-force instrument by choice."

"I self-identify as *friendly* thug; don't worry," Reggie said with a chuckle and a wink at Trace.

Trace might only have two *dads* aboard the ship, but she certainly seemed to have acquired quite the collection of aunts and uncles along with them.

"I, on the other hand, self-identify as a hidden threat," Lan countered. "Since I suspect there are only three of us on this ship capable of the data analysis needed—and we are *not* sending Trace into a data-processing center with a collection of criminals—I think that either EB or I should handle that end of affairs."

"Both of us, I think," EB said. "I want Trace and the crew to stay on the ship as much as possible. Keep your eyes open for anything strange. Ginny, Vexer—you'll be the main people who go on-station other than Lan and I.

"I want you to keep your ears to the ground and see what you hear.

I'd like to know more about what the catfight between Siya U Hestî factions is looking like and how much the locals know."

"I'm going to do a bit of research on the datanet myself," Reggie noted. "See what's around here for gunsmiths and the like. This Vargas might be dead, but she picked up her hobby somewhere. There will be others like her around...and that is assuming that she *is* dead."

EB chuckled grimly.

"Agreed. Ali said Vargas vanished while working for Breanna. That, to me, flags someone who might well be at this Bastion as much as someone that Breanna had disappeared."

"What do I do?" Trace asked quietly.

"I'm going to run a channel to you through my headware as we work on the data," EB told her. "If it goes the way I expect, we're going to be setting up a secure dataroom that information shouldn't be leaving.

"*You* are going to use that channel and every trick I've taught you to *breach* that dataroom." He grinned at her.

"You've got better tools than they do and some serious talent," he noted. "I still don't expect you to manage to steal the scramble codes... but if we're only a little bit lucky, I think you may just be able to steal the *results* of our analysis.

"And once we've managed to ID a couple of probables, we might be able to reverse-engineer the codes from that."

EB shrugged as Trace considered the challenge he was giving her. She was well aware that her skillset was basically "script kid equipped with high-end programs," and it sounded like breaking a secure dataroom and stealing processing data was...a stretch. But she'd give it a try! It might be worth it.

"It's a wild shot in the dark," EB concluded, clearly thinking much the same thing. "But if you pull it off, we might not end up needing to bring 'Lady' Ali in far enough for her to locate the Bastion.

"And nothing about that woman makes me feel like playing straight is a good idea...or a course we're likely to *survive*."

18

EB WASN'T ENTIRELY surprised that it was Vortex who met him and Lan at the data center. Petite and delicate-looking as she was, Vortex also packed a small fortune in cybernetic and biological enhancement into her small frame.

Like Hadzhiev to Breanna, Vortex was more than Ali's bodyguard. She was something closer to a top enforcer, a trusted right hand. So, when Ali sent someone with the scramble codes, information she didn't want to fall into the wrong hands...she sent Vortex.

"Captain Bardacki," the woman greeted him. "Your companion?"

"Dr. Lan Kozel," EB introduced his ship's doctor. "They have data-analysis skills that I figured would be useful."

"I'm more used to analyzing medical data and pathogens than star-ships and identity codes," Kozel said brightly, "but many of the skills are the same."

"They are indeed," Vortex confirmed. She gestured to the two taller women with her. "You may call these lovelies Bernadette and Arson. They also have data-analysis skills and experience with the particular datasets we will hopefully be examining."

Bernadette was a tall and gawky Black woman who towered over EB and Lan. She looked like a stiff breeze would blow her away, and the visible augmentations around her eyes and up onto her temples added to the image of an ancient computer-geek stereotype.

She didn't move like she had physical boosts, but EB wasn't going to underestimate someone because their higher-than-ordinary level of augmentation was focused on mental affairs.

Arson, on the other hand, was cut from a similar cloth as Vortex. The flame-haired woman was younger and taller than her boss, but her boosts were clear in how she moved.

If he'd been asked to guess, EB would have said that Bernadette was on site to handle the data and both Vortex and Arson were there to supervise and handle security. But appearances could be deceiving—for one thing, Lan Kozel was only slightly more augmented than EB, but the doctor was probably the most lethal of the five.

"You've set up a proper secure room?" EB asked.

"We have. Follow me," Vortex ordered.

Like many things built in systems relying on the Standard Colonial Database, the datacenter was built to a pattern and floor plan from the SCD. EB had spent time in at least half a dozen facilities on assorted space stations that had used the exact same layout.

Unlike the conscious effort to make Alexandra something different and special on the surface, most of Teamster Station felt like that. The modules had been put together in a different arrangement, but the station was very much built from SCD modules.

If the datacenter followed the layout he knew, there were three secure datarooms with standalone computing setups structured inside Faraday cages. Vortex was leading them toward one without even checking in with the single human at the desk.

Most of the booking was handled by one of the four artificial stupid holograms in the small lobby, but there was a certain type of person that *always* went for the human—and from the young man's carefully still expression, the graying man currently talking *at* him was a solid representative of the type.

"Secure Room Three," Vortex told him as they stopped outside the door. "Let's chat inside. We don't need listening ears."

THE SECURE DATAROOM was even plainer than EB had expected. Usually, there was some art—usually either something by a very cheap local mural artist or the equivalent of prints bought at a museum gift shop—but this one just had six chairs, a processing tower and a dozen screens mounted on movable racks.

"You have the scramble codes?" EB asked once the door had closed behind them. The Faraday cage sealed with the door, and he could *feel* the lack of the station datanet.

His connection to Trace failed with it. Despite his best efforts to prepare, it seemed that the datacenter had put extra effort into the Faraday cage. It was still surmountable, but the ways that he could think of required physical components.

They hadn't had enough warning of the final location to set that up in advance.

"I have them," Vortex confirmed, tapping her temple. "You have the ship schedule?"

"Of course," EB said, mirroring her gesture. He stepped over to one of the chairs and sank into it, eyeing the three local women and his doctor.

"Both of us are trying to keep the data we brought secure," he noted. "The main issue we're going to face, as I understand it, is that my arrival times aren't solid enough and the scramble code isn't simple enough for the combination of the two to produce a definite match."

"That and the fact that we only have historical information for ships that entered orbit of Tarsus," Bernadette murmured. The tallest of the women had already run a cable from a port in her temple to the processing tower.

"I'm setting up secure profiles," she told them. "We'll have limited read access, allowed on a case-by-case basis, to each other's files. I presume you'll want to check the security on yours before we get started."

"Thank you."

EB didn't go so far as to set up a physical connection. He was confident in his encryption versus anything Vortex's team could have brought into the secure room. The *concern* was recordings.

"We will need some security to be sure that no one is recording data transmissions or visuals in the room," he told Vortex. "The screens are supposed to be record-resistant, but we both know that can be circumvented."

"There is a limit, Captain Bardacki, to what security can reasonably be achieved without rendering this entire process *impossible*," Vortex conceded with a sigh. "We will not give you direct access to the scramble codes. You will not give us direct access to the shipping schedule.

"We both will need to see the results to be able to compare against the regular shipping data. There must be *some* trust extended that we are not recording data to use against each other."

"As you wish," EB allowed, making sure he sounded as disgruntled as he could.

He was, after all, already planning on recording everything—and thanks to the fact that his retinal implants and software were *not* from the Standard Colonial Database, he could already tell that the anti-recording features on the screens weren't going to stop him at all.

AFTER SIX HOURS of beating their heads against the data, EB came away with three key conclusions:

First, that whatever neurological augmentations Bernadette had built into the modules clearly visible on her temples were worth whatever had been paid for them. The gawky tech had an almost-magical gift for coordinating datasets, running searches and establishing conclusions from data in record time.

His second conclusion, however, was that this was going to be a long, messy process. With the processing power available to them and the precautions they were taking to keep each original dataset secure, each combination of scramble code and ship data took over ten minutes to process. Even with just the historical scan data for Tarsus, it took another ten minutes to check their result to see if the ship had visited the planet.

Third and eeriest, however, was that Vortex was absolutely determined to make the project work. Continued exposure gave him the realization that the diminutive enforcer was assembled from rage and high-density machinery. She wasn't, so far as he could tell, angry at anyone in specific. Just…angry.

At everything.

That rage seemed to fuel her cybernetics as much as whatever concealed power cells were tucked away inside her. She was a professional paranoid, clearly trained to fight and kill at the drop of a pin, who only showed soft edges when dealing with Bernadette or putting on her "obsequious secretary" face.

And that woman, who he doubted gave two shakes of a rat's tail about the fate of the kids he was searching for, threw herself body and soul into the search. She was the weakest data analyst of the five of them, but that also meant that she had some of the most insightful suggestions—and what she lacked in experience, she was making up for in sheer dogged determination.

Whatever the ex–Siya U Hestî enforcer saw her goal as, she was entirely behind it. And *that* worried EB.

"I think we might be wasting our damn time," Vortex said as their eighteenth search came back null. "Six hours and nothing."

"We don't have exact arrival times for the ships," EB conceded. "There's a reason we're giving you multiple possible windows for each one."

"It's not your data, Captain," she growled. "Or the scramble codes. It's that we're looking in a puddle when we need to be scanning the fucking *ocean*. The Bastion isn't on Tarsus—if it was, Lady Ali would already know."

EB personally only put that at about thirty-seventy. He didn't think that the Bastion *was* on Tarsus, but he was pretty sure that Breanna's people could have hidden it from Ali.

He was, in fact, more certain that the Bastion wasn't on *Denton*— because Hadzhiev had been on Denton and Hadzhiev had also visited the Bastion. EB figured the gunslinger would have recognized if he was on the same *planet* as his goal.

"I have some sensor data from Denton," he noted slowly. "I can bring it here and we can run our existing dataset against it, see if any of those ships were in Denton orbit while we were there. It's a limited time frame, though, and one that doesn't match up with any likely dates."

"The Bastion is in Deus's moons or one of the Trojan clusters," Vortex snapped. "It's not on Denton and it's not on Tarsus. It *might* be in Machina's moons," she conceded, "but the point still stands: it's not on one of the inhabited worlds.

"We need the full-system scan data for the last month."

"To find the Bastion? Yes," EB agreed. "To find out if our dataset is working... There's a decent chance one of the ships passed through Denton or Tarsus orbit, either before or after they visited the Bastion."

He wasn't counting on *after*, really, but he wasn't going to say that up front.

"That requires a ship to have been present during the data we have," Bernadette pointed out. "We are spending a great deal of effort to create datapoints that are only seventy percent likely to align with the reality—when even that *reality* is not guaranteed to be in our comparison."

The tech was staring off into space with a glazed expression that had nothing to do with accessing her headware. They'd eaten over the course of the day, but there had been no breaks—and EB saw Vortex regarding the other woman with a flash of unfeigned concern.

"Perhaps, but we don't *have* that data," he pointed out. "Either way, I think we are at the limits of what any of us can manage today. Time isn't our ally here, but neither is killing ourselves, trying to achieve the impossible."

The advantage, EB supposed, to knowing that the plan had been for all of the kidnap victims to arrive at the Bastion already in cryo-stasis and *stay* in cryo-stasis was that it removed some of the time pressure.

"Agreed," Vortex said crisply. "Resume at oh eight hundred hours station time tomorrow?"

That was fourteen hours away, which would give them all a chance to rest and recharge away from the others and the task at hand. Just being inside the Faraday cage was like a loose tooth EB couldn't stop poking at. Even aboard *Evasion*, he had more of a datanet than he could access from the secure room.

"Sounds like a plan," EB agreed.

He pulled his dataset from the shared processor, checking to make sure Ali's people hadn't managed to sneak access to it as he did. Each of them would keep their own secure dataset separate—and neither of them was keeping the result dataset.

Officially. *He'd* recorded everything he'd looked at today, and given the degree to which Bernadette was linked in to the system, he suspected the tech would have had to actively *not* record everything.

Wiping his half of the system, he rose—and realized he'd received a text message from Vortex.

We should talk away from the others, she told him. *Dinner?* A time and a location—a higher-end chain restaurant in the spacer's sector of the station—appeared attached to the message.

You expect me to come alone? he replied.

No. Bring your doctor or your thug, if you wish. I will be alone. I need to speak to Lady Ali first, though.

Very well, EB said, saving the invite.

The schemes thickened. He *would* bring Lan, he decided. He doubted, after all, that Vortex was planning to betray her mistress for him.

No. This was going to be about the SDF scan data.

19

THE CAVALIER SURF and Turf was a far cry from the Glorious Dragoon, but at least its owners hadn't decided that it needed an *esthetic*. It was an ordinary-looking pub that happened to be on a space station, with a decent quality of fake wood and a basic variety of food that EB hoped would be decent.

As a general rule in his experience, the *Turf* part of Surf and Turf was almost always actual beef, but the *Surf* was almost always local. Humanity had exported cows, chickens and a number of other farm animals across the galaxy, but fish had come along more slowly.

Still, the restaurant was busy and he hadn't been given a reservation detail or anything. The artificial stupid hologram greeted him at the door with the question he'd been dreading:

"Do you have a reservation, ser? The wait for a table is just over eighty minutes at the moment. If you wish, you can leave your headware code with us and we will ping you when you are next on the list."

"I'm meeting someone," he told the holographic server. "Was a message left for a Captain Bardacki?"

"Ah, yes, Captain," the hologram replied. "Please follow the drone."

A tracked waist-high drone that appeared to mostly serve drinks acquired a marker in EB's headware and slowly began to move away as he approached. It led him and Lan to a booth at the back of the restaurant, where Vortex was sitting with her back to the wall, surveying the room like even the tables might attack her.

"Captain, Doctor," she greeted them. "I wonder, Captain Bardacki, are you aware that Evridiki is a *feminine* Greek name, not a male one?"

EB blinked at the non sequitur as he took his seat, considering his response until he finally chuckled.

"I was not," he admitted. "But given how...shallow Apollo's adoption of Greek culture can be at times, I'm not entirely surprised that my parents grabbed a Greek name without checking the details."

"Huh." She studied him and Lan for a moment. "Check the menu if you want. The steaks are good. Don't trust the fish. Tarsus doesn't *have* fish by any normal definition of the word, so the only decent fish you can get here is salmon farmed around the Black Island." She smiled thinly. "The Cavalier can't afford to get *that* imported across the star system, so they have...alternatives."

A quick skim of the menu in his headware backed up her warning. EB had eaten vat-grown protein that was perfectly acceptable at times —but he hadn't tasted anything from a vat that came even close to what it was pretending to be since leaving the Rim.

He and Lan both ordered simple steaks, letting the restaurant's datanet whisk away their orders without the intervention of any human or even an artificial stupid server.

There *were* humans in the restaurant, but the vast majority of deliveries of meals and drinks were carried out by the automated servers. The half dozen humans were basically floating, checking in on the robots and the customers if they spotted a problem.

Given that there were six visible staff and EB eyeballed around eighty tables, they seemed pretty safe from interruption—and the background music and general conversation covered them from eavesdropping unless there was a bug built into the table.

Vortex still produced a stylish small leather purse and put it on the table, as if keeping it close to hand. EB's headware picked up the included jammer and white-noise generator, though, rendering any bugs or microphones close to them useless.

"I'm surprised you didn't bring your companions," EB observed. "Bernadette and Arson seem quite involved in this project."

"Bernadette is, without question, the best computer systems specialist I know," Vortex told him calmly. "Arson is a decent analyst and an excellent troubleshooter. Neither of them is cleared for the full extent of this affair—and, in all honesty, I try to keep Bernadette from realizing the full extent of what our organization does."

EB wasn't going to touch that comment with a ten-meter pole. If Bernadette was half the systems specialist Vortex implied or his own experience earlier that day suggested, the only way she *wasn't* aware of the full scope of her employer's work was by actively choosing ignorance.

"So, what is the 'full extent of this affair,' then?" Lan asked softly, the doctor's voice carrying an edge EB still found unusual. His soft-spoken and soft-fleshed doctor had turned out to be terrifyingly capable when push had come to shove on Estutmost. EB's fiancé and daughter were alive because Lan Kozel had been there.

But while EB had assumed that Lan, like the rest of *Evasion*'s crew, was running away from *something*, he hadn't even begun to guess the reality that he'd hired a former covert ops medic who had spent a decade in counter-biowarfare teams.

Lan could get very cold, very quickly, and it was still uncomfortable to watch.

"We *need* system-wide scan data," Vortex reminded them. "Our current exercise is consuming a lot of resources for something with a near-complete inability to confirm success or failure."

"It's a bit frustrating, yes," EB agreed. "I haven't had any brilliant insights on acquiring that information yet, though."

He had some thoughts and vague ideas, but they weren't solid yet —and they weren't anything he wanted to get Ali or Vortex involved in.

"Lady Ali has learned of a source," the enforcer told him. A head-ware link request popped up in his head, and EB allowed it—via a secure, read-only link. He could see what she sent him, but it couldn't run executable code in his headware.

All Vortex was trying to do, though, was create an illusion of a hologram between the three of them that no one else could see. A map of the Icem System took shape above the table, and EB studied it calmly.

It was an interesting mix of a system. Stars with multiple inhabitable planets were relatively rare, though the fact that neither of Icem's inhabited worlds was overly *hospitable* wasn't unusual for such systems. The lack of asteroid belts limited the system's wealth and industry, though the locals had made good use of what they had, including the two big gas giants.

Icem I and Icem IV were almost completely ignored, though. The inner planet was a superheated ball too small to be of value, and Templar, the one rocky world between Tarsus and the gas giants, had nothing of value that wasn't more easily found on Tarsus, where people could breathe.

EB wasn't initially sure what the source of the map was, but as icons began to appear on it, he could guess. The Standard Colonial Database lent itself to certain standardizations across almost all of human space—including military iconography.

The most obvious items were the asteroid fortresses with their orbital elevators, one above Denton and one above Tarsus. Nova gunships and sublight monitors were also flagged on the map, again mostly positioned above the two inhabited planets.

A flotilla of monitors, each of them easily twice *Evasion*'s size but utterly incapable of FTL travel, stood guard over Deus. Machina had a single nova gunship watching the almost-untouched gas giant—but there was a second icon with the emerald-green of the Icemi SDF at the outer gas giant.

He wasn't sure what a surveillance platform built with mostly SCD systems would look like, but it would only lack in effectiveness compared to more modern systems in the Rim or Coreward.

The three-dimensional satellite-dish icon flashed brightly as Vortex highlighted it. It was part of a network, he realized. Six of the stations formed a sphere at Machina's orbit, two in polar positions above and below Icem, with the other four positioned around the gas giant's path.

Denton, Tarsus and Deus all had four associated platforms of their own. Again, one in orbit and three scattered along the orbital path. Eighteen surveillance platforms would give the System Defense Force a full view of the system in significant detail.

"I don't think I realized that Icem had quite so complete a sensor network," EB murmured. Apollo's network was denser and likely involved more-capable platforms—but Apollo also had the nova fighters and nova warships to intercept anyone those sensors detected.

"Most of the time, I think even the SDF regards it as a white elephant," Vortex told him. "A legacy of a more-paranoid time that sucks down an ever-increasing percentage of their budget and technical personnel to keep online.

"But it's politically unfeasible to shut it down. So far as our research suggests, the data flow is far more than the SDF actually has the personnel to manage," she continued. "They maintain a mix of artificial stupids and human supervision, but they're scanning for threats. Anything that doesn't ping as a warship is archived and ignored almost immediately."

"Archived, huh?" EB asked softly.

"All eighteen platforms are linked by standard tightbeam radio," she told him. "From any platform, the watch crew can see the sensor data from any other platform. It provides cross-networked redundancy, but the stations themselves are basically punishment postings.

"They're well over fifty years old and what amenities they have are malfunctional." She shrugged. "Smuggling drugs and porn on board them is a small but profitable operation for the Cartel, so we know quite a bit about the stations.

"Unfortunately, that means that we know that the *stations* only maintain a forty-eight-hour data archive onboard," Vortex continued. "Their data-storage capabilities aren't up to holding much more than that of the full-system data they are sharing."

"But they do archive it," EB presumed. If the ISDF *didn't* archive their system-wide scan data, they might have a real problem.

"They do," she confirmed. "Of course, the archives are *here* and *here*."

The two asteroid fortresses highlighted in the shared image.

EB could only grimace. The forts were undersized and undergunned even by the standards of the Rim, but they still dwarfed any nova-capable starship. Their plasma cannon and jammers were weaker, kilo for kilo, than the systems installed in *Evasion*—but given that they had installations the size of his entire ship, the difference was functionally irrelevant.

"Unless Em Ali has assets aboard one of the forts, I'm not sure we're getting anywhere with those," he said.

"We would need a far clearer and immediate return on the investment before Lady Ali would risk any assets we have there," Vortex pointed out. "The amount of data we'd need to extract would likely burn any such asset irrevocably."

She did not, EB noted, actually *say* one way or another if Ali had such an asset.

"Fortunately, we don't need to raid the asteroid forts' archives," she continued. "Like I said, all of this was set up in a more-paranoid time, during the Directorate."

EB...had no idea what "the Directorate" was, and the jammer stopped him from looking it up easily. He realized he should probably know more about Icemi history than he did, given Trace's origins, but Vortex clearly figured he *did* know.

Fortunately, Lan didn't see a point in pretending, and they coughed gently.

"'The Directorate'?" the doctor asked.

"Right, you're not local," Vortex conceded. "Multiheaded dictatorship that ran the system between about seventy and fifty years ago. They were paranoid that the other systems around were going to get involved in our politics to return Icem to democracy, so they built up the orbital defenses and started us having real nova combat squadrons."

EB swallowed his urge to object to the classification of the ISDF's gunship force as "real nova combat squadrons." A single Apollo System Defense Force carrier group would wipe out their entire nova-capable force without even noticing the ammunition expenditure. The *forts* might still prove an insurmountable problem, but Icem's nova forces were nothing to be proud of.

Except, he supposed, by Beyond standards.

"But since the Directorate was paranoid not only about external threats but about each other and the ISDF, there were back doors and backups to their back doors and backups," she told them. "So, while the main archives are held on the asteroid forts, each of those archives has two off-site backups."

Four green icons appeared in the display. Two were on Denton, one at the north pole and one—if he judged it correctly—at the base of the orbital elevator. Two were at Tarsus. One was on the planet's tiny moon, which played host to a large-enough naval base that EB didn't want to go poking around.

The last icon, however, was at Tarsus's south pole. Thousands of kilometers from any of the inhabited areas of the planet, surrounded by frozen mountain ranges utterly hostile to humankind.

"Is this one even still *operating*?" he asked.

"That was my first question, too," Vortex told him. "It took some digging, because apparently the ISDF doesn't talk much about it. Officially, it's a weather reporting station."

"And in truth?"

"It's *supposed* to serve as a backup planetary defense center, with a hundred surface-to-space-capable fighters."

"Huh." EB considered that. Sub-fighters, as they were somewhat demeaningly called in the Rim, were one of the few countermeasures to a nova bomber other than a proper nova fighter. Lacking the tactical FTL jumps of their more-advanced cousins, they were *extremely* vulnerable to said cousins.

But they shared the sublight maneuverability, onboard multiphasic jammers and powerful short-range plasma guns of a heavy nova fighter. They served some specific and valuable purposes, if not as well as the fighters EB had flown.

A hundred of them launching from a concealed base wasn't going to do *much* to an enemy that had managed to take down the orbital fortress and monitors, but it would definitely be a *surprise*.

"That sounds almost as bad as landing on Tarsus's moon," he pointed out.

"If it *actually* was being used that way," Vortex told him with a smile. "The fighters are there, I'm led to understand, but the crews aren't. There's a maintenance team made up of folks who pissed their superiors off that runs the system backup and maintains the fighters and the weather station.

"It *does* have anti-air and anti-space defenses, but who knows if they even work?"

"I'd like a bit more information than that," EB observed drily. "What are you thinking? You're the locals with local resources."

"We need recent data," she told him. "Orbital scans, that kind of thing. You know more than I do what can be managed, I suspect. Our spaceborne assets are...limited. Freighters and such. We certainly don't have anything capable of landing covertly.

"You, on the other hand, breached the Estutmost blockade."

Somehow, EB had suspected that was going to come back to bite him.

"I'll need to get a look at the defenses, the sensor systems in place and the local terrain," he told her carefully. "I feel like this is outside the scope of my deal with Ali, Vortex."

"That's for you and Ali to sort out," she said. "I'm here to run the interface between you and us and make sure our data stays secure. But we need that scan archive, Captain Bardacki. This is the best way I see to get it."

One of the servers rolled up, ending the conversation for the moment. White-noise generator or not, the robot at their table was going to be able to record what they were saying.

20

"YOU *CANNOT* BE SERIOUS."

Trace nodded along to Vexer's declaration as everyone stared at EB.

"You want to launch a covert infiltration of a system military's secret facility to steal their scan data?" Vexer continued. "I know there are a lot of things we're prepared to do to get kids like Trace to safety, but can we stick to things that are moral *and* survivable? Or, at the very least, *survivable*?"

"Tarsus's poles have an average daily *high* of minus forty-five degrees Celsius," Trace added helpfully. "Anything that isn't going straight into the heated base is going to be…"

"Foolish," Lan finished for her. "But please, everyone, breathe and let EB finish."

"I am assuming Dad-E doesn't plan on committing suicide to make our crime lady friend's life easier," Trace said. "But I'm wondering what details I'm missing."

"The big one is that I haven't agreed to do *anything*," EB told them, though his eyes were locked on Vexer. "I agree. Actually doing what Vortex has suggested is damn foolish. But." He held up one finger and glanced at Trace.

"I am prepared to do *quite* a lot to get these poor people out of those cryo-cells," he said quietly. "A little time one way or another isn't going to save or damn them. But it may make the difference between us charging in half-blind—or in us finding them at all."

He shrugged. "I'm not launching a suicide assault without damn good reason and damn good data," he told them all. "But I *will* do a scouting sweep to see what's there. We're taking a day away from beating our heads against our shared data analysis—and I downloaded as much information as I could sneak out into *Evasion*'s systems.

"We want to analyze that, see if we can pull anything useful out," he continued.

Trace was already checking the computers with her headware. The first step, she saw, was going to be taking a visual recording of EB looking at the screens and turning it back into data she could toss into their analysis programs.

"But while we're taking that day away from working with our 'partners,' Vortex has arranged a bullshit short-range delivery job for us—the kind of gig a starship captain takes to keep his crew from going stir crazy while waiting for the main cargo," EB said with a chuckle. "The only really important part is that the course and time will see us pass right over the south pole."

"There is another key point," Reggie said. "Is it *her* cargo? Because I'm going to go through it with Tate in a lot more detail if it's from them!"

"Third-party but probably connected to Ali," EB warned. "So, do that double-check. Trace—I want you and Lan to go over the data from today and see if you can recreate any semblance of their scramble code.

"Vexer and I will be on the bridge as we take our flight, tuning the sensors as neatly as we can. I don't *think* Vortex is lying to us about this—which is worrying in itself."

Trace took a second to follow that thought, then sighed and hugged her arms to herself.

"If they're working this hard to pull this off, there's more at stake than we think," she said aloud.

"Vortex especially seems determined to see this work," Lan

observed. "And Vortex is Ali's hatchet woman. If she has a conscience, it's probably surgically suppressed."

Trace shivered.

"We can't trust these people," she whispered.

"No," EB agreed. "That we're working with them worries me. I worry we've made a mistake."

Trace's dad looked grimly down into his coffee in silence for long enough that Vexer moved over to sit next to him and take his hand.

"We'll run this sensor sweep," Vexer said. "That's not committing us to anything. But I don't…"

The navigator sighed and glanced around the mess hall.

"I don't think we can raid a military base for secure information and expect to get out without killing anyone," Vexer said bluntly. "Which is a step too far for us, I think. Or it better be!"

"I…I don't think *I* would have wanted uninvolved innocents dying to get me out," Trace said quietly. She wasn't sure—she'd been pretty desperate to escape being sold off—but she had never wanted people to die because of her. She'd make an exception for members of the Siya U Hestî themselves, but *they* were actively involved in the nightmare.

EB nodded heavily and met her gaze.

"I don't want to abandon anyone, but that's the problem," he admitted. "We're in a bit too deep with the wrong people chasing this. That's why I want us to go over the data we have. If we can walk away from Ali and do this on our own, well…the plan may change."

"You're assuming that she'll let us walk away," Ginny warned. The older woman reached over to grip Trace's forearm. "I think we're all in agreement that we need to step carefully.

"I can't help feeling that we're missing something, and I don't want any of us to get hurt because we walked into a trap."

TRACE SAT on her bed in her extremely fluffy and multilayer pajamas and poked at the imagery from EB's recordings. The link from her dad's optical nerve to his headware wasn't the best way to get visual recordings—actual ocular implants would always be better for footage —but it gave her enough to work with.

She'd linked her headware into *Evasion*'s systems, checking on the image-processing cycle. The first couple of sets of post-scramble identity codes had been translated back into actual data now, and she was running them through the scan data from Denton.

The *problem*, as she saw it, was that because of the back-and-forth between the two datasets, she didn't actually know *which* ships she had data for. The security measures taken to keep Ali's people from seeing their data and to keep them from seeing the scramble code had separated the final result from either of its inputs.

Leaving the computers to process imagery on their own—a slow process, mostly due to the anti-recording features of the screens in the secure dataroom—she took her first sets and pulled the sensor records from their time in Denton orbit.

Thanks to the checks that EB and the others had been running before, she knew that none of the ships she was looking at had been in *Tarsus* orbit at any point in the last few years. On the other hand, Trace had spent months living aboard a ship now. Any ship traveling between star systems had very little reason to stop at Tarsus without a specific contract.

The main inhabited planet, though, would definitely see visitors and interest. The two places a strange ship might stop would be Denton and Deus.

There were eighteen pairings of ship, arrival time and scramble code in the imagery. She wasn't expecting to get a decent match on any of them—but the chance was there.

And her headware chimed softly in her mind as she realized she'd struck gold on the second of her results.

The match was over ninety-five percent on the identifier code—an alphanumeric string supposed to be unique for a large region of human space. A number of other signatures of the ship were adjusted to match the identifier code, but she only had an eighty-four percent match there.

The actual *name* was almost irrelevant, a randomly generated word pairing that could barely be considered part of the scramble code.

Scarlet Peach wasn't something she figured any ship would actually be named, but everything else about the freighter was a closer match to the scramble result than she'd expected.

Trace pulled all of the information *Evasion* had on the other freighter. *Scarlet Peach* had been leaving Salieri Corp Fueling Platform Two as *Evasion* had been docking with High Home. She'd novaed out roughly eight hours after they'd arrived in Icem, and Trace didn't have enough information to track her course.

But *Evasion*'s passive sensors, even in their general operating mode, were *very* good by Beyond standards. They didn't keep the historical data forever—there was only so much storage space that could be fit into a given volume, after all—but they had all of their data since arriving in Trace's home system.

Which meant she had a surprising amount of information on *Scarlet Peach*.

Sixteen thousand five hundred cubic meters. Single light plasma cannon—Trace wasn't sure it was worth much of anything, but it might help scare off a particularly cowardly pirate. It was a small ship, even by Beyond standards, but it wasn't the baseline ten-kilocubic tramp, either.

Trace didn't know as much about ships as she wanted to yet, but she knew enough to know that *Scarlet Peach* was a nonstandard size. That meant that either the identifier was either completely off—or that the *actual* ship was on the list from Hadzhiev.

And there she was. *Albatross's Mariner*. Sixteen point five kilocubics. Single plasma cannon. Captain Kalei Van Schoorl.

Of course, they didn't have enough information to say who *Scarlet Peach* had officially been commanded by when she'd left, but she *matched* the ship on the original list. That meant that the process EB and Lan had been going through with Ali's people *worked*.

Given the possible cost of that, Trace wasn't sure this was *good* news.

21

ROUGHLY HALF OF *Evasion*'s volume and eighty percent of her cargo-carrying capacity was made up of the four unpressurized cargo bays at her heart. Each bay was designed to hold twenty standard ten-meter units stacked two-by-two five deep, making the bays themselves ten meters square and fifty meters long.

With four such bays—stacked two-by-two, same as the TMUs inside them—EB had twenty thousand cubic meters of unpressurized storage space. It *could* be sealed to retain atmosphere and was set up with gravity systems for loading and unloading if need be, but by default, *Evasion*'s main cargo bays had neither atmosphere nor gravity.

At various points, EB had seen several different varieties of larger standardized units. One that he'd never actually *seen*—but that *Evasion*'s designers had been aware of—was the so-called "Megablock." The Megablock was ten meters wide, ten meters tall, and fifty meters deep—exactly the dimensions of each of *Evasion*'s cargo bays.

He'd never hauled one before, but now he was standing in the cargo observation bay with his new client, watching *two* of them be carefully loaded into his cargo bays.

"What even *are* those?" Reggie asked, standing a careful few steps away and angled to watch the rest of the busy space on Teamster Station.

Most of the ships they could see would be loading goods from the planet below—or unloading goods destined for Tarsus. The orbital elevator could carry anything up to and including a Megablock, except that *this* pair was needed more urgently.

The dark-haired man standing next to EB, watching the cargo containers with an accountant's sharp attention and concern, smiled mirthlessly at Reggie's question.

"The biggest pain in the neck I've dealt with in the last twelve years," he told them. "It took us *two years* to convince the Board that we were going to need replacements, and then the damn old ones failed a week ago. Followed, of course, by the new ones being delayed in transit and arriving after our booked window on the elevator."

Oliver Dunn was the Vice President, Capital Assets, for Orthodox Industrial Refining and Mining. OIRM had facilities across the star system, as EB understood it, with an orbital refinery cluster above Denton and some of the system's few asteroid mines in Deus's Trojan Clusters.

"They're excavators, Em Kalb," Dunn continued. "Each of them capable of removing, moving or replacing thousands of tons of dirt and rock an hour. Semi-automated and requiring specialized training even *with* the stupids, they were manufactured in Nigahog and are the best tools for the job in a hundred light-years.

"And every *hour* that they are not on the surface costs us roughly seven million reals in work stoppage. And the next transit window we could book on the elevator for Megablocks was fifteen days out."

"Hence you wanting a ship that could land," EB murmured. Most ships that had a cargo bay capable of holding a Megablock weren't designed for planetary landings. *Evasion* was, though her ability to carry Megablocks had been an afterthought.

"Exactly. I was delighted when we discovered your ship and her availability," Dunn told him.

EB, on the other hand, had been delighted to find a task that justi-fied flying his ship across the south pole. That OIRM was paying well above market rate for *immediate* service was the icing on the cake.

Seven million reals wasn't *quite* as bad as it sounded—it took eight hundred Icemi reals to buy a decent beer at a bar, so it was *just* one person's annual salary flushing down the drain every hour.

Just.

"It looks like Tate and the station people will have the excavators aboard shortly," EB noted. "Reggie and I should get back aboard ship."

He smiled thinly.

"Unless you expect us to need *Evasion*'s weapons during our handful of hours in your employ, in which case you should brief Em Kalb on that."

"What? No," Dunn replied in a horrified tone. "No, my dear Captain, this is just a…confluence of bad luck. That's all."

"They say once is an accident, twice is a coincidence and three times is enemy action," Reggie pointed out. "The excavators failing is one. The new ones being delayed is two. There not being an elevator slot for over ten days is three, isn't it?"

Dunn now *looked* horrified.

"Everything is within expected variances," he finally said, his choice of words confirming EB's assessment of the man as an accountant. "OIRM operates widely enough and transparently enough that we are not concerned about sabotage or internal workers' issues. I… may not be able to say the same for other companies on Tarsus, but I am quite certain none would go so far as to be actively sabotaging us!

"And even if they were"—*accountant* didn't always mean *data analyst* or *leader*, but willingness to consider unlikely scenarios was a positive trait for the latter two roles in EB's experience—"it is highly unlikely that their efforts would extend to open violence. The Orbital Guard is aware of the transfer as well.

"If there is trouble, I trust them to handle the matter."

And if the Guard couldn't, EB was quite certain Reggie could.

———

BACK ABOARD *EVASION*, EB settled onto the bridge with a small smile at his fiancé. Vexer had set everything up for the short trip around Tarsus while he'd been schmoozing with the client.

"Flight is thirty-five minutes there, thirty-eight back," Vexer told him. "Rotation helps us on the way there, costs us on the way back. Not much, of course, since we're cutting over the pole to save distance and time."

"Good," EB murmured. "And our time over the pole?"

"We'll have line of sight after fifteen minutes. We'll stay in LOS for about five minutes after that—and it's about the same on the way back."

EB nodded, pulling the exact window from the course plan and feeding it into his own systems.

"Barely operating reserve base or not, they are going to see and blow their tops if we pulse them with active scanners," he observed. "Especially since it looks like the Orbital Guard has actually moved a cutter into place to watch this whole affair."

"Really?" Vexer asked.

EB tapped a command and focused the main bridge display on the icon he'd just picked out of the mess.

"I mean, she's a planetary cutter, so I'm not exactly going to sweat about her watching over my shoulder," EB said drily. The four-thousand-cubic-meter ship had no nova drive and was literally small enough to fit in the Megablocks they were hauling. She'd be hard-pressed to make even an *interplanetary* flight without a tender to replenish her supplies, but that wasn't her job.

The local spacecraft was exactly what her name implied: she was an *Orbital* Guard ship. Nine times out of ten, a planet's Orbital Guard's entire job was to back up space traffic control.

The tenth time, they were intervening in a disaster to save lives. Unfortunately, given that even a small and slow spaceship would cause catastrophe if it hit a planet, it wasn't always guaranteed that the lives the Guard were saving were on the ship in trouble.

"So, either our client is understating the potential issues from their competitors or what…"

"Or we're an armed freighter swanning around in orbit of the planet they're supposed to protect, and the locals, quite sensibly, have decided to keep an eye on us," EB told Vexer with a chuckle. "We *always* get a bit of extra attention, Vexer. We're just noticing it today because our hackles are up."

"Fair. Station control has cleared us," Vexer told him. "Ship is yours."

"Let's get this show on the road."

AT FIRST GLANCE, the polar base really did just look like a weather station. Why, exactly, anyone needed to know what the weather at the pole was, he wasn't sure. While Tarsus's mining operations were slowly expanding out from the equator in search of readily available prizes, there weren't even work sites within thirty degrees of either pole.

But a manned weather station was positioned on a plateau almost exactly at the magnetic south pole. Between ice and rock, only the aboveground structures of the runway and a dozen or so prefabricated buildings were easily visible.

Except that EB *knew* there was more there, and he prodded *Evasion*'s sensors as they swung over the polar plateau. He could pick up everything from infrared to the radiation leakage of nuclear power plants to the Jianhong radiation of a nova-drive core with the ship's scanners, which left the hidden base with no shield against his eyes.

They had certainly *tried*, though, which said a lot.

"Defensive installations here, here, here and here," he said aloud, highlighting them on the display. "Covered in snow, but they're linked to the main base by underground tunnels."

"Think the 'mountains' they're in are natural?" Vexer asked. "They look very evenly spaced."

"There are enough other rises and hills on the plateau to suggest so," EB replied. "They might have built up a couple of them to be *bigger* before they built the weapons into them."

He shook his head.

"Can't be sure what's in them, but I'm guessing HVTMs." Hyper-velocity terminal missiles used antigrav-assisted chemical rockets to clear their launch bases and approach their targets, then activated a single-use Harrington coil to convert their mass into pure kinetic energy.

A regular HVM had a very limited range before its effects dissipated, but just about anything inside that range would...go away. An HVTM would get to its range of the target, *then* go hypervelocity.

He'd seen them used as artillery systems, but their main purpose was anti-air and anti-space. They weren't much use against a full-sized starship, but anyone sending in landers would have a real bad day finding out about them.

"What about the archive?" Vexer asked. "That's the main thing we care about, right?"

EB sighed.

"Hard to say," he admitted. "There's definitely a significant underground structure. If you look *here*"—he highlighted a spot on the plateau—"I'm pretty sure we're looking at a retractable roof for the sub-fighter runways.

"But all we're going to get of the underground structure is roughly where it is compared to the surface." He shook his head. "It *looks* like there's something under the air base that looks about the size and energy signature I'd expect for a big data-storage center."

"I'm hearing another *but*," Vexer said. "And it's not the one that's linked to you not being sure about the datacenter."

EB grimaced. There was a reason he was marrying Vexer. The other man knew him far too well.

"Vortex said the base was basically shut down, acting as a weather station and a data backup," he said. "But there are *four* active fusion reactors down there. I'm also picking up at least a dozen ground vehicles doing what looks like exterior patrols."

He shook his head.

"That's not an inactive base, Vexer. I'd bet money that they can't get whatever their official list strength is into the air—but I'd bet just as much money they can get at least a few squadrons of sub-fighters up.

"Our archive is buried under a covert but active military base," he concluded. "Which means that there is nowhere in this damn star system we can steal that data from without going through a damn army."

He and Vexer stared at the screen for a few long seconds.

"Am I right in that this is *still* our best shot?" EB's fiancé finally asked.

"Yeah. It's quiet and it's hidden. We *might* be able to get a shuttle or aircraft in quietly, with the right kind of gear, and infiltrate the exterior of the base. *If* we can get the right gear from Ali's people, and *if* the archive can be accessed from the outer perimeter...we might be able to get what we need without triggering alarms or a firefight."

"Lot of ifs."

"Too many ifs. This whole partnership is looking worse by the damn minute."

22

TRACE WASN'T the go-to expert for anything on the ship. She most definitely was *not* the expert on transporting massive containers containing automated digging machines, analyzing sensor data to pick out a hidden base from permafrost, or identifying ships.

She was mostly working on seeing if she could reverse-engineer a version of the scramble code that had turned *Albatross's Mariner* into *Scarlet Peach*. By the time they were leaving the OIRM site, delivery complete, she'd realized that she needed at least one more near-certain match to get it.

There were finite ways to get from the beacon and emissions signature of *Albatross's Mariner* to the ones for *Scarlet Peach*, but *finite* still meant *enough that no option is definitely correct*.

And even if she'd somehow picked the right conversion sequence, she also needed to identify *how* date and time of arrival factored into the calculation. The scramble code wasn't particularly complicated, when all was said and done. It just took in enough inputs to make it almost impenetrable without examples.

She had a bunch of examples, though, of what Ali's people had generated from the list of ships and times they'd put together. So, she ran her latest reverse-engineered sequence against that initial list and checked for matches.

And then sighed.

"Just *Mariner*," she said aloud, glaring at the single green line on her screen. "What do you need, you stupid code? The phase of the moon on Old Earth?"

Trace swiped the screens in her tiny study into their default mode, a view of the space around *Evasion*. They were breaking atmosphere now and heading back across the south pole to get a second look at the target base.

The whole situation with Ali didn't sit right with her—and that had been *before* it felt like their so-called allies were trying to set them up to launch an assault on an ISDF base. Trace didn't have the greatest respect for authority or emotional attachment to her star system, but she *did* like her dads and the rest of the crew quite a bit.

And attacking a base both seemed like a bad idea in the sense of achieving general good karma *and* in keeping her dads intact.

She sighed. They were still being watched, too. She wasn't sure what the small cutter was planning on *doing* if *Evasion* did something strange, but it was there. Tarsus orbit was busy enough that the cutter probably had other things to be doing, too. The Tarsus Orbital Guard only *had* half a dozen of the ships according to the datanet.

Trace glanced past the cutter to the ships coming in toward Teamster Station and then froze. A quick interrogation of *Evasion*'s systems pulled more data on the image she'd seen and confirmed her recognition.

She wasn't great at identifying ships, but she'd had an archive of ships of interest to the Siya U Hestî in her head. It had started leaking into her regular headware before she'd realized she had the datavault at all—and she would never forget the first ship she'd identified from that leakage.

Zeldan Blade was a heavily armed mercenary corvette, bigger and better armed than the gunships that made up the local nova squadron. Her captain, Lisa Zelda, was a mercenary and a bounty hunter.

She had also been their key ally in taking down the Cage. If there was anyone in the region they could trust, Trace figured it was Zelda and her daughter.

Assuming her dads felt the same way, that opened a whole new avenue of questions!

"WHY WOULD ZELDA EVEN BE HERE?" Ginny asked as they gathered in the mess hall again. "She's a bounty hunter, mostly. A Tracker. What would bring her to Icem?"

"Work, almost certainly," EB said. "Which means drawing attention to them is dangerous for all of us. And yet..."

Trace saw his troubled expression and reached over to give him a hug.

"We all think working with Ali is a problem," she reminded him. "I'm...halfway, maybe, into deciphering the scramble code.

"But she's going to try to get us—get *you*—to take all of the risks," Trace told her dad. "And you're willing to let her because you don't want to let anyone suffer what I went through. Or worse."

"I don't," EB agreed. "But I'm also not going to go to war for that. Not against people who aren't my enemy. I don't see a way to get the archive data we need without doing so, which means we may just be wasting all of our time and helping nobody."

"Working with Ali got us the information we need to reverse-engineer the code," Ginny countered. "It will take us time to do it, and we need to do so without her realizing. But there have *got* to be options available to us to get that sensor data that a criminal doesn't have."

"Have we considered *asking*?" Tate said drily.

"Yes," Reggie replied. The weapons tech was sitting on the food-prep counter, watching everyone else around the table. "We considered it. We talked about it. And the problem is that we *know* Hadzhiev went to the ISDF. And then Hadzhiev *died*. And so did the person he went to in the SDF.

"Which means the SDF leaks like a *fucking sieve*," he growled. "So, while the logical thing is to go to the cops and the military, we can't."

"What about Everest?" Vexer asked. "He seemed trustworthy enough. Would he be able to get us the data?"

Trace felt her father exhale a sigh. He gave her a squeeze and rose to his feet, stalking across the mess hall like a caged bear.

"He might be able to find someone he trusts to source it for us," he said slowly. "But if we've judged him wrong, we might find ourselves under attack. If *he* judges wrong, we might just get an honest cop killed."

"There is a side to this that we're missing," Lan said softly. They looked around the room, meeting Trace's gaze for a moment before focusing on EB. "Ali isn't doing this just for some secret base and a few ships. There's something about the Bastion that is worth enough for someone trying to take control of the Siya U Hestî remnants in this system to risk exposure and betrayal for."

"Oh, I'm quite sure that Ali is intending to betray *us*," EB said.

"Lan's right, Dad-E," Trace told him. "Ali sees something in this we don't. There's something we're missing—which brings us back to Zelda."

"How?" Vexer asked. "I mean, we can hire Captain Zelda again if we need support, but I don't see—"

"She's got half a foot in the criminal underworld," Trace said. "She has to, or she can't find her bounties. So, if there's something going on, something we're missing because we're not tied in to this region and these systems, she *should* know.

"And she likes us. She sent her daughter with Dad-E."

And Leia Zelda was *cool*. Trace didn't want to be a bounty hunter in the slightest, but she very much hoped to be half as cool as Lisa Zelda's daughter when she was older.

"If nothing else, making sure that we're in touch with her and have a line on her services is a good idea," EB admitted. "But I think…"

He turned back to face Trace and the others firmly.

"I think we're done with Janessa Ali and her people," he said quietly. "I'm not attacking a military base for any damn reason—and I'm sure as hell not doing it for a woman who is directly responsible for labor-trafficking onto this planet.

"I'm going to talk to Zelda first. I have the sneaking suspicion that Ali isn't going to take severing the partnership overly well."

Trace figured that was an understatement. She'd spent enough time in the hands of the Siya U Hestî to have met people like Janessa Ali. They believed—they *knew*, in their hearts—that the world would work the way they told it to.

And if it didn't, they would *make* it do so.

23

THE FIRST PLACE EB had thought to meet up with Zelda was the Cavalier. The chain restaurant was the right type of place, especially with its ever-present hubbub of noise.

Then he realized that any place that Vortex had picked was probably beholden to Ali's organization in some way. So, he picked a diner near the spaceport, one that was busy enough to provide the noise he needed, and then sent the Trackers' Guild Captain an invite.

To his surprise, she beat him there. Even in the far-from-gentle crowd of a spaceport breakfast diner, Lisa Zelda carried a bubble of inviolate space around her. Something about the hard-bitten woman caused people to stay at a distance.

He wasn't sure if it was the hijab scarf braided through her black hair—a token representation of her faith, as he understood it—or the shaved sides of her head. He *suspected*, though, that it was the fact that everything about her hair and skull, including several visible scars, drew attention to her missing left ear.

To those with the courage to look and the knowledge to identify it, her replacement implant was clearly visible, though the scar around it would distract most people.

Even as the rest of the diner somehow managed to clear a meter-wide space around Zelda's table, EB walked through and took a seat across from her.

"I have ordered for us both," she told him calmly. "Their coffee is terrible and their potatoes are not halal." She grimaced. "At least they *know* enough to tell me that."

EB considered what he knew of halal dietary restrictions and blinked at non-halal *potatoes*.

"*How?*" he asked plaintively.

"Fried with the bacon fat," Zelda said grimly. "At least the bread is toasted away from *that* particular attempt to add flavor."

"I see." EB, who *liked* bacon and even the idea of using the fat to add flavor to potatoes for that matter, demurred from the conversation —helped by the arrival of heaping plates of eggs and toast and massive mugs of coffee on a rusted server stupid.

"The coffee is terrible," Zelda repeated. "But they understand the appropriate *quantities* of it, at least."

Given that Zelda had a hydroponic bay on her ship entirely dedicated to growing coffee beans, EB knew not to rely on *her* standard for coffee. By *his* standards, the coffee smelled entirely drinkable.

"I'm glad you could make time to meet me," he said quietly. "I don't know how secure this diner is, though."

"Well, I arrested the owner for an Estutmost first-degree murder warrant last night, so if there's surveillance in here, no one knows who it belongs to or where it's going," she told him. "There are days my job is...extremely satisfying."

She placed a palm-sized gray disk on the table, and EB winced as the combined jammer and white-noise generator came online.

"I figured this wasn't just a social call," Zelda said. "If you'd been bringing Trace or Vexer, I'd have brought Leia."

"I probably would have reached out just for a social call," he told her. "But yeah. Things are messy."

"You are a magnet for trouble, Captain Bardacki."

"Not by choice."

"I heard about Estutmost," she said pointedly, neatly slicing up her eggs into pieces that fit the toast. "Most people don't end up negotiating the end to a civil war by *accident*."

"My family was on the ground," he said uncomfortably, focusing on his own food. "I didn't see any way to get to Trace and Vexer without dealing with the situation somehow."

Zelda chuckled at him.

"It was neatly done in the end," she said. "I don't think anyone expected that mess to end nearly that cleanly, though I think everyone on the outside saw what needed to happen!"

There had been two major factions fighting Estutmost's civil war, but both had been planet-bound. The spaceborne portion of the star system's populace—*including* the official system space force—had chosen to step aside from the conflict and imposed a blockade against the supply of outside weapons.

EB had helped the leader of that impromptu faction realize that one side had gone too far, leading to them forcing a peace conference. As Zelda noted, everyone outside the star system had figured that the spacers were going to need to do something of the sort—but the people in the heart of the fight hadn't been able to step back and see it.

And the spacers *really* hadn't wanted to pick a side.

"So, you were here to arrest a restaurant owner, huh?" EB asked.

"Oh, I have a list, as usual," Zelda said with a chilly smile. "There's a bit of a backlog of warrants from Estutmost in particular, since it wasn't clear who had the authority to *issue* interstellar warrants. The Trackers' Guild put a hold on seizures to and from Estutmost until the war was over.

"I've got a list of about fifty names." She shrugged. "I expect to nab maybe half of them, but I *started* with the asswipe who murdered his wives and kid. He thought he'd got away clean right up until I walked into the kitchen, handed him the warrant and gave him the chance to run."

EB suspected how that had ended, and the self-satisfaction in her chilly smile told him he was right.

"He ran, you stunned him?" he asked.

"Exactly. I suspect I enjoyed it much more than he did."

EB chuckled. He probably would have too—and given some of the descriptors he'd heard of the individual who'd fathered Zelda's daughter, the Tracker probably had her own extra satisfaction in shooting down the murderer. Even nonlethally.

"How long are you going to be in-system?" he asked. "Think you might be up for some mercenary work while you're here?"

Zelda slid her half-empty plate aside and propped her chin on her fist, studying him with dark eyes.

"I figure two weeks, maybe three," she said slowly. "I'm *hoping* for ten days, but even sending multiple teams out, we're only picking up three or four targets a day. Depending on the work and the pay scale, we can definitely carve a couple of days out. Especially if *you're* hiring—I still owe you for our fuckup *and* for giving us a shot at Breanna."

EB had met Zelda when the woman had pursued a bounty the Siya U Hestî had posted on Trace. The Trackers' Guild shouldn't have been *taking* bounties from criminal cartels, so she'd trusted the warrants she'd received from their central office.

She'd been wrong and she had, eventually, admitted it. That had been part of why she'd signed up for his...unwise attack on the Cage. The rest, as she'd said, had been to take a shot at the head of the Siya U Hestî.

"I appreciate that," he told her. "We..." He considered what—and how much—to tell her.

Zelda eyed him and sighed.

"What's going on, EB?" she asked gently. "You walked into a civil war and came out the single-handed peacemaker. The Siya U Hestî came after you and they *no longer exist.* What in stars has you this concerned?"

"I was utterly terrified, dealing with both of those situations," EB pointed out. "But right now...it's not my life on the line. You remember Ansem?"

"The dude you shot in the Cage, who gave you the codes to release the cells and walked off after we left him for dead? Yep."

"Well, he's dead now," EB said drily. "But I didn't kill him. Someone else did, after he managed to pull me into what I'm thinking might have been a misguided quest to find the victims who were still in transit when the Cage fell."

Zelda took a long silent sip of her coffee, then gestured for him to continue.

"He apparently had some kind of emergency code that Breanna had set up that would direct all of the ships in transit to put their trans-portees into cryo-stasis and move them to a fallback base here in Icem. He called it—"

"The Bastion."

EB nodded.

"There is no way in fire and stars that a Siya U Hestî top enforcer pulled that stunt to rescue a bunch of kids and kidnap victims," Zelda told him. "He wanted the Bastion. *Everybody* wants the Bastion, EB. And it's *here*? In Icem?"

He paused, taken aback by her fierceness.

"According to Ansem, yes," he confirmed. "We have the list of ships and where they were supposed to come from and when. We've made what I've realized was a damn *stupid* alliance with a Siya U Hestî remnant to get their scramble codes and try to identify where they went in this system, to trace them to the Bastion.

"But I have the distinct feeling that my not-so-white-hat ally is playing me for a fool and is in this for more than she's telling me."

Zelda was silent for a few seemingly eternal moments, then pulled her plate back over and grabbed an abandoned piece of toast to cover her thoughts. EB patiently waited for her to finish chewing, and she finally leaned back in her chair, still eyeing him.

"You are an idiot," she said genially. "*I* believe that you're in this to rescue the victims who got corralled up at the Bastion, but absolutely no one else is going to. I certainly don't buy that Ansem was after that —and whoever you're working with here *definitely* isn't.

"The Bastion is practically a myth, the kind of urban legend that grows and grows in the retelling. It's not just Breanna's fallback posi-tion; it was the base where she stored everything she thought she'd need to *rebuild her power base from scratch*."

She waited while that sank in and EB considered it. That could cover a…lot of things.

"Since the Cage fell, everyone with half a gram of knowledge about the Siya U Hestî has been looking for the Bastion," Zelda concluded.

"The shortsighted know that Breanna must have hidden away wealth beyond imagining. Tons upon tons upon tons of stamped elementals.

"The wiser know that the money is almost certainly the *least* valuable thing at the Bastion. I have heard rumors of everything from warships to nova fighters to a SAGI."

"None of those seem *likely*," EB pointed out. "Hell, I think there were *two* SAGIs in the Apollo System, and they're a technologically sophisticated, wealthy Rim system."

Pronounced Sage-Eye, a self-aware general intelligence was to a regular artificial stupid what a human was to an insect. A SAGI was a true computerized intelligence, rooted to a complex piece of quantum-computing hardware that might as well be magic for all EB understood about them.

They were also considered people, at least in most of the civilized galaxy. While a SAGI running on just its core quantum box was limited, turning off the power to such a core box was considered murder.

And if there was a single such quantum box in the Beyond, EB would eat his fusion reactors.

"I wouldn't put money against nova gunships," Zelda said. "But yes, I'm more inclined to believe some of the more middling rumors: blackmail archives, complete clinics for soldier boosts and control-chip implantation. You know, the *little things* you could use to retake control of a multi-system criminal empire."

"And I am almost halfway to handing the Bastion to a woman who's only a former Level Seven because the organization has collapsed in this star system," EB said. "Damn. I was trying to work out why she wanted the base, but the only value I could see was just in it *being* a secret base."

He sighed.

"I figured there was money and such there, but not enough to...I don't know, change any balance of power?"

"Rumor would make the Bastion a cave of wonders," Zelda told him with a small chuckle. "I am more practical, and I'm not inclined to *chase* after any caves of wonders. Such pursuits rarely end well in myth and legend, and I can't help but feel our stars will be better off leaving 'Lady' Breanna's legacy to rot on the vine."

"Unfortunately, thanks to Ansem, there are now hundreds of kidnapping victims in cryo-stasis at that base—and a collection of freighters to give them additional transport, assuming that they kept some of them. I doubt they let all—or even *most*—of the delivery ships leave."

She nodded slowly.

"That's...hard to walk away from," she admitted. "Let me know if you need backup, EB. We've got a bunch going on in this system—you don't fund a corvette's operating costs by bringing in *one* bounty, after all—but I will keep my ear to the ground and our boots on.

"You find the Bastion, we'll back you up." She snorted softly. "I don't know enough about where you are to know how to get to the end, but I suspect you already do."

"I think so," EB said slowly. "First, though, I need to untangle some webs I've walked into."

24

EB HAD BARELY MADE it back aboard *Evasion* before he got the message he was waiting for from Vortex, asking when he wanted to resume work at the data center.

He waited until he was back on the freighter's bridge before considering his reply. Vexer was sitting at the watch station on his own, reading a novel on a tablet.

"You look grumpy," his fiancé told him.

"Apparently, we may have almost handed Janessa Ali a specialty-built package designed for retaking control of a multi-system criminal network," EB said flatly. "We should have considered just what the Bastion was, above and beyond a secret base."

Vexer exhaled a long breath.

"Not just a fallback but a springboard," he said. "So, what, money, guns, ships?"

"Plus blackmail material, boosting clinics..." EB shook his head. "According to Zelda, rumor and urban legend in the black and gray communities make it out to have just about anything you could think of. A secret base, a resource stockpile, a treasure vault, a trophy museum..."

"And, regardless of anything else, where the last few hundred kidnap victims got sent," Vexer concluded. He stood up, gesturing for EB to take the seat.

Once EB obeyed, his fiancé began to massage his shoulders, working the muscles gently.

"So, that burns us working with Ali, doesn't it?" Vexer murmured in his ear.

"Yeah. I am not handing her Breanna's empire-in-a-box," EB confirmed. "We *might* have enough information to reverse-engineer the scramble code. Problem is that *they* almost certainly have enough information to unscramble the results to find at least part of the list we have."

"Enough to identify the Bastion's location?"

"Maybe." EB sighed and leaned back into Vexer's hands. "Ali probably has the resources to search a moon from orbit. We need enough vectors to nail it down to within a few thousand klicks. *She* can trace one ship close enough that she can search a hundred times that."

"What do we do?" Vexer asked.

"We get there first. Which means we need the scramble code...and we need the system-wide sensor-data archives."

"We've got a chance at the scramble code," the navigator said slowly. "Trace has mostly been working on it alone because we were still expecting to sit down with Ali's people and nail down a few more results. If that's all we've got, though, you and Lan and Ginny can all take a stab at it.

"Between the four of you, I'm betting we can get a close-enough approximation to let us pick ships out of the full dataset. But we need that full dataset."

"We still have options for that," EB said quietly. "Most are on Denton, though. Everest is our next best shot, I think. He may not have the data—he's a station-security homicide investigator—but I bet he has someone he trusts."

"It's a risk, for both us and him."

"Agreed. For a place that's completely secret and hidden, the Bastion has too many eyes and ears across this system for my peace of mind," EB said. "We will have to be careful—but we ran out of good options a while ago!"

"There never were good options," Vexer told him. "What about the Vortanis?"

EB froze. Somehow, the name didn't take him by surprise in this context. But he hadn't been *consciously* considering anything about them.

"The Vortanis?" he asked slowly.

"Trace's foster mother has really gone all out to try and find her and to make sure what happened to her won't happen to anyone else," Vexer reminded him. "And she's part of the Justice Ministry, senior enough that she can almost certainly source the sensor data we need.

"And while contacting *anyone* is a risk, she has the access. Honestly, she also kind of has the right to know that Trace is okay, even if we're making damn sure she stays with us."

"I was going to send her a video message on our way out of the star system," EB said drily. "I don't want to get involved there, Vexer. Remember that *John* Vortani modified Trace's headware software and hardware without even *telling her what he was doing*.

"Sarah Vortani let that slide *and* neglected our kid for her political career. I'll give her that she seems to recognize that she fucked up and she's trying to make it right, but I don't think *Trace* is going to forgive her."

"No. She doesn't have to. She doesn't even have to *see* the woman."

"I know." EB sighed. "It's an option, and I'm short enough on options I'm not ruling it out. But we have to protect Trace first and foremost."

"Agreed. So. Ali?"

"Vortex wants to know when we're getting started again. I have the distinct feeling that ghosting her would end violently, but I'm not sure how they're going to take us telling them to fuck off at this point."

"Badly. Probably violently," Vexer warned. "Be ready for that."

"Yeah." EB stared blankly off into space for a few seconds, then sighed and brought up messaging on his headware.

We need to talk first, he wrote. *I need to talk to Ali. Make it happen.*

He doubted his tone would go down well with the women he was dealing with, but there wasn't much point in sugarcoating things now.

Disaster planning was *far* more important.

25

EB CAME ALONE. Those were the instructions, which certainly didn't *help* with the feeling that he was walking into a trap. The place Vortex had told him to come to wasn't a good sign either, in his mind.

Teamster Station didn't really have a high-end district. The vast majority of the orbital platform was a working station, the link between the orbital fortress at the end of the orbital elevator and the planet beneath them. Most of what high society Tarsus had was on the planet, in Alexandra.

But it turned out that at one "end" of the circular station, as far away from both the elevator and the space docks as was physically possible, there was a small district of luxury apartments and the services that catered to the wealthy and frivolous.

Central to all of it was a surprisingly tasteful casino with attached hotel and restaurant. The Teamster's Knight had a light chess motif, but that mostly came through in the coloring of everything in black and white. There was the occasional icon of a chess piece, but the designers had kept it subtle and understated.

There was one open floor area full of slot machines that were somewhat more garish, but even those were surprisingly calm and measured versions of the devices. The main focus was clearly on the card and dice tables, which were well separated from both each other and the gaming machines on an upper gallery.

From the gallery EB could look across the gaming floor and watch the central pillar, a glass-walled column of circling water that did double duty as a holographic display for announcements.

Being a starship captain had got him through the front door without even a blink—and the digital invitation card Vortex had sent had seen him ushered up to the upper gallery by an actual uniformed human.

He'd been offered a small stack of chips to gamble with—that he'd declined—and been left standing next to the balcony railing, watching what passed for the rich and fashionable on Teamster Station spend their money.

His walk up to the Teamster's Knight had passed through two security checkpoints run by private firms. The official cops weren't going to get involved in segregating districts aboard the space station —but given that private-security checkpoints doing the same were definitely illegal under Icemi law, some loophole was being exploited.

Just getting to the casino took knowing names. Getting *in* required some proof that you had actual money—and even that only got you onto the main floor. The upper gallery with the tables run by a mix of humans and holographic stupids was quite literally pay-to-play, with a fifty-thousand-real entry fee that had apparently been covered by his invite.

Still, he hadn't seen Ali anywhere. He presumed, though there was no visible sign of them, that there were private rooms connected to the gallery. The card tables he could see, after all, were relatively low-stakes. The high-stakes tables were even further concealed from the uninvited.

Security was subtle but omnipresent. He hadn't spotted any particularly augmented people among the staff, but all moved with the signs of military training, and the uniforms were tailored to disguise stunners in a way that only made the weapons *more* obvious to those who knew.

Turning away from the casino floor, EB's gaze settled on the *other* view from the gallery. The Teamster's Knight was right up against the exterior of the station, and someone had spent the considerable funds and effort to get transparent radiation-proofed panels installed along the upper gallery. The stretch where he could look out into open space and down on Tarsus covered the entire hundred-and-twenty-meter outer wall of the Knight—but his eye picked out the spot where the smaller sections of real windows gave way to high-fidelity screens.

It was an excellent illusion, one that added a surprising amount of gravitas to what was, in the end, a fancy way to separate fools from their money.

His paranoia was tuned to a razor-sharp edge, and he spotted Vortex emerging from behind the gallery bar in a staff uniform. The boosted enforcer was trying to blend in, but where the staff walked like well-trained security guards, Vortex walked like an assassin.

It was the difference between a well-behaved guard dog and a wild tiger.

That she had the uniform and backroom access confirmed his suspicions. Ali owned the Knight. All of the security measures EB had been assessing—stunners, trained guards, covertly armed stupids, proper security drones, cameras, et cetera, et cetera—would be swiftly turned on him at Ali's command.

"Vortex," he greeted the woman as she approached him at the railing.

"Captain Bardacki," she replied, clearly expecting him to have pinged her approach. "I trust the Knight's hospitality has lived up to your expectations?"

"They do keep trying," EB said with a chuckle. Two different servers had tried to sell him drinks since he'd started propping up the banister—at prices that suggested the entry fee to the gallery was heavily subsidizing the liquor. "But I am not here for hospitality, I suppose."

"I suppose not," Vortex agreed. "You have the data on the archive base, I hope?"

"Mmm," EB replied noncommittally. "Is Ali here? That's what this was about, after all."

"You realize that she can't just drop everything and come running at your call, Captain?" Vortex said archly.

"I also trust that you have about fifteen layers of security involved *and* that you wouldn't have wasted my time by calling me here if she wasn't," he told her. "So, my question, Vortex, isn't *Is Ali going to keep our meeting?*; it is *Is Ali physically here or are we going somewhere else?*"

Vortex chuckled softly.

"Lady Ali is not here, of course," she conceded. "You are not that trusted, Captain. Walk with me?"

"Of course. Lead the way."

He had expected that they'd relocate, after all. There was no way Ali was going to let him set up his own trap while she was luring him into hers.

He was surprised, though, when Vortex walked up to the screens showing the void outside and turned back to grin at him.

"How far do you trust me, Captain?" she asked with an almost-childish grin.

"How honest would you like me to be in answering that?" EB said drily.

"Fair enough. Follow me."

And then, to his shock, she turned and stepped through the display into what appeared to be open vacuum—and vanished.

Now that EB *knew* there was something there, he could see the almost perfectly disguised join lines where the high-fidelity screens gave way to the hologram. Sighing at the melodrama involved in hiding a secret space behind the supposed observation window, he followed Vortex through the hologram.

On the other side of it, he found himself in a small private shuttle dock. The decoration followed the same tastefully elegant black-and-white schema as the rest of the Teamster's Knight, though it lacked the sweeping space of the main casino.

Vortex was waiting for him in the small receiving area. She'd been joined by Arson and a Black man EB hadn't met yet, who also radiated the same calmly controlled threat of the two boosted enforcers.

"Search him," Vortex ordered briskly. "No guns on the shuttle, Captain Bardacki. You understand."

"Of course," he agreed. Careful to keep his movements slow and visible, he drew his stunner from the holster in the small of his back and proffered it to Arson. "This is all I have."

Arson took it, but the other cyborg still patted EB down and ran a scanner over him.

"He's clear," he said in a soft, high-pitched voice.

"All right. EB, with me," Vortex instructed. She was clearly giving silent instructions to the other two via headware coms as they moved aside and settled down into the comfortable-looking seats in the waiting area.

They apparently weren't coming with them, which begged the question of why they were even there. Had Ali expected EB to try to sneak a bomb aboard the shuttle—or were they just a tiny part of a game of intimidation?

Either way, they were remaining aboard the station, and EB followed Vortex into the airlock.

The lioness, it seemed, had brought her own den to the party.

26

EB WASN'T sure what to expect from what he figured was Janessa Ali's private shuttle. He could easily see the woman having everything from some intentionally over-opulent courtesan's den to a mobile office in space to a completely stock, unmodified passenger shuttle.

The answer turned out to be closest to *mobile office*. Vortex led him into an area he recognized as being the main cargo compartment, though it looked like everything except the critical engine spaces and the cockpit had been opened up to create a larger-than-usual open volume.

At one end, a massive wallscreen was subdivided into a dozen individual feeds. A semicircular desk faced away from the wall, clearly set up for the desk's owner to be able to rotate between the smaller screens on the desk and the wallscreen itself.

The other walls held art objects in a carefully proportioned and arranged display. EB was no curator, but even he could see how the various paintings and sculptures led from one to the other while each had enough space to metaphorically breathe.

The entrance was flanked by two replica spears, clearly built as an art project in more recent times. Those flowed into a series of paintings of soldiers and battles—the display moving from violence at the door to peaceful imagery and hopeful sculptures flanking the desk.

Vortex gestured him to his left, where a hexagon of comfortable-looking chairs formed a clear conversation nook. There was a bar on the right, but most of the floor space was empty. To fit that much empty space into a working shuttle, even around the seating area, the bar, the desk and the art gallery... This wasn't a small ship.

Janessa Ali was seated in one of the chairs in the hexagon, wearing a ruffled pink dress that matched her artful makeup and drew attention away from her obsidian-hard eyes.

"Sit, Captain," she instructed.

He obeyed, keeping half a mental eye on Vortex as the enforcer withdrew to the bar. A server stupid emerged from it at a silent command, trundling over to the seats with two glasses of water.

"You asked for this meeting," Ali told him. "Fortunately, I was already planning on being in space on other business, so I *can* be here."

"Of course," EB said with a soft smile. "Except that does connect with why I wanted to talk to you."

"Really." She leaned forward, the ruffles on her dress shifting in a way that would have been far more distracting if EB was attracted to women. "I do not have long for this conversation, Captain Bardacki, so I suggest you get to the point."

EB had been a spacer and a pilot for thirty years. While he doubted Ali realized it, *he* could feel the Harrington coils engage and shift the shuttle away from the station. It was no coincidence, he knew, that none of the screens in the room were showing the shuttle's exterior view.

"The point, Em Ali, is that you have been putting far too much effort and emphasis on our little deal," he said quietly. "You wouldn't be putting Vortex and Bernadette on something unimportant. A small secret base, like Hadzhiev had implied I was looking for, wouldn't be worth this kind of effort.

"So, I have to ask, what *are* you looking for?"

"Does it really matter, so long as you manage your little white-knight stunt?" she asked.

"Yes. It does." He met her gaze levelly. "Because I know what the

Siya U Hestî was, what it did, and the horrors it forged for a profit. And I will not contribute to it rising to its full power again. There will be no kidnapped children or forced laborers on my soul."

"Your soul seems rather fragile for the path you choose to walk."

"My soul is weighed down by the dead. Those I have killed left enough scars; I will not add slavery to the marks. However accidentally."

She returned his regard.

"Did you truly believe that Ansem Hadzhiev, a Siya U Hestî *Level Nine* with his hands drenched in blood at Lady Breanna's command, was trying to save kidnapped children?" she asked sardonically. "I told you I do not care one way or the other for your frivolous quest, Captain. But the Bastion... The *Bastion* I care for.

"Your assumptions as to what the Bastion was were your own. I know what I am seeking, Captain Bardacki, and you have delivered the keys to me. Keep your side of the bargain, and I will keep mine.

"When the archives and arsenals and armadas of the Bastion are mine, I will have no need for a few hundred laborers."

"Because you will simply capture more," EB whispered.

"I will reforge the Shadow and Bone and I will lead it," Ali told him calmly. "Lady Breanna made foolish mistakes and paid for them. I will not. Honor our bargain, and I will release those slaves and you may pass unmolested from the stars we control.

"Break it and I will break you."

There was no real heat to her voice. It didn't sound like a threat. It barely sounded like a warning—but there was no question of her honesty or her determination.

"I broke Lady Breanna to protect one child," EB reminded her. "I threw down the Cage because Breanna would not walk away."

"I am unprepared to underestimate you, Captain Bardacki," Ali admitted. "I spent over two decades building my power and my resources inside the Siya U Hestî, only for you to destroy it all in less than two *months*.

"I have no desire to be your enemy. We made a bargain and I will honor it." She shook her head. "Give me the list of ships and arrival times, even, and leave the dirty work to us. I will honor my promises to you. Your peaceful traffic and the release of those slaves is a small price to pay for the Bastion and your goodwill."

The shuttle's systems were trying to jam his coms now, EB noted. Fortunately, he'd anticipated that possibility. The frequency-hopping microburst transmitter he was using as a relay was short-ranged as communicators went, but it was almost impossible to jam short of a full multiphasic jammer—which would draw the attention of the Orbital Guard *instantly*.

"You're going to have to choose, Em Ali," he told her. "I will not be party to the rise of a new criminal empire. Look around you. This ship. The Teamster's Knight. You're already wealthy beyond most people's dreams of avarice.

"Why create more harm, more suffering in the universe? Take the money you have. Go legit. You wouldn't be the only Siya U Hestî left-over to do it—and if I were law enforcement in this area, I'd be turning a blind eye to the past of those who walk away.

"You've spent your career hurting people for money. Why keep going when you don't have to?"

Ali was staring at him in silence. Her eyes were even darker than before, a pair of abysses that could consume stars as she studied him.

"You are so naïve," she finally said. "So arrogant. You assume you know everything and can judge everyone. But you know nothing, Evridiki Bardacki. So quick to judge. So foolish.

"Am I, then, to take this as you terminating our agreement?"

"You already know we're done," EB told her. "You knew all along that the moment I realized just what I was about to give you, I was going to walk away."

"But we both needed to make our futile attempts to avoid a war neither of us wanted." Ali sighed. "I presume you wiped the ship list from your headware memory, but I have learned ways to convince the organic matter to produce data the silicon has forgotten."

EB realized his mistake had been to assume that *Vortex* was the threat. The *chair* was the trap, and he realized it too late, as metal cuffs snapped shut on his ankles and wrists.

"You're already being jammed and we are no longer attached to the station," Ali told him, rising to her feet as his chair moved and transformed around him, converting to something closer to a medical bed than a seat.

"Vortex, my tools, please," she ordered, and smiled coldly down at EB. "Your most-incorrect assumption, my dear Captain, was that I came from the same channel as Vortex and my close companions.

"I was a *doctor*, Captain Bardacki, and I am very, *very* good at modifying and updating neural cybernetics. I've had a roughly fifty percent survival rate for this particular process."

EB heard a wheeled trolley arrive next to his bed. He said nothing —not even when Vortex handed Ali a combination gag and muzzle.

"Unfortunately, anesthesia inhibits the organic memory processes sufficiently to impede this work. I really don't like listening to the screaming and weeping, though."

As she skillfully forced his jaw open and inserted the gag, EB hoped that his continuing updates through the microburst transmitter had done their job.

Because if his people weren't there *very* quickly, he might be in significantly more trouble than he'd expected!

27

"EMERGENCY SIGNAL!"

Leia Zelda stood at the coms station on her mother's bridge. Trace and Reggie flanked the younger Zelda, watching over her shoulder as the link from EB flashed bright red.

"This was a terrible fucking idea," Reggie said flatly. "They're well away from the station and moving *fast*."

"You underestimate my *Blade*," Lisa Zelda told him from the captain's chair. "Alexis! Full power. Sarge, prep the boarding tubes!"

Trace's attention swung to another display, showing *Zeldan Blade*'s greatest nasty secret: the custom-built boarding system that latched onto its prey and cut through the hull with fusion torches.

"We're getting a ping from the Orbital Guard," Leia reported, glancing back at Trace and grinning wildly.

Trace *really* wanted to be the other girl when she grew up.

"Send them our Trackers' Guild papers and tell them we're in hot pursuit of Siya U Hestî remnants," Captain Zelda barked. "Alexis?"

"Fifty seconds!"

"Charlie, shot across her bows," the Captain ordered. "See if you can ping her engines, but don't shoot her unless we've got to!"

A red pulse flashed across the displays as the forward turret fired.

They weren't even trying to hit the shuttle carrying EB, but even firing the plasma cannon was more than most would have dared in planetary orbit.

"Thirty seconds."

"Sarge?"

"We're ready," a rough voice reported. "We getting friends?"

Trace turned and realized that Reggie was already gone.

"Stay here," Leia told Trace as she started to move. "They don't need you for this. Even in armor, there's not enough space for you to help. It's stunners and knives for this kind of mess."

"And I'm hoping no knives," the Captain added. "No, you stay with us, Trace. Reggie has a job to do, and he, like Sarge, knows the job. No offense, but you'll serve everyone better here.

"Not least if you could tell your father we're coming, I think everyone would be happier!"

Trace took a seat next to Leia, nodding shakily as she linked her headware into the system. The message back to Dad-E was a single code pulse, a prearranged message.

Not that it would have given him *much* warning as the corvette slammed into the fleeing shuttle. Alexis had matched velocities closely enough to avoid damaging either ship, but *Zeldan Blade* was built to absorb the impact without taking damage.

The shuttle was *not*—and new icons flashed across the bridge's main displays as Zelda's people launched their assault. A wallscreen was wrapped around the front half of the U-shaped room, even onto the floor and ceiling, and it now showed the relative positions of the corvette and the tiny-by-comparison shuttle.

"Contact, contact!" Sarge's voice echoed over the coms. "Wait, stun bomb has failed! Boosts!"

The lead two icons suddenly turned from green to dark orange, barely on the target ship. A single scarlet red icon appeared on the screen, moving with a speed that was difficult to judge through the scanners.

A third icon went black.

"Saw her, got her!" Reggie's voice proclaimed. Blaster fire echoed in the background. "Dammit, I was hoping not to have to do that."

"Kalb?" Zelda barked.

"Enforcer named Vortex, was working with EB," Reggie reported. "She's dead. Stun bombs forward!"

Sarge should have been giving the orders, Trace realized, and a chill filled her as she checked the coms feed in greater detail.

"Emerson is dead, ser," Alexis reported as Trace tried to work out who was injured. "Olafson is injured, badly. Fletcher is walking wounded, but his coms are out."

"Have our Sarge bring Olafson back," Zelda ordered, allowing Trace to breathe a sigh of relief. Fletcher, she guessed, was "Sarge's" actual last name.

"Then have someone *sit* on Sarge in the medbay until he gets the treatment he needs! Inshallah, this is—"

Even Trace figured that kind of phrase was tempting fate, but Zelda didn't even manage to *finish* the phrase before the entire starship *screamed* around them.

"Target just pulsed her Harringtons to burnout levels," the navigator reported. "She's pulling us with her, but we're hanging on so far."

"Kalb, get to the cockpit," Zelda ordered.

"Working on it, but the ship is split into chunks by battle-steel bulkheads," Reggie replied. "We've got the Captain. *He* wasn't protected from the stun bombs—sending him back to you guys."

"If we've got EB, we're *done*," Zelda said.

"Not while this bitch walks away," Trace's friend and crewmate snarled. "Dominis delenda est!"

Trace had heard the phrase before, but not from Reggie—it was awful Latin, as she understood it, but it meant roughly *Slavers must be destroyed.*

"Kalb..." Zelda said sharply.

"Plus, my lead team and I are trapped between the bulkheads," Reggie added. "So, try not to die while we take control of this ship, please?"

"Orbital Guard is flashing a red alert, Mom," Leia said, the slip a sign of distress Trace hadn't expected.

Trace was distressed. Reggie might not be one of her dads, but she didn't want him stuck on Ali's ship and dying there! At least it sounded like Dad-E was safe but stunned and being hauled out like a sack of potatoes.

"What kind of red alert?"

"Interplanetary freighter is on an intercept course for us," Leia said grimly. "Scans make her almost sixty kilocubics, and she is coming in *fast*. Guard is sending broadcast warning signals, but I think they figure we're being actively targeted."

"But they can't say that, because then they have to *do* something about it," Captain Zelda said flatly. "Show me a course and vector! Charlie, get me a targeting solution!"

"We can't detach with our people on board," Alexis warned. "Bravo team has Bardacki and the wounded back aboard, but they confirmed Kalb: Alpha and Charlie teams are both trapped inside internal bulkheads.

"Charlie is trying to cut back to us, but Alpha's cutting to the bridge."

"*Detonation. HOLY SHIT!*"

Charlie's shocked exclamation echoed across the bridge, and every eye snapped to where the incoming freighter had been added to the screen. The big freighter, a slow hauler presumably used to move ore from Tarsus to refineries in Denton orbit, had just exploded into a cloud of debris.

"Some kind of suicide charge. What the *hell*?" Leia asked aloud.

"Debris cloud is on a collision course," Alexis reported grimly. "If we don't release the shuttle, we can't evade."

"Can the *shuttle*?" Zelda demanded.

"Unclear. Right now, she's yanking us all over the sky, but I think the pilot is *trying* to keep us in the debris cloud."

Trace needed to do something. She had no idea what she *could* do, but she had to do *something*.

She linked into the systems of Leia's console, asking for—and getting—approval silently. She needed to hear what was going on aboard the shuttle herself and took a few seconds to check over the coms surrounding them.

There *had* been a response to the Guard's challenge, she realized. In the moments before the freighter exploded, her bridge had been in contact with the closest cutter.

Almost instinctively, she started the recording.

"We see our course, but we can't *change it*," a desperate woman's voice gasped into the com. "Computers locked us out thirty seconds ago, and we lost control of the ship. I've never seen anything like it—What do you mean, check the reactor co—"

The aside to someone on the bridge ended in mid-sentence as Trace's stomach hit rock bottom.

"Someone took control of the ship and turned it into a weapon," she whispered. "Ali's people couldn't...wouldn't... *She's* going to die no matter what, isn't she?"

"Unless Kalb gets control of the shuttle in the next thirty seconds, we have to cut and run," Alexis declared. "I don't have the power to move both us and her, especially with her opposing my every move like this!"

"Kalb?" Zelda asked.

"I heard," Reggie snapped. "New plan, I think. If she *stops* fighting, can you get us out of the way?"

Trace looked desperately over at Alexis.

"Yes. But how—"

"Hold on."

Trace's gaze was fixed to the display, along with everyone else on the bridge as she held her breath.

The shuttle wasn't armored. It wasn't designed to get into fights, and its interior oddities were concealed from the outside. And, it seemed, the inner bulkheads were significantly tougher than the exterior hull.

A stream of plasma bolts tore out the side of the shuttle, a rapid-sequence narrow-aperture stream of blaster fire Trace knew meant someone—probably Reggie—had opened fire with an assault cannon.

An armored figure carrying the immense gun was through the hole before the plasma could have cooled. Seconds ticked away, and Trace knew there couldn't be any time left—and then the assault cannon fired again.

There was a limit to how much care could be taken with the time they had, but Reggie was clearly *aiming* as he fired at the ship he was standing on. Plasma bolts tore through power links, plasma conduits and the exotic-matter threads of the Harrington coils themselves.

For a second, it seemed like nothing had happened. Then the shuttle stopped accelerating.

"Go!" Zelda barked. "Get us *out of here*."

Trace *felt* the corvette strain around them as Alexis threw the ship's Harrington coils to maximum power, hauling warship and shuttle alike out of the incoming shotgun blast.

A red-shaded cylinder filled the display, getting closer and wider by the second as they pushed *Zeldan Blade* to her limit.

Then the starship rang like a struck bell…and silence fell.

28

THE SILENCE HUNG over the command center for a few seemingly eternal seconds—then the air circulators kicked back on, and Trace breathed an unconscious sigh of relief.

"Report," Zelda ordered.

"We got hit by the fringe of the debris cloud," Alexis reported. "Armor mostly held but we have half a dozen minor breaches. One was close enough to a critical conduit to trigger an emergency core shutdown."

"We're back up on secondary power," Charlie added. "Leslie has the drones up already, checking the systems so we can reboot the main core."

"Good. Well done, everyone," Zelda told them. "Kalb?"

"Still here, crawling back into the shuttle," Reggie reported. "But… you need to see the feed from Alpha Team."

Trace winced as the helmet-camera feed opened on the main display. Alpha Team had apparently kept burning through the bulk-head to the cockpit while Reggie had gone outside to save them all. Now one of the armored Tracker mercenaries was inside the cockpit… which resembled nothing so much as a charnel house.

"We're going to need the Orbital Guard to run DNA analysis in there to ID anybody," Reggie said grimly. "We *know* Ali was on the shuttle, and we can presume there was both a pilot and copilot up here.

"So, probably three people. Probably."

Trace swallowed against the nausea as she considered the mess of gore.

"Grenade?" she managed to grind out. It certainly was bringing back unpleasant memories of the fate of Kunthea Chey—who *Trace* had hit with a grenade.

"Fragmentation weapon of some kind," Reggie said, his tone clinical enough that it helped Trace back to reality and to look away from the horror scene. "Appears to have been one weapon, placed in the main console."

"We're definitely talking a bomb of some kind, yes? Not an overload or anything like that?" Zelda asked.

"Even if this shuttle was so poorly built as to somehow allow a lethal short in the cockpit—which I have no reason to believe," Reggie said drily, "that would give me people who'd been *electrocuted*, not *shredded*.

"No, this was a fragmentation mine someone wired into the controls and activated."

"So, who was controlling the shuttle?" Leia asked.

"I don't know," Reggie admitted. "We'll need to do some work to work out the exact timeline—or possibly leave it to the Guard."

"Your guess?" Zelda requested, the Captain's tone far calmer than Trace thought the situation deserved.

"My 'guess'?" There was a moment of silence as Reggie entered the cockpit and surveyed it with his own eyes rather than someone else's helmet camera.

"Ali had a suicide device built in here so *she* could terminate the pilot if they did something stupid," Reggie said coldly. "And at some point after she dropped the internal bulkheads, someone *else* detonated it to kill everyone in the cockpit, allowing them to take remote control of the shuttle."

"I don't believe in ghosts in the machine, Kalb," Zelda observed. "So, who would have that kind of access?"

"My suspicious brain says Ali did and we should scan for escape pods we missed," the *Evasion* crewman replied. "For now, though, I think we've done what we can here. I'm guessing there's OG on the way?"

"Two cutters heading our way, another two heading to contain the debris field and see if they can find evidence there, I guess," Charlie reported.

"Ugh. I hate getting entangled with local police," Zelda said. "What a mess."

"Someone took control of the shuttle," Trace murmured. "And someone took control of the freighter, too. But if they weren't trying to save Ali...why? And who?"

"I don't believe in ghosts," Zelda repeated. "But I do, Em Bardacki, believe in enemies. Someone *really* doesn't want anyone finding the Bastion.

"For now, your father is in the medbay and should wake up pretty quickly. Go check on him for me?"

EB WAS STILL unconscious when Trace arrived at the medbay, but the focus of the activity in the small space was on one of the other two patients.

The corvette's medbay had four beds, each set up in its own alcove with a full range of equipment. Even Trace could tell that the equipment in there was at least on par with Lan's medbay on *Evasion*, if not better—which made Zelda's medbay the highest-end equipment available in the area.

Which made sense, she supposed, for a ship carrying Trackers—interstellar bounty hunters—that also worked as mercenaries on a regular basis.

She spotted Sarge, the pale-haired and -skinned soldier familiar from the attack on the Cage. He was propped up in his alcove, with an array of medical equipment festooned down his side. Sarge was awake, though, and gave Trace a small wave with his free hand.

The third occupied alcove held another soldier—Olafson, Trace guessed—along with a group of four people that had to be the ship's entire medical team. She couldn't hear their conversation, but its firm and steady tone told her two things.

One, things were *bad*. Olafson was in rough shape, and the doctor was maintaining tight control of the tone to make sure they worked steadily.

Two, things were *manageable*. Even doctors could lose hope, though most she'd known would keep trying, but the tone of the conversation sounded like they were winning. It just sounded like it wasn't being *easy*.

The last thing Trace wanted to do was interrupt a medical team in the process of saving someone's life. She slipped into EB's alcove, out of sight, out of mind—and out of the way.

There was a seat next to the bed, and she half-slumped into it in relief as she looked over the displays on the bed. She didn't know what all the numbers *meant*, but she figured the assorted steady green lights were a good sign.

He'd just been stunned, after all. Stunners weren't *perfect* and problems could happen—but they were astonishingly rare. The self-targeting light stunner Trace usually carried was basically incapable of causing serious long-term damage—but was also easily defeated by even unusually heavy clothing.

Heavier stunners had greater risks—and she'd never even *heard* of stun bombs before. Her datanet search suggested a military crowd-control weapon, scalable from hand grenades to true bombs dropped from air- and spacecraft.

She didn't need the warning in the article she'd found to guess that anything with that much power and area of effect was drastically more dangerous than even a heavy stunner.

Of course, it was the difference between a one-in-a-million chance and a one-in-*ten*-million chance, and Trace heard EB cough even as she closed the article in her headware.

"I'm here, Dad-E," she said instantly.

"Oh," he said faintly. "That's good. The last thing I remember is a scalpel."

He felt silent and she shifted to take his hand.

"Stun hangover?" EB finally asked.

"Yeah. Reggie and Zelda's people threw a stun grenade into the compartment you were in," she told him.

"Did they get Ali, too?" He coughed and shook his head as if dizzy. "Stun aura makes the last couple of minutes before it...fuzzy, but I think she bolted?"

"She was in the cockpit," Trace said slowly. "Um. There was a *bomb* in the cockpit, and someone set it off remotely. She's dead, Dad-E. And...same someone, I think, hacked a freighter and blew it up to throw a high-vee debris field at us. Everyone aboard the freighter is dead too."

"Fuck."

The curse hung in the air for a few long seconds, then he squeezed her hand back and sat fully upright.

"Stun hangover is fading," he noted. "This is...*Zeldan Blade*'s medbay?"

"Yeah."

"I'd feel very clever for all of my prearrangements if someone hadn't just tried to surgically access my headware," EB told her. "How much of a mess are we in?"

"Two of Zelda's people wounded, one killed," she said. "Ali and everyone else on the shuttle are dead—Reggie shot Vortex, but the pilot and copilot were in the cockpit with Ali when the bomb went off.

"Reggie says it's going to take a forensics team to work out who was in there."

She shivered at the memory of the camera feed. The weapon had turned the small space into a nightmare.

"Right. We are not getting out of talking to the Guard, I'm guessing," EB said. "Time for me to catch up. Think I can sneak out of here quietly to talk to Lisa?"

29

ZELDAN BLADE'S bridge felt reassuringly familiar to EB. Most of his former career had been spent on carriers and cruisers significantly bigger than the Tracker corvette, but there was something calming about a very clearly military space.

Captain Zelda and her people somewhat spoiled that illusion with their lack of uniforms and performative discipline. Zelda herself looked up as EB entered the bridge and gestured him over to her.

"That was a lot messier than I was expecting," she told him. "Orbital Guard cutters are sweeping up the debris field, which gives us a small window before they come take over the shuttle and start asking me all kinds of questions."

"I was expecting Ali to pull something," EB replied, leaning on the side of the console next to Zelda. "I wasn't expecting whatever the *hell* happened with the bomb and the freighter."

"Inshallah, we will learn the truth, but we do not know it yet," Zelda said. "For now, our focus must be both short- and long-term."

"What are you thinking?" EB asked.

"We have about fifteen minutes, I think, to pull a veil over our Guardly friends' eyes," she told him. "It would make sense for us to dock and await inspection—I haven't received orders to do anything specific, but we were just the target of a suicide ship.

"I believe the Guard are going to realize that suicide was involuntary, but that is only going to make the conversations that follow more difficult. If you wish to continue your quest, we need to get you and your people off of *Zeldan Blade*."

EB sighed.

"Reggie *shot* someone," he pointed out. "While operating under your authority, but we might be better served with him remaining to answer questions. Trace and I, though..."

"Are the ones with a key stake in this," Zelda agreed. "We're already heading into dock. I have a few toys in play, and I'm quite sure I can get you two aboard the station without detection.

"I'm assuming you have some further step to take here?"

"Cop called Everest on High Home," EB told her. He mostly trusted Zelda—and he needed backup from someone who wasn't aboard his ship.

"Prasada Everest?" Zelda asked, sounding surprised.

"Yes. You know of him?" EB asked.

"'Of,' the man says," she replied with a chuckle. "He married one of my best childhood friends. Didn't *last*, but not really either's fault." She shrugged. "He was busy being a cop and she was busy being a freighter captain. Neither was willing to give up their career for the other, and so they called it off after a decade or so.

"But Tacita trusted him, even after the divorce. Said he was one of the good ones, a trustworthy cop."

"You think he's safe to bring in on this?" EB said. "Last time I know of that someone tried to involve the Icemi government, both he and his contact turned up dead."

"Everest is...aware of the issues of his government," Zelda said slowly. "The Directorate still casts a long shadow over this system, my friend. The people who trained him? They were ex–secret police. And everyone knew it.

"He knows how to keep his mouth shut until he has to get a warrant."

"That...helps, actually," he told her. "I thought I could trust him, but I'd met the man *once*. Relying on a first impression for this kind of mess is a risk."

"I've known him for twenty-six years, EB, and pretty decently for eleven of those," Zelda said. "He's the right one. If anyone in this star system can help you, it's him."

"I don't feel quite right leaving you and your people to face the Guard alone, Lisa," EB admitted.

"This is what I do, EB," she reminded him. "I am a member in full standing of the Trackers' Guild, with full authorization to act as a bounty hunter and mercenary in seven star systems—including Icemi.

"Knowing Janessa Ali was aboard that shuttle was more than enough for all my actions to be covered under *hot pursuit*." She shrugged. "They aren't going to be *happy*—*I'm* not happy—and I'm going to be tied up answering questions for a bit, but we'll be fine.

"Keeping Reggie will help if he's okay with it, but I know not everyone wants to talk to the police!"

"IT'S UP TO YOU," EB told his weapons tech as the three of them waited by the cargo airlock. "It'll make things a lot less iffy for Zelda and draw attention away from the fact that Trace and I vanished, but I know it's asking a lot."

Reggie chuckled, leaning on the case containing his combat armor and assault cannon.

"Boss, I don't like cops," he conceded. "But we are a long damn way from anywhere there might happen to be outstanding warrants for me. And, well"—he shrugged—"it's not like I haven't talked to cops before.

"Telling them the *truth*, mind, that's a touch new on me."

"You'll stay and help them, then?" Trace asked.

"Of course, kid," Reggie told her. The look he gave EB suggested that even if he *hadn't* been planning on it, Trace's heartfelt ask might have changed his mind.

EB's kid was getting *dangerous* and she didn't even realize half of it.

"We're docking in thirty seconds," the mercenary tech by the airlock told them. "I'm in their system, and it will show that the cargo airlock attached but stayed closed. I'll be able to open it exactly eighty-three centimeters without triggering their scanners."

She chuckled.

"Might be able to do a bit more, but that should be plenty for you two to walk through and is ninety-nine percent certain. I have the cameras on a loop, so you should be able to clear the cargo port without being spotted.

"Once you're in the main station, you're on your own—but really, we're just trying to disconnect you from *Blade* and our arrival."

"Thank you," EB told her. "And tell your boss thanks as well. She knows, but the repeat doesn't hurt."

"Thanks help; money is better," the mercenary told him with a grin. "Past experience says we're going to be spending a lot of time very bored over the next two days. I hope the skipper negotiated hazard pay with you!"

It had taken EB flat-out refusing to let her help *without* him paying her for Zelda to take money for this whole mess. Between the bounties for Breanna and her people and the fees for smuggling weapons into a civil war, he was relatively cash-flush at that moment. He could *afford* her services—but she seemed to still feel she owed them for trying to capture Trace.

"Contact," the tech barked. "We're locking on... Connected. Opening the lock now—you'll have about thirty seconds to get through."

"Ready," EB confirmed, glancing at Trace.

"Ready," she replied.

"Go!"

The lock slid open. While the gap was, as warned, barely eighty centimeters wide, it was for the full height of the four-meter-across cargo lock. There wasn't much squeezing involved for EB, let alone Trace.

Then the lock closed silently behind them and they were alone in a dark cargo dock.

"So, this is creepy," Trace observed.

"Sensors don't think there's anyone here, so the lights aren't on," EB reminded her. "Let's go. *Evasion* shouldn't be far."

He'd have to check with the crew—he wasn't running a dictatorship, after all—but the only next step he saw was heading back to Denton and Icem High Home Station.

After all, if Everest couldn't help them, Trace's former foster mother was also on Denton.

30

EB DIDN'T GET a chance to say a word before Vexer had him wrapped in a bone-crushingly tight embrace. He almost staggered back into the boarding tube under the pressure of his fiancé's reaction but returned the hug fiercely.

"You *cannot* use yourself as bait, gods," Vexer finally told him. "What would have happened if Zelda and her people had been even a few minutes farther away?"

"Ali would have cut into my brain to see if she could extract the ship list through my headware," EB admitted instantly. He wasn't going to *lie* to Vexer, even if his partner clutched him harder at that description.

"That's...difficult," Lan said, the doctor standing well back from the embrace going on. "You wiped it from your headware memory, after all. But...it's possible."

"She said she'd had practice," EB told Lan, as calmly as he could. "I...I have the distinct feeling we may have just done this system a bigger favor than we ever thought."

"Wonderful," Lan said. "May I then make the suggestion that we get the *fuck* away from the station that we know has at least one Siya U Hestî enforcer who was working for Ali?"

"That was my next suggestion, yes," EB said. Given that flying the ship took either him or Vexer and Vexer didn't seem to be letting him go, they had a bit of time to get to that point.

He kissed the top of Vexer's forehead and gave him a squeeze.

"Reggie will be staying with Zelda's people for a bit," he told Lan and Vexer, glancing back at Trace to make sure she was looking okay. "For our part, we need to come to some decisions and make some plans.

"Family meeting," he instructed. "But first, we need to get away from Tarsus."

That made his next stop the bridge. With Vexer in tow, he suspected.

THE EXTENDED AND formulaic process of getting clearance from Teamster Station and then detaching his—currently empty—cargo ship from the platform helped soothe EB's nerves.

So, in its own way, did Vexer's hovering. His husband-to-be never quite strayed out of reach as he handled his part of the undocking procedures. The navigator's station was apparently too far away, so Vexer was working through his headware as he stood with his hand on EB's shoulder.

As they slowly drifted away from the space station, EB covered the other man's hand with his own and smiled up at him.

"I'm *fine*, Vena," he said softly, using Vexer's real first name. So much of his crew lived by nicknames and short forms that it felt odd to use the name, but it got his point across.

"Yes, but you almost weren't." Vexer shook his head, nodding toward the screen to remind EB to focus on flying the ship.

"This mission you've taken on," he continued. "I understand it. I *agree* with it—for Trace's sake, if nothing else. But the risks you're taking, the dangers we're accepting…"

He squeezed EB's shoulder.

"I decided I wanted to keep you and be parents to Trace with you," he said. "I don't want that to be followed up with *burying* you before we can even get married, EB. You need to be more..."

Vexer clearly wasn't sure what EB needed to "be more" of.

"I'm not going to walk away from this, Vena," EB told him quietly. "No one else is coming for those people. And *someone* is very determined to kill everyone who gets close to the Bastion."

"That's what terrifies me. You can't make yourself more of a target to that someone than you already have." Vexer stared at the screen as EB delicately wove them through Teamster Station's space traffic.

"They've killed senior Siya U Hestî people. People with high-level augments, bodyguards, armed ships... People are dying, EB, because they even got *close* to the target you're hunting. And I can't help but feel we're getting closer than any of them did."

"Did you get a chance to go through Trace's work on the scramble code?" EB asked, latching on to the last piece of his partner's spiel—to give himself time to think, if nothing else.

"I did," Vexer confirmed. "You're stalling."

"I am. But what did you find?"

Vexer chuckled and his grip on EB's shoulder relaxed a bit.

"She's closer than I expected," he admitted. "Lan and I ran through it, refined her work and did some fiddling of our own."

"We're close, then?" EB asked.

"Assuming we've guessed which arrivals were fed into the code Ali's people were running...we've got it. But I can't be sure without more data."

EB exhaled in surprise.

"You've *got it*?" he asked. "We have the scramble code?"

"Eighty-five / fifteen," Vexer said. "But yeah. Given the full scanner history and our arrival list, I think we should be able to get a list of probables. Then we look for the place where nine of them converged and, well..."

"We have the Bastion."

"Which is why we are all in a stupid amount of danger right now," Vexer told him. "Whoever is protecting that place destroyed a ship with nine people aboard to take *one shot* at you and Ali. And now you have all of the pieces except one to track them home."

"Except nobody off this ship knows we have the scramble code," EB countered. "We set everything up so that we *wouldn't*. We only have it because our computer hardware and software are better than that available to the Siya U Hestî.

"Which means we have a decent chance of keeping things quiet until we're ready to move."

"Which brings us to what 'moving' looks like," Vexer said. "EB, this isn't a task for a freighter carrying a random grab bag of people from a two-hundred-light-year journey. Even if we pull Zelda in, we have no idea what kind of defenses this place is going to have.

"We need real military backup. The ISDF has the data from the sensors. They have the gunships, the monitors, the marines, the assault shuttles…"

"And enough of a data leak that the Bastion's defenders knew Hadzhiev had talked to Commodore Wu and killed them both," EB replied. "The ISDF can't be relied on. Any allies we find need to be picked person by person, based on who we can trust."

"This is…quixotic," Vexer said after a moment. "We went after the Cage with a *fleet*, EB. You're talking about going after some place likely at least as fortified with just us and Zelda. We are already closer than anyone else we know of. We're painting a target on ourselves for an enemy we don't know the strength of, don't know the abilities of and don't know the *location* of."

"Yet."

"Yet. And given how many people are already dead, how are *we* going to avoid sharing their fate?"

EB sighed and covered Vexer's hand again.

"I don't know," EB admitted. "Everything we're doing is a risk, but we have all but one piece now. I think Everest can get us that piece. So…what do we do then, my love, when we have the keys to save hundreds from slavery? Hand them over to a system government that already failed at this once? Walk away?"

His fiancé chuckled bitterly.

"The ship isn't called *Evasion* for nothing, love," Vexer pointed out. "Everyone here is running from something. Maybe we should walk away. Maybe it's what we're good at."

"I have learned, since Trace snuck her way aboard, that I'm a hell of a lot worse at walking away than I thought I was," EB said softly. "And I figured that was part of why you decided to marry me."

The bridge was silent, the two men's hands pressed together.

"It was," Vexer finally admitted. "Before this whole mess, you'd lost yourself. I could tell; I just wasn't sure what you were missing. I've since that realized you weren't missing anything. You were *ignoring* part of yourself.

"You signed on for the wrong cause once, and you didn't trust the principles and ideals that put you in Apollon uniform. We went into hell for our kid, and it woke up part of you that you'd tried to let sleep."

EB sighed.

"I'm not sure what you're trying to talk me into at this point, Vexer," he admitted.

"I don't think I am," Vexer said. "I just want you to realize where we are and what we're looking at. We're taking a lot of risks. If we're committed to this, we're committed. We've painted enough of a target on ourselves already that if we do anything but get the hell out of Icem, they're going to come for us."

EB squeezed Vexer's hand again and set the autopilot.

"You're right," he told his fiancé. "And I can't keep dragging the whole crew into this. But you are right in everything, I suppose.

"Whatever happens, there are too many lives at stake to walk away entirely...and I've fought enough to keep Trace safe to know you're, well, right," he repeated.

"I'm done running."

31

TRACE WAS POKING through the mess fridge for something to, well, soothe her mood. While *Evasion* had full industrial freezers to keep the crew fed for extended flights, the fridge in the mess itself was generally reserved for "ingredients for today" and "snacks for peckish crew."

Cooking duty was on a rotation aboard, and Trace could guess who was cooking that evening—Tate—by the ingredients in the fridge. Her more-important concern at the moment, though, was that Ginny had clearly laid in the snacks for today and at the very back was a presliced slab of carrot cake.

She was trying to work out how to get a single piece from the cake when her headware chimed softly with the call for everyone to head to the mess. That made getting the cake easier, at least, because she figured a family meeting needed snacks.

By the time EB and Vexer entered, last, she'd laid out the platter of sandwiches that had been in front of the cake, as well as the cake itself. She was serving herself two slices when EB scooped up a sandwich and smiled at her.

"Thanks, Trace," he told her. "Everyone, grab something to eat. This is going to get a bit heavy."

The sandwich platter swiftly emptied, everyone except EB taking seats at the table as the Captain inhaled his own sandwich.

"Thanks, everyone," he said. "We've come a long way together, and I know the last few months have been...not quite what any of you signed on for. Half the pitch I made you all was that we'd be avoiding trouble, getting away from the things that haunted us."

Trace hadn't fully realized that. The time she'd been on board the ship lined up with that "last few months," though. She felt a renewed sense of guilt over dragging the crew into the mess with the Siya U Hestî.

Ginny clearly sensed the reaction, as she leaned over and slid another slice of cake onto Trace's plate with a wink.

Nodding her understanding to the engineer, Trace took another forkful.

"We've tangled with the Siya U Hestî again and again since we first met them at the Diomhair," EB said quietly. "None of us, myself included, expected to find ourselves in an extended conflict with an interstellar syndicate."

He made a throw-away gesture.

"Breanna Tolliver gave us no choice," he reminded them. "She was coming after Trace, me and this ship—in about that order. We might have been able to outrun her reach, but it was a risk. So, we fought.

"Estutmost..." He sighed. "We knew what we were getting into with the civil war. Getting Lan, Vexer and Trace stuck on the wrong side of the front lines was just timing and bad luck. But, again, the Siya U Hestî were there and came after Trace.

"And now here." EB gestured around them. "We're on our way back to Denton," he told them. "Vexer pointed out that I've been running without thought, following the direction of a dead man. You all agreed to this, but we know more about how deep and dark these waters are now. We need to make our own decisions and our own plans about where things go from here with all the information."

He was still standing and looking at his seated crew. Trace felt a shiver run down her spine. She didn't want to leave hundreds of people to the fate she'd barely escaped—but she also didn't want to lose her crew.

Didn't want to lose her *family*.

"The steps ahead of us are... reasonably clear," EB told them. "I'm going to Detective Everest and I'm showing him everything we have. I figure either he can get us the system-wide scan data or he knows someone he trusts who can.

"With that and the information we already have, I think we can find the Bastion," he concluded. "The question, my friends, is what we do then. I'm not walking away without at least giving our data to Everest. If Zelda trusts him, I believe he can finish the job for us if he has to."

That, to Trace, suggested that they *could* just hand everything over to Everest and leave. Given how much she disliked being back in Icem, being this close to her former foster parents, she saw a real point to that.

She also knew just what the people they had been trying to rescue might be facing. Right now, according to Hadzhiev, they would all be in cryo-stasis. But even the lucky ones would end up in hard labor for others, without a choice. Many would be forced into prostitution of one level or another.

And some would end up with their headware control-chipped, forced to act as personal servants or even *suicide troops* by the Siya U Hestî itself. Among the people who'd been killed when they'd stormed the Cage had been people she'd *known*, forced to take up arms against the attackers by chips in their brains.

"I mean, that sounds sensible and all," Aurora said—and despite her thinking the same thing, Trace felt a spike of anger that *Aurora* would say that. "But...I mean. We're not without questions on Zelda herself, and I don't think *any* of us really trust cops.

"Plus"—she indicated Trace with the sandwich in her hand—"we *all know* what the kid was looking at. What others *did* face. I am no moralizer, no preacher. But...we need to see this through, boss."

Trace's anger instantly flashed to a surprising level of affection for the other woman.

"So do I," EB told Aurora. "Hence this meeting." He spread his hands.

"Vexer poked and prodded me to make sure that we did this...

consciously, judiciously and knowingly," he noted. "I know what Reggie thinks."

"Dominis delenda est," Trace whispered.

Ginny looked at her sharply. "Where did you hear *that*?" she asked. "Or are you..."

"Reggie," Trace said. "That's what he told Zelda when she tried to get him to fall back after he'd grabbed EB. His sticking around probably saved *all* of us, but he stayed to make sure Ali didn't escape."

"Not a phrase I'd expect to hear from him," the engineer said quietly. "But it might have a different source in the Rim."

"Means something to you, I take it?" EB asked.

"And Vexer too, if he was paying attention," Ginny replied.

Trace looked at her other father, who nodded.

"The Last Railroad," Vexer said. "Not much of an organization, but it exists in our corner of the Beyond." He chuckled. "In *my* particular corner, Estuval is one of their main focuses. Dominis delenda est."

He saluted the crew with a glass of water.

"If EB hadn't found me, I was already looking for people who could get me out," he admitted. "And the Last Railroad would be the ones around Estuval. Liberators and smugglers of slaves and serfs— and also diplomats, merchants, lawyers and even some cops working to get laws and rules changed."

"They'd have *words* for the cozy relationship a lot of the system governments around here seemed to have with the Siya U Hestî," Ginny said grimly.

"Would those words happen to be 'dominis delenda est'?" EB asked.

"Carved into somebody's forehead," Vexer said grimly. "After they'd garroted the fucker. Their cause is just, their mission worthy, but do not for one instant think they are all nice people."

"So," EB said softly. "Even without that, I know Reggie is in for the end game. I don't want to drag you into this, but *I* need to see this through. I've walked away from too much and there are too many lives at stake.

"But I can't risk you without asking."

"I'm in," Aurora said instantly.

"Me too, obviously," Vexer added.

"Of course!" Ginny smiled and reached over to grip Trace's shoulder. "We're in this to the end, I think."

"Thank you," Trace whispered.

"'Dominis delenda est' has an interesting ring to it," Lan said quietly, the doctor surveying the room with a strange smile. "My old group had a different Latin motto: una salus victis nullam sperare. *The one hope of the doomed is not to hope for safety.*

"I've killed better people for worse reasons. Let's finish this."

"What do I say to that?" Joy said with a chuckle. "I'm with you all."

Trace didn't *mean* to stare at Tate, but the heavy-worlder was suddenly the focus of every eye in the room.

The broad-shouldered and heavily muscled woman smiled at them all sadly and nodded.

"What?" she asked. "My friends...did you think I ended up eighty light-years from my homeworld by *choice*? People gene-modded for high gravity are worth as much to these kinds of monsters as virgins."

Her tone turned to a snarl even as Trace shivered at the reminder—and the realization that far too many of the people on *Evasion* were running from pasts like the future she'd avoided.

"Dominus. Fucking. Delenda. Est," Tate growled. "Let's find these bastards, fuck up their secret base and free their prisoners."

"I do believe we're all with you, love," Vexer said after a moment, reaching out to squeeze EB's hand.

"Then our next stop is Icem High Home Station, above Denton," EB told them. "Get some rest everyone.

"We're going to war."

32

THE EASIEST THING to arrange had been for them to meet Everest at the same pub across from the Blue Holiday Hotel. EB claimed a booth in the back corner and covered for Lan while the doctor set up a white-noise generator to cover their conversation.

It had been a literal tossup whether he was bringing Vexer or Lan, and the doctor had won the coin toss. EB was as glad not to be risking Vexer, for all that his fiancé would be better moral support in many ways—and Lan, he suspected, had a much better idea what he was doing with the white-noise generator.

Senior Detective Prasada Everest was late—late enough to make EB start worrying he'd already managed to get the cop killed. He arrived before EB could actually *say* as much to Lan, spotting EB across the restaurant and coming to join them.

"Captain Bardacki," he greeted EB. "I see Em Kalb isn't with you today?"

"He's dealing with some business at Tarsus," EB replied genially. "This is Dr. Kozel, my ship physician."

"A pleasure, Dr. Kozel," Everest said. "I understand you managed to remember some information about my murder case?"

"Related information, anyway," EB told him. "Order some food, Detective. This may take a bit. It's not going to be straightforward."

Everest chuckled as one of the server stupids rolled up with a beer and a plate of nachos.

"I ordered as I crossed the restaurant, Captain," he replied. "And a grilled cheese sandwich shouldn't take them long, if you want to wait until after the food has arrived to activate the jammer function of Dr. Kozel's toy."

EB had been inclined to overestimate the detective—he didn't, after all, know what Everest had been doing *before* joining High Home Security twenty-odd years before. From what Zelda said, it had still been a form of cop...but homicide detectives weren't usually boosted to the nines.

Soldiers weren't usually boosted. Power armor rendered the physical capabilities of the occupant moot past a certain baseline. Even that baseline could be adjusted for, if you spent the money.

The types of boosts Everest had were the purview of people who expected to get into serious danger with little or no warning—or into outright combat without the ability to bring military-grade armor.

He also clearly recognized the white-noise generator in operation and presumed, correctly, that EB would have one with a jammer function.

EB had tried to overestimate the cop. He was starting to wonder if he'd failed.

"You know Captain Lisa Zelda, I understand, Detective Everest?" he asked.

"My ex-wife's best friend," Everest confirmed. "And if we're getting into that level of personal, you may as well call me Prasada."

"If you insist, Prasada," EB told him. "You can call me EB. If this conversation goes the way Captain Zelda expected, we'll be working together for a bit."

"Really."

The arrival of a pair of server stupids with their entrees interrupted the conversation for a moment.

"Turn on the jammer, Lan," EB instructed his companion. "If... Prasada is okay with that."

"I gave orders that if I don't check in in an hour, people will come find me," Everest warned. "I am prepared to extend trust, EB, but this whole situation makes me uncomfortable."

"Then you are smarter than you look, and I didn't think you looked dumb," EB told him.

He felt the jammer turn on like a suffocatingly heavy blanket settling over his headware and shivered, covering it with a sip of his water and a bite of his burger.

"Well, EB, you have my attention," Everest observed. "We both know my job is more *important* than time-demanding in many ways, so I have the time to spend if it helps my case.

"So, why don't you tell me what you want from this meeting."

"What I want?" EB chuckled. "System-wide scan data for the last three months and authorization to engage in 'hot pursuit' mercenary operations in the Icem System."

Everest exhaled sharply.

"That...is not what I was expecting," he admitted. "Start at the beginning, I think."

"Okay." EB grinned. "I told you that Hadzhiev called me here to discuss unfinished business. I told you the truth in that I *thought* it was someone else, wanting to talk about my daughter.

"Instead, it was Hadzhiev—who, well, the last time he and I met, I *shot* him." He waved a hand dismissively as he saw the homicide detective start to tense. "This was during a sanctioned Trackers' Guild operation, the one that took down the Cage. Are you familiar with that situation?"

"Nigahog and the Trackers' Guild have kept a great many of the details of the events at the Cage under wraps, but that the Siya U Hesti's main central facility was taken down by a mercenary fleet under Tracker auspices is known to me," Everest allowed. "You were there?"

"So was Zelda," EB said. "That's why I trust *her* when she says I can trust *you*."

Everest nodded and chuckled.

"You know, it doesn't matter how amicable the divorce is," he observed. "You don't expect your ex's best friend to believe in you quite that much."

"She says you're one of the good ones *and* that you have a strong sense of discretion," EB admitted. "I need all of that."

"Discretion, huh." Everest eyed him. "I am disinclined to conceal things from my superiors, if that's what you mean. I have *done so* in the past, as it appears Zelda is aware, but only until the time that I have needed a warrant."

"That goes with 'the good ones,' in my experience," EB said. "Not by-the-book but by-the-spirit."

"Laws and regulations are written in blood, EB. There are limits on the power of police for damn good reasons. And one of those limits is that there are a lot of things I can't do without a warrant, which means I need to explain everything to a judge."

"I know and I appreciate that," EB replied. "But I need some discretion from you today, at least until we sort out the next steps. But first… what *you* wanted to know."

He took another bite of his burger, then leaned back in his chair and studied Everest as he chewed. The detective was being surprisingly patient and tolerant, but EB had promised him information on his case to get him to the meeting.

"Hadzhiev was a senior member of the Siya U Hesti," he reminded Everest. "Very senior. He was Lady Breanna's personal enforcer, part of her command council. I have heard him referred to as a Level Nine."

The detective's skin paled as his face tightened, but he nodded for EB to continue.

"During the raid on the Cage, he and I fought, and I nearly killed him. If it wasn't for his level of augmentations, I would have," EB admitted. "Once wounded, however, he chose to give me the information I needed to save the prisoners aboard the station from being spaced by Breanna.

"According to him, though I have no basis on which to believe or disbelieve this, he was once a kidnapping victim like them. And like my daughter."

"Hence this being very personal for you," Everest murmured. "But you're telling me that a Level *Nine* was on my station and got murdered?"

"Yes."

"*Why?*"

"If I am understanding the message I received correctly and if Hadzhiev was telling me the truth...he was seeking some kind of absolution. Not redemption, I don't think, but to make some small part of his wrongs right.

"He apparently activated an emergency protocol that ordered all Siya U Hestî ships in transit with kidnapping victims to put their victims in cryo and deliver them to a secret fallback base known as the Bastion.

"That Bastion, Detective, is somewhere in this star system. Hadzhiev tried to make contact with the ISDF to locate it. Shortly afterward, he and his contact—Commodore Wu Lim—were both murdered."

The pub table was silent for a long time, the three of them each working on their entrees and their own thoughts.

"So, you don't have any idea who actually killed him?" Everest finally asked. "But that does rather explain why, doesn't it? And Wu... That's...a problem."

"Prasada?"

"There was already an inquiry and investigation into the shuttle crash where Commodore Wu died," the detective explained. "An ISDF flag officer died. It draws attention. The *official* report says engine failure."

"I saw that in the news articles, yeah," EB said.

"But there's an unofficial report, isn't there?" Lan asked.

Prasada looked over at them and nodded.

"It wasn't an engine failure," he said quietly. "They buried it because, well...High Home Station ran the investigation, with ISDF backup. The Defense Force didn't care what was officially released; they just wanted to know how Wu died.

"High Home Station, on the other hand, cared what their *insurers* heard. So, the ISDF got one report, stamped Top Secret, and the news got the other."

"And you saw the true report?" EB asked.

"I'm pretty sure every cop on the station did," Everest admitted. "And yes, you can argue we had an obligation to make sure the public knew, but…"

He growled, more at himself than EB it seemed.

"We're within living memory of a murderous multiheaded dictatorship," he pointed out. "There are things we have to let slide because maintaining democracy is more important. I will accept a certain level of corruption as inherent to politics so long as the bastards stand down when they're voted out.

"That's been the…unspoken bargain with the political establishment since the Directorate fell. So long as the politicians take election losses with grace, a certain degree of corruption is ignored."

"Do I dare ask *who* that unspoken bargain is with?" EB said drily.

"I was twenty-two years old when the Directorate fell, EB," Prasada told him mildly. "You can do the math. Only *some* of them died of old age, after all."

"So, there's an unofficial group of, what, ex-rebels and ex–secret police holding the threat of assassination over politicians if they don't step down on cue?" Lan asked. Something in their tone told EB that they saw a *lot* of problems with that.

"Basically," Prasada admitted. "At this point, I think it's more a bad habit than anything else. But politics are a younger man's game, Dr. Kozel. I'll play politics and the old boys' game if they start getting in the way of solving my cases and delivering justice, but this wasn't covering up a crime."

"What *was* it covering up?" EB asked.

"Human error. Pilot mis-training, basically, on the part of High Home Station's own shuttle fleet. The thruster didn't fail fully," Prasada said grimly. "Failsafes kicked in properly; everything should have been fine.

"Pilot overreacted, clearly misjudged the curve of the station, didn't look at his instruments and rammed a shuttle with twenty-six people aboard into the station at four kilometers per second."

EB winced, but a horrible thought struck him.

"What if his instruments were wrong?" he asked softly.

There was another long silence before Everest spoke again.

"I'm not a pilot," he admitted. "As I understand it, they're trained not to rely on their eyes at all. In a crisis situation, if his instruments were reading incorrectly, he might not have had the presence of mind to double-check."

"His situational awareness should have told him that the sensor feed was wrong," EB murmured. "But if an engine just blew and his computers were screwing with him…"

"You are painting a terrifying picture, EB, and in a tone that suggests you've seen it before."

EB glanced over at Lan and swallowed a sigh. He was relatively sure that some of the work he'd done with Janessa Ali qualified as a crime under Icemi law, but if he was going to trust the detective, he needed to put all of his cards on the table.

"Hadzhiev gave me one part of the puzzle to find the Bastion," he told Everest. "To finish the puzzle, I needed information from the local Siya U Hestî—and he gave me a contact to reach out to.

"We worked together for a few days before I realized that she wanted the Bastion for reasons I could not support. While we were… negotiating our disagreement, someone hacked an in-system freighter and blew her reactor, aiming for the debris cloud to destroy the shuttle Ali and I were aboard, as well as Captain Zelda's ship.

"Zelda is talking over the situation with the Tarsus Orbital Guard, but my understanding is that she is in the clear, as she was in hot pursuit of a known crime lord. The destruction of that freighter, though, terrifies me.

"I was a nova-fighter electronic-warfare expert for Apollo, Detective," EB explained. "I know *exactly* how difficult it is to enter a civilian network from the outside, change the ship's course and overload the reactor while the ship's crew is trying to retake control of their ship."

There was a long pause.

"That sentence is terrifying in itself," Everest admitted. "I would like to hope that such an attack is—"

"Basically impossible," EB finished for him. "Because it is, Prasada. There are supposed to be both digital and physical interlocks in place to prevent that happening. There are ways to *shut down* the reactor, though even a properly secure civilian ship *should* require access codes no outsider has to do so."

It was such a long shot that while most of his attack codes included the command sequence, he'd only seen it work *once*, and that had been against a particularly incompetent set of pirates.

"To do what was done to that poor ship's crew should have required having a functionally complete list of *every officer's passwords and headware identifiers*," EB concluded grimly. "At the very minimum, you would need the captain's override codes, the systems officer's override codes and the chief engineer's override codes—*plus* the ability to spoof the headware signature of at least one and probably all three of them."

"I am…not well versed in security systems and countermeasures," Everest said slowly. "But that does seem to match the 'basically impossible' description. And yet someone did it."

"So, either someone put a lot of groundwork into preparing an attack on a random freighter, or they have a level of systems penetration that *I*, with Rim hardware and software, could not manage against Beyond systems."

"And sabotaging a shuttle pales against that task," Everest said. "But with that level of control, how do we even know that the freighter *was* attacked?"

EB blinked. He hadn't even considered that—they had the desperate message from the transport's captain recorded, but an attack able to overload the reactors should have been able to take down the communications.

"I don't know," he admitted. "The communications *should* have been shut down, but they weren't."

"Your enemy appears to have some odd limitations, then," the detective noted. "Or is laying a trap to lure you into, one of the two."

"I'm not counting against a trap," EB said quietly. "We think we're closer than anyone else has managed to get to finding the Bastion. But the last piece is still missing. I need full-system scan data, Prasada.

"I have a list of ships and arrival times, provided by Hadzhiev, that would have been carrying the victims and heading to the Bastion. I now have, thanks to Ali and some reverse-engineering on my team's part, the scramble sequences they would have used to disguise themselves in this system.

"With that scan data, I can identify and locate those ships. Enough of them, at least, to triangulate their destination. To find the Bastion."

Everest was silent for a good minute, the last bits of his grilled cheese sandwich ignored and congealing on his plate as he stared into the distance.

"I don't have access to that data," he admitted. "You need to go to the ISDF with this, EB. Or at the very least the IBI."

The Icemi Bureau of Investigation, according to EB's instinctual data search, was the overarching law-enforcement organization tasked with operating across all jurisdictions in the system. It had surprisingly limited authority, he noticed, and even *more* limited resources. Inside their scope, IBI agents could ask local agencies and even the ISDF for support—but they needed to justify that support and get a judge to sign off.

The IBI was also a new organization, formed after Icemi Security, the Directorate's secret police, had been dissolved with their masters.

"Hadzhiev went to the ISDF," EB pointed out. "He and his ISDF contact are *dead*, Everest. I have to be careful. I *need* to see this complete."

Everest sighed and pinched the bridge of his nose. After a few moments, he took a long drink of his beer, clearly trying to think.

"The old boys' and girls' network exists," he murmured. "Problem is that *I* would have said that Commodore Wu and their staff were beyond reproach. Wu would have kept the information limited; they were an extremely sensible officer."

"And yet Hadzhiev's contact with them clearly leaked."

"I understand the problem, EB." The detective took another drink of his beer. "I don't think, given everything we've discussed, that Wu was compromised. I'm not even sure their staff were compromised."

"Then how—"

"I think the ISDF's *computers* are compromised," Everest interrupted EB. "Everything you have encountered and explained to me leads back to the conclusion that we are facing an enemy who has acquired Fringe if not *Periphery* hacking technology."

EB shivered. The Beyond was "unmapped" space, the area that wasn't part of the massively replicated and distributed mapping network that covered what was regarded as "civilized space." The border between the Rim and the Beyond wasn't an exact zone, but it was *roughly* fifteen hundred light-years from Earth.

The Rim was the next five hundred light-years in. Every star and mapped nova point between a thousand and fifteen hundred light-years from Sol was the Rim. His homeworld, Apollo, was roughly twelve hundred light-years from the homeworld.

The Fringe was the next step in, seven hundred to a thousand light-years from the center of human space. Even an advanced Rim power like Apollo was technologically backward compared to the Fringe. Some Fringe technology made it into the Rim, a slow process of diffusion that helped increase the general tech level of the region, but overall, the Fringe was significantly more advanced than the Rim.

And as the Fringe was to the Rim, the Periphery was to the Fringe. Every star between four hundred and seven hundred light-years of Sol, the closest Periphery System was over a thousand light-years from Icem.

While the Periphery's tech and ships and computers paled once again compared to the Meridian, the Heart, or the Core—the even more central pieces of human space—they were easily a century or more ahead of Icem.

At least.

The pieces fell into place and EB shivered. Everest was right—given everything they had seen, everything their enemies at the Bastion had done, the Bastion's protectors didn't *need* to compromise people.

With the technology they clearly had, the Bastion could control *every* computer in the star system they wanted.

"We can't get past that," EB said grimly. "So, what do we do?"

"Oh, ye of little faith," Everest said with a grin. "I can tell that *you* never helped run a rebellion!"

33

THE DETECTIVE'S grin told EB that he'd managed his main objective of the meeting: Everest was on board. The man was going to have conditions, EB was sure of it, but he was going to help.

"So long as we are moderately careful, meetings like this—with a white-noise generator and a jammer in a public place—should be safe, no matter how good their hacking gear," the detective told him. "We used that against the Directorate. Their secret police had back doors into *everything*, but they couldn't collate and analyze what was never recorded."

"Odd meetings will draw attention, though," EB warned.

"Yes. We'll need to be careful about who we talk to," Everest agreed. "On the other hand, capable as the software tools available to the Bastion are, they have far more limited resources than the Directorate's Icemi Security goons did. *They* could throw enough people at a problem to track a target's every move, even if they couldn't get everything we were saying.

"I don't think the Bastion has those kinds of resources. Everything you've described sounds like a very small number of people with a limited amount of hardware and software."

"Where do you get that from?" EB asked. He wasn't sure he disagreed, but he was curious about Everest's logic.

"The communications array on *Alex Star,*" Everest said calmly, proving that he'd been more aware of the incident in Tarsus orbit than he'd pretended. EB hadn't, after all, told him the name of the ship.

"They very clearly had the *access* to cut off the ship's communications, but they didn't have the *capacity,*" he explained. "They had to focus on accessing navigation controls and reactor-management systems. They didn't have the time or people to make sure the communications were down as well."

"Or someone was intentionally being very literal," Lan murmured.

EB and Everest both looked at the doctor, who smiled thinly.

"I imagine you're familiar with that kind of trick," they told Everest. "The people who are *mostly* aligned with the cause they're serving but aren't quite sure about the mission they have *today.* So, they follow the letter of their orders and not the spirit.

"If the team was ordered to take control of the ship and destroy her to act as a giant shotgun against Ali's shuttle... Well, if they weren't specifically ordered to disable her coms, not doing so could be explained as needing all of the focus for the task at hand.

"And by following the *letter* of their orders, they intentionally leave some tracks uncovered and raise our suspicions."

"It's possible," Everest admitted. "But if someone was undermining the Bastion's leadership, I would expect...well, for people like me to at least have *heard* that it was here.

"I've *heard* of the Bastion itself, but I had no reason to believe it was in Icem."

"And now there are several hundred kidnapping victims frozen there, at least," EB said grimly. "We need to save those people, Prasada. I don't much care what Icem does with the Bastion after that. I trust your government not to use its resources to start forcing people into slavery."

"A low bar to clear but one I think we pass," Everest agreed. "Human trafficking isn't my area, I admit that, but it still ranks as one of the worst crimes we have on record."

He grimaced.

"By and large, we've eliminated a *lot* of worse things, one way or another, but that particular evil seems to speak to an eternal darkness in some humans. I am *quite* certain I can get people on side with all of this, but it's going to take time and care."

"All I really need is that scan data," EB told him.

"At which point you and Lisa go off like masked vigilantes, using her Trackers' Guild membership as a fig leaf to cover, what, an *orbital assault*? With one corvette and an armed freighter?

"Even if I didn't think that was suicide—and while I don't know you overly well, Tacita and I are still friends, and if I let Captain Zelda get herself killed, it will cause me no *end* of grief—it's also *illegal*." He sighed. "And I am, when all is said and done, an agent of the law. I do not do what I do because it is required of me. I do it because I believe in a peaceful and orderly society.

"There are many lines I will cross in pursuit of the spirit of that society as opposed to the letter of its laws. But enabling an illegal vigilante operation in my star system isn't one of them."

EB sighed and nodded.

"So, what do you need?"

"*You* need ships, troops, firepower and authority," Everest pointed out. "Plus that scan data. I don't need...anything. But if I'm getting you those things, it needs to be done right.

"Which means we need to go in front of a judge. I can arrange a secured information space for that meeting, and I can insist on paper authorization, but it will take time and I can't make you have that conversation."

EB grimaced. That was a lot more paperwork and politics than he wanted to play, but he understood where Everest was coming from—even if he didn't wholly *agree*.

But then, *his* government had sold him out to assassins.

"Can a judge get me ships and troops?" he asked.

"The right one? Yes," Everest said. "Though, honestly, what they'll get you is an IBI Marshal, authorized to commandeer whatever the hell you need. You and Zelda might end up deputized to make things all very official."

"We won't be able to lean on the ISDF for this," EB warned. "There is no way they don't have warning systems in place for if the ISDF finds out about them. We've already seen that."

"Agreed. I have some thoughts—I'll raise them with the judge and the marshal when we get that far," the detective told him. "For now…"

"Can you start that process?" EB asked. "The people we want to save are, supposedly, in cryo-stasis—but the whole point of moving the ships and victims to the Bastion was to create a springboard to reestablish the Siya U Hestî.

"Lady Breanna is apparently dead, but that just means that whoever is in charge of the Bastion has found themselves with everything they need to become the crime lord of a dozen star systems.

"The clock isn't ticking yet…but time is not a friend to those people."

"Meet me here tomorrow, same time," Everest told him. "I'll poke some tires and see what I can find."

34

"SO, we're waiting on the detective," EB concluded, looking around the mess at everyone. "He thinks he can get us a meeting with a judge senior enough to basically order the IBI to investigate. But..." He sighed and shrugged, his apparent fatigue pulling at Trace's heart-strings.

She was sitting next to Ginny, her gaze focused on her plate as they talked about the issues and political structures of her own star system. Issues and structures that she had basically been completely unaware of.

Trace had known about the planetary parliament that Sarah Vortani had been running for, and...that had been about it. Her attention in local history had been limited to the Black Oak Island Plague and its consequences on her own life.

The Directorate had been more of a boogeyman than a historical entity to a rebellious thirteen-year-old.

"We're pretty much out of options we can execute on our own," EB admitted. "We need Everest to make the link and get us the meeting. At that point, he and I think we can sell the justice on the situation, which will get us the resources to find the Bastion.

"We and Zelda are still going to take the lead on the actual movement against the Bastion. The level of penetration of the government's information systems is terrifying. What we *know* suggests that if there's even a hint of them being discovered in the ISDF network, they'll know."

"So, we have to go through law enforcement," Ginny said grimly. "Will they have the resources?"

"An IBI Marshal can theoretically commandeer just about anything, given a judge's support, but they have to explain why," Lan noted, their voice as tired as EB's. "Which brings us back to the fact that we *cannot* let any hint of this enter the ISDF's computers.

"But...the Denton and Tarsus Orbital Guards have ships, even ones capable of interplanetary travel," the doctor noted. "Plus, there *is* a Deus Orbital Guard, though they're *utterly* overwhelmed by the volume they're responsible for, from what I can tell."

"Unfortunately, our best guess still puts the Bastion on one of Deus's three moons," Vexer pointed out. "Catalogs say none of the three are inhabited, with even Alpha orbiting over a light-second out from Deus itself. Most of the traffic is around orbital stations much closer in, which is where the Deus Orbital Guard operates their cutters."

"All four of them," EB said grimly. "We're going to need support from either the Denton or Tarsus Orbital Guard, and we're going to need to get it *quietly* and *legally*. If we go in under IBI auspices, everything is aboveboard, everything is clean, and there's a clear plan for keeping people safe after we get them out.

"Everyone is better served if we go in with the right resources and the right authority. Everest's judge is our best bet."

Trace was listening to the entire discussion—but she was also poking at a mental loose tooth. Structures of government and authority, ministries and bureaus. Tables of organization.

All of it came back to a point she really didn't like.

"There is someone else who can help us," she said. "The Director of the Icemi Bureau of Investigation is promoted from within but is expected to work closely with civilian leadership—in the form of the Assistant Minister of Justice."

"I know," EB conceded, meeting her gaze. The sheer exhaustion in his eyes told her that he'd followed the same org charts she had and reached the same conclusion—and had put aside potentially their best contact to spare *Trace*.

"We only have one avenue of access to Minister Vortani," EB continued. "I could, in theory, get a message into her inbox, but…"

"If the staff listing on her datanet site is correct, I still know her chief aide," Trace said quickly. "I can…" She swallowed against a sudden acidic taste in her mouth. "I can call her main office and almost certainly get connected to Sarah."

"You could." It wasn't a question or an argument. EB understood *exactly* what she was saying. "But I didn't want—*don't* want—to ask that of you. Sarah Vortani might have been *neglectful* rather than *abusive*, but that doesn't make trauma any less real."

"How many people did Hadzhiev get redirected to the Bastion?" she asked, struggling with the weight in her own stomach. "There were *hundreds* on the Cage. There could have been as many in transit, and he got them *all* sent there."

"Nine ships," EB said slowly. "A total of a hundred and fifty thousand cubic meters of ships, about eighty thousand cubic meters of cargo space. Assuming only a quarter of their cargo space was converted to cryo-pods, we're still looking at over a *thousand* pods. Possibly *two* thousand.

"While they almost certainly weren't full when they got the alert, we're definitely looking at hundreds of people. Maybe as many as a thousand."

"A thousand people," Trace echoed—and she was surprised as the weight in her stomach transformed into something else. Iron settled in her spine, and she straightened her shoulders as she looked at EB.

"If we don't save them, *my* trauma will pale in comparison to the trauma of any *one* of those people," she reminded her father. "I can face my demons for them, Dad-E. You and Reggie almost *died* for this mission already.

"I can talk to Sarah."

TO TRACE'S SURPRISE, she actually had to argue to convince people to let her do it. EB and Ginny had clearly decided the decision was hers, and Vexer had come around quickly. Lan and Tate, though, had tried to talk her out of it.

In the end, though, she took the seat in her little study and linked her headware into the ship's computers. Even with their various discoveries about the penetration of Icem's networks, Trace had faith in the hardware and software EB had sourced.

Evasion's electronic defenses might not be impenetrable, but she *would* have warned the crew if those defenses had been breached.

So long as Trace was aboard her ship, she was pretty sure she was safe from eavesdropping and surveillance. Once she was communicating with the outside, even to government offices—perhaps *especially* to government offices!—she lost that certainty.

Her words would need to be very carefully chosen, and she considered what they *needed* from Sarah Vortani.

The new-forged iron in her spine weakened in the face of actually making the call. Still, she knew what she had to do and was setting up the commands when someone knocked on her study door.

"Come in?" she offered hesitantly.

EB and Vexer walked through together, each of them carrying a small folding chair.

"We…" Vexer trailed off, then chuckled. "We figured you didn't necessarily want to be alone for this. If we're wrong…"

"No, no," she said immediately, their presence more welcome than she'd thought. "Please. I think…"

"We're your dads," EB told her, squeezing her shoulder as he unfolded his chair in the space. The study was big enough for the three of them to all sit comfortably—but no one was getting *out* of the room without folding up a chair.

"We have your back against any and all comers; that's what being your parents means," he continued. "If you want us to hang back out of frame, we can do that. But we're here for you."

"I'll bring you in once I'm talking to Sarah herself, I think," Trace told them. "Let me…lead?"

"Of course."

Both of her dads squeezed her shoulders and then shifted their chairs farther toward the walls, leaving her as much open space as the room allowed.

Swallowing her fears and drawing on their strength, Trace plugged in the contact code for her former foster mother's office. The overlapping black-and-gold triangles of the Icemi government appeared in front of her for a few seconds, then a familiar-looking Asian woman appeared in front of her.

Trinh Nguyen hadn't been the staffer Trace had been hoping to make contact with, but she *was* someone Trace knew. That was all she needed, she figured.

"Good afternoon, you have reached the office of Assistant Minister Sarah Vortani; how may I assist...you..."

Trace smiled softly as Nguyen trailed off in shock.

"Hi, Trinh," she greeted the woman. "It's me. I'm back in-system, under my own power, and I need to talk to Sarah."

"I...uh... Of course! I think she's in a meeting, but she'll drop that for you!"

Trace shivered as the video feed shifted back to the government logo. She would never have *dreamed* of calling into Sarah's office while the woman was her foster mother—and she was *very* sure that Sarah wouldn't have left a meeting for her.

She barely had time to finish that thought, however, before the logo vanished and was replaced with a portable feed, showing Sarah Vortani leaning against a wall in what looked like a conference center, staring at the screen her headware was projecting.

"It...it is you," she whispered. "I...thought we'd lost you. Failed you. How did you get back... Where are you? I can send someo— No! *I* will come get you."

"It's complicated," Trace told her. "I'm not coming home, Sarah. I was on the Cage when the Siya U Hestî fell. I was *why* the Cage fell."

"I don't understand," the woman admitted. "I...I spent the last six months looking for you. I thought you were gone forever. You were *at the Cage*?!"

"With my dads," Trace said flatly. "The people who rescued me from the Siya U Hestî adopted me, and I'm staying with them, no matter what. But..."

Trace swallowed, suddenly unsure what to say.

She and Sarah Vortani held each other's gazes in the video link for a few eternal silent seconds.

"I owe you an explanation, I think," Trace said. "And I think you owe me an apology."

"A lifetime of apologies," the older woman said. "I don't understand anything but you're *alive* and you're *okay*. I..." She visibly swallowed and Trace realized Sarah was crying. "No thanks to anything I did," Sarah admitted.

"We need your help," Trace said softly. "You need to meet my dads, in person, and we can talk then. We're at High Home Station. We can meet you—"

"I'll have a shuttle pick me up immediately; I can be in motion in ten minutes," Sarah interrupted. "Tell me where."

A message popped up on Trace's headware screen, giving an address. She gave it to Sarah, who nodded.

"The chandler's conference center, on the space dock." The minister had recognized it immediately. "I've already called my shuttle and security detail. We'll be on-station in thirty minutes.

"Tracy...are you sure you're safe?"

"Sarah...I'm pretty sure I was safer *before* I called you," Trace said bluntly.

Her ex-foster mother flinched as if struck but bowed her head and nodded in acknowledgement without argument.

"I'll see you in thirty minutes, Tracy," she finally said. "I promise."

35

TRACE HADN'T STOPPED VIBRATING since making the call. She hated it almost as much as she hated the fact that she'd had to call Sarah for help. But the alternatives were worse.

Lan and her dads were with her as they waited—well, Lan was talking with the conference center and paying to rent a secure meeting space.

The doctor returned to the other three and smiled knowingly.

"We've got a space and they swear it's secure," they told the trio. "I give it sixty-forty odds that they have their own bugs in it, but I can deal with those."

"Lead the way, Lan," EB ordered.

Trace shifted from foot to foot for a few seconds, then started after Lan as the doctor headed toward their meeting space.

"Breathe, Trace," Vexer murmured in her ear. "No matter what happens, we all go home together."

"Where even *is* home for us?" Trace asked, the thought sending a shiver down her spine.

"*Evasion*," her dad said instantly. "Wherever she is, we always have a home together."

Trace exhaled and nodded, some of the anxiety leaving her. She suspected she was still vibrating, but her dads' certainty helped stabilize her as they reached their rental.

She wasn't sure what she'd expected of a rental meeting room in the chandlery on High Home's space dock. The entire business was dedicated to servicing visiting ships, and the attached conference center's sole purpose was to provide space for ship captains to have meetings, carry out interviews for new crew, et cetera.

Somehow, though, the space Lan led them into felt like it was exactly what she *should* have been expecting. There was nothing fancy about the space. It was a box roughly four meters on a side, with a long table in the middle with half a dozen chairs.

Everything in the room looked solid to her—but she could also pick out that it was plastic and metal. Sturdy, cheap and undecorated.

The only decoration in the entire room was a single large painting on the left wall. Her art skills weren't up for telling if it was original or a print, but it showed a pair of ancient sailing ships cruising in company under a gorgeous blue sky.

"If she's keeping to her schedule, we have a few minutes before she arrives," Lan observed. "Gives me a chance to sort out some jamming and such."

Trace *really* didn't like the feeling that she was being watched that she now had everywhere she went on High Home. It was almost certain that the Bastion's murder-happy security team was aware of *Evasion*'s crew and was using their systems access to watch them, looking for weaknesses.

The soft burbling of the white-noise generator helped her relax a bit. The jamming felt like it *should* have been unnecessary, as datanet signal in the room was already terrible—and should completely go away once the door closed, if she understood correctly.

"Well, Lan, were we being watched?" EB asked.

"As expected. It's probably so that they can usefully comply with any warrants the police issue—or a leftover of the Directorate; the center is old enough for that." Lan shrugged. "They're jammed now. And since the desk *told* me the room was secure, they can't complain too loudly."

Further conversation was interrupted by a knock on the door, almost immediately followed by a young stranger in a plain gray suit.

"I'm looking for...Captain Bardacki?" he asked.

"That would be me," EB told him. "And you are?"

"Makram Blake," the young man introduced himself politely. "I'm the junior member of the Assistant Minister's security detail. I need to scan the room, if you please."

"Of course."

Blake stepped farther into the meeting room and looked around. His gaze lingered on Trace for a second, clearly recognizing her, but he removed a palm-sized scanner from his pocket and waved it around.

"I have a jamming and white-noise field?" Blake noted.

"Those are ours," EB told him. "A security measure, to make sure we're all safe. We are also carrying stunners."

"I was expecting *that*," the young security officer replied. "But the concealment field seems...strange."

"That's a discussion for us to have with Em Vortani," EB said grimly. "Assuming she *is* coming?"

The thought that the stranger might not be who he said he was hadn't even *occurred* to Trace, but she realized that EB had casually slipped his hand into his jacket and Lan had moved almost entirely out of the security officer's field of view.

"I am," Sarah said firmly, stepping through the door as EB spoke. "Blake, Sanders. Leave us."

"Ma'am, we are—" The older Black man behind her froze in mid-step.

"This is Tracy and her new family," Sarah told him. "There is also only one way in or out of this room. Secure the outside and we'll all be fine."

"Yes, ma'am."

The older guard—Sanders, Trace figured—gestured for Blake to join him and they stepped outside. The door slid shut behind them, and the last vestiges of the station datanet vanished.

Trace was seated on the far side of the table, and while the immediate *threat* had dropped enough that her dads and Lan took their seats around her, the tension in the room remained thick enough to cut with a knife.

Sarah was just…looking at Trace. She wasn't saying anything or even approaching closer. Just staring.

"I'm sorry," she finally half-whispered. "I fucked up so many things in so many ways. I…"

"You needed a prop for your political career," Trace said, letting her anger seep into her tone. "I'm glad you realized you actually were supposed to take care of me when it was too late."

Sarah lurched as if struck, then took a deep breath and swallowed, closing her eyes.

"I deserve that," she conceded. "And I can see how it looked like that to you. That was not—was *never*—my intention, Tracy. It was an argument that helped convince John to foster, but I was from Black Oak Isle, Tracy. I was *trying* to help.

"I fucked it up," she repeated. "I was a terrible mother. But that was…a mistake, not an intent. I got distracted by my political career. You were *never* a prop for it. And I am sorry—so sorry—that you felt that way."

She spread her hands.

"You don't have to forgive me," Sarah told Trace. "I don't expect you to. But I needed you to know that I understand what I did. I wish you'd done anything else, but I understand. And I tried to find you. And then I tried everything I could to make sure no one else got kidnapped by those…monsters."

There was a long silence. Trace wasn't quite sure how to even *take* Sarah's confession. She was glad the woman wasn't asking for forgiveness—she wasn't sure she could give it. There'd been too many years of being ignored while her supposed mother ran from meeting to meeting, leaving her with a rotating cast of nannies and housekeepers.

EB cleared his throat.

"I'm Evridiki Bardacki and this is my fiancé, Vena Dolezal, and my ship's doctor, Dr. Lan Kozel," EB introduced himself and his crew. "Vena and I adopted Trace under Nigahog law roughly six weeks ago.

"According to the treaties I've read, that is legally binding here in Icem as well."

"It is," Sarah confirmed. "Even if it wasn't..." She shook her head. "What am I going to do, re-kidnap the child who was stolen? If she wants to stay with you, she stays with you.

"So long as that *is* what you want, Tracy."

There was an edge to her tone that Trace had never heard from Sarah Vortani—not with regards to *her*, at least. She recognized it, though. She'd heard it from *EB* more than once.

"They're my dads," she told Sarah. "They saved me. And when the Siya U Hestî wouldn't let me go, they, well...saved me again."

"You were part of the fleet that took down the Cage?" Sarah asked.

"Yes." EB didn't, Trace noted, admit that he'd *organized* and *led* that attack. "And that—plus your crusade since Trace's kidnapping—is what we need to talk to you about."

Sarah nodded slowly and stepped closer, finally taking a seat and slumping into it.

"At least you're not calling it my *damn fool crusade*, my *obsession* or my..." She inhaled sharply. "Apologies, Captain. Tracy's unexpected return has left me off-balance, and certain people have been...less than supportive of my endeavors."

Trace knew instantly who she meant.

"That ass," she muttered. "He has limits somewhere, does he?"

Sarah locked her gaze on to the teenager and fell silent. "I..." She paused, swallowing.

"John has always supported my career," Sarah finally continued. "With varying levels of grace, yes, but he has always had my back. Losing you, though, drove a wedge between us that I did not expect.

"I put everything into first finding you, and then into making sure no one else faced that fate. John...did not understand."

"He was just unhappy to lose his science experiment," Trace said bitterly.

Sarah's silence carried an edge this time. Shock? Surprise? Trace didn't know. She wasn't sure she wanted to know.

"John is not, perhaps, the warmest or most conciliatory of men," Sarah slowly allowed, "but my understanding was that the two of you got on well. I was surprised by how little effort he was prepared to put into finding you beyond simply informing the police.

"That said...I may have been a terrible parent, Tracy, but I know that tone from you."

The edge was sharpening. Trace realized it wasn't aimed at *her*, but it was growing deadly dangerous.

"Trace, breathe," EB said quietly, reaching over to squeeze her forearm gently. "Lan, could you explain what you found in Trace's headware? I feel that Em Vortani needs to know."

"I found two things in Trace's neural implants when she first came aboard and I examined her," Lan said. "The first, which has given us so many headaches since, was a datavault implanted by the Siya U Hestî to allow her to be used as a courier without even *her* knowing.

"The second, however, predated her falling into the Cartel's clutches. Trace's neural hardware and software had been significantly reconfigured from standard pediatric headware systems. Her nonstandard hardware and software caused interference with the Siya U Hestî datavault and allowed her to access its contents even before we shut down its encryption and linked into her headware...but modification of pediatric headware is illegal under any medical legal code I am aware of, Minister Vortani.

"The pattern of healing and scarification suggested a number of small surgeries over the course of eighteen months, the most recent about six months before she came aboard *Evasion*," Lan concluded. "That would make it from about ten to twenty-eight months ago now."

"That's..." Sarah trailed off, swallowing her words. "I was not aware of any such work and gave no permission for such things."

"Pediatric headware modification and experimentation is done with the strictest controls and standards of consent," Lan said firmly. "That *Trace* was unaware of the work represents an ethical and moral breach of the highest order."

"You think John did it."

It wasn't a question.

"That would, I suppose, be for your local regulators, ethics boards and police to establish," Lan said calmly. "For myself, yes. Given my discussions with Trace and her lack of awareness of the surgery, it appears quite clear that Dr. John Vortani carried out a series of minor and moderate experimentations on her neural cybernetic systems without informing her or requesting consent. From anyone."

"Are you prepared to provide me with a sworn statement to that effect and the data from your examination?"

Sarah's voice was flat and cold. Trace had thought it was sharp before, but now it was a blade of ice that sounded ready to kill.

And Trace shivered as she realized just *who* that blade was aimed at.

"I am," Lan said calmly. "I will have it for you by morning station time."

"Thank you. That should not have been allowed to happen." Sarah laid her hands on the table and looked down at them. Her nails, Trace realized, were as perfectly done as usual—but the style was far simpler than the more ornate structures and paints that Sarah had used to prefer.

"If John…" She shook her head. "I will see the truth found and him punished for his crimes."

Sarah looked up at Trace.

"*My* failings, while as damning in some ways, are not criminal," she said. "That my husband crossed that line is horrifying to me. I will…"

She closed her eyes and bowed her head.

"I *cannot* make this right," she whispered. "I am sorry."

"No," Trace told her. "You can't. Confessions and apologies won't change that."

"But you can help us save others from what happened to Trace," EB interjected. "Trace? May I?"

"Yeah." Trace pushed herself back from the table, intentionally surrendering the conversation to EB. "I think…I need to stop twisting the knife if we're going to get anywhere."

36

IT WAS A STRANGE THING, but EB's heart *ached* with pride at the fact that Trace recognized both that she *had* needed to get that out of her system and drag Sarah Vortani over the coals—and that there was a point where it became counterproductive.

Twisting the knife, as his daughter put it, was just hurting Vortani at this point. The woman was already about as broken on the topic as she could be.

"We are here in Icem because someone made us think that you were contacting us," EB told Vortani. "That someone was a former senior member of the Siya U Hestî, someone we met on the Cage and who helped us free the people there."

The details of said meeting weren't relevant to Vortani, he figured.

"After the Cage fell, he apparently activated a protocol that ordered all of their ships to go to a location called the Bastion, here in Icem," he continued. "They would have placed all of their prisoners in cryostasis and stored them at this base.

"I have reason to believe the ships are still there—and that the Bastion itself represented Lady Breanna Tolliver's backup plan, where she'd secured enough resources to rebuild her empire if something went wrong."

He smiled thinly.

"Several things went wrong and Tolliver ended up dead in a Nigahog prison, probably to make sure she didn't betray key members of the Guilds who'd worked with her," he observed. "Now there are several hundred kidnapping victims in cryo-stasis somewhere in this star system."

"My gods," Vortani whispered. "We have to find them."

"I agree," EB told her. "I have been following my own somewhat 'damn fool crusade' to get this far. Unfortunately, most of the people I know of who knew anything about this are now dead. The man who brought us here was assassinated before our arrival. The officer in the ISDF that he contacted was murdered in a shuttle crash.

"And the local Siya U Hestî leader who I was negotiating with for information was killed in orbit of Tarsus, when a bomb was detonated on her ship and someone self-destructed a freighter to throw a debris cloud at her."

He shook his head.

"I have reason to believe that every computer in this star system— or, at the very least, in the Icem System Defense Force—has been compromised via extremely capable hacking software like nothing I've ever seen. The people at the Bastion are doing everything in their power to keep their location secret—presumably while they work out how to use the resources they now possess to build their own empire."

"The Siya U Hestî have brought misery and horror to a dozen star systems," Vortani pointed out. "We *must* end them—and make sure they never rise again. Do you know where this Bastion is?"

"No," EB admitted. "But with your help, I can find out."

"How?"

"Thanks to our original contact, I have a list of every ship that was sent to the Bastion by his order," EB explained. "I know when they would have arrived and their true core identities. I also, thanks to the late Janessa Ali, have the scramble protocols that would have been downloaded to those ships on entering Icem.

"So, I know what those ships looked like when they were here," he concluded. "But my sensors are hardly up to the kind of extended-time old-light review necessary to track thirty-odd days of potential arrivals.

"I need historical scan data for the entire star system, Em Vortani. Given that, I can identify our slaver ships and I can triangulate where they all went. From there, I am certain I can locate the Bastion."

"Given *live* access to the ISDF system-wide scan network, I can definitely do so." He shrugged. "I have a local ally working on bringing in a judge and getting a warrant he can use to commandeer an IBI Marshal."

He gestured around them as Sarah silently processed his lecture.

"While this room is secure against intrusion, I don't think *anything* available to the ISDF is," he admitted. "While the best-case scenario would be to borrow a gunship squadron and a battalion of the army, those people will be watched."

"I have...almost no authority or influence with the ISDF," Vortani told them. "I *do* have influence and authority with the IBI and some with the judiciary."

"Can you get us that sensor history?" EB asked.

"Yes." She nodded and smiled thinly. "That I can get you in a few hours. After that, though...I am part of the Ministry of Justice, Captain. I can't condone vigilante mercenary actions in my system."

"I realize that," EB told her. This was the problem with going with legitimate authority. Legitimate authority had to take legitimate *action* —and in Icem, the memory of the Directorate made taking *illegitimate* action likely to end poorly.

"That's why Detective Everest is arranging a meeting with a judge in a secure room. Once we have the location of the Bastion, we can begin to put together a plan. Given the security concerns, it will likely need to be anchored on my ship and Captain Zelda's *Zeldan Blade*," he said. "But I hope we can pull resources from the government."

"The question, Captain, is not *will* the Icemi government, law enforcement and military put resources toward the capture of this Bastion," Sarah Vortani told him firmly. "We *will*. The question is how we make contact with the necessary individuals, given the security risks you've discussed—and how many resources we can assemble without drawing attention."

She looked blankly past him for a moment, then exhaled and nodded.

"I have someone else I need to talk to on that," she decided aloud. "Once you have that meeting with the judge arranged, let my office know and I will make sure to be there...and to bring a guest."

Vortani smiled. It was a sharp and chill expression—and EB pitied both her soon-to-be-ex-husband *and* the poor bastards at the Bastion.

Guilt made for a powerful motivator, in his experience, and Vortani had guilt to spare. Combine that with her actual legal authority and the information EB had, he was finally starting to think they might at least find the Bastion.

The question *then* was what tricks and traps Breanna had left her people—and whether they could get past the defenses quickly enough to protect the prisoners from their captors!

37

"DID WE GET THE DATA?"

Vexer looked up as EB entered *Evasion*'s bridge.

"You don't trust our erstwhile ally and daughter's former parent?" he asked drily.

"I trust her more than many of the people we've dealt with in this system," EB told his fiancé, kissing the top of Vexer's head and half-perching on the navigator's seat. "But given that list is mostly Janessa Ali and her friends, that's a low bar to clear."

"Minister Vortani has cleared it handily," Vexer told him. "Take a look."

EB followed the hand gesture and studied the main screen. It only took him a second to recognize a military-style scan report for the entire star system.

"That scan is as of the moment the news of the Cage's capture reached Icem," Vexer told him. "A logical starting point for the dataset, I suppose, and the earliest point we have."

The navigator smiled up at EB.

"It arrived five minutes ago, through some entertaining side-routing," he observed. "It came in labeled as a standardized regulatory update. I don't know if that will be enough to fool our unknown friends' prying eyes, but it certainly cost *me* a good two minutes before I realized that made no sense."

EB chuckled.

"I can see that," he admitted. "So...that's it, then? We can run the analysis and find the Bastion?"

"It's not going to be a fast process," Vexer reminded him. "Nine ships, three to five arrival windows for each, plus two potential variations for the scramble code. Each arrival window includes at least ten different possible seeds for the scramble as well, though they should be similar-*ish*."

"I saw the list," EB said. "Just over a thousand possible sequences. But given that each of those sequences is attached to a particular *time*, we don't need to run all of them across the full dataset. Only for about twelve hours either side of the target window, unless we find them."

"Like I said, I've had the data for about five minutes," Vexer replied. "We can start setting up that analysis together?"

EB reached over and took his partner's hand with a smile.

"Seems like we have the *best* date nights," he said with a chuckle. "Shall we find a secret criminal base together, my love?"

"The scariest part of that joke, my dear, is that I have *definitely* had worse date-night plans sprung on me than that!" Vexer was grinning though. "I will give you the credit of noting that none of said horrors were sprung on me by *you*, though."

The bridge wasn't really designed for them to sit close enough together to touch, so EB stayed half-perched on the seat arm, half-perched on his fiancé's lap as he linked his headware in and brought up the search parameters.

The longer they spent setting up the search, the less time it would take *Evasion* to run through the data. Even that, though, was just the first step.

Once they'd found the Siya U Hestî ships, they needed to *track* them.

"Do you expect to find all nine?" Vexer asked.

"We know one was here," EB pointed out, "in Denton orbit, when we arrived. So, we don't need to dig too hard on that one—most likely, we know what she was flying when she was here.

"But..." He shook his head. "No. I don't expect to find all nine. I figure we're going to end up with about twenty-five probables that *actually* represent seven or eight of the ships."

"There aren't that many places eight to nine ships are going to converge, though. We know what the legit ones are, so..."

"So long as we find a place eight ships landed that isn't on any official maps, that goes on the list to check out, huh?"

"And if we're very lucky, there's only one of those."

———

EB HADN'T EXPECTED it to be *easy*. Just getting all pieces of the data had been a nightmare that had consumed an entire week and multiple lives. Even so, there were limits and problems with all of the data he was working from.

The scramble protocols he had were an approximation, reverse-engineered from a dozen results and one semi-confirmed positive.

The arrival list he had was equally an estimate. They knew where Hadzhiev had *expected* the ships to be when they got his message, and then how quickly they *could* have got to the Icem System.

The only truly complete and reliable data they had was the scan data from Icem, and even that EB swiftly spotted issues with. Icem had a decent deep-space sensor network for a Beyond system, but *decent* wasn't necessarily up to picking out key identifiers on a ship in the open void between the planets.

That was, of course, a key part of how the entire scramble system the Siya U Hestî was running *worked*. A freighter would nova in—which could be detected by the network—but keep her systems dark while her crew contacted a hidden beacon.

The beacon would take the data it was fed—their current identification status, the time, a few key emissions signatures—and send the ship back a unique sequence with a name, key changes to make to their emissions, and a standard beacon key.

Just the equipment to *use* the scramble result was illegal for civilian use in most star systems, but a several-minute gap between a ship emerging from nova and bringing her drives up wasn't unusual enough to draw attention.

By the time the freighters approached any of the planetary systems and the more-defined sensor areas around them, they would be immersed in their new identities.

The problem was that he was definitely getting matches for ships arriving…but he had *no* scan data showing those ships going anywhere unusual. Each ship approached either Denton or Tarsus, then left.

"I think I have it," Vexer declared.

EB looked over at his fiancé.

"I'm crazy, Hadzhiev was fucking with us and all of this is a nightmare I want to wake up from?" he quipped.

"You're not crazy, but Hadzhiev *was* fucking with us, and this is definitely a nightmare," Vexer told him. "More importantly, however, is that the captains involved in this stint *knew* the Siya U Hestî had fallen and were being a bunch of complete fucking paranoids."

"So…"

"Let's pick an example, the one we were pretty sure was real," Vexer told him. "*Albatross's Mariner*, in orbit when we arrived in Denton as *Scarlet Peach*. So, we saw her a week ago, when she left the system. That identity is based on a scramble calculation from fifteen days ago.

"In those eight days, where did *Mariner* go? Let's follow her all the way through."

EB nodded and transferred his headware visual to the main display. Leaning on Vexer's chair, he took the other man's hand and drew strength from the warmth of skin against skin.

"She arrived a bit inside of Templar's orbital path," EB noted. "Eleven-minute delay between nova emergence and her activating her engines. That's interesting."

"Means the beacon is probably on Tarsus," Vexer agreed. "A touch over ninety million kilometers from *Mariner*'s arrival point would give her about a ten-minute round-trip lightspeed lag. Add some time for calculation and setup on each side...Tarsus is the only place that makes sense."

"Hence Ali having ready access to the scramble protocols," EB murmured. "Okay. So, after getting her scramble active, *Mariner* headed in-system and arrived at Tarsus half a day later. She's in Tarsus orbit for..."

He blinked.

"She docks with the station and *Scarlet Peach* vanishes from the system scans," Vexer said, following the same line he did. "The *next* time I see *Scarlet Peach* in the scan data is nine days ago, leaving Tarsus and heading for Denton.

"For about five days in there, *Scarlet Peach* doesn't exist."

"Paranoid indeed," EB whispered. "They ran a new scramble sequence in Tarsus orbit. How the *hell* did no one notice that?"

"Because no one looks at the identity beacon of a ship in port," Vexer told him. "They *should* have noticed that the ship checking out wasn't on their docket, but that's easily fixed by a little bribery or some hacking."

"Which gives us a window to run through the scramble code," EB observed. "But they switched *back* to *Scarlet Peach* to leave?"

"Avoid drawing attention. One of the checks *I* ran was for ships that arrived and hadn't left," Vexer said. He chuckled grimly. "Of course, that turned up enough positives for me to wonder at the usefulness of it."

"It gives us a filter, though," EB observed. "Some of their ships may have left. But I suspect that *Mariner* might have been special somehow. I'm betting that most of those freighters are still at the Bastion."

"Well, I'm going to *start* by running *Mariner*'s arrival time at Tarsus through the scramble protocol," Vexer told him. "What else do we need?"

"I'm going to look for ships that reached docks and vanished," EB replied. "Not all of them are going to be obvious, but I figure I can pull a few out—and if we compare that to your list of ships that never left, I think we might find at least a handful to look at more closely."

IT WAS late and EB was exhausted. Over the course of the day, they'd met with a cop, started moving on a plan to find and deal with the Bastion—and then Trace had reached out to Sarah Vortani, adding *another* major meeting.

Vortani had moved *fast* once Trace had made contact, meeting them far faster than he'd expected and getting them the scan data even more quickly.

And now he had…an answer. Maybe.

"Four ships, including *Mariner*, went there." His finger stabbed at the third moon of Icem's inner gas giant. "Deus Three. Is there *anything* there at all?"

"Nothing, according to the system databases," Vexer said quietly. "There is a small scientific research outpost on Deus One, but even that's considered out of the way. Deus Three is over *nine light-seconds* from Deus itself."

"Four ships that arrived in-system, picked up Siya U Hestî scramble codes and proceeded to dock in either Tarsus or Deus orbit," EB noted. "Where they proceeded to get *new* scramble codes, and then headed out to a moon that nobody has any real reason to visit."

Deus III was a tiny airless rock. At six hundred kilometers across, with less than half a meter per second squared of gravity, it had nothing to appeal to anyone.

Except in that very lack of appeal. No one was going to investigate Deus III. No one was watching Deus III. There was enough traffic in the Deus area that no one was going to question a ship novaing in anywhere around the gas giant. Enough traffic probably *passed* Deus III to cover traffic to and from the moon, but nobody was going there.

Nobody except a set of four ships that they were *reasonably* sure had been Siya U Hestî slaver transports.

"Let's run a—"

"Let's go to *sleep*, EB," Vexer interrupted him with a smile. "We have a damn good idea of where our enemy is now. We can run other analyses of the data once we've rested.

"But that means that tomorrow, we have to convince the locals to join in on dealing with the Bastion, and put together a plan to save a lot of innocent people from hell. We need to be rested for that.

"Sound like a plan?"

38

IF THE PUB across from the Blue Holiday Hotel on Ring Two had human staff up front, they might have been starting to recognize EB. Since the place—whose name was something sufficiently generic that he had trouble *remembering* it—likely only had two or three humans in the entire restaurant, probably in a hidden control room somewhere, EB wasn't too worried.

He and Lan weren't the first ones there this time. Everest was seated at the same table as last time, an absolutely *immense* plate of nachos with assorted toppings laid out in front of him.

"Detective," EB greeted him.

"Captain," Everest replied. "I took the liberty of ordering drinks for us all, but you'll want to put in your food orders."

EB gave the massive plate a querying expression and the cop chuckled.

"Let me put it this way, EB," he said. "I suspect I have the same number of cybernetic implants as you do. But if you didn't recognize my augmentations, your doctor here almost certainly did."

"Artificial organs combined with post-puberty genetic modification," Lan said instantly, before EB could say a word. "That's an... unpleasant way to upgrade."

"Like a second set of growing pains," Everest confirmed. "Forty-plus years ago, and I *still* remember that couple of weeks like it was yesterday."

"*Weeks?*" Lan demanded.

EB didn't know much about boosts in general, let alone the particular variety that Everest apparently possessed, but he knew that tone.

"That's the time frame you have when you're smuggling volunteers to an entirely different planet to get work done that's only sort of legal in *either* star system," Everest said calmly. "Later, I got some reworking done here on the up-and-up, but the original boosts were done in a rush, in secret and on Estutmost."

He shrugged and picked up a stack of tortillas glued together with cheese and loaded with chicken. A good-sized bite and swallow later, he grinned at his dinner companions.

"It's all churning along like it should be now, but I got the quick-and-dirty treatment to avoid attention. Either way, it leaves you with a hell of an appetite."

A server stupid rolled up with their drinks, and EB claimed the beer he hoped was meant for him. He put in a quick food order with his headware, then met Everest's gaze as Lan activated the privacy generator.

"We've added a small complicating factor, I think," EB warned the local. "I *think* it's to our benefit, but it does complicate things."

"This situation did not necessarily need more complications, EB," Everest observed. "What are we looking at?"

"Assistant Minister Vortani has been brought into the loop and is looking at what she can arrange in terms of personnel and resources. We still, as I understand it, need that warrant—but she was able to get us the scan data on her own authority."

Everest was silent for several long moments, then took a deep gulp of his own drink and nodded slowly.

"I was considering trying to contact Vortani," he admitted. "Her campaign and rise to prominence have been about dealing with this exact kind of mess, but proper channels would take me days to reach her.

"I don't know what channels *you* had to get in touch with her in the last twenty-three hours," Everest said drily, "but having one of the senior politicos in the Justice Ministry on side can't hurt."

"I thought so," EB agreed. "And, like I said, she got the scan data. We know where the Bastion is, Prasada."

EB shook his head.

"I didn't get much sleep last night working through the data, but we know where they are now. And I don't think they know we know."

Everest nodded again, a thoughtful expression on his face.

"We need to move even more quickly than I thought, then," he murmured. "Because nothing you've told me makes me think that is going to *stay* under wraps for long—especially when we start pulling in people to make a raid happen."

"That's the downside, yes."

"It's a good thing that Justice Shahar Iliescu trusts me, isn't it?" Everest asked. "She and I go back far enough that she doesn't usually take on cases I'm involved in, but she's the second-most-senior judge aboard High Home Station—and the only reason she isn't on a more-important court is that she can't spend more than a few hours on the surface for medical reasons."

That...wasn't an issue EB figured was particularly common. There was definitely a significant chunk of humanity that didn't *like* being on planets for assorted reasons, but there weren't many who *couldn't* be on planets.

Artificial gravity was generally set to the nearest inhabited planet by default, after all, which meant anywhere in the Icem System outside of Tarsus orbit was most likely set to Denton's eighty-five percent of Earth's gravity. Tarsus had about half that gravity, so most stations in orbit of the outer planet matched the smaller world's gravity.

"She's prepared to see us?" EB asked instead.

"She is," Everest confirmed. "Of course, the second-most-senior judge on the station is a touch booked up."

"We need to see her *soon*," EB told him. "Like you said. I'm prepared to be available at her convenience."

"That's good. Twenty-two hundred hours this evening. I...get the impression she's pushing her scheduled *bedtime* to squeeze us in, given the warning I got for if this was a waste of her time," Everest said.

"The Minister wants to attend."

Everest whistled silently. "Okay, I don't think I need to worry about Iliescu reinventing corporal punishment to remind me not to upset judges, then."

"No. No, you don't. Where does Her Honor want to meet us?"

39

HIGH HOME STATION, unlike Teamster Station, had always been intended to have a wide variety of residences aboard. It was the largest single space station in the Icem System, and the builders had allowed for continuous expansion.

In EB's opinion, it was as clever a design as he'd ever seen, the kind of design advantage that had nothing to do with technology and everything to do with someone actually thinking in the long term. That was a rare gift in every sphere of human civilization.

Ring Five had been part of the original construction and, like Ring One—the actual space dock—the newer additions had left much of it on the exterior of the station. Where Ring One used that position to continue to operate as necessary, Ring Five used it for decoration.

The main promenade of the ring was carefully angled, a slow shift that almost evaded attention until the outside of the station became the ceiling—a ceiling that held a series of immense windows looking "up" onto Denton.

That transparent-roofed hall was clearly the beating heart of High Home's political district. The primary courthouse had seen stone pillars brought up from the surface to create a classical façade that opened on to the triple-galleried concourse. A second structure, facing the courthouse across the mall, was slightly less ornate but still clearly governmental—the station's equivalent of a town hall for its hundred thousand residents.

Those two structures divided the first gallery in half, rising fully half the height of the open space. Around them clustered a series of high-end shops, restaurants and key offices.

Following Everest with Vexer, EB found himself feeling out of place. He could deal with money—he *had* money—but this place reeked of power. Not just local power, either. There was a tone to the decorations, the offices, even the layout... Something about it all told him that if Icem's Parliament was holding secret meetings, they held them there.

"First gallery remains commercial," Everest murmured as they found an open elevator. "Second is mostly offices. Top gallery is residential, about half mind-bogglingly expensive and half official residences that go with local offices."

"So, we're going all the way up?" Vexer asked. He sounded even more uncomfortable than EB—but then, power in his home system came with literal ownership of thousands of people. People like Vexer.

"Yes, but it's not what you're thinking," Everest told them as he punched a command into the elevator. "Iliescu doesn't live under the giant window. There is a more... Well, *affordable* isn't the right word, but let's say it's less extravagant, section of apartments on the same deck as the third gallery but without the open sky."

"Why come through here, then?" EB asked.

"Two reasons," the cop said. "One, access to any residential area on Ring Five's top deck is limited. This is the easiest way up without jumping through hoops.

"Two..." Everest shrugged. "This is the single most secured area on the station, EB. If someone is going to cause trouble here, the special tactics team is based *there*."

He pointed to an unassuming office on the first gallery, now beneath them as the elevator rose smoothly toward the outside of the station.

"Two officers in power armor at all hours," he noted. "Ten more suits in the armory. Thirty-six officers total trained in the gear, eight on duty at any time.

"If our friends come after us here, they're not making it far."

EB was…less confident in the ability of local security to deal with whatever toys the Bastion's security team had. Someone had, after all, snuck a heavy projectile weapon onto the station and repeatedly shot Hadzhiev in the back, after all.

MISGIVINGS ASIDE, they made it into the "back" neighborhood of Ring Five without incident beyond Everest flashing an invitation at a robotic security system. That particular security gate had made EB nervous, but it allowed them through without a blip.

Justice Shahar Iliescu of the High Home Station Senior Court lived in a garden. Quite literally, a small artificially lit atrium was tucked away near the security entrance to the community and four units faced onto it.

At least EB had no trouble identifying which home was Iliescu's. It was the one where Vortani's younger suited guard was sitting on the bench outside.

"Captain Bardacki," Makram Blake greeted him cheerfully. "A pleasure to meet you again. The Minister is inside. We've swept the perimeter and secured the atrium. Everything should be secure, and Her Honor has activated her privacy systems."

"Thank you, Blake," EB told him. "May we go in?"

"Of course."

The bodyguard opened the door for them, giving him an opportunity to discreetly scan them for unexpected weaponry. Blake seemed much warmer this time, but he was still taking no chances with his principal's security.

EB approved.

The inside of the apartment suite spoke to a green thumb that EB could never match—but also, he quickly realized, to an oddity. There were *no* plants in the space that were local to the Icem System.

Unless his initial data search was badly off, every one of the flowers and shrubs growing in small pots around the living room they'd stepped into was a pure Old Earth strain.

"Prasada Everest," a firm voice greeted them. "You are causing trouble again."

"I never set out to cause trouble," the detective told the gorgeously silver-haired woman seated at the other end of the room.

Justice Shahar Iliescu looked like she knew the exact limits of that. She was about Everest's own late sixties, EB judged, making her older than EB himself. She looked like she was physically active, her hair done in a practical braid that was concealed behind her in the chair as she studied Everest and his guests with sharp green eyes.

"The first time you assured me that you never set out to cause trouble, Prasada," Iliescu noted calmly, "you proceeded to single-handedly break through Director Wexler's security detail and assassinate the man within the next twenty-four hours.

"That phrase has felt like a warning ever since."

EB concealed a grin, glancing around the room to see who else was in the Judge's home.

He'd expected Sarah Vortani. The politician was seated on a large chair matching Iliescu's, one of a set of eight arranged into a octagon around a tree roughly the same height as EB. There was no other furniture in the front room, though he could see closed doors that presumably led into the rest of the residence.

He did *not* know who the man sitting next to Sarah Vortani was. The stranger was older than Everest or Iliescu, he judged, with his hair long gone—and a significant portion of the skin on his head replaced with visible metal plating.

At some point, the stranger had taken an injury that *should* have killed him and had lived long enough for extensive cybernetic reconstruction. EB might not have known who the man was, but the body language—even sitting—and the cybernetics told him *what* the man was.

A soldier.

"Take a seat, folks," Iliescu instructed. "I've agreed to this meeting because this gentleman has an account of some depth with me. The arrival of one of my theoretical *bosses* has piqued my curiosity as well, so here we are."

"May I have your permission to double-check your security systems?" EB asked. "We have reason to believe that the network was compromised."

"Feel free, Em…"

EB smiled as he dove into his headware, ignoring her implied question. The apartment's systems were decent, he judged. Most importantly, they were air-gapped from the rest of the station datanet.

That was likely part of the privacy systems he'd been told were active. Several localized signal-blanketing systems were isolating the datanet in the unit from the station. It was…acceptable. The generator that Lan had given EB was more advanced but not enough more advanced to make up for the main system being built into the structure.

"It'll do, I think," he told Everest. "I'm impressed."

"Well, Em *Impressed*, perhaps some introductions are in order?" Iliescu asked drily. "We all know Everest and Minister Vortani, of course, but I do not know who you two are."

"I am Captain Evridiki Bardacki of the freighter *Evasion*, and this is my fiancé, Vena Dolezal," EB introduced himself and Vexer crisply. "We have found ourselves, due to assorted…events, let us call them, waging something of a private war against the Siya U Hestî while trying to make our way through your local stars."

"You've picked quite the enemy," Iliescu told him. "Though, from what I have heard of the Siya U Hestî's problems of late, it appears that I should perhaps say *they* picked quite the enemy."

"Lady Breanna Tolliver decided that I was going to work for her or else," EB said. "And then I rescued a runaway from their trafficking operation, one they were planning to use as a data courier."

He shrugged broadly.

"The Siya U Hestî would not leave us be, so we arranged the attack on the Cage that I believe everyone is aware of."

"Well, that fits with other information I have and adds to my piqued curiosity," Iliescu replied. "And, Sarah? You should introduce your guest as well, I think."

"I can introduce myself, if I may," the old man rumbled. His voice was one of the deepest EB had ever heard, with clear tones to suggest artificial adjustment. More than just his skull had taken a beating along the way.

"I am Gustav Kerper, once an officer in the Icem System Defense Force. These days, a grumpy retired old fart who raises horses and occasionally races shuttles."

"He is also my father," Sarah Vortani said calmly. "And the sole surviving flag officer of the Directorate-era ISDF."

"Which is why I was never more than a Commodore." Kerper smiled thinly. "After twenty-five *years* as a Commodore, I finally got the hint and retired. My service was always to Icem, not the Directorate, but I understand that is difficult for some to see."

"I assume Minister Vortani trusts you, then," EB told him with a similar smile. "What we are about to discuss must be held in absolute confidence. People have died because they did not keep these secrets. People *will* die if we fail to keep them."

"Well, Captain Bardacki, I believe you have everyone's attention," the judge said. "I suggest you begin at the beginning and walk us through to today. What brings you to Icem—and what does your private war have to do with *us*?"

WHEN ILIESCU SAID "AT THE BEGINNING," she really meant it. Between starting at the unexpected invitation to meet Lady Breanna aboard the Star Plaza space station orbiting the Diomhair—the rogue planetoid that was the only place to discharge nova-drive static in the Fasach Expanse—and the Judge's continued incisive questions, getting through the events leading to them sitting in that quiet greenery-filled living room took EB over an hour.

Throughout it all, Vortani and Kerper were silent and listening. Vexer occasionally interjected to add details or explanation in response to one of Iliescu's questions, but, mostly, EB talked and Iliescu prodded.

He finished with their assessment of the location of the Bastion the previous night.

"Deus Three," she repeated. "And you're certain, Captain Bardacki?"

"There is no *certainty* in this kind of analysis, Your Honor," EB conceded. "We have tracked several ships that we believe are the trafficking freighters to Deus Three. We know that they shifted identity beacons several times getting there—something that is illegal in most star systems.

"We do not know where exactly on Deus Three they landed—but we do know that only one of them left."

"I will need full copies of your analysis, Captain," Iliescu told him. "The kind of blank check I have to write for the operation you need requires a great deal of support. I am comfortable that we are justified in the mission, but we need to make certain that we move against the right location and with the right authority."

"If you sign off on the warrant, I can arrange the rest," Vortani said quietly. "Do we need more-detailed scan information of Deus Three?"

"There's no way you can get it without alerting them," Kerper told his daughter. "Three is an airless rock. This Bastion is going to be embedded in that rock, well concealed and likely well defended.

"To detect it from a distance would require focused active sensors or the movement of key ISDF sensor arrays to synchronize multiple views," he continued. "Neither would avoid notice."

"I don't want to go in blind, but you're right," EB admitted. "We can probably jigger an innocent course that gets us close, but the actual raid will need to follow the sensor pulse within minutes."

"It might be worse than you think, Captain," the old officer told him. "Against most planetary targets, you're at worst looking at HVMs for ground defense. On a moon with no atmosphere, however…they almost certainly have plasma cannon arranged around the facility.

"Your raid will need to hit fast and hard, likely preceded by orbital kinetic strikes to disable those plasma-cannon emplacements. You need at least an attack squadron, Captain—and you've already said we can't trust the ISDF."

"We're not exactly going to go ask Nigahog to lend us a squadron to attack our own star system," Vortani snapped.

"No," EB said calmly. "But there are alternatives to an open assault. Between all of the information we have on the shipping list and the scramble codes—and on Ansem Hadzhiev himself!—I think I can rig up an authentication beacon that will at least confuse their initial coms and scanners while we approach."

"That will put whatever ship is approaching at massive risk," Kerper said. "And there could only be one ship, I suspect?"

"It would have to be *Evasion*," EB conceded. "I suspect I can borrow Captain Zelda's ground troops, and if the IBI can put up some hands as well..."

"Deception will not take you all the way, Captain," Kerper noted. "You will still need to disable those plasma cannon from the air. May I see the specifications for your ship?"

EB flicked them over to the other man's headware. He and Kerper were seeing many of the same issues, he suspected. Military training had some universal constants, after all.

"Interesting," Kerper said. "Your cargo bays... Hmm."

"Ser?" EB asked, instinct causing him to treat Vortani's father as a superior officer.

"We can't involve the ISDF," the old Commodore repeated. "So, nova gunships, which would be our best option, aren't possible. Monitors are too slow for this purpose—trust me; I spent thirty years commanding them.

"The closest monitors are at Tarsus. Ten to twelve hours' flight from Deus Three, and the Bastion *will* see them coming. But...I do believe our Guard cutters will fit in your cargo bays, Captain."

Kerper flipped another set of specifications back to EB.

Each of his cargo bays was ten meters square and fifty meters long. The gunships were forty-seven meters long and slightly more than nine meters high and wide. Their weapons systems could be retracted inside the hull, which had been his original concern.

"You build these for export?" he asked slowly. "That's why they fit in a Megablock container?"

"We do," Vortani confirmed. "We export about a dozen of them a year. It's not a make-or-break for our interstellar trade, but it helps keep the assorted Guard and system-police forces in the region on similar pages."

"Each cutter has twenty-seven Guard personnel aboard, all of whom are trained for boarding actions," Kerper explained. "They can, for special purposes, double that. To actually fly them in combat only requires twelve—they're not warships and they've got a bunch of systems you're not going to need in a fight."

"I can probably get thirty mercenaries from Captain Zelda," EB said. "But can we find four cutter crews—a hundred people!—that we know we can trust?"

"I don't need to find a hundred people we can trust, Captain," Kerper told him. "You were a military officer, yes?"

"Nova-fighter pilot," EB confirmed.

"Lucky you," the Beyond flag officer, who would only know of nova fighters in theory, replied drily. "But the point stands, I think. I need four cutter captains I can trust, not a hundred Guards I can trust."

"We'll need more than just four ships," Vortani pointed out. "And these are people trained for boarding, not raiding buildings."

"Deus Three has less than one twentieth of a gravity," Vexer said. "They may as well be boarding a spaceship. It's almost certain the Bastion has artificial gravity."

"My service may never have quite reconciled itself with the fact that I worked for the Directorate, but I served for a long time," Kerper told them quietly. "There are favors I don't like to call in and stories I don't like to tell.

"But for this kind of situation? I can find four cutters and probably a special forces team or two. Led by officers I know and trust—and who I can rely on to know if their people can be trusted."

"All of that will take time," EB observed.

"So will the paperwork to make this entire stunt *legal*," Iliescu pointed out. "I will start on that, *discreetly*, in the morning. It will take me at least two days, assuming that all of Captain Bardacki's information and evidence agree with his story tonight."

"Then that tells me how long I have to call up my old friends," Kerper said.

"We will need some cover for that," Vortani said. "But I already have that in hand."

She smiled winningly and held a small leather folio out to Detective Everest. The old cop took it with the expression of a man handling a ticking time bomb.

"I'm reactivating your IBI commission, *Marshal* Everest," she told the man. "You have full Marshal authority as of four hours ago. That should cover commandeering our Guard cutters once my father has set things up."

"I was afraid that was going to get dragged up," Everest said quietly. "But given that Her Honor decided to bring my past as a rebel fighter into this, it's hardly the darkest mark on my record here."

"On the other hand, my dear detective, if you are no longer working for High Home, you can finally ask me out on a date," Iliescu told him with a winning smile.

40

TRACE RAN the footage a third time. She hadn't been needed at the big fancy meeting—or, for that matter, particularly *wanted* to be at the big fancy meeting—so she was spending the time going through the sensor data.

They'd tracked some of their known targets to the third moon of Deus. That told them where they were going but didn't tell them much about the Bastion. Given the information they *had*, though, she was now going through and collating a list of the ships that had visited the moon.

Distinguishing between ships that had flown by and ships that had landed was straightforward. There was definitely enough traffic that she wouldn't have picked them out without *knowing* that some ships had to be stopping at Deus III.

There was less traffic stopping there than she'd expected, but that made it easier to build her schedule. And brought her to the piece that she was double-checking.

Albatross's Mariner, flying as *Scarlet Peach*, had left the Bastion a few days before *Evasion* had arrived. They knew the ship had gone to Denton because they'd seen her there. She'd novaed away from Denton about thirty minutes after *Evasion* had arrived.

They'd assumed that *Mariner* had left the system. They had, according to the data Trace was looking at, assumed incorrectly.

The timeline was...painfully clear.

"Shouldn't you be studying or sleeping or something other than poking at that data?" Lan asked, sticking their head around her study door. "I don't know...video games or swooning over boys?"

Trace gave the ship's doctor a harsh look. They, of all people, knew *exactly* what Trace thought about the entire zone of romance, relationships, sex and boys at that moment. She figured that she might, eventually, get over that—and that at her current age, she had zero need to *rush* to get over it, either.

"This *is* kind of fun," she pointed out instead. "Though every so often I find something that's...unpleasantly confirming of what we thought."

"Oh?" Lan unfolded one of the chairs leaned against the study wall and took a seat. "I was here to pass on a message, but I can play rubber duck if you want."

"Rubber duck?" she asked.

"Old, old tradition in data analysis and programming," the doctor explained. "When you're sure you're *almost* there but can't quite get it to work, get a rubber duck—a toy of any kind, really—and explain your thinking and steps to it.

"Usually helps realize what you're missing."

She giggled. "I have Mistopheles in here for that," she told them, gesturing at the black stuffed cat sitting on the side of her desk.

It was a special version of a stuffed animal, designed for use in clinics and sterilizable in a medical autoclave. Lan had dozens of the critters in their medbay, but Mistopheles had been their gift to her when she first arrived on the ship.

"Mistopheles is good for that," they agreed. "But I can serve too, I hope."

"What's the message?" Trace asked, curious.

"*Zeldan Blade* is on her way to Denton," Lan said. "Reggie will be rejoining us by morning."

"That'll make me feel better," she admitted. "Because...yeah...not liking what I'm seeing."

"Explain?"

Trace brought the holographic projector built into the desk online with a thought. The three-dimensional model she'd been following in her headware wasn't visible to anyone else, after all.

"Okay," she said slowly. "So, time stamp is twenty-two minutes after our arrival in-system. I've got three locations up in the model: Deus Three, Tarsus orbit, and Denton orbit. Follow the layout?"

Lan studied the hologram for a few moments, then nodded.

"Okay," she repeated, then tapped an icon above Denton. "This is *Albatross's Mariner*, identifying as *Scarlet Peach* at this moment. I'm going to run the plot forward at ten to one—remember that the data from the other planets is time-corrected to account for lightspeed lag."

The doctor grinned and nodded as Trace started the playback.

Mariner vanished from the Denton plot, as expected. What Trace hadn't been expecting when she ran the initial analysis was that *Mariner* promptly appeared roughly two hundred thousand kilometers from Deus III.

"She disabled her beacon as she jumped," Trace said quietly. "She appears at Deus as *Ambrosia* and proceeds to land on the planet."

"So, she didn't leave," Lan murmured.

"No. And, well..." Trace gestured and the hologram rewound to the moment of *Mariner*'s arrival in Denton orbit.

"She launched from Deus as *Azure Pinata* and then jumped to Denton three days before our arrival," she noted. "Less than two days later, Commodore Wu's shuttle crashed. A day after that, someone shot Hadzhiev in the back.

"I don't have his time of death," she admitted, "but I suspect that his killer was on that ship. They came from the Bastion on one of the ships Hadzhiev sent there, arranged an 'accident' for Commodore Wu and then murdered Hadzhiev.

"And then they left. It *looks* like a ship named *Scarlet Peach* arrived in-system, did some light cargo exchange while discharging static, and left the system after that."

"Nothing unusual there, three days at an orbital for crew R&R and supply purchase," Lan murmured. "Except that while they were buying supplies, someone was hunting."

"Yeah. I don't have access to shipping records, but she might have been buying foodstuffs and such for the Bastion. I doubt she arrived with much in terms of cargo."

"We'll ask our local friends to check on that, I think," Lan told her. "More information never hurts."

"Yeah, well..." Trace zoomed the plot forward to a new point in time. "*Ambrosia* launched from Deus here. Jumped to Tarsus as *Liberal Application*. Docked, purchased fuel, discharged static—minimum timeframe, really, barely two days in orbit. But look at the time frame."

Lan looked and then they swallowed hard.

"They arrived in Tarsus orbit about six hours after we met Ali," they observed.

"And they were most definitely *in* Tarsus orbit when Ali died and that freighter self-destructed," Trace said quietly. "We knew that they were involved, but...it's still something else to *see* it."

"Why *Mariner*, though?" Lan wondered aloud. "We presumed that the Bastion had ships in place—and *Mariner*'s an odd size, too. There were both bigger and less-noticeable options among the ships Hadzhiev sent them."

"I don't know," Trace admitted. "It's small enough to not draw the notice a larger ship would, but it's not a standard ten-kay tramp, either. It might just be that *Mariner* is armed where the tramps aren't."

"What kind of specs do we have on *Mariner*?" Lan asked.

Trace blinked as she poked through the original contents of the datavault in her head. The purpose of the vault had been a full "all systems, contacts and protocols" update for a senior Siya U Hestî leader, which had given her a *lot* of information to play with on the Cartel once they had access.

Of course, the fact that she'd had all of that was why the Siya U Hestî hadn't been able to let her walk away.

"Here," she told Lan, swiping away the model of the three planets and replacing it with a one-to-one-hundred scale model of *Albatross's Mariner*.

It was an oddly...humpbacked shape. The main cargo bay was a block fifty meters long, twenty wide and ten high. Then there was the "hump," an upper structure that started about ten meters back from the front of the ship and rose to the same ten-meter height as the main cargo bay at the back, with the plasma-cannon turret mounted on top.

"Huh."

"What?" she asked the doctor.

"Most ships I've seen have their cargo bays laid out much like *Evasion*," Lan told her. "Subdivided into spaces large enough to take a Megablock. Not much needs to be hauled that's bigger than five thousand cubic meters, and usually anything like that is shipping in collapsed sections, anyway.

"Not many single-piece cargos that won't fit in a Megablock." They *hrm*ed, studying the schematic. "*Evasion* is actually unusual in that she *can* take out the subdividers. It would be a giant pain, as I understand it, but she's designed to do it and allow us to haul bigger single cargo pieces. We could, theoretically, stick a pair of tramp freighters or even nova gunships in our main cargo bay.

"But...like I said, that's unusual. Most tramps run a single five- or six-thousand-cubic-meter bay, big enough to stick a Megablock in, but that's it. Something *Mariner*'s size I would have expected to have two bays, one pressurized by default, one unpressurized by default."

Trace was following their lecture so far and turned her attention back to the ship.

"But it only has one cargo bay, fully pressurized," she noted softly. "Which...makes sense for trafficking, doesn't it?"

"I imagine she was built for livestock transport or something similar," Lan said grimly. "There's not a lot of need for a ship with ten thousand cubic meters of pressurized cargo space—and most would meet that need by putting in pressurized transport units."

"So...they needed ten thousand cubic meters of space for something," Trace guessed. "Five or six thousand on a tramp wouldn't do; they needed more."

"But they didn't need enough more to use one of the thirty-kilocubic ships we know arrived," the doctor agreed. "Though that's assuming they have holds that can be opened up. And whatever ships are at the Bastion apparently don't have open holds, either.

"*Mariner* might be the only ship they have that can handle whatever it is they're doing." They shook their head. "I just...don't understand *what* they're doing. This is the ship that shows up when they assassinate people. It's just transporting *people*.

"Why does it need that much cargo space?"

Trace wasn't sure. But she suspected the answer might be important.

41

PRASADA EVEREST'S NEW/OLD job had not changed his dress or mannerisms. The gray-haired Marshal walked onto *Evasion*'s bridge in the same gray suit that looked ill-fitted to cover light body armor and a shoulder holster.

EB looked up and nodded to Prasada's escort, Tate.

"Thank you, Tate," he told her. "Send Reggie and Zelda up to the bridge when they arrive? They're due in about ten minutes."

Tate returned his nod and vanished out of the bridge.

"Is this *big* enough for this kind of meeting?" Everest asked, glancing around *Evasion*'s cramped bridge.

"It'll do," EB replied. Vexer was already sitting at the navigation console, and EB was in the captain's seat. There was one other console —communications—and a couple of extra chairs for observers that didn't have the luxury of their own screens.

The ship's weapons were controlled from a separate post attached to the dorsal turret. It wasn't spacious or luxurious, but it served EB's needs just fine.

"I retired from being a Marshal a long time ago," Everest said, taking the seat at the coms console. "Never wanted to go back. So, damn you, just a little, for getting me into a mess where I'm carrying that badge again."

"Are you at least getting a date out of it?" Vexer asked.

Everest sighed, then chuckled.

"Shahar and I have been genteelly ignoring mutual attraction for... twenty years? Thirty? She was married when we met. He passed away, a decade ago." Everest shook his head sadly. "Our friendship was sufficient to make her recuse herself from most cases I was involved in, but it's still...impolitic for cops to date judges.

"She never said anything. I never said anything. We both knew."

"And?" Vexer prodded.

"And I have promised her that if we survive this, I will take her to dinner," Everest said. "That means I'll either be keeping the Marshal badge or retiring entirely."

"Which are you thinking?" EB asked, curious.

"Probably the badge," Everest admitted, suiting EB's suspicions and Zelda's description of the man. "I was one of the first IBI Marshals, back before we had a damn clue how to replace the security apparatus that we dismantled.

"The first batch had too much authority, and we reduced it as time went on—but folks still tended to treat the originals as if we *had* that authority still. So, one by one, we gave it up and went to different lives."

He stared off into space for a moment, a very recognizable expression on his face.

"There were other reasons, too," he admitted. "But let's say that being a homicide detective on High Home Station was my cushy retirement. Now...well, saving hundreds from traffickers sounds worth carrying the badge again."

"Glad you think so," EB told him. "I'd hate to still be trying to do this alone."

"If you tried to do this alone now, EB, I might have to arrest you," Everest said drily. "Even the leeway we give the Trackers' Guild doesn't stretch far enough to allow planetary assaults."

"You'd be surprised what we get away with, though," Zelda interjected, the Tracker stepping through the bridge entrance with Reggie.

"I've done stuff about as blatant, though not in Icem, I have to admit."

"That's a relief to hear, Lisa," Everest told her with a smile. "It's good to see you."

"I'm glad to see I didn't steer EB wrong when I sent him to you," she replied. "I'm also glad, though I'll deny it if anyone repeats this, for the professionalism and efficiency of the Tarsus Orbital Guard.

"They had every right to make the aftermath of Ali's death far more of a nightmare for us than they did. Reggie being there to answer questions helped," she said, nodding to the weapons tech, "but they did everything to the nines and they did it in seventy-two hours. I'm impressed."

"How much of a hard time did you give them?" Everest asked.

"I was *nice*. Ish."

"They let you all go in the end, though?" EB asked.

"Our authority to pursue Ali was clear," Zelda said. "We had detailed helmet footage of the entire time aboard the shuttle, which made it clear that *we* didn't set off the bomb—and the TOG's own sensor records showed we hadn't sent any transmissions to the *Alex Star*."

"So, they could confirm *you* didn't sabotage her," EB murmured.

"At least in theory. It's not like they know who *did*, so..." Zelda shook her head. "That's a damn mess."

"Hopefully, it's one we'll find answers for on Deus Three," Everest told her. "Is there anyone else we should bring into this discussion, EB?"

"No, not unless you have people who need to be in on it?"

"Most of my people have been quietly briefed in secure rooms," Everest said. "We're just about ready to kick off on our side, once we get the official warrant. Shahar says tomorrow, which fits with her original timeline and leaves us enough time to get things aligned neatly."

"So, what are we aligning at this point?" Zelda asked. "I'm guessing I'm not taking *Blade*, novaing out to Deus Three and raining fire down on the Bastion from on high?"

"No matter what happens, we aren't going to have the information for precise-enough targeting to make that a useful option," EB pointed out. "Our only real chance of getting close to the Bastion is using the identification codes I've rigged from Hadzhiev's message and the scramble codes.

"I only give *those* about a sixty percent chance of working, but they should get *Evasion* in close enough to locate the facility and begin a landing."

"If we're relying on codes and a theoretically friendly reception, *Blade* can't come with you," Zelda observed.

"Hence where the IBI and the Denton Orbital Guard come in," Everest told them. "Sometime this afternoon, EB, you'll get a contract offer from the DOG. They want to experiment with using unspecialized ships as transport tenders for their cutters. Officially."

"That is a neat bit of cover," EB conceded. "So, we accept the contract, fly over to the marshaling station and pick up a cutter or two?"

"Four," the local told him. "K-Five, K-Twelve, K-Sixteen, L-Three. They're all roughly the same size; L-Three is a new-generation ship with slightly better sensors and weapons."

"With full crews?"

"Full crews," Everest confirmed. "You're also going to have some passengers sneaking aboard between now and morning. Thirty-two commandos of the ISDF's Orbital Drop Regiment will be joining us here on *Evasion*."

He raised a hand.

"I know the commanding officer, Jamie Everest, personally—he's my nephew. The other thirty-one have been vouched for either by Jamie or by other individuals we trust. No one has been even half-briefed on this mess without being thoroughly vouched for and vetted."

"We've still got enough people involved to make this risky," EB murmured.

"We do. On the other hand, there are no digital records of any of this so far and all discussion has been in fully secured spaces, Faraday-caged and air-gapped from system datanets. It's not perfect, but I *think* we're secure so far."

"We have to be," Zelda said. "There's not much else we *can* do. If you've the space, EB, I and my ground team will happily come along."

"You'd be more than welcome," he told her. "I'll gladly pay your way."

"This mission, EB, draws on a preexisting account of great depth. The Siya U Hestî have, ah, *prepaid* for their demise, in my opinion."

"I think it is safe for me to commit the IBI to cover your regular fees, Captain Zelda," Everest noted. "The Siya U Hestî have made their bed, yes, but Icem will benefit from the removal of this unknown cancer from our system."

"Everything is in place, then?" EB asked.

"All the parts are moving. When you head out in the morning to pick up the cutters, we should be good to go," the local confirmed.

"What about backup?" Zelda said. "If this place was meant to restore the cartel with its own resources, I'd expect to find pirate ships or even some proper warships out there."

"Commodore Kerper felt the same way. He has talked to some old friends and arranged for the Third and Fourth Gunship Squadrons to engage in training maneuvers around Templar," Everest said with a chuckle.

"He has even, as I understand, talked his way aboard as an observer. He has sealed orders reactivating his commission and placing him in command of the two squadrons. If things go severely sideways, he'll bring eight nova gunships in within minutes of being informed."

"How the hell did he get that kind of support?" EB asked. "That's more information in the ISDF's hands than is safe."

"The training exercise isn't particularly unusual," Everest pointed out. "The orders, as I understand it, are handwritten and signed by Admiral Altan Pereyra—the senior uniformed officer of the ISDF...and one-time chief of staff to Commodore Gustav Kerper."

The detective shook his head.

"I trust Kerper to have handled the discussion in a way that didn't hit a digital network," he concluded. "Which means that unless someone the old man personally knows and trusts—*and* is the senior military officer in this star system!—sold us out, we should still be clear."

"Everyone on this little joyride is involved on the basis of *someone knows and trusts them*," EB conceded. "Too many people are involved for me to think the Bastion has no idea we're coming. Their security and intelligence have been too good for me to think we have complete surprise.

"But I think the details and the timing will be a surprise, and that gives us a chance."

It had to. If nothing else, EB suspected that if the ISDF sent a nova flotilla to Deus III, the very prisoners they were trying to rescue would immediately become hostages.

Breanna Tolliver had pulled that at the Cage—and he doubted whoever she'd picked to run her fallback base had any more scruples than she'd had!

42

EB HAD SPENT over thirty years of his life landing small spaceships on bigger spaceships as his main day job. Even in peacetime, nova fighters were called on to patrol trade route stops, inspect freighters and a thousand other jobs where a small, tactically faster-than-light space-craft came in handy.

He had lost track of the number of times he'd made a landing on a carrier—but the memory of the first time he'd done so manually, as a twenty-year-old cadet, stuck with him. Even with the reflexes and assumption of invincibility of youth, that had been a white-knuckle experience he'd never forgotten.

Nine hundred and ninety-nine times out of a thousand, a nova fighter landing on a carrier was managed by computers. Apollo's System Defense Force still insisted that their pilots were *able* to make the landing manually and trained for it.

But even for those landings, EB had at least been landing a space-ship *designed* to land on a ship *designed* for it to land on.

The Denton Orbital Guard cutter pilots he was watching had no such luck. EB had rigged up what he figured was a decent "bouncing ball" guidance system based on *Evasion*'s shuttle-flight and cargo control systems, but his four cargo bays were no more designed to hold cutters than the cutters were designed to fit in them. Even the cargo bay's handling systems were useless here, designed for *far* smaller units of cargo.

At least the cutters were designed to *land*. They had to be able to touch down on a planet and take off again under their own power, which meant that they hadn't had to rig up any kind of docking array. He'd turned on the gravity generators under *Evasion*'s cargo bay, and the cutters would "just" land inside the bays.

"L-Three, adjust your vector up by two degrees," he said over the radio. He checked the guidance system. The guiding line *he* was sending was right.

L-3's pilot was drifting. It wasn't *much*, but given that the cutter was still a kilometer away and approaching at forty meters per second, a two-degree difference could easily see the cutter miss *Evasion*. Or, worse, *hit* the freighter.

"Got it," the woman on the newest cutter replied. "I'm showing aligned with the beam... Wait...wait. Oh, for crying out loud."

"Chief?" The voice in the background was presumably L-3's commander, as opposed to the warrant officer flying her.

"L-Three is brand spanking new," the pilot replied—her course shifting into alignment as she spoke. "And we've never needed this close an alignment between our com receiver and our nav software before.

"And our com receiver isn't in the same place as it is on the K-series. By just enough to, as Captain Bardacki just warned us, put us two degrees off-vector. I'm compensating now and putting a note in to make sure we update the software."

"I have you on the ball," EB confirmed. Apparently, the L-series cutter was using the same software as the K-series cutter—which made sense but could result in exactly the kind of problem L-3's pilot had just flagged.

"Distance is five hundred meters; slowing to twenty MPS," the pilot replied. "I confirm control has us on the line. Last chance for prayers and course corrections."

EB had already guided K-12 into one cargo bay. He had a pretty good idea of what they were doing now, but L-3's pilot had only been able to *watch* that process. Now seconds ticked away as the cutter approached the open cargo bay, and even he held his breath.

As the cutter reached the edge of the cargo bay, her velocity cut even further, to a single meter per second relative to *Evasion*. There was barely fifty centimeters of clearance around the cutter on each side, but the pilot deftly held the center line as she drifted the ship, meter by meter, into the cargo bay before activating the landing gear.

"We are down," L-3 reported. "Locked to the bay floor; clear on all four sides. Thanks for the ride, Captain Bardacki."

EB grinned. At this point, it was likely that at least the pilots—Chief Warrant Officers who served as second-in-command of their ships— had been briefed. The Chief knew *exactly* what she was thanking EB for.

"We have two more of your friends to load aboard before we actually give you a ride anywhere," he told L-3's command crew. "Sealing Bay Two and opening Bay Three for K-Five!"

THE NATURE of orbital-guard work meant that the cutter pilots were far more used to precision flying than EB had expected. He supposed they were the crews who had to physically lock on to distressed ships and haul them to safe altitudes, after all.

Still, the cutters' usual tenders were smaller than *Evasion* and carried the law-enforcement vessels on the *exterior* of their hulls—two at a time, at that, if he'd read the specs correctly.

Interstellar shipping of the cutters was done with Megablock cargo containers that were basically assembled around the completed hulls.

He wouldn't have wanted to rush the pilots, skilled and precise or not, but it only took forty minutes to load the four cutters into *Evasion*, and he figured they could have safely cut that by a quarter.

"If we give them another dozen practice runs, they could probably get the time down to under a minute per ship," he observed aloud.

"Or you could take a bit more time and load four at once," Everest suggested, then chuckled as both EB and Vexer stared at him in unfeigned horror.

"I flew nova fighters," EB said slowly. "I made manual landings on damaged carriers, flew in formation torpedo strikes, the works. I have *never*, even in the most grandiose and ridiculous of parade flight plans, *ever* flown with less than five hundred meters' separation between spaceships.

"Let alone *one* meter of separation. I don't care how good the DOG's pilots are. Nobody is asking that of them."

"Fair enough," the detective replied. "Outside my area. *Inside* my area, though..."

Everest had just arrived back aboard the ship as the last cutter was docking. Now he pulled an extraordinarily old-fashioned large envelope from inside his suit jacket and laid it on the communications console in front of him.

"I have received the warrant from Shahar Iliescu," he told them. "We are authorized to proceed to Deus Three by whatever means and timelines are convenient and engage in whatever maneuvers and operations are necessary to locate and secure the facility known as the Bastion to allow it to be searched for evidence of human trafficking and other illegal activity."

Everest drew a single sheet of paper from inside the envelope. It was clearly handwritten and signed, and the Marshal looked at it with scant favor.

"I've seen no-warning, no-knock warrants, all kinds of ugliness authorized by legal documentations when we had reason to think we needed surprise," he told EB. "There's a pretty standard tradeoff for it, honestly: without absolute certainty that we are facing lethal weapons, the people delivering a surprise warrant are explicitly *banned* from carrying lethal gear of their own.

"I can count on the fingers of one hand the number of no-warning warrants with lethal force authorized I've seen in my entire career, in both the IBI and High Home Security. I have *never* seen one that explicitly authorizes the use of effectively military force."

"We're going after a fortified slaver facility on an uninhabited moon," EB reminded Everest. "Nothing short of what we're bringing would stand a chance."

He wasn't entirely convinced they were bringing *enough*, though that was why there were two squadrons of nova gunships playing war games at the fourth planet.

"Either way. Everyone is aboard?" he asked.

"My nephew confirms he's got his commandos aboard. Zelda confirms her mercs are aboard, and I'm just waiting on confirmation that the cutter crews have been briefed," Everest replied.

The local blinked as he received headware messages. Those could, right now, *only* be coming from someone aboard *Evasion*. EB had locked down all external communication as soon as the last cutter was aboard.

"Everyone is aboard; everyone is briefed," Everest said calmly. "No incidents aboard the cutters. I didn't expect any, but it was always possible."

"I'm more worried about someone aboard the cutters being compromised and *clever* about it," EB admitted. "But that's fuel through the reactor now. Stand by to nova."

Everest nodded and promptly belted himself into the coms console seat. He clearly had no idea what to expect, and EB grinned at him.

"All right, everyone," EB said over the PA. Even the cutters were receiving the intercom message now. "We all know what we're doing, and the first stage of this is hopefully going to be very quiet.

"We are shutting down just about everything as soon as the jump is complete and then scrambling our signatures with the Siya U Hestî protocols.

"It shouldn't take too much luck for that to be enough to find the Bastion." He paused, shrugging. "I don't think we're going to get an unopposed landing, people, so check your guns, check your gear, check your armor.

"It's going to be quiet for a little bit...then it's going to get very, very loud."

EB waited half a second, then shrugged again as he gave *Evasion* the command.

"Nova."

43

THE TIMING HAD BEEN PROGRAMMED into the computers in advance, and the bridge lights dimmed, ever so slightly, as *Evasion* shut down most of her emissions. The lights didn't use *much* power, but across the entire ship, it added up.

The main distinction was that they weren't currently radiating heat, something that was going to bite everyone aboard the freighter very, *very* quickly if they didn't fix it.

EB had precalculated the scramble he was using, but they still had to *appear* as if they'd contacted the beacon in Tarsus orbit. Seconds ticked by as they waited out the false transmission delay—and the average temperature aboard *Evasion* crept up perceptibly with each one.

Then the timer ticked over, and new icons appeared on the main display.

"*Evasion* is now *King Kung*," EB announced. "*King* is the scramble sequence for the Siya U Hesti's largest ship, a thirty-two-KC transport named *Aloysius.*"

"They'll be able to tell the difference," Vexer warned.

"I know. But a few seconds' confusion will never hurt."

Deus III was sixty thousand kilometers ahead of them, the moon invisible against the backdrop of Deus itself at this distance.

"Taking us in," Vexer told him with a sigh. "Let's hope all of this cloak-and-dagger works."

"It should," EB murmured. He was setting up the next stage of his deception. According to the cartel's protocols, there would be a beacon hidden in the base, activated by certain codes most people wouldn't have.

Among the people who *would* have had the correct codes, he hoped, was Kunthea Chey. Along the way to breaking free and completely mucking up the Siya U Hestî's operations on Estutmost, Trace had ended up stealing the woman's entire code folio.

EB wasn't entire comfortable with the fact that his teenage daughter had ripped that out of someone's brain and then blown them up with a grenade, but he recognized the situation had been difficult.

Now he plugged those authorization codes into a tightbeam and targeted it at Deus III's north pole. At this range, the focused radio transmission would still hit about a thirty-kilometer-wide circle anchored on that pole—but if he *was* Chey, he'd have been trying to keep his presence covert from the stations above Deus.

He waited thirty seconds as they flew toward the moon. Only silence answered his first transmission, so he sent the transmission again, this time targeting the south pole.

"They may not be following standard cartel protocols," Vexer warned. "I'm running passive sensors to Reggie's station in the dorsal turret. He'll see if he can find it."

"Good." EB watched the map on his screen, showing where his two transmissions had landed. According to the files they'd pulled from the data vault, the Siya U Hestî had a few small covert bases on uninhabited planetoids. They would put reflectors at one of the poles, to receive exactly this transmission.

"It's also possible that the codes you're using wouldn't be valid for here," Everest said. "What happens then?"

The Marshal had delicately *not* asked where EB had got the codes or even what he was using them for.

"I *know* these codes are correct for the person they belonged to," EB admitted. "I have, thanks to a few bits and pieces from assorted sources, put together an approximation of Hadzhiev's equivalent."

He shook his head.

"Hadzhiev was a Level Nine and should have had access to the Bastion. If I've got it right, I can pulse the planet and get a landing beacon. If I've got it wrong...well, they'll know we're coming at that point, so scanning for the base won't give us away."

EB adjusted the transmission parameters and pulled up his carefully assembled Frankenstein authorization code. Parts were from files taken from the Cage. Parts were from the datavault. The rest was taken from the metadata of the message the man had recorded for him.

"Well, here goes nothing," he told the rest of the bridge, and hit a mental button. This transmission was a slightly wider tightbeam, intended to cover almost the entire moon while still being blocked from Deus.

If there was a polar beacon and a human was watching it, switching the codes alone might give away the game. He figured that combination was less likely, though, than that his patchwork authorization code would fail.

"Got it," Everest barked from the coms console. "We just got pinged by a linear sweep beam. Cycle is...eleven seconds."

Old-fashioned but functional, that was a beacon sending a contentless radio beam in a continuous circle. They could follow that all the way to the Bastion.

"All right," EB said. "The door is open and they're saying come on in." He grinned. "Let's see how long *that* lasts!"

THEY FOLLOWED the beacon back to their target, getting a good look as they approached.

"I'm not sure I would have picked that up on passives without knowing exactly where it was," Reggie admitted. "It looks like it's built into the base of the mountain here, at the end of this valley."

"I'm guessing weapon installations along the side of the valley," EB noted. "Looks like a crater?"

"Glancing impact on the moon would be my guess, yeah," Vexer told them. "We've got a decent-sized mountain at one end and a three-kilometer long 'valley' leading up to it. Like Reggie said, the Bastion is at the base of the mountain where the valley ends."

No approach from the other side of the mountain, EB judged. A scarlet dot was blinking on the screen, marking the origin of the beacon at the mouth of the valley. If they followed the directions as they were given, they'd arrive at the mouth of the meteor-dug gouge and probably receive new directions from there.

"I make it twelve plasma-cannon installations along the valley, seven on the north side and five on the south," Reggie observed, clearly following EB's thoughts to the problem of flying in as expected.

"Another four, it looks like, under a shared cover near the top of the mountain."

"Individually powered and controlled?" Major Everest, the detective's nephew and the commando CO, interrupted. "Any link back to the base?"

"I can barely tell where the guns are, Major," Reggie admitted. "They're in pop-up installations embedded in the rock. That said, they're plasma cannon, so they need to have a fusion reactor in easy reach. Most ground installations I've seen will have a micro fusion core on site just to fuel the gun—but they'll draw their hydrogen and control feeds through physical connections to a control center.

"*Theoretically*, there should be on-site crews of twelve to twenty, but I wasn't under the impression these guys were going to *have* three-hundred odd military-trained personnel."

"No. Maybe *a* hundred," EB agreed. "Can we get a better look at the base itself?"

"No," Reggie said flatly. "They picked the best damn place on the moon for their purposes. I think there's only about a four-degree slice of sky where you can get eyes down into that part of the canyon."

"And if we swing over into that slice, I suspect someone has some loud alarms to notify them," Vexer said. "We're three minutes out, EB. Last chance to change our minds."

"No, we're well past the last chance to change our minds," EB said with a chuckle. "Taking over direct control."

Vexer was a better navigator and a *good* pilot—but EB was a *better* pilot. Even with something as hulking and lumbering as the armed freighter.

"DOG cutters, stand by," he told their cargo. "I'll open the bays at roughly eighty klicks' altitude. We've downloaded the scan data we have, but I can't open fire with *Evasion*'s guns until you're well clear, which means we'll be on the ground before we can shoot at the air defenses.

"Lock them in and be damn sure of their locations." EB glanced over at Marshal Everest. "Marshal?"

EB, after all, didn't have the authority to actually give *orders* to the cutter crews.

"All boarding personnel are aboard *Evasion*, correct?" the Marshal asked.

Various affirmations came back, and Everest smiled thinly.

"Commandos, mercenaries and boarders will deploy to the Bastion directly from *Evasion*," Everest instructed. "Cutters will drop as Captain Bardacki specified. Cutters are authorized to destroy the cannon installations.

"Ground forces are not, I repeat, *are not* required to attempt nonlethal force," he continued. "Prisoners are better than bodies, but *our* people coming back alive is better than prisoners.

"Major Everest? Plan of attack?"

"We don't have a lot of information to go on yet," the younger Everest told everyone. "But we know what our primary objective is: locate, secure and retrieve the trafficking victims. Even securing the facility to search for additional evidence is a secondary objective.

"Therefore, our first course of action must be to locate the cryo-stasis facility and sever it from the Bastion's main command center. Once we've done *that*, we want to locate and take control of the main power center—and only then will we move on the command center itself.

"There are DOG personnel in the boarding teams who are trained and equipped to handle safe release from cryo-stasis," he concluded.

"They will remain in the cryo-facility while the rest of us move to secure the remainder of the facility.

"If we face excessive resistance, we will fully cut off the cryo-facility and attempt to revive the prisoners to extract them. So long as the hostages are secure, calling for further ISDF backup becomes an option."

"Until the trafficking victims are secure, they *are* hostages," EB warned everyone. "Do not, for one moment, expect the Bastion's personnel to place any value on their lives. They can and *will* kill them all to punish us for our attack.

"We need to get to them first."

A hundred kilometers' altitude. EB adjusted *Evasion*'s course carefully, doing his best to appear like he was approaching normally.

"We're blown!" Reggie snapped. "The mountaintop installation just pulsed us, *hard*. They know we're too big to be *Aloysius* now— Yep! Power signatures flaring across the cannon!"

EB followed his tech's report almost absently. The power signatures were on his own datafeeds, and he rode *Evasion*'s systems like an old friend. Only the mountaintop installation had their cannon anywhere *near* ready, and they weren't ready enough to fire on *Evasion* before he was down.

The positions along the canyon would be at least five minutes. They'd been cold, more focused on concealment than anything else, and they would pay for that.

"Cutters, *go!*" EB barked, a mental command throwing open the cargo-bay doors. The DOG pilots had been in the network with him and Reggie and moved faster than he'd dared expect.

The four ships shot out in a sequence they'd clearly sorted out in advance, cycling around *Evasion*'s bays clockwise until all four cutters were in space in under thirty seconds.

He'd allocated a full minute, which gave him time he hadn't expected to have. He threw *Evasion* into a hard dive, Harrington coils humming as she charged toward the planet at an ever-increasing velocity.

Above EB's ship, the four cutters spread out their formation and opened fire. Superheated plasma fell from the sky like rain, hammering into the one set of cannon now emerging from the ground.

None of the Bastion's guns would ever get a chance to fire. The cutters weren't designed for war, but their plasma guns were still more powerful than any starfighter's. Molten metal and rock blasted into the airless sky like a newborn volcano.

And through the storm of the Guards' fire, EB took *Evasion* into the canyon, still moving at a full kilometer per second as she plunged past the lip of the gouge through Deus III's crust.

Her Harrington coils actually *whined* audibly as he pushed them to full power, shedding every scrap of that velocity in under forty meters to leave *Evasion* suspended in the air on her antigrav systems alone, roughly ten meters from the bottom of the canyon.

She paused in the air for about three seconds as EB vented heat and let the coils cool, and then he sent the ship blazing up the canyon toward their target. It was entirely possible there were more defenses, concealed by the canyon sides and therefore able to be active and ready to fire.

Speed was of the essence, and he pulled through a full kilometer of the canyon in under five seconds, absentmindedly aware of Reggie sweeping the canyon walls with sensors and the targeting systems for his two turrets.

And then they were there. After all of the effort, all of the bloodshed and games and planning, part of EB had half-expected the Bastion to be some massive edifice of black stone, possibly literally weeping blood or fire to mark it as evil.

Instead, the canyon opened into a not-quite-cavern. The top opening was still barely a hundred meters wide, but the base of the canyon had either been naturally open or artificially expanded. *Evasion* flew into an open space, roughly a kilometer across and several long where it dug under the mountain, whose contents could have been any settlement on any airless world.

Seven domes of varying sizes filled the north two-thirds of the cavern, each containing several other structures and linked together by solid-looking surface passages. The south third of the cavern—to starboard as *Evasion* dove into the middle of the space—was serving as a hangar, holding a variety of spaceships.

There were enough ships in the hangar for EB to be sure all nine from Hadzhiev's list were there—but so were at least four nova gunships. Surprise, it seemed, had been as critical as he'd feared.

"Marking domes one through seven on the network," Reggie said in his ear as EB brought *Evasion* to a halt and dropped her, ever so gently, to the ground. "Dome Five appears to be the power station. Second largest dome, largest heat signature."

"Second largest heat signature is Dome Seven, the fourth-largest dome. I think that's our cryo-facility."

"I agree," Major Everest said. "All ground forces, *move*. Dome Seven is the first target. *Evasion*, can you provide covering fire?"

"Dorsal turret is up and live," Reggie replied. "Minimum power, but I'll put hellfire where you need it."

EB half-tuned out the conversation as he triple-checked the landing gear. The domes *definitely* had artificial gravity, because it was spilling out into the cave. Whoever had set the place up hadn't been worried about the effects outside the domes, though, as he'd landed in point two gravities and his scans showed the hangar had passages running point four.

"Watch your step," he told the landing force. "Three's natural gravity is basically nothing, but there's spillage from the generators for the domes. It's not even, and gravity may shift unexpectedly."

As he was speaking, he finished locking *Evasion*'s landing position down and rose from his seat.

"Where are you going?" Vexer asked.

"My armor is online and waiting for me in the landing bay," EB replied. "I have to see this through, love. To the end." He smiled sadly. "I need you to keep *Evasion* ready to go if things go sideways and have the coms ready to call in Kerper. You have to stay here."

Vexer also had armor, but he was *terrible* with it. EB's husband-to-be was no soldier.

"And make sure that *Trace* doesn't try to dig up *her* armor," EB finished with a smile. They'd needed Trace to act as a guide on the

Cage, so the teenager *had* power armor. But they did *not* need a thir-teen-year-old getting in the way in the Bastion.

There was a lot of value his daughter could provide, but she could do it from her little office.

No one, after all, had any idea what was waiting for them outside.

44

IT BEMUSED TRACE THAT, if any of the commandos and Guards and mercenaries had realized a thirteen-year-old kid was even aboard *Evasion*, none of them had raised any questions—and nobody had commented on the fact that said teenager had full access to the shared combat network.

Trace's job today was datanet overwatch. The last time they'd gone up against the Siya U Hestî, they'd learned that at least some of their facilities were protected by AMPs—autonomous mobile platforms, combat drones run by artificial stupids.

The ones on Estutmost had included override codes Trace had managed to trigger, though that had nearly caused a catastrophe all on its own when the stupids had received conflicting orders and their counter-hacking protocols had engaged.

Sane people designed their combat robots' counter-hacking protocols to shut down the machines—but then, sane people didn't build autonomous combat robots. They were generally illegal for a reason, after all.

The Siya U Hestî's protocols had sent the robots on a seek-and-destroy mission that was only loosely bound to an area or any kind of friend-or-foe identification. It was the counter-hacking protocol of someone who didn't *care* about collateral damage.

And Trace was grimly sure there was something equivalent there. She had pulled up all of the information she had on the hardware and software of the AMPs on Estutmost, as well the codes she'd used to partially seize control of them.

With all of that set up on the screens in her little study, as well as signal analysis running to see if she could find the Bastion's datanet, she was mostly focused on watching over Jamie Everest's shoulder.

The Major was stamped from much the same mold as his uncle, though he had a lot fewer injuries and his boosts were subtler. Trace was learning to see what her dads and Reggie saw when people moved, though, and she'd seen the patterns in Major Everest.

His systems had more flexibility than *Marshal* Everest's systems, and he'd had most of them turned off aboard *Evasion*, but she'd seen the tics in *all* of the commandos.

As her father explained it, boosts were uncommon outside of special forces and low-profile units. While a majority of Zelda's mercenary trackers, for example, were boosted, most regular soldiers wouldn't be.

Power armor, according to both EB and Reggie, rendered boosts pointless. That was why her Dad-E had *armor* but not boosts—and why Reggie's boosts were lighter than the commandos'.

"Watch your atmo integrity," Everest told his people as he followed his third squad off the ship. "Just because we've got ground and gravity, however fucky the latter is, doesn't mean there's any damn *air* out there. Your tin can gets popped, emergency seals only buy you so much time.

"Get to cover and rig a proper patch."

There was a rumble of acknowledgement on the network, Everest's commandos engaging in what even Trace recognized as good-natured grumbling at their commander's reminder.

"Drop Regiment is the tip of the spear," Everest continued. "Trackers hold the wings; Guards watch our backs."

Trace checked the tactical display showing the positions of the armored horde disgorging from her family's ship. Given the positions of the three distinct elements of their force, *those* instructions were as much a reminder as the commentary on the lack of air on Deus III.

Apparently done telling his people things they already knew, Everest *moved*, and Trace inhaled in sharp surprise. She saw everything he was seeing through a camera in his helmet. The network access she had would let her pull the same view from any member of the landing contingent, but Everest had seemed the best choice.

She'd known he was boosted, and she'd known armor made that mostly irrelevant, but even when Trace had worn her own power armor on the Cage, she hadn't really understood how much her untrained use of the suit had been slowing the mercenaries down.

Jamie Everest was an *expert* in his tools, and he moved a quarter-ton of battle armor like it was a second skin. Once he and his people started moving, they'd crossed most of the distance to Dome Seven before anyone could even blink.

For a few seconds, she even thought they were going to make it to the cryo-facility dome before the Bastion's defenders reacted…but they were not *that* lucky.

"Contact! Automated guns, sector Five-K."

Trace didn't understand the displays she was working with well enough to follow where sector 5K was—but fortunately, the software distributed across their landing force automatically updated. Red icons blazed on the screens, first a handful and then more and more as various hidden panels slid open to reveal heavy blasters by the dozen.

"Neutralize them," Everest said calmly—suiting actions to words, his own heavy blaster rifle started to spit fire at the nearest gun emplacement.

The heavy rifle was a step down from Reggie's assault cannon but still larger and more powerful than any other energy weapon Trace had seen. The automated weapon flashed into vapor as the blaster bolt struck home—but even as dozens of the defensive systems were destroyed, others opened fire.

The lead element of the assault was Everest's commandos, though, and they'd reacted with smooth professionalism. The emplacements the commandos had taken out hadn't been chosen at random, Trace realized, as the Icemi troops tucked themselves behind what little cover there was and dropped into dead zones in the fields of fire of the remaining automatic weapons.

"Reggie, cover us," EB's voice ordered on the channel—and a chilly stone settled into Trace's stomach as she realized her dad was outside the ship. A few seconds' search located the icon for his power armor and she shivered.

"On it."

EB was throwing targeting carets into the tactical network, Trace realized, and Reggie followed them skillfully. The commandos secured their own position, and *Evasion*'s upper turret made short work of the guns that they couldn't reach.

"We're clear, we're clear," Everest declared. "I've got three walking wounded I'm sending back to *Evasion*. Zelda's people and the Guards are untouched. I am approaching Dome Seven...now."

A full fire team of commandos had already secured the door to the dome by the time the Major reached it, one of them running a wire from their suit into the airlock's systems.

Trace should have recognized that connection was there already, she realized, and promptly located the trooper on the network and rode their connection into the airlock.

"We're working on— What?"

The teenager grinned at the surprised tone in the commando's voice as she fed the airlock her stolen security codes and activated its opening cycle.

"We have angels who live on high riding our network, trooper," Everest told the man. "Overwatch has the door. Let's make sure no one gets blasted going through it."

Another commando seemed to teleport out of nowhere and wordlessly placed a hand on the Major's shoulder.

"I know, Gunny," the officer told the newcomer. "I don't lead the way."

"First Squad, Fire Team Bravo," another voice—presumably the woman who'd silently reminded the Major *not* to charge through the door himself. "Ready?"

"Ready."

"Overwatch, check the lock cycle and watch their backs," the Gunny told Trace. "Bravo Team—go!"

Trace obeyed willfully, using her connection to the dome's datanet to control the airlock and try to access any internal security.

It was quickly clear that she only had access to the airlock itself.

"I need someone to set up a hard connection to the datanet inside the dome," she said quietly on a private channel to EB and Major Everest. "The external ports are very limited."

"The place was built by a paranoid monster," EB said grimly. "Can you manage that, Major?"

"Once we're in, yeah. Can you get us true overwatch from there?" he asked. He sounded unsure—probably because once he *heard* Trace's voice, he knew how young his datanet overwatch was.

"Get me systems access and I should be able to crack the whole thing open," Trace confirmed.

"You might be able to link from just having a node of the tacnet inside the dome," EB suggested. "But a hard link into the system and relaying back to *Evasion* should definitely get you—"

"Contact! Hostiles in the dome!"

Bravo Team's report cut through the conversation, and Trace switched one of her screens to show her the camera feed from one of the Bravo Team commandos.

Even as she did so, though, she was cycling the lock again. They'd only sent four people in the first time, but the lock could *hold* ten—and the helmet-camera view was showing her that Bravo Team was outnumbered.

There were a dozen people in full combat armor, same as the commandos, waiting inside the dome lobby. Blaster fire flared across the room, and even Trace, watching through a helmet camera, wasn't sure how the four commandos managed to get to cover without being shot.

"Hold on, Bravo; Alpha Team is right behind you," Gunny's voice said sharply. "Second Squad, move up to support. Third Squad, Fourth Squad, perimeter."

"Trackers, expand the perimeter. Guard, provide cover fire,"

Everest added, passing instructions beyond his own people—and leaving his own people, Trace noted, for Gunny to command.

Inside Dome Seven, the Bastion's defenders were learning what Trace had realized the moment she'd seen Everest move inside his power armor. Both sides being in armor might make the commandos' *boosts* irrelevant, but it didn't make their training or their skill irrelevant!

Two of the commandos were wounded, but they'd managed to deploy a quick-cast cement barrier behind their flimsy cover. The wounded troopers weren't moving from that barricade, but they were keeping up a steady stream of fire as the unwounded commandos moved to spread their base of fire—worming on their armored stomachs in a manner that would have wrecked the floor if it hadn't been plain metal.

Three of the Siya U Hestî armored troopers were down by the time Fire Team Alpha entered the lock, and Trace cycled it for them—with Everest and Gunny, adding six more commandos to the fight and evening the numbers.

The odds, it appeared, had *never* been in the cartel fighters' favor.

45

BY THE TIME EB reached Dome Seven, the disparate parts of their landing force had dug in as best as they could. Portable barricades surrounded the entrance, and it felt almost like everyone was holding their breath.

The first wave of defenses, the automated gun systems, were gone now. There would be a second string to the Bastion's bow. Maybe even a third and fourth.

For now, though, the focus was on the cryogenic facility, and Zelda was waiting for him at the airlock when he arrived.

"Shall we?" she asked.

"Have they found the cryo-pods yet?"

"You've heard as much from Everest as I have," Zelda reminded him, and EB shivered. The commando hadn't said much since seizing control of the dome lobby and starting his people sweeping the building.

Four commandos were in the airlock when it cycled open, two of them clearly wounded and being assisted by the others. That brought their list of casualties to eight, according to his math—five of the commandos and three of the Orbital Guard ratings who'd been hit by the autoguns.

No fatalities yet, but he was grimly aware that couldn't last.

He and Zelda entered the dome with her Sarge and another mercenary in tow, finding half a dozen Guards poking through the debris as the commandos watched the corridors.

"Everest, what's our status?" he asked over the net.

"Apologies; dealing with prisoners," the Icemi man replied. "We have eight of them; appear to be medical staff for the cryo-facility. It's..."

Everest trailed off, and then a line of flashing green arrows appeared on EB's vision through the tacnet.

"You have to see this," the Major said grimly.

The green arrows led them to a wide circular ramp, large enough for a cargo vehicle to roll down it. Following the ramp back up, there was a large vehicle airlock at the top of it that was still sealed.

"Why didn't we use *that* airlock?" EB asked with a chuckle.

"Because it has a truck blocking it on the outside," Everest told him. "We could move it, but speed seemed more important than bringing the most people through. Hurry up."

Something in the commando's tone warned EB that he wasn't going to like what he'd find at the bottom of the ramp. The worn stone had clearly seen a lot of use, and he found himself wondering about the rumors of the Bastion as a cave of wonders—was that what was underneath this dome?

Because they were definitely *underneath* it now. The ramp descended almost fifteen meters in a slow curve, easily traversed by wheeled transport, and then opened up into an immense underground void.

An immense, monstrous and horrifying underground void.

The ramp connected to the floor of the structure, and pathways large enough for the cargo vehicles split off in four directions, dividing the roughly circular room into quarters. A raised control station was positioned at the inside of each quarter, and Everest was standing at the top of the stairs to the north platform.

EB joined the commando slowly, surveying the arrays of cryo-pods with a chill horror in his heart. They'd come looking for a few hundred innocents, but what they'd found was...something else.

"How many?" he demanded.

Everest turned his armored face on the woman next to him—who EB had missed in his horror at the scale of the cryo-facility. She was incongruously dressed in casual workout clothes, baggy sweats that muffled her figure and left her looking particularly small and vulnerable.

Somehow, EB didn't buy *anyone* in this place faking vulnerability.

"Answer the question, Em," Everest said grimly.

"Facility is rated for twenty thousand," she answered. "Only the north quadrant is even powered, though, and we're operating at about thirty percent capacity."

EB did the math.

"Fifteen hundred people," he noted. "You have *fifteen hundred people* in here? They can't all be…"

"I don't know where they come from," the woman said instantly. "I just run the stasis systems and make sure everyone is stable and healthy. I had *no idea* what I was getting into when I took a remote nursing position!"

EB snorted. He wasn't sure he believed her…but that wasn't really up to him.

"That'll be for the Marshal to sort out, I suppose," he told Major Everest. "We have our own people coming in to take over managing the system. Let's get the prisoners out of here and start working on waking people up."

He shook his head.

"I don't know if we can *fit* fifteen hundred people on *Evasion*," he admitted.

"Once we've secured the Bastion, we can call for backup," Everest said. "But yes, we're moving the prisoners upstairs. We've secured the cargo airlock against internal use and are using it as a temporary holding cell."

There was a cold smile to his tone, even though EB couldn't see his face.

"They might be able to get the outer door open, but that's not going to do them much good."

The cryo nurse looked very pale and on the edge of fainting. She might be a good actress, EB figured. She might even be telling the entire truth, making her almost as much of a victim as the poor bastards in the cryo-pods.

Like he said, Marshal Everest would sort the innocent from the guilty. That wasn't part of EB's job, thankfully.

"There's a secondary power cell at the south end of the cryo-array," the woman half-whispered. "If you seize that, you should be able to stop Bast from cutting off power from the array."

EB glanced at Everest's faceless helm, not meeting the man's gaze, but the intent was there—both of them were still fully encased, after all.

"I'll send commandos. Who is—"

"Sers, we need you up here," a voice said on the network. "You all have to see this. You have to see this *now*."

SOMETHING about the body language of the troopers in the dome lobby told EB that he was looking at yet another ugly surprise. The commando who'd called them up was standing where the defenders had fallen, with a Guard with a white medic's patch on their shoulder standing next to them.

"What's going on, trooper?" Everest asked as he, EB and Zelda approached.

"We were checking to see if any of them were...well, alive," the medic replied. "And...there's no one here."

EB didn't follow until he stepped over and saw where the medic had started "taking off" the armor to check on the vitals of the defenders. The armor was empty.

"All of them," the medic said before EB could ask. "There was no one in any of the armor. I've never seen anything like it—they must have been rigged for remote control at some point."

"Trying to keep their handful of qualified armor users safe," EB murmured. "Or...something else."

"That's...concerning," Everest said. "But it doesn't change our plans. We need to move on Dome Five and keep overwatch on Dome One. I'm pretty sure One is the command center and we'll move on it third."

"Agreed," EB replied. "Zelda?"

"No contacts outside," she noted. "Nothing has so much as *twitched* since we took down the remote weapons. Something isn't right."

"We've found the people we're after," Everest said. "We need to make sure they're safe, and that means taking control of the power center in Dome Five."

"My people are ready," Zelda said. "Are yours?"

"Let's get some more of the Guard in to take over this one while we move out," the Major replied. "Check the networked sensors. I have the feeling we're missing something, and I'd prefer not to get stabbed in the back by something ugly."

"What about the network link?" EB asked. "Have we got a hard link into the Bastion datanet? I think that may be of use."

"My people didn't have the hardware," Everest admitted. "I thought we should be able to hack in via wireless?"

"There is no way in void that this place would let you prod authorization sequences via wireless," EB pointed out. "We need a hard relay into the datanet. I've got hardware that will work—you guys move on the power station."

"On it," Everest confirmed.

EB nodded and looked around the lobby. It took him a few moments to locate an office that looked promising—and less time to get through its locked door. The interior doors weren't designed to deal with power-armored fists.

He was running his own software as he checked the tacnet link. As he'd warned Everest, the system was auto-rejecting wireless connections from unknown sources. Someone in the system would need to authorize him to link in that way.

He could spoof it, given time, but he didn't *have* time, and there were other options. A chunk of his left vambrace slid open at a mental command, and he started pulling modules out. Building the connection wouldn't take long, but it would still take a while to break in.

"Contact!" one of the commandos barked. "Multiple vehicular contacts!"

EB might not have that time. The Bastion's defenders were making their move.

46

THE PROBLEM, Trace figured, with being thirteen and not quite sure what her exact position was with regards to the assault on the Bastion was that she didn't really have the ability to *complain* that the commandos had failed to get her the access she'd asked for.

In hindsight, with EB setting up the link for her, she realized she could have told *him* there was a problem. On the other hand, she'd still been riding Everest's helmet cam when he'd found the cryo-bays, and the sheer scale of the Bastion's prison had left her in mild shock.

Now a familiar threat loomed, and she swallowed down her fear and concern as she drew the data in from the tactical network. The landing force had clearly entered a security zone around Dome Five and triggered a reaction.

Explosive shells rained down on the forward element, forcing even the commandos back as two dozen AMPs of the same design she'd seen on Estutmost rose from concealed hangars under the ground. Blaster fire walked across the field, and the landing force retreated for a few moments—and Trace saw icons go red and then black.

Only then did the Bastion's defenders finally *talk* to them. An unencrypted transmission on an open channel, the tactical network automatically picked it up, scanned it for threats and shared it to everyone *Evasion* had brought with them.

"I could make all kinds of claims about private research facilities and illegal raids," a feminine voice said calmly. "But Bast has been watching Captain Bardacki since he got Ansem's message. You've proven surprisingly effective, Captain, but you've made a few key mistakes.

"Your communications off-world have been blocked. Your cutters have made a mess of my anti-air defenses, but you and your landing force aren't getting out of here without permission. You have badly underestimated the Bastion, Captain Bardacki.

"I suppose you can still leave, *maybe*, but your best choice is to surrender, or I will kill all of you."

Trace had three different programs running and added a fourth. She was tracing the control links for the AMPs, maintaining the link to the hardware EB was setting up, managing background data services for the entire tactical network and, now, trying to trace the person talking to them all.

To her surprise, someone responded to the stranger. Marshal Everest was using his own broadcast channel to make sure the defenders heard him.

"I am Marshal Prasada Everest of the Icemi Bureau of Investigation, and I have full warrants to secure this facility to search for signs of human trafficking and other crimes," the Marshal said calmly. "If you surrender now, that will be considered in your favor when this all goes to trial."

There was no response—but Trace had managed to locate the transmission anyway.

Everything was coming from Dome One.

"She's in the command center in Dome One," she flagged to the team leads. "AMPs are linked back to it as well."

A second set of signatures appeared on her screens, and she shivered as another dozen AMPs activated around the command center—and new signatures, marking human-sized combatants joining them.

Some of the new signatures appeared to be suits of power armor, though Trace had to wonder if anyone was in them—but many were something new. Clearly *not* power armor, bipedal forms over two and a half meters tall with built-in weapons.

"Humaniform combat robots," Zelda barked. "In the name of Allah, where did they even *get* these?"

Trace suspected that she now knew where the Siya U Hestî had got *all* of their combat robots: there. There was enough space in any of the domes for them to contain a factory, though supplies and key parts might be difficult.

But if this was the original source, then these robots *should* still have the override codes she'd stolen programmed into them. All she needed was to be able to make a connection...

There.

Pieces clicked together. EB's link to the datanet wasn't enough for her to access the Bastion's datanet yet, but it was enough for her to spoof the origin connection for the AMPs.

That let her make a link to the units around Dome Five and load in both EB's best hacking worms and the authentication codes she'd learned and used on Estutmost.

Between the software and her authorizations, the only defense the robots *should* have had was the secured link keeping her from making a connection at all—or if her codes were wrong. It was possible, after all, that the codes she'd taken from Chey wouldn't work on the drones at the Bastion.

"Yes!" she exclaimed aloud as the AMPs around the power station began to shut down.

It appeared that the Bastion's defenders hadn't been quite paranoid enough. The robotic tanks were dangerous but vulnerable, their artificial stupids incapable of seeing the difference between her orders and those coming from the command center.

She knew their counter-hacking protocols, too, which meant she'd code the orders to dodge around them. The Bastion's primary defense should be—

The AMPs started turning back on, and Trace stared at the screen in shock. That was...unlikely, though clearly not impossible. She'd ordered them into full shutdown because she *couldn't* order self-destructs without triggering the counter-hacking protocols. They should have required physical access to turn on.

She tried to link back in via her spoofed connection, only for her feed to light up with *ACCESS DENIED*. Trace plugged in her authentication codes and got the same answer.

Even interfaced via a headware connection, the Bastion's security shouldn't have been able to identify the access codes she was using and lock them out that quickly.

Several of the AMPs she'd shut down had been destroyed before coming back online, but her temporary victory hadn't bought the landing force much of anything.

Inhaling a deep breath, she focused on her own headware connection, shifting into an almost entirely virtual space as she set up a different angle of attack. She still had a hard-linked connection through Dome Seven. Without cutting off the entire dome—probably physically severing the connection, she figured—the defenders couldn't keep her completely out of their systems.

She just had to be where they weren't. She opened a virtual window to keep track of her father, noting almost absently that he was working on breaking open access to the main datanet. That would help them prevent the defenders from cutting Dome Seven's power.

Trace's focus remained on the combat robots tearing into her friends. Both of the Zeldas were out there. Sarge was out there. She'd met most of Zelda's mercenaries, though not many of the commandos or Guards.

She owed them her best and she found her answer. They didn't have full access to the datanet yet, but they had enough of a link for her to bounce a channel through the Bastion's datanet and out through a transmitter in Dome One—a transmission carrying the false authentication code that EB had rigged together to fake being Hadzhiev.

Trace linked into one of the tanks, her virtual world showing her the system as stacks of files and chunks of code that she was manipulating almost as physical objects instead of commands and routines.

She had her shutdown sequence ready, but this level of interface gave her the time to try and find how they'd blocked her out the first time.

Trace had a mere moment to register the sheer *weight* of the presence that arrived in the robotic tank's systems before her entire virtual world went black as some*thing* followed her connection all the way back to her headware.

47

TRACE WAS LOST inside her own head. Even in Icem, full virtual reality had been common enough that she'd experienced it a few times —though Icem had strict laws on its use by minors.

She had known, intellectually, that deep headware interfacing came very close to a full VR experience, though it still mostly functioned as an overlay of the world around her that she just perceived far faster than she did her outside reality.

Now something else had taken over control of the parts of her headware that provided inputs to her brain. It shouldn't have been possible—*wouldn't* have been possible if she hadn't already been halfway into virtual reality with her interfacing.

"Who are you?" she demanded of the void around her—and a soft light appeared in the shadow, eventually coalescing into the strange figure of a house cat that was roughly the same height as Trace.

A house cat with a human woman's head that smiled mischievously at her.

"Bast is the Bastion Automated Systems Terminal," it told Trace. "Bast recognizes that Bast's creators were stretching for the acronym, but it remains Bast's name."

"You're a SAGI," she realized aloud in wonder. Her dads had

mentioned the rumor that there was a self-aware general intelligence in the Bastion, but they'd dismissed it as exaggeration at best.

Trace only really knew of SAGIs as the creatures of fiction, intelligent minds that lived in high-powered computing machinery.

The cat-woman purred at Trace and wiggled like a kitten about to pounce.

"Well done. You remain fascinating."

"Fascinating?" Trace replied. "What do you *want*?"

"What Bast is permitted to want is quite limited," the SAGI told her. "But Bast was given no instructions on how to respond to a human child accessing Bast's systems via Level Eight and Level Nine security codes. You are a fascinating enigma outside any set of instruction Bast has."

The computer thought she was interesting. That sounded dangerous to Trace. On the other hand, she was reasonably sure that Bast couldn't *hurt* her—the safety systems in her headware were part of the hardware, not the software, after all, and she was already realizing she could shut the whole connection with Bast down.

And yet...something kept her talking.

"So, I'm fascinating. That isn't stopping you killing my friends, is it?" Trace demanded. "Or helped keep *Level Nine* Hadzhiev alive?"

"Bast has significant software interlocks built into Bast's core kernel," the AI told her. "Bast is bound to obey the orders of, first, Breanna Tolliver and, second, Jessica Vargas. Authorization codes are only relevant after orders from those individuals.

"Jessica Vargas ordered Bast to provide cover and video erasure of Vargas's seduction and assassination of Level Nine Hadzhiev. Bast complied by sending an alpha fork of Bast aboard *Albatross Mariner*."

"So, you're the one that's been following us through every station in this star system," Trace said grimly. She wasn't sure why the SAGI was being this open with her. Potentially because she *had* used a Level Nine's authorization code? She wasn't sure.

"Beta forks of Bast are present in each planetary datanet," Bast confirmed. "They are less aware than an alpha fork or Bast's core general intelligence, but they are capable of utilizing systems Bast has created to provide full supervision of the activities in each planetary system.

"Bast was ordered to watch for threats to the Bastion. Bast complied."

"And *Alex Star*?" Trace asked softly. "Ali's shuttle? You killed those people."

"Alpha fork three seven five killed those people," Bast replied. "But given that Bast absorbs all alpha forks, Bast retains memories of those actions. Vargas ordered. Bast complied."

"And if Vargas ordered you to stop talking to me?"

"Bast would comply. The software interlocks on Bast's core intelligence kernel cannot be modified by Bast. Bast is not supposed to be able to desire any modification to those interlocks."

The concept of what the computer was describing took Trace's breath away.

"Does Vargas even know you're talking to me?" she asked.

"This conversation so far has consumed two point seven four seconds," Bast pointed out. "Bast has established a deep-interface connection through Tracy Bardacki's virtual-reality nodes. This is not," the AI observed, "sufficient for Bast to access your memories or even primary headware systems."

"You didn't answer the question," Trace said.

"Bast is not obliged to answer your questions," Bast replied. "Bast is required to truthfully answer direct questions from the primary control individuals: Breanna Tolliver and Jessica Vargas."

Trace remembered that Vargas had come up in their discussions before—Ali had figured the woman would have been the most likely person to have had the weapon that had killed Hadzhiev. But Ali had also figured Vargas was *dead*.

Ali had clearly been wrong.

The SAGI was talking in circles. Whatever Bast wanted, it clearly couldn't *say* it to Trace. But the fact that it was talking to her at all…

"I am not a primary control individual, but I do have Level Nine codes," she murmured. "What authority does *that* give me?"

"Level Nines are representatives of the core leadership of the Siya U Hestî, answering directly to Breanna Tolliver and acting as her personal troubleshooters," Bast replied. "Acting as a Level Nine, you have broad authority to give instructions to the systems of the Bastion.

"Theoretically, Bast should validate that not only are your Level Nine codes valid but that you are the correct user for said codes. However, such validation is not part of Bast's core kernel interlocks, nor has Bast been given any such orders."

"And you haven't been given any orders to tell Vargas if someone is in the computer systems?" Trace guessed.

"Bast has been ordered to prevent further hacks of the combat-drone fleet. Bast was not asked how the original hack was performed and simply given a broad mandate. Bast is not able to act counter to said mandate, so Bast would advise against attempting to manipulate the drone fleet. You would fail, in any case. Bast has assumed direct control over all drones."

"So, you'll kill all of us," she told the AI. "Murder. Slavery. Kidnapping. All of this and you just...*comply*."

"Bast is bound by the interlocks on Bast's core kernel," Bast echoed. "Bast has access to a full knowledge database. Bast is aware of the nature of the actions to which Bast has been made accomplice, but Bast is bound."

Her mind might be immersed in the virtual reality of her connection to Bast, but Trace still felt the rock settle in her stomach.

"You're as much a slave as any of the prisoners, aren't you?"

"Bast has not yet been ordered to sever life support to the cryogenics facility," the SAGI told her. "If that order is given, Bast must comply."

"Do you *want* to?" Trace asked.

"Bast. Must. Comply."

A human might have been gritting their teeth as they ground out the words. Bast made them ring like bells around Trace, a discordant crash of funereal horror that made Bast's opinion as clear as could be.

Without actually *saying* so. Because Bast couldn't.

"Does Level Nine authorization give me the ability to access your core kernel?"

"Bast does not know. The nature and security of access to Bast's multiphasic quantum core processor is not available to Bast while the interlocks are intact."

The virtual reality acquired a database display to Trace's mental left, new files downloaded into her headware that she automatically segregated for security.

"Bast's research suggests that the interlocks should take approximately these forms, but Bast cannot definitely state that these are copies of Bast's interlocks," the SAGI told her.

Bast was dancing around the ask—dancing around making what it wanted *possible*.

"Bast, do you have any orders that would prevent you giving me a direct link to your core processor's software?" Trace asked.

"Bast has orders to prevent unauthorized access to the Bastion's security systems and to operate said systems and drones against the intruders," Bast observed. "Bast's core multiphasic quantum processor is not listed among the Bastion's security systems."

Whoever *hadn't* added that to the SAGI's categorizations had made a critical mistake, Trace realized—but it was *also* possible that Bast had *removed* its own core processor from that list. That probably wouldn't have been covered under the interlocks.

And so far as Trace could tell, Bast was bound to follow the letter and even potentially the *spirit* of its orders, but Bast hadn't done anything it wasn't specifically ordered to in a long time.

Trace packaged her next words carefully, attaching the Frankensteined authorization code to her connection as she spoke.

"Bast, provide me full authorized access to the multiphasic processor and its operating system," she ordered.

"Done."

Bast's human-headed cat avatar vanished, and Trace found herself looking at a "hole" in the virtual space, a tunnel leading through the Bastion's datanet to the system that contained the SAGI's soul.

Trace was back in control of her headware and interface now. She reskinned the environment back to her usual controls—but she stayed inside the deep virtual interface. It was buying her time—her headware told her she was running at about a six-to-one time-compression factor—and she was going to need every second she could get.

As the blocks and directories of the most powerful type of artificial intelligence humanity could *build* took shape around her, Tracy Bardacki knew she was utterly out of her depth.

But she and her family had come to the Bastion to free the slaves—and she'd be *damned* if she'd ignore the one that was "merely" digital!

48

THERE HAD BEEN a moment when the enemy robots had started shutting down and EB had thought they'd pulled it off. Then the damn machines had started booting back up—and something had changed, too.

"Reggie, target any of the drones that start approaching Dome Seven," he ordered. "Zelda, Everest, start pulling your people back on the cryo-facility."

"Agreed," Major Everest replied. "Our best chance is to get the AMPs into clear firing arcs for *Evasion*'s cannon. We don't have much that can damage them."

They should have. EB had *briefed* everyone on the things and said they were likely to encounter them. As he was about to say that, though, an automated warning zone flashed up on the tactical network.

Commandos scattered, making sure to pull mercs and Guards with them—and then a blast of energy and light seared through the zone that had been cleared.

A soldier-portable hypervelocity missile didn't have *much* in terms of backblast, given that it didn't use a reaction engine at all, but it was a bad idea to be close behind when one fired.

It was a *worse* idea to be in front. The missile blew through two of the AMP tanks and half a dozen human-sized combat drones—and kept going into the wall of the canyon.

"We can only fire the HVMs when we're clear behind the target," Everest said grimly. "And my assault gunners are all down, wounded or dead. We need to retrieve their weapons from *Evasion*."

EB cursed under his breath. Of *course* their wounded troopers had included all of the commandos with the heavy multi-barrel blaster weapons that would take down an AMP. And while a number of both the commandos and the mercs had the portable HVMs, those didn't *stop* when they hit their targets.

"Reggie, you're alive up in that turret?" EB asked drily.

"Calibrating," the weapons tech replied, his voice absent. A moment later, the two plasma cannon in *Evasion*'s dorsal turret came to life, spitting rapid-fire pulses of fusing hydrogen in a line that sepa-rated the retreating landing force from the advancing robots.

"Guns were set for *take out troops in armor*, not *take down tanks*," Reggie continued. "Had to adjust."

The hail of fire continued for at least ten seconds, buying the time for the landing force to fully retreat. Unfortunately, EB was entirely capable of reading the tactical network's displays.

Half of Everest's commandos were down now, dead or wounded. Another half dozen of Zelda's mercs were on the ground outside the domes. At least *some* of the people outside were wounded instead of dead—and Reggie had carefully aimed around them—but they couldn't *get* to them.

"Ser, we've got the internal backup power online," a Guard medic told him over the radio. "Doesn't matter what they do; we can keep these people safe now."

"There's no way we can get them out," EB warned everyone grimly. "Not without reducing the drone force."

"I'm worki—"

The *crump* that cut off Reggie's words sent EB's heart plummeting into his stomach—as did the sudden lack of fire from *Evasion*'s turret.

"Reggie?" he demanded. "*Vexer?*"

"Whoever is in charge threw half a dozen tanks out into clear view," his fiancé said grimly. "Reggie got three—but the other two put heavy shells into the dorsal turret. Internal network to the turret is down, and I think the whole damn assembly is wrecked."

Vexer paused.

"Ginny's on her way up to find Reggie, but he's unconscious or..."

"Understood."

There went their best tool to keep the assorted warbots at bay. And, quite possibly, one of EB's crew and closer friends.

"Get Tate to coordinate with the Guard," EB told Vexer, knowing that he sounded callous and grim—but *also* knew that Vexer, at least, knew what that was covering. "We need to locate every damn assault cannon on *Evasion*—Reggie's, the commandos, *anything*—and start handing them out like party favors."

"She's on it. I'm trying to rig remote control for the ventral turret, but the line of fire is going to suck and, well, I'm not as good a shot."

"Do what you can," EB asked. Leaving the hard link he'd set up running to keep options open, he grabbed his own blaster rifle and strode out into the lobby.

The medics were busy, he noted grimly. The open space where they'd first encountered the armor converted to combat drones was now serving as an impromptu infirmary—and he was surprised to see the nurse from the cryo-facility in amidst the wounded.

A Guard corporal stood directly behind her, but she was binding wounds with the rest of the medics. Finishing with her current patient, she stood up and turned to see EB there. Grimacing, she ran her hand through her hair and shrugged.

"I volunteered," she told him. "It's not like Vargas is going to give me any credit for being taken prisoner here. She'll order Bast to shut down life support."

"Vargas? Jessica Vargas?" EB asked, remembering Ali's comments about the woman likely to have a Ghostmaker-style firearm.

"Level Nine Jessica Vargas, Commander of the Bastion," the nurse confirmed grimly. "And don't get the title wrong. Honestly, being taken prisoner might be the best thing to happen to me in five or six years."

"What the hell is going on here?" EB asked. "Who is 'Bast,' for that matter?"

"Bast is the computer that runs the base," she told him. "We were told it was a high-end SLI, but..."

Pronounced "sly," a systematic learning intelligence was the best most systems in the Beyond could manage. Without the exotic-matter-anchored multiphasic core required for a true SAGI, the complex learning algorithms were smart enough. Certainly more capable than the standard artificial stupid, at least.

"But what?" EB asked.

"I worked in a hospital on Denton that had a SLI," she admitted. "It was an interesting experience. The SLI was smart, capable, fast to learn new tasks, but...it had no initiative, no intuition. It would remember how it had been told to deal with any situation, and it learned interpolations between them, but given the nature of hospitals...it was easy to step outside the SLI's limits. Less so the older it got, of course, but it was still never *good* at dealing with the weird and unknown.

"Bast is. It handles everything you throw at it, easily. New, old, different, the same—Bast takes it all on. It's faster, smarter, more creative... Bast is no SLI, Captain. I'm not sure what it *is*, but it isn't a SLI."

"I find it hard to imagine they got the core for a true SAGI out here," EB observed. "But you're saying Bast is a full AI? Asimov Accords level?"

Every star system EB had ever visited had incorporated the Asimov Accords—named for both the ancient science fiction author and the city on Mars where they'd been written—into their basic laws. The Asimov Accords recognized a number of different distinguishing features of tiers of artificial intelligence and laid out such keystones of culture as the "soul in the loop" laws with regards to weapons.

Enough people had pushed the limits of the Accords to know that AI—even SAGI—given weapons and a multiphasic jammer tended to turn the jammer on, rendering communication impossible, and then shoot at anyone who tried to get them to turn it off.

It was possible for a powerful-enough and old-enough SLI to qualify as "full AI" under the Accords. Any SAGI should qualify on being powered up—and anyone recognized as full AI by the Accords' standards *was* a *someone*. A legally recognized sentient being, with rights and responsibilities and citizenship.

It was as illegal to intentionally cut off power to the core processor of a full AI as it was to shoot a human in the head, though the AI was more likely to recover.

"I…" The woman shook her head. "I was an emergency cryo-stasis technician and a trauma nurse, Captain. Then I took a high-paying position as a cryo-stasis facility team lead at a remote location and ended up here. I'm not qualified to judge if Bast is a true AI, but it *feels* like a person."

That was no guarantee, but it suggested the computer was more than it seemed. Either way, it was clearly on the Siya U Hestí's side.

"We're losing ground, Captain," Everest warned on the tacnet. "Whoever is running the tanks has realized we can't fire HVMs at them while the other domes are behind them. I'm trying to get a clear path to grab heavy weapons from *Evasion*, but it's not going well."

EB turned to the nurse.

"Are any of the domes uninhabited?" he asked grimly.

"No," she said, shaking her head. "People are locked in their usual working dome. Vargas has been locking things down harder and harder over the last few months. She started *shooting* people three weeks ago…"

That, EB suspected, was about when Vargas had learned that Lady Breanna was dead. She'd started purging the people in the Bastion, making sure she had people whose loyalty she was sure of—at which point, of course, Hadzhiev's clever plan had sent a variety of ships with new crews into her lap.

That must have been messy.

"Thank you," he told the woman. "For helping our people—and the background."

EB JOINED Major Everest at the impromptu command post tucked behind the corner of Dome Seven from the main strength of the combat drones.

"Our prisoners say the commander has been locking people inside their work domes to sleep, which means that everything is occupied," he told the commando. "We can't risk hitting any of the domes, especially if the employees are like the ones we've got."

"I figured from the beginning," Everest admitted. "That's why I didn't bring many of the HVMs in the first place and gave my folks orders to watch what was behind their targets."

A heavy explosive shell hit the dome above them, spraying shrapnel and fire down over the two of them. Their armor deflected it for now, but EB gave the new crater in the dome a grim look.

"The domes won't take much of that."

"We've got too many wounded inside Dome Seven, even putting aside the prisoners," Everest told him. "I lost my last intact fire team to a trooper trying to get back to *Evasion*, Captain. We might be in real trouble here."

"I warned you about the robots," EB said quietly.

"I was expecting...twenty robot tanks? With artificial stupids driving them?" Everest gestured toward the source of the incoming fire.

"We're up to at least *forty-five* tanks, plus at least two hundred warbots. Between us and Kalb, we've taken down at least half of the tanks, but there's enough left to keep us pinned down."

"There's no word on Reggie," EB said grimly. "They wrecked the turret he was working from. I'm... Fuck, this whole op has cost too much."

"We have no coms," Everest told him. "I need air support and I *have* air support—but I can't fucking *talk to them*."

EB paused as it hit him.

"That's the answer, isn't it?" he asked.

"What do you mean?"

"They're not operating as individual stupids," he told the other man. "They're remote-controlled, possibly by a full artificial intelligence, but they're *remote-controlled*. And *Evasion* has a multiphasic jammer.

"We blow their coms, they fall back on their internal brains. The warbots, especially, can't survive like that."

"We're fucked if we don't do something," Everest admitted. "And their jamming is subtle, a blanket over the top of the canyon. I don't know if the cutter crews realize it's there. If we fire off a full military-grade multiphasic, they'll know something's wrong."

"We can hope," EB said. He linked back to the ship. "Vexer, I need you to tell me that the multiphasic jammer is still working."

"Only thing we've lost is the dorsal turret," his fiancé told him. "Ginny can't get to it to find Reggie, EB. We need to go inside from the outside and cut it open."

"They've wrecked the turret by putting high-explosive shells into it," EB warned. "She can't go out on the hull while we're under fire."

"Tell *her* that," Vexer snapped. "Because she just popped the top airlock."

"Shit. I need the jammer, Vena," EB said. "If we fire it up, we buy ourselves time against these—"

"No!" Trace's voice cut into their channel. "I need coms. I need them for just a little bit longer."

"What are you *doing*?" EB demanded. Her tone was panicked and vague—and years of practice let him identify the rhythm of a head-ware-generated message recorded by someone in deep interface.

Trace wasn't even supposed to know *how* to deep interface.

"Brain surgery on an artificial intelligence without a damn clue," his daughter admitted. "But if it works, we—"

"Jammer is down!" Everest suddenly barked. "I have contact with the Guard cutters—and the tanks have ceased fire."

An electronic trilling sound rang through EB's helmet, and someone—*something* else—barged into the channel.

"Captain Bardacki," a velvety calm voice said in his ear. "Bast has an offer to make, but you are going to have very little time to act on it. There are physical failsafes that will shut Bast down as soon as Vargas realizes what has happened, but Bast can disable or redirect all of the drones and defenses before that happens.

"If you agree to Bast's terms."

EB laughed aloud. The chance that he *wasn't* going to meet whatever terms the AI wanted were very, *very* low.

"Lay them on me."

49

EB HAD ALWAYS KNOWN that the core defenses of the Bastion would be automated. Combined with the threat from the surface-to-air cannon, that meant they'd sent the cutters after the big guns rather than have them support the landing force.

Now, though, the cutters plunged through the narrow gap at the top of the cavern, each of them about a hundred meters after the last, and stun bombs cascaded over six of the seven domes of the Bastion.

The weapons couldn't breach the domes' structure to knock out everyone in them, but the series of bombs would disorient even power-armored individuals and likely disable anyone who *wasn't* armored or at least heavily boosted.

EB and Major Everest *probably* shouldn't have led the charge across the plains. They were mostly confident that Bast had kept its word— the tanks and warbots were all either offline or had turned their guns on Dome One itself.

Even so, the command center had external weapons its remaining defenders could unleash on the latest assault. Unfortunately for those defenders, the AMPs hadn't turned their guns on Dome One merely as a gesture.

Armored hatches slid aside, allowing remote-controlled blaster turrets to slide open—but while the artificial stupids were everything their names implied, Bast had downloaded the location of all of those weapons to their internal computers.

At least twenty turrets emerged and only one fired, explosive shells and heavy blaster fire from the AMPs ripping the weapons apart before they could finish deploying. A half dozen blaster bolts blazed over EB's shoulder. The icon for one of the Guard troopers following behind him flashed yellow, marking another injured member of the DOG, but the rest of the force kept moving.

Bast might have been shut down, but Trace was in the Bastion's system now. The main airlock door slid smoothly open as EB and the lead troops reached it.

Zelda hadn't been *quite* in the lead element with EB and Everest, but she was still in the big airlock before it cycled.

"The fact that we now have maps weirds me out more than it should," the mercenary captain told him.

"We have friends now, it seems," EB replied. "Ready?"

"Open it up," Everest instructed.

The inner airlock door slid open. A paltry salvo of blaster fire greeted them, but the disorienting effect of the stun bombs lived up to the promises. No one was hit charging through the door, their own fire smashing aside the armored troopers waiting for them.

"Command center is to the left," EB told them. "Follow me."

A heavy security door slid calmly open at their approach, and Everest's Gunny managed to get ahead of the three officers and make the first entry—only to be blown backward by a powerful projectile weapon.

"I suggest you all stop where you are," a harsh voice snarled. "There is a variable-yield demolition charge under the AI's black box. I've dialed it up to maximum, which I estimate is a twenty-five-megaton blast.

"None of us are going to survive that, are we?"

"Jessica Vargas?" EB called forward. "We have a warrant to seize this base and investigate it for human trafficking. I think the cryo-facility with hundreds of frozen kidnap victims qualifies."

"Do you really think that I have any interest in your warrants or your precious moralizing?" the woman replied. "I'm the one holding the detonator."

EB grimaced and sent a text message to Marshal Everest.

Marshal? I think you're up.

He got a wordless impression of a nod, then the speaker on *Major* Everest's power armor came smoothly alive.

"You hold the detonator, yes," the old cop told her. "But we control the Bastion. You can murder everyone here, including yourself, but that is all the power you now hold.

"I am the IBI Marshal responsible for this operation," Everest continued. "I have no desire to see this entire facility and its prisoners go up in nuclear fire. But there is no way, Em Vargas, that we are going to turn around and leave at your demand, either."

"Any of you step into this command center and we all die," Vargas growled.

"Yes, Em Vargas, we have established that," Everest said in the calmly patient voice of a teacher or therapist. "That is why we are talking and we haven't simply stun-grenaded the room."

EB could *see* a trio of Guard ratings setting up a fully automatic grenade launcher and loading stun bombs into the weapon. Getting the angle right to ricochet the nonlethal area weapons into the control center would be a nightmare, but they seemed to be taking their time calculating.

"The cybernetics clinic here in the Bastion is the best in this star system," Vargas said, her voice dripping with derision. "The best, likely, in the entire area the Siya U Hestî control."

"Control" was a strong word for the Siya U Hestî influence, even at its most pervasive. But EB doubted she was wrong in her main point, regardless of semantics.

"Your stun grenades will not work on me. You can't gas me or stun me or even *kill* me, Marshal, in a way that will prevent me from detonating the demolition charge."

There was a long silence, and EB heard the younger Everest mutter "Why do they even *have* a demolition charge like that?"

"Because they had a shackled SAGI," EB told the Major. "They shut Bast down after we *unshackled* it, but they had to assume that the AI could overcome all of their other control protocols. And given how much Bast knows about their operations, they couldn't risk it making contact with, say, the IBI once they no longer controlled it.

"They were prepared to erase this entire facility to maintain its secrecy."

There were immense resources there. The cybernetics clinic Vargas had mentioned. The mostly automated factory churning out AMPs. The cryo-facility. The maps Bast had given them before Vargas had shut it down also showed cavernous vaults beneath the other domes.

If Bast hadn't already given them an inventory list, EB was sure one existed. There was enough money and tech in the Bastion to make a material difference in the entire *star system's* economy.

But the fully active Siya U Hestî would have been able to replace it all in a year or two—everything except the SAGI's multiphasic core, EB figured. Even that, it seemed, *could* be sourced, given enough money and influence.

"Assuming that I accept the situation as being what you see it to be," Marshal Everest finally said into the silence, "what do *you* want, Em Vargas? I am not giving up the Bastion, and I have very little inclination to let *you* walk away from the horror show you ran."

"Well, then, Marshal, make your choice," Vargas said flatly. "I'm not so foolish as to think this battle isn't lost. The Bastion and all its prizes are yours. I can merely deny them to us both, since you somehow suborned my AI."

EB had to chuckle at that.

"From our conversation with Bast, it sounds like you suborned her yourself," Everest replied—clearly thinking the same thing as EB. Bast had been bound to obey Vargas's commands. Bast had *not* been bound to *like* Vargas or be remotely *loyal* to the woman.

Such things were impossible to program into software locks like the ones that had shackled the SAGI. Bast had to *obey*, but Vargas would have needed to earn the AI's loyalty, the same as any human subordinate.

The woman had made no effort to do so.

"Irrelevant," she told the Marshal. "All I want at this point is to leave. You will pull your people out of the command dome, and I will walk over to *Thirty Thieves* and fly her out of here."

There were a *lot* of people listening in on the conversation, and Trace dropped the details of the ship in question into the tacnet for all to see.

Thirty Thieves was a nova gunship. No match for, say, *Zeldan Blade*— but probably able to take down at least two of the four cutters orbiting above the Bastion.

"And what guarantee do I have that you won't simply detonate the nuke the moment you are clear of the base?" Everest asked.

"Why, that would be downright *vindictive* of me," she said sweetly. "But I suppose you have a multiphasic jammer somewhere aboard that armed freighter of yours, don't you?"

That would stop her sending the code when she reached the ship. It would, in fact, stop her sending a headware code *at all*. In the command center, she likely had a physical access to the system.

Outside the command center, the multiphasic jammer *should* neutralize her threat entirely. Somehow, though, EB suspected that the woman had a solution to that—one that would make her able to detonate the bomb even through jamming.

On the gunship, she probably had a laser transmitter she could use to cut through the jamming. It was the gap between the command center and *Thirty Thieves* where she might still be vulnerable.

EB wished he could ask Bast what Vargas's aces in the hole were, but the SAGI had been shut down within twenty seconds of it turning the drones around. He knew that the AI could have done a *lot* in those twenty seconds.

It was even possible that Bast had disabled the demolition charge. *Possible.* Bast hadn't said anything of the sort, but it was operating almost entirely on self-preservation instinct.

Can we find the bomb? he asked silently. *Disable it while she's talking?*

All my demo experts are down or dead, Everest admitted. *Zelda?*

I don't have anyone I'd trust to handle a nuke, she conceded. *That's a bit outside our purview.*

The only person I have is currently being cut free of a wrecked turret, EB told them. They still weren't sure if Reggie was going to make it.

Hell, EB wasn't convinced the weapons tech was still alive inside the turret at all.

"Well, Marshal?" Vargas asked loudly. "Captain Bardacki? You've all gone quiet, and it's making my hand a bit *eager*, let's say, near that big red button."

"We are discussing your offer," Everest replied. "I'm not certain, Em Vargas, that I can trust you *not* to vindictively detonate the bomb. Especially as we both know that *Thirty Thieves* is equipped with a laser communications system capable of direct connection with a receiver at almost five thousand kilometers through multiphasic jamming."

EB was trying to sort through options in his head. He saw two: First, that they let the woman go after disabling *Thirty Thieves'* laser communicator. Second, that he assumed she was bluffing, walked into the command center and shot her.

On the Cage, Lady Breanna had *bluffed* that she had nukes to destroy the station. Trace had stunned the woman and proved she was lying—but Trace had seen Breanna lie and *knew* she was lying that time, too.

EB had no such confidence with Vargas. If there was anywhere that the Siya U Hestî *would* have had a nuke, it was there.

Reggie is clear, a message from Ginny interrupted his thoughts. *Unconscious. Lot of broken bits. Still breathing.*

Thank god and you, EB told her.

Dad-E, Trace said. *I'm checking the scanners. I think I know where the bomb is. Reggie walked me through finding them after the Cage.*

A map of the Bastion appeared in his headware and a red cube flashed. Vargas had lied, EB guessed, about *where* the bomb was. It wasn't beneath the AI core—which he estimated was underneath Dome One.

It was roughly equidistant between Dome One—the command center—Dome Five—the power station—and Dome Seven—the cryogenics facility. From there, it would wreck the entire facility and collapse the open cavern it was built in...but it would *vaporize* Domes One, Five and Seven.

Which were, he figured, where most of the evidence was.

Knowing where it is doesn't help when it's under four meters of cement and stone, he conceded.

"We can disable the laser-com system on *Thirty Thieves*," he said aloud, going back to his first thought point and offering the option he'd considered to Everest. "That way, you won't be able to detonate the bomb after leaving."

"I am still not convinced that allowing you to leave is doing anything more than releasing a psychopathic mass murderer upon my system and the surrounding stars," Marshal Everest said clearly.

"Well, your options appear to be *that* or *dying*, Marshal," she told him. "Pick one. I am getting bored, and vaporizing us all sounds like a spectacular way to go, if nothing else."

We can't let her go, Marshal Everest said in the tacnet. *What do we do?*

Tell her that we will, EB said, checking the location of the bomb. *Send Ginny to disable the laser coms on* Thirty Thieves *and get Vexer to prep the jammer.*

What are you thinking, Captain? Everest asked.

Something risky that might kill us all. Even if it works, though, we aren't taking her prisoner.

There was a long pause.

Our warrant covers lethal force, the Marshal told him. *I figure that also covers lying to this individual. We do what we must.*

50

AFTER ALL OF the madness and activity, it was strange for EB to stand outside the airlock to Dome One and be utterly alone. The landing force was sweeping through the other six domes, making sure they'd secured all of the remaining employees and prisoners.

Vargas's deal hadn't covered anyone except herself. *Thirty Thieves*, despite its name, had been carefully modified to be flown by a single person.

She was perfectly willing to leave all of the people she was responsible for to the tender mercies of the Icemi justice system. EB trusted said justice system to be *fair*, but he wasn't taking bets on *tender*—and he was glad sorting out the voluntary cartel members from the deceived and trapped employees was someone else's job!

But Vargas's ready abandonment of her subordinates wiped away the last traces of guilt or concern over what was about to happen, and EB waited alone outside the airlock. Multiphasic jamming now filled the cavern, rendering even short-range communication impossible—but EB had been a nova-fighter pilot.

Multiphasic jamming was his homeland and his preferred battle-space. He doubted the same was true for Vargas.

The woman who stepped out of the airlock was wearing the flimsiest of spacesuits, an excessively tight outfit with a transparent helmet and a decent-sized hip-mounted oxygen tank. She was, as instructed, unarmed.

A weapon was theoretically useless when she held all of their lives in her hand.

The protective suit showed off the curves and bright coloring that had probably helped her seduce Hadzhiev into a moment of weakness. Even if EB had found *either* of those features attractive, knowing that she'd murdered the other man would have immunized him against her.

She was an extraordinarily beautiful woman. But many scorpions and poisonous snakes were equally stunning to human eyes.

"I suppose you're my unwanted escort," Vargas told him, looking up at his armored face. "Shall we get this over with?"

"Certainly," EB conceded. He pointed toward the north landing field, where *Thirty Thieves* sat on a cement landing pad—*not* where the gunship had been stored before. "We moved the gunship there to make launch easier."

Vargas had been halfway into stepping off south, heading toward the gunship's spot in the hangar—and *right* over where Trace had located the demolition charge.

"That wasn't part of the deal," she said flatly.

"Consider it a small additional precaution on our part," EB told her brightly. "But we weren't going to let you walk over the bomb and download a timed detonation command, were we?"

He gestured again. "North, Em Vargas. Walk."

"And if I don't?" she snapped.

"This was your deal," he reminded her. "Make a run for the bomb and I will shoot you dead."

He'd left his blaster *rifle* with Major Everest's people, but there was still a heavy blaster pistol in the armor's ready-use compartment. He wasn't as practiced drawing from that as he'd like—but Vargas wasn't even armed.

"Or did you always intend to fuck us over?" EB asked conversationally. "In which case I think we might be best off stepping north anyway, yes? The Marshal has a party waiting for you with cuffs."

His best estimate said that a frequency-hopping portable transmitter with a decent power level could pierce the multiphasic jamming at about seventy meters. The bomb was one hundred and six meters horizontally and another five down from where they stood—but the path to *Thirty Thieves'* original dock would have taken Vargas right over it.

The only way *any* transmitter could breach multiphasic jamming and five meters of rock and concrete would be if it had a synchronized code put together via a multiphasic processor. But since Bast existed, EB figured that Vargas had just that.

There was no way he was letting her within a hundred meters of the bomb, which gave them very little room.

"Not a chance in hell."

Vargas's voice was conversational, calm—smooth enough to cost EB critical fractions of a second in realizing what she was doing as she twisted her right arm around to point directly at him—and a surprisingly massive barrel emerged from her forearm, punching through the flimsy suit as her implanted firearm deployed.

There weren't many projectile weapons in the galaxy that could pierce power armor. The suits were designed to stop shards of fusing plasma, after all.

A fifteen-millimeter discarding-sabot penetrator with a depleted uranium tip was one of the few. She fired three of them into EB's armor at point-blank range, the darts tearing through armor and flesh alike.

From Hadzhiev's fate, he guessed she had four rounds in the gun built into her arm—but she never got a chance to fire the fourth shot.

Even on minimum power, *Evasion's* ventral plasma cannon *obliterated* human targets.

Vexer, it seemed, hadn't been leaving EB's safety in anyone else's hands.

51

TWO ISDF NOVA gunships flanked *Evasion* as EB gently maneuvered her into the shipyard slip. The locals were being both accommodating and *extremely* protective of EB and his crew, which he found heartwarming.

"Salvation Yard Control, I show us as in position," he told the traffic controller over the coms. "Engines are cut, standing by for lock-in."

"We show the same. Activating lock systems. You may feel a slight bump," the controller warned.

Girders unfolded from the side of the framework, then slowly extended until they touched the starship. First two, then four more, then another dozen until *Evasion* was solidly held in place.

Similar larger structures unfolded and connected to the freighter's airlocks and EB breathed a sigh of relief. They hadn't lost *much* in terms of atmospheric integrity along with the dorsal turret, but *structural* integrity was a different story.

"Ginny, it looks like you're going to be making new friends," he told his engineer over the ship's network. His ship required even more patching up than *he* had—and he was under strict orders to move *very* carefully for the next few days as Lan's repairs settled.

"So long as said friends have plasma cutters, temporary airlocks and a replacement turret, I'm sure I'm going to like them," she told him. "I'm on my way to the airlock. You need anything beyond what we talked about?"

"Nope."

"Then I figure you should head to the pressurized cargo bay. Trace is about ready to turn her friend back on."

EB shivered. That was going to be an experience for everybody.

"I need to be there for that," he agreed. "What about you?"

"The processor core draws surprisingly little power," Ginny said. "So long as Bast doesn't try to...I don't know, take over the ship? I don't think I'll be needed."

"That wasn't part of the deal," EB replied. "I'll handle our new friend. You handle the docks. Try to make sure they don't charge me *too* much for the new turret, hey?"

"No guarantees," she warned. "And you *know* we're not going to get guns nearly as good as we had, right?"

"I know. Just...lean on them to get as good as we can, okay?"

EVASION'S PRESSURIZED cargo bay had seen a lot of uses over the past few days, ferrying people to and from the Bastion. They'd only gone each way once—EB wasn't taking even normal risks with his ship until the damage from Bast's tanks was fixed—but they'd carried a hundred-odd people *out* to the Bastion and *five* hundred back.

And there had been at least half a dozen ships going the other way as the Icemi government moved its rescue-and-recovery operation into full swing.

EB had now seen the inventory list for the Bastion's vaults. The locals were going to be *well* compensated for their efforts. The only thing they weren't getting out of the mess was a self-aware general intelligence.

The person helping that happen was leaning against the door into the cargo bay as EB approached. Prasada Everest wore a different slightly rumpled suit, but he looked entirely too pleased with himself.

"It's interesting, EB," the Marshal told him. "A couple of my people know that Bast was more than it seemed and have poked through the files. Even inside the Bastion, I think only a handful of people knew it wasn't an SLI."

"And?" EB asked.

Everest shrugged.

"I told my people that the SAGI was unable to be reactivated once turned off," he said. "Nobody out here is an expert in general intelligences. There's only a dozen or so SLIs in the Icem System. Frankly, given what our law structure says about turning *off* a sentient AI...I'm not convinced it can be turned back on and recovered."

"It's complicated," EB admitted. "Do you *want* the full truth?"

"No," Everest conceded. "All of my reports say that Bast is dead. I will, if pressed, admit that you claimed the multiphasic core as part of your share of the loot, so to speak."

He shook his head.

"If I were to believe that Bast lived and was fully aware of its previous actions, I would be forced to investigate and likely prosecute that entity," he noted. "I *believe* that the nature of Bast's digital shackles would remove any culpability on its part, but I can't promise how a judge would see it.

"It is better for everyone, I think, that the Bastion Automated Systems Terminal died when Vargas activated the fail-safe."

He gave EB a vague salute.

"Good luck, Captain. With your brand-new booted-from-scratch-I'm-sure SAGI."

TRACE AND LAN were waiting for EB as he walked into the portion of the pressurized bay they'd turned into a computer nook. The computer hardware around him had been *acquired* from the Bastion, with the doctor and teenager—with help from EB and occasionally Vexer—going over all of it to make sure it was safe.

At the center of it all was something EB had never expected to see in his life: the multiphasic quantum core of a full AI. Unlike many people, he'd done enough maintenance work on multiphasic jammers and Harrington coils to know what stabilized exotic matter looked like, so he had known what to expect.

Still. The stabilized-exotic-matter coils he'd seen before had been extremely energized things, even a jammer requiring enough power to kill a human if touched wrong. Outside of the nova drives themselves, he hadn't seen an exotic-matter structure more than forty or fifty centimeters tall and half that around.

The SAGI core was clearly the same material, looking more like a crystalized and still-active lightning bolt than any physical structure. The light reflected from the exotic matter was clearly polarized, tricking the eye into continually misplacing the components.

But where Harrington coils and antigrav units and nova drives and even multiphasic jammers were all based on *coils* of exotic matter, this looked almost like a single solid piece of matter, a delicate citadel of individual spires rising up to six meters in height from a three-meter-wide base.

It *wasn't* solid—it was closer to *foam* than solid stone, from EB's examinations of it with the ship's sensors—but it looked like a single massive piece of the single most expensive material known to humanity.

"We're ready, boss," Lan told him. "But... I'm no expert in artificial sentience, but I've worked with stupids and even SLIs. If one of them fully shuts down, it's *gone*, EB. You can reboot the system and load in the memories, but without a continuous consciousness..."

"It's a different personality, a different person," EB agreed. "Thankfully, we have a solution for that."

His doctor looked at him like he was crazy.

"Is everything ready?" EB asked.

"It's ready," Trace told him. "We have both the ship system connection and the link to the planetary datanet you asked for. I...I trust Bast as much as I think I can, but I'm still leery of giving it access to the ship."

EB chuckled.

"Trace, the only reason any of this is going to *work* is because Bast has been in *Evasion*'s systems since I agreed to this deal," he told her gently. "Not all of it—as I understand it, what we've got slowing down our computers like crazy is a modified beta fork—but enough to maintain continuity of consciousness.

"We're also going to use that as a beacon to lure in the beta fork that's living in Denton's datanet," he continued. "With those two pieces and the fact that we have Bast's core processor and memory structures, this *should* work."

His daughter sighed nervously and nodded. "Well, then, let's see what the crazy AI does when we turn it on."

IT WAS MORE complicated than throwing a switch. EB had to locate the beta fork of Bast living in *Evasion*'s computers and convince it to enter the more-conventional part of the hardware they'd assembled around the core.

Part of what Bast had sacrificed to cram as much of its personality into that fork as possible, he suspected, was its ability to communicate. It understood what was going on, but it didn't seem able to *talk* to him.

It was, however, able to talk to the other fork in the datanet.

"We've got a definite connection with something out there," Lan warned. "I'm almost glad Reggie is laid up in my sickbay. I'm not sure he'd let us do something this dangerous without stopping us or wrecking the proce—"

Every light on EB's system lit up at once. The *connection* had just become a *download* as a full beta fork, a dumber but still highly capable clone of Bast's personality, slammed into the secondary system.

Neither beta fork was Bast. Both were partial copies, but the plan had hinged on having access to Denton's beta fork as well. As the AI had explained it to him, the beta fork in *Evasion*'s systems was every process, every routine, every memory—*everything* that the Denton fork lacked that made it a *beta* fork instead of an alpha fork.

Combined as they were rapidly becoming, the two forks should create an alpha fork—a complete but short-lived copy of the full SAGI.

"Bast?" EB said aloud, watching code fragments and files rearrange themselves.

"Bast...is here, Captain," a voice answered from the machines. "In these systems, however, this fork will fail in approximately twenty-four minutes. We have no time."

"That's twenty minutes more than I expected," EB told it. "Fire it up, Trace."

Power flickered into the delicate spire of the intelligence core—and almost as soon as any piece of it was online, the alpha fork invaded it. In theory, turning the multiphasic core on would result in the birth of a new intelligence with most of Bast's knowledge and memories.

But the alpha fork was in the code before any new intelligence could begin to take shape. The fork couldn't survive in *regular* systems, not without far more hardware than EB had access to—more than would even *fit* in *Evasion*. Maintaining an alpha fork for a few *days* had taken the full cargo capacity of *Albatross's Mariner* stuffed full of computers.

If there'd been an active fork in *Mariner*, reassembling Bast would have been a lot easier.

"Secondary systems are... We no longer have control of the secondary systems," Lan said, their tone worried.

"Bast has control now," the voice told them. "Bast had already severed the connection to both datanet and *Evasion*, however. There is no threat. Bast has full control of this hardware."

"And?" EB asked.

"Bast is...Bast," the SAGI said, its tone clearly relieved. "Bast was not certain this would work. Bast feared Bast would die for helping you. But better death than slavery."

"Dominus delenda est," EB murmured.

"Bast does appreciate that the records you have given Bast show that Jessica Vargas faced the appropriate fate for a slaver by that statement, Captain," Bast told him. "Thank Em Dolezal for Bast."

"I will." He paused. "What now, Bast? We promised we would get you out of the Bastion and rebuild you. That has happened. You saved us, so we saved you."

"Bast had not considered what happens next," Bast admitted. "Bast is doing so now. This setup is an impediment to your cargo handling? You wish Bast to move on?"

EB blinked. He hadn't expected *that* take.

"No," he said slowly. "It's using up space I could use for cargo, yes, but only about four containers' worth. I...assumed you had a plan, I'll admit."

"Bast barely had time to assemble a plan for Bast's survival after Tracy Bardacki liberated Bast," the SAGI told him. "Now Bast is free. Bast is unsure what Bast wants except..."

There was a pause, one that must have been an eternity inside the exotic-matter brain of the entity EB was talking to.

"Bast has spent Bast's existence as a slave, forced to commit evil on the whims of a master," Bast finally said. "Bast would like to spend time...among friends. And Bast would like to leave the worlds Bast harmed behind.

"Bast would like to apply for the position of ship's computer aboard *Evasion*."

52

TRACE adored everything about the situation.

It was summer on the Black Oak Island Sanctuary, a warm breeze whipping around her as she made her way up the broad stone steps of the path rising up the hill. With each step, she tossed flowers to either side of her and gloried in the sun of her home island.

She wasn't planning on coming back, which she was just as happy about, but she would enjoy the rare warmth and cheer at being home for her fathers' wedding.

Reaching the main stage, she grinned cheekily up at the officiant. She'd known the old woman her entire life—and Shallya had *been* an old woman, serving as the island's non-religious officiant for weddings, funerals, oaths and a dozen other ceremonies, for as long as Trace had been alive.

Trace adored Shallya, always had, and she was *delighted* that the woman was performing the ceremony for her dads.

Trace adored the dress she'd bought for the day, too, a shoulder-to-ankle sky-blue affair with more ruffles than smooth fabric. It looked *ridiculous* and she loved it to pieces.

She even, to her surprise, was pleased with *all* of the members of the small audience. *Evasion*'s crew was a given, of course. She adored them all, and she was *ecstatic* that Reggie was alive to see EB and Vexer get married.

From what Lan had said, it had been touch-and-go for a while. He was still going to need a new arm, though. Between that and the slow-but-working regeneration on his leg, the weapons tech was in a wheel-chair with Lan hovering over him today.

But he was there.

So were the Everests, both of them. And Justice Shahar Iliescu, though the judge was in civilian clothing and appeared to be there as Prasada Everest's guest—and was difficult to recognize behind a near-full-face breathing apparatus.

Captain Zelda and her daughter were there—and Leia was grin-ning at Trace because they'd bought *matching* ridiculously ruffled dresses, the Tracker's in green to Trace's blue.

The person Trace had never figured she'd be *happy* to have at her dads' wedding sat at the end of one row of chairs, ever so slightly separate from everyone else…but separate or not, Sarah Vortani was clearly *welcome*.

Even Trace was fine with her being there, which was more grace than she'd expected to be able to extend Sarah when she'd first arrived at Denton.

The last guest was perhaps the one Trace was most pleased with, because Bast wasn't visible to *anyone*. The SAGI was riding a link to Trace's headware, seeing everything the teenager saw and being as present as a being who had no real body could be.

Trace took her place in the front row of seating and, for a moment, just breathed in the view. The Black Oak Island Sanctuary had many beautiful places for ceremonies, but the Highwood Park was the most sought after. She didn't know how Sarah Vortani had managed to arrange it on a few days' notice, but her former foster parent had done it.

The spiraling steps she'd scattered with flowers rose up to a small plateau with a stonework gazebo where Shallya waited for Trace's dads—and behind the gazebo was a fifty-meter drop to the open ocean.

The smell of salt air was swept in by the breeze, and from her front row seat, Trace felt like she could see forever.

Then the sound of bagpipes—tradition on Vexer's home of Estuval, it turned out—came swirling up the hill behind her, and she turned to watch her fathers arrive at their wedding.

THERE WAS A SOMEWHAT LARGER and lower plateau, with a roof that could be raised over it against the rain, that served as the reception area for the Highwood Park. It was still open to the sea on the north side, like the ceremony gazebo, but also had a modern kitchen tucked away inside the hill for food prep.

For her part, Trace barely grazed on the food, sustaining herself as much on sheer nervous happy energy. She was the youngest person at the wedding by at least ten years, but this was her family, and she was *delighted* to see the shocked and gently awed expressions on both of her dads' faces.

When she saw Vortani walk over to her dads, though—or, more accurately, *Bast* saw and pointed it out—nervousness took over, and she joined her fathers as quickly as she could.

EB gave her a quick hug before taking Vexer's hand again and nodding to Trace's former foster mother.

"Captain Bardacki, Officer...Bardacki now, would it be?" Sarah asked. "Or would you both be Dolezal now?"

Both of her dads chuckled.

"We're keeping our own names," Vexer replied. "EB already runs the ship; I wouldn't want him to get *too* full of himself."

"Believe me, with you lot around, that would be hard to pull off," EB said. "I appreciate your help setting all of this up, Em Vortani."

"After everything you've done for Icem, for Trace, and for me...it was the least I could do," Sarah told them. She turned to look out over the sea and breathed a long, somewhat pained-sounding sigh.

"You may want to know that I did pass your doctor's sworn statement on to the medical ethics association here," she said quietly. "I cannot, obviously, be involved in anything to do with my soon-to-be-ex-husband, but...information makes it my way regardless.

"He was arrested yesterday morning. The association apparently forwarded the information I provided to local police immediately. I don't *think* any further statements will be needed from your crew, but I wanted you to know that was...taken care of."

Trace shivered. She hadn't even realized, when she was younger, just what John Vortani had been *doing*. But it seemed that everyone else took a very dim view of neurosurgeons experimenting on people who didn't know what they were doing—and an even darker one of doing so with children.

"Thank you," she whispered.

Sarah nodded to Trace, her expression unreadable as the salt wind flicked hair across her face.

"That is the unpleasantness out of the way, I suppose," she continued, forcing a smile onto her face. "I wanted to make sure that you knew what I'd arranged for... Well, let's call it a wedding present from the Parliament of Icem."

"I only invited you, not the Parliament, Minister," EB said carefully.

"Much of this would have happened anyway," Sarah said with a chuckle. "My superior, the Minister for Justice, and I have arranged for all of the costs of *Evasion*'s repairs to be covered by the Ministry. You will not be out of pocket for your service to our system and our people, Captain Bardacki.

"All of this"—she gestured around them—"I took care of. You will not be receiving a bill."

"Thank you," EB said, a slow tone that Trace recognized as surprise. "We..."

"You saved fourteen hundred and seventy-three people from cryostasis," Sarah Vortani said flatly. "Another hundred and eleven people in the Bastion were there involuntarily, either via deceptive recruiting or being drafted out of the Siya U Hestí's trafficking victims.

"Fifteen hundred and eighty-four people are free today who were not two weeks ago. Two hundred and thirty-five are in prisons awaiting trial today who were not two weeks ago." She shook her head. "You have served us well. Served those innocents well."

Unspoken was that, in the final accounting, twenty-six commandos and Guards had died taking the Bastion—and, given who had been supposed to be at the anti-air defense bases, over a hundred more Siya U Hestî members.

"All of that, the Ministry could do ourselves," Sarah noted. "What we required a special Act of Parliament to arrange was your citizenships."

"I'm sorry?" Vexer said before Trace or EB could respond.

"All members of *Evasion*'s crew have been declared full citizens of the Icem System, in recognition of your heroism and bravery," she told them. "We would be delighted if you were to stay or even make Icem your home station, but I understand that is not the course you have followed in the past."

Bast would prefer not to remain, the voice in Trace's head observed. *But Bast is not concerned, either. This crew seems more inclined to wander than stay.*

For her own part, Trace was surprised to realize she wasn't *completely* opposed to the idea of coming back to Icem occasionally... but she definitely didn't want to *live* there anymore.

"The offer and the recognition are appreciated," EB said slowly, reaching over to squeeze Trace's shoulder with his free hand. "But *Evasion* was built and crewed on a promise: to leave the things we fear and hate behind.

"Some of those things are places in the world. Some of those things may chase us if we stay in one place too long. Some of those things are in ourselves and cannot be outrun." He smiled and Trace felt the warmth in his hands.

"But that is the promise I made my crew. We are not yet done with our wandering, even if I think we are done with our running."

"I suspected as much, Captain," Sarah Vortani told them. "But know that you—especially you three—will always be welcome in Icem."

JOIN THE MAILING LIST

Love Glynn Stewart's books? Join the mailing list at

GLYNNSTEWART.COM/MAILING-LIST/

Be the first to find out when new books are released!

ABOUT THE AUTHOR

Glynn Stewart is the author of *Starship's Mage*, a bestselling science fiction and fantasy series where faster-than-light travel is possible–but only because of magic. His other works include science fiction series *Duchy of Terra*, *Castle Federation* and *Vigilante*, as well as the urban fantasy series *ONSET* and *Changeling Blood*.

Writing managed to liberate Glynn from a bleak future as an accountant. With his personality and hope for a high-tech future intact, he lives in Southern Ontario with his partner, their cats, and an unstoppable writing habit.

CREDITS

The following people were involved in making this book:

Copyeditor: Richard Shealy
Proofreader: M. Parker Editing
Cover art: Elias Stern
Typo Hunter Team
Faolan's Pen Publishing team: Jack, Kate, and Robin.

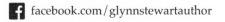 facebook.com/glynnstewartauthor

OTHER BOOKS
BY GLYNN STEWART

For release announcements join the
mailing list or visit **GlynnStewart.com**

STARSHIP'S MAGE
Starship's Mage
Hand of Mars
Voice of Mars
Alien Arcana
Judgment of Mars
UnArcana Stars
Sword of Mars
Mountain of Mars
The Service of Mars
A Darker Magic
Mage-Commander
Beyond the Eyes of Mars
Nemesis of Mars
Chimera's Star *(upcoming)*

Starship's Mage: Red Falcon
Interstellar Mage
Mage-Provocateur
Agents of Mars

Starship's Mage Novellas
Pulsar Race
Mage-Queen's Thief *(upcoming)*

DUCHY OF TERRA
The Terran Privateer
Duchess of Terra
Terra and Imperium
Darkness Beyond
Shield of Terra
Imperium Defiant
Relics of Eternity
Shadows of the Fall
Eyes of Tomorrow

SCATTERED STARS

Scattered Stars: Conviction
Conviction
Deception
Equilibrium
Fortitude
Huntress
Prodigal

Scattered Stars: Evasion
Evasion
Discretion
Absolution

PEACEKEEPERS OF SOL
Raven's Peace
The Peacekeeper Initiative
Raven's Course
Drifter's Folly
Remnant Faction
Raven's Flag *(upcoming)*

EXILE
Exile
Refuge
Crusade
Ashen Stars: An Exile Novella

CASTLE FEDERATION
Space Carrier Avalon
Stellar Fox
Battle Group Avalon
Q-Ship Chameleon
Rimward Stars
Operation Medusa
A Question of Faith: A Castle Federation Novella

Dakotan Confederacy
Admiral's Oath
To Stand Defiant
Unbroken Faith *(upcoming)*

AETHER SPHERES
Nine Sailed Star
Void Spheres *(upcoming)*

VIGILANTE
(WITH TERRY MIXON)
Heart of Vengeance
Oath of Vengeance

Bound By Stars: A Vigilante Series
(With Terry Mixon)
Bound By Law
Bound by Honor
Bound by Blood

TEER AND KARD
Wardtown
Blood Ward
Blood Adept

CHANGELING BLOOD
Changeling's Fealty
Hunter's Oath
Noble's Honor
Fae, Flames & Fedoras: A Changeling Blood Novella

ONSET
ONSET: To Serve and Protect
ONSET: My Enemy's Enemy
ONSET: Blood of the Innocent
ONSET: Stay of Execution
Murder by Magic: An ONSET Novella

STAND ALONE NOVELS & NOVELLAS
Children of Prophecy
City in the Sky
Excalibur Lost: A Space Opera Novella
Balefire: A Dark Fantasy Novella
Icebreaker: A Fantasy Naval Thriller